CHAPTER

7

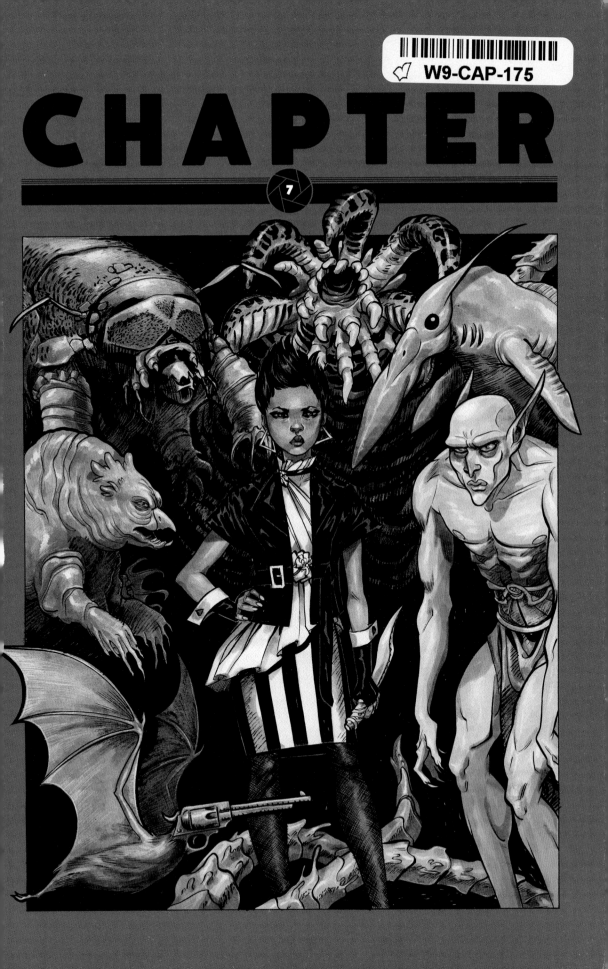

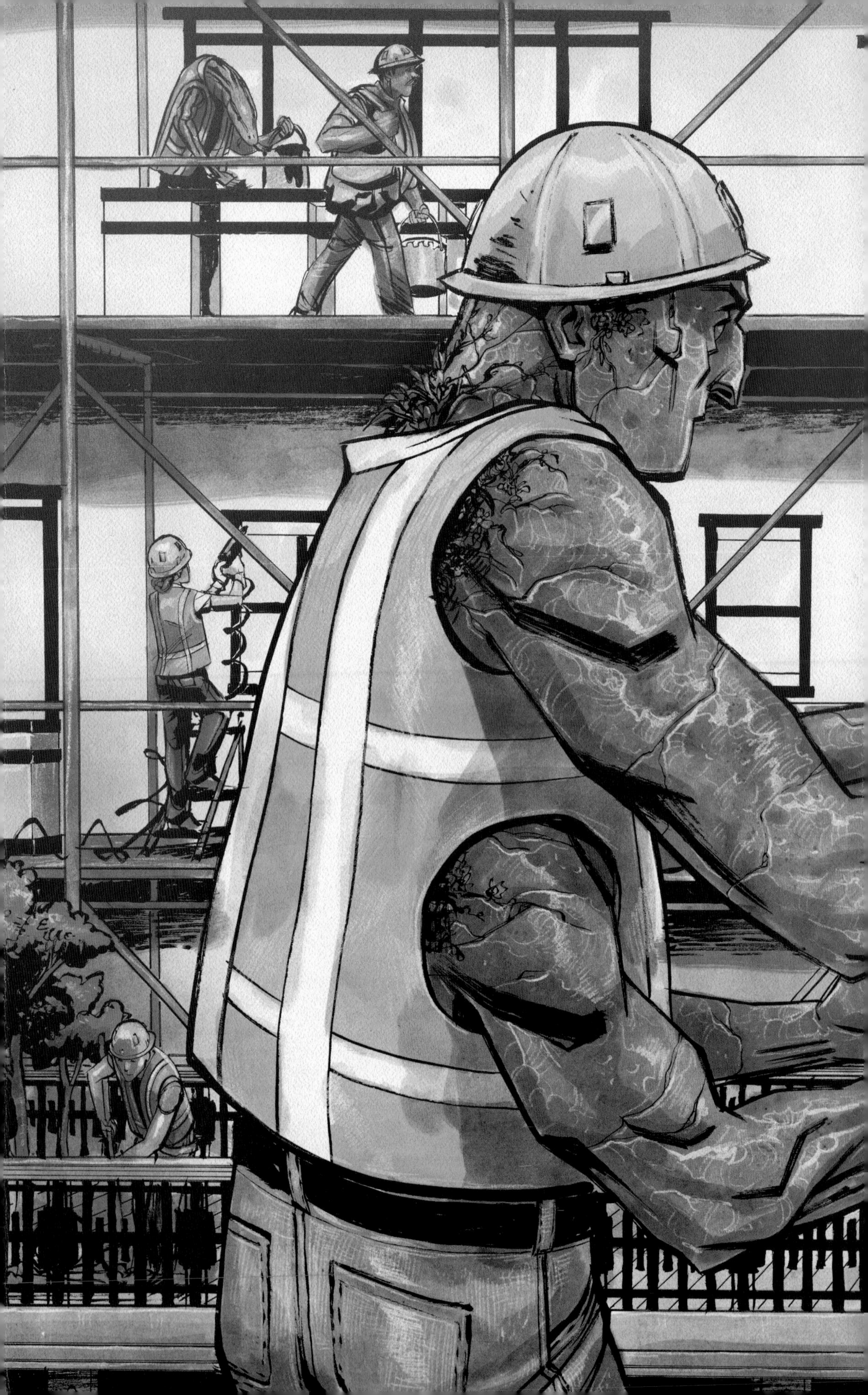

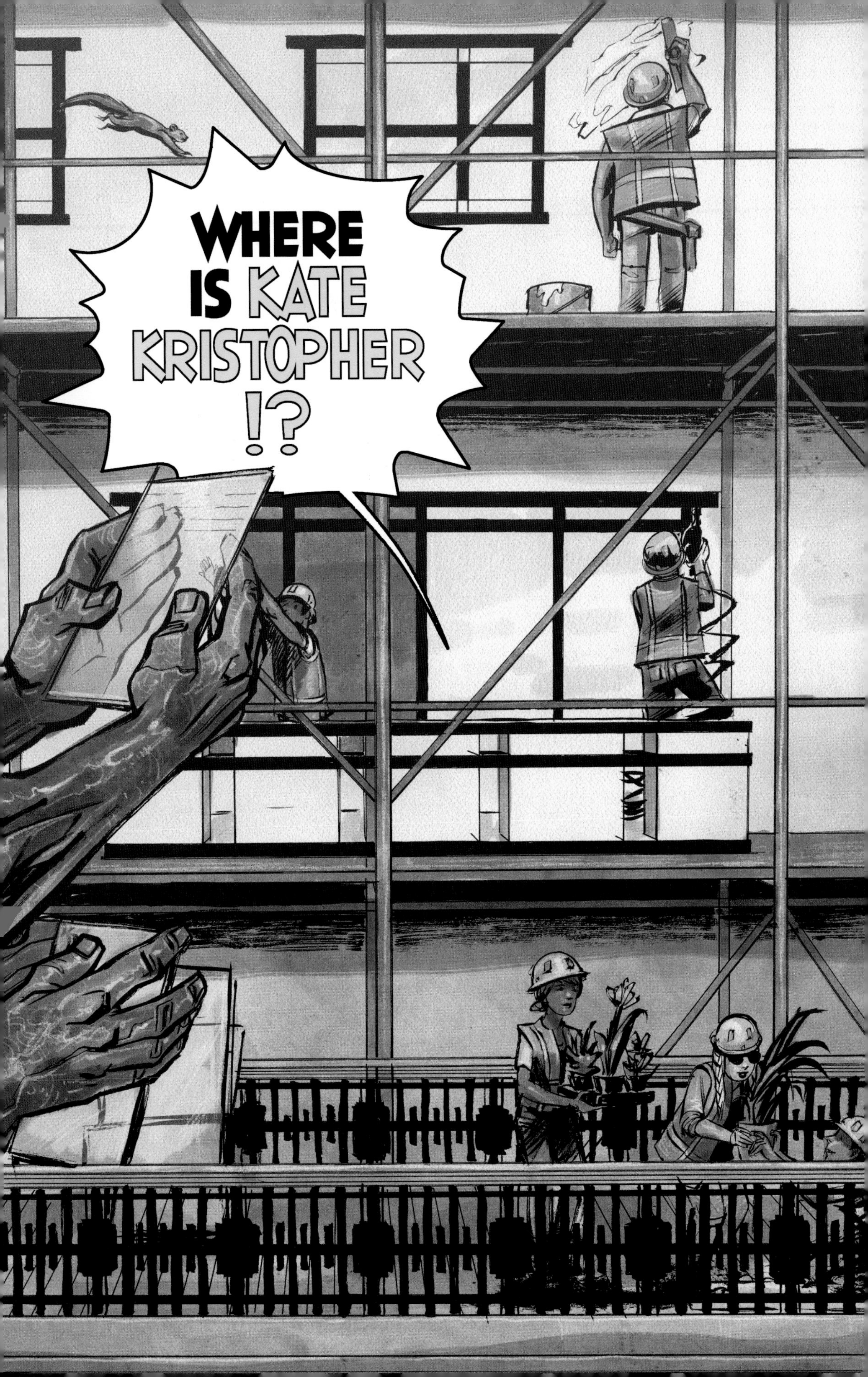
WHERE IS KATE KRISTOPHER !?

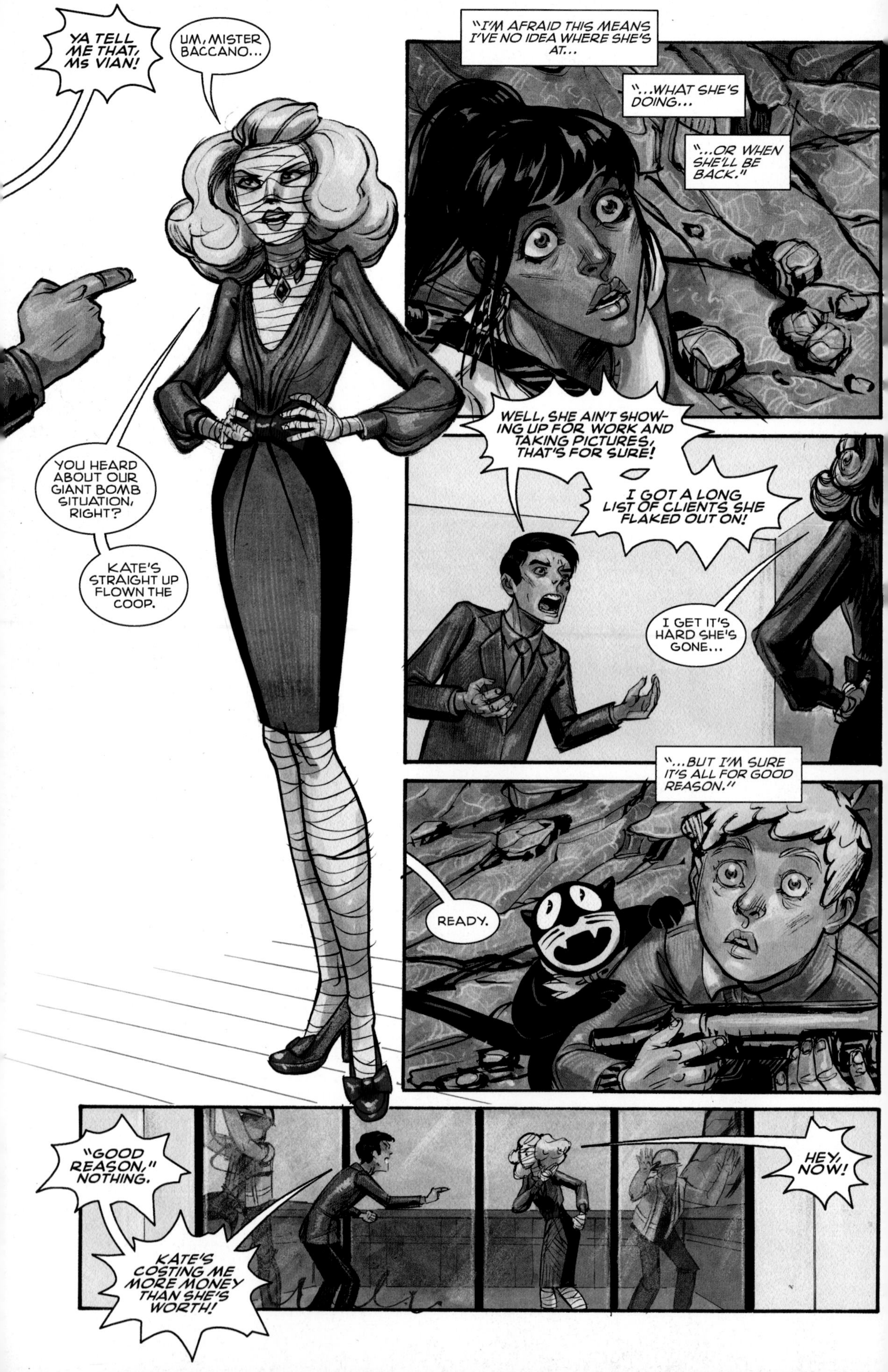
YA TELL ME THAT, Ms VIAN!
UM, MISTER BACCANO...
YOU HEARD ABOUT OUR GIANT BOMB SITUATION, RIGHT?
KATE'S STRAIGHT UP FLOWN THE COOP.
"I'M AFRAID THIS MEANS I'VE NO IDEA WHERE SHE'S AT...
"...WHAT SHE'S DOING...
"...OR WHEN SHE'LL BE BACK."
WELL, SHE AIN'T SHOWING UP FOR WORK AND TAKING PICTURES, THAT'S FOR SURE!
I GOT A LONG LIST OF CLIENTS SHE FLAKED OUT ON!
I GET IT'S HARD SHE'S GONE...
"...BUT I'M SURE IT'S ALL FOR GOOD REASON."
READY.
"GOOD REASON," NOTHING.
KATE'S COSTING ME MORE MONEY THAN SHE'S WORTH!
HEY, NOW!

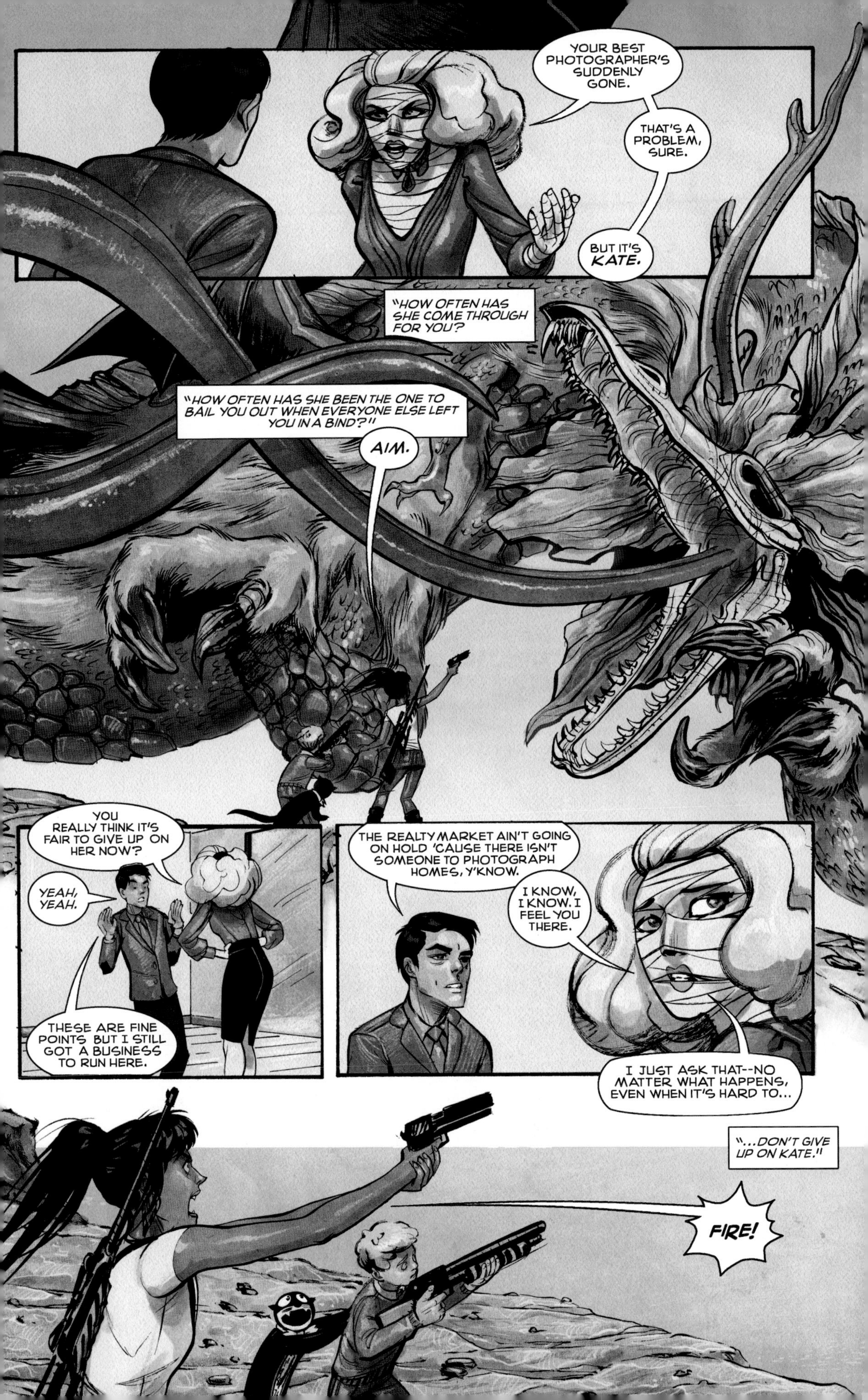

YOUR BEST PHOTOGRAPHER'S SUDDENLY GONE.
THAT'S A PROBLEM, SURE.
BUT IT'S *KATE.*
"HOW OFTEN HAS SHE COME THROUGH FOR YOU?
"HOW OFTEN HAS SHE BEEN THE ONE TO BAIL YOU OUT WHEN EVERYONE ELSE LEFT YOU IN A BIND?"
AIM.
YOU REALLY THINK IT'S FAIR TO GIVE UP ON HER NOW?
YEAH, YEAH.
THESE ARE FINE POINTS BUT I STILL GOT A BUSINESS TO RUN HERE.
THE REALTY MARKET AIN'T GOING ON HOLD 'CAUSE THERE ISN'T SOMEONE TO PHOTOGRAPH HOMES, Y'KNOW.
I KNOW, I KNOW. I FEEL YOU THERE.
I JUST ASK THAT--NO MATTER WHAT HAPPENS, EVEN WHEN IT'S HARD TO...
"...DON'T GIVE UP ON KATE."
FIRE!

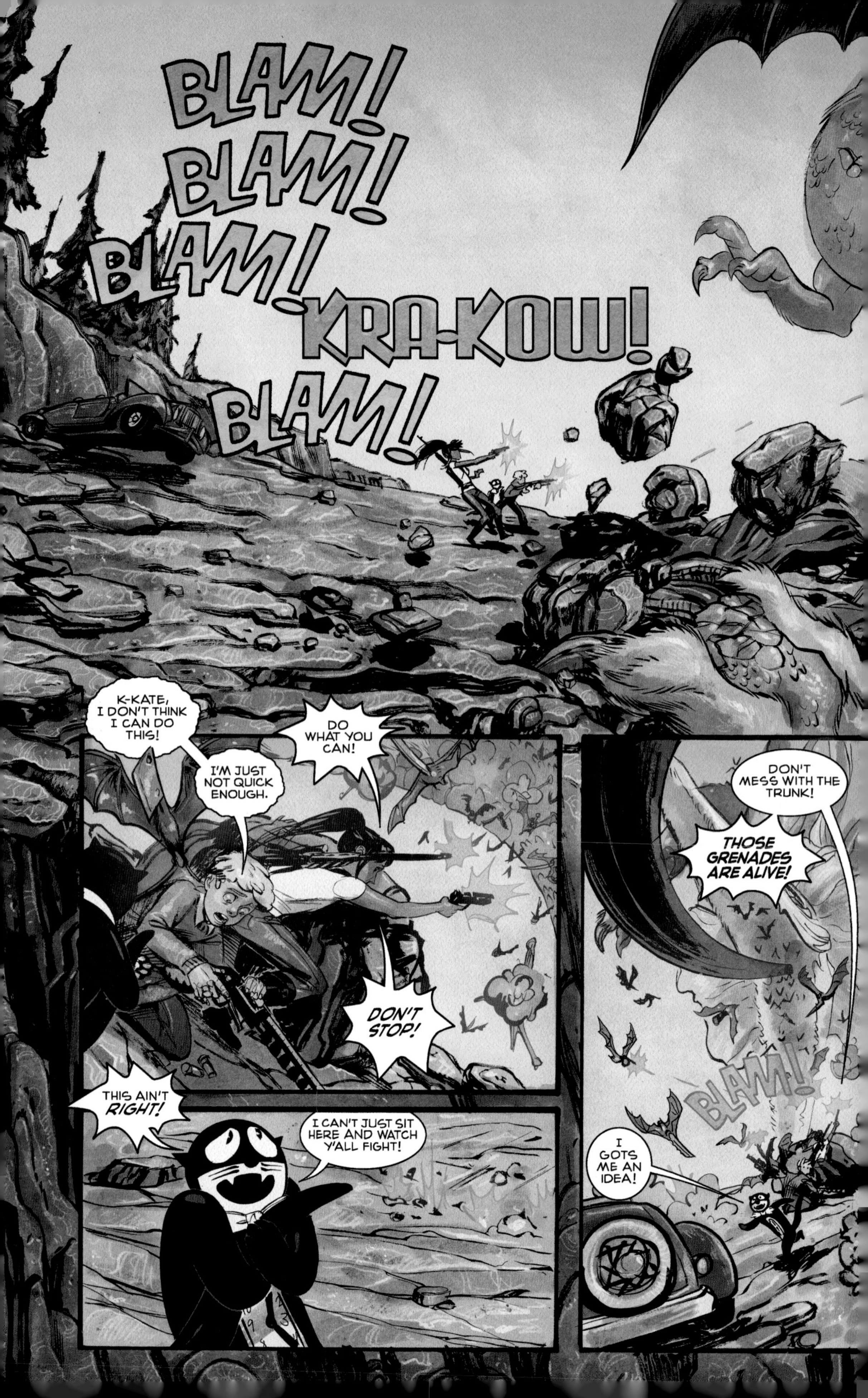
BLAM! BLAM! BLAM! KRA-KOW! BLAM!
K-KATE, I DON'T THINK I CAN DO THIS!
I'M JUST NOT QUICK ENOUGH.
DO WHAT YOU CAN!
DON'T STOP!
DON'T MESS WITH THE TRUNK!
THOSE GRENADES ARE ALIVE!
BLAM!
THIS AIN'T RIGHT!
I CAN'T JUST SIT HERE AND WATCH Y'ALL FIGHT!
I GOTS ME AN IDEA!

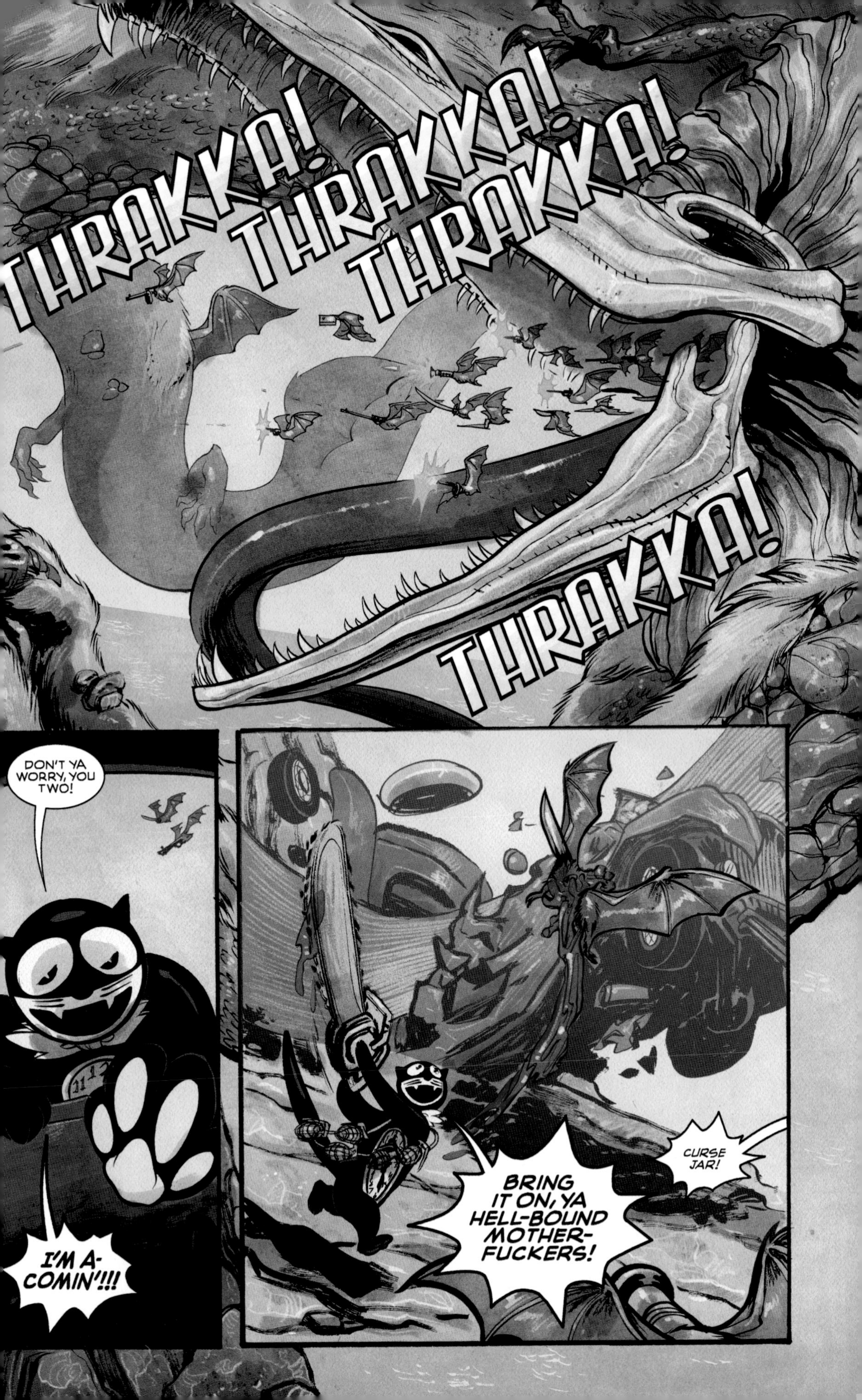
THRAKKA! THRAKKA! THRAKKA!
THRAKKA!
DON'T YA WORRY, YOU TWO!
I'M A-COMIN'!!!
BRING IT ON, YA HELL-BOUND MOTHER-FUCKERS!
CURSE JAR!

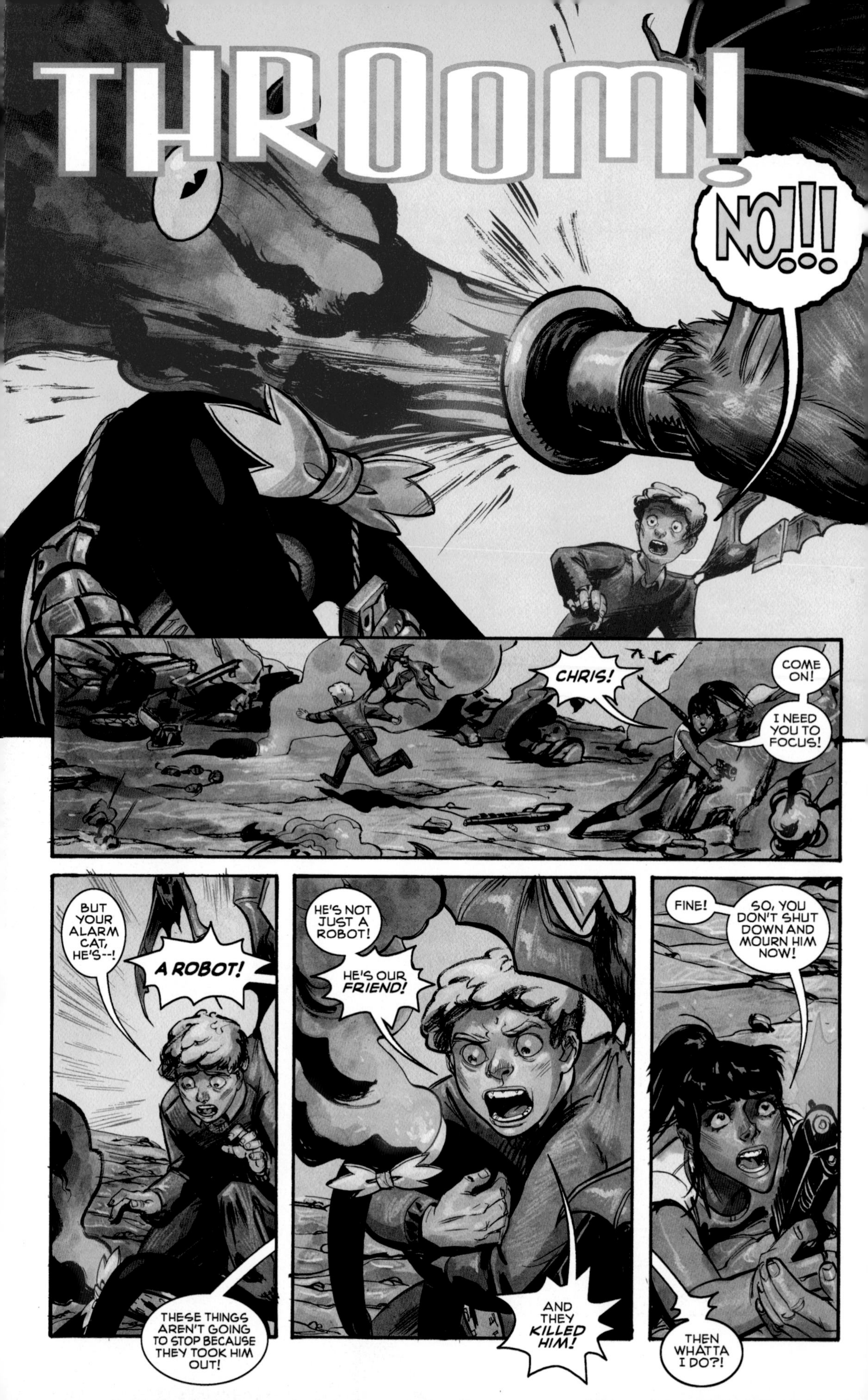
THROOM!
NO!!!
CHRIS!
COME ON!
I NEED YOU TO FOCUS!
BUT YOUR ALARM CAT, HE'S--!
A ROBOT!
THESE THINGS AREN'T GOING TO STOP BECAUSE THEY TOOK HIM OUT!
HE'S NOT JUST A ROBOT!
HE'S OUR FRIEND!
AND THEY KILLED HIM!
FINE!
SO, YOU DON'T SHUT DOWN AND MOURN HIM NOW!
THEN WHATTA I DO?!

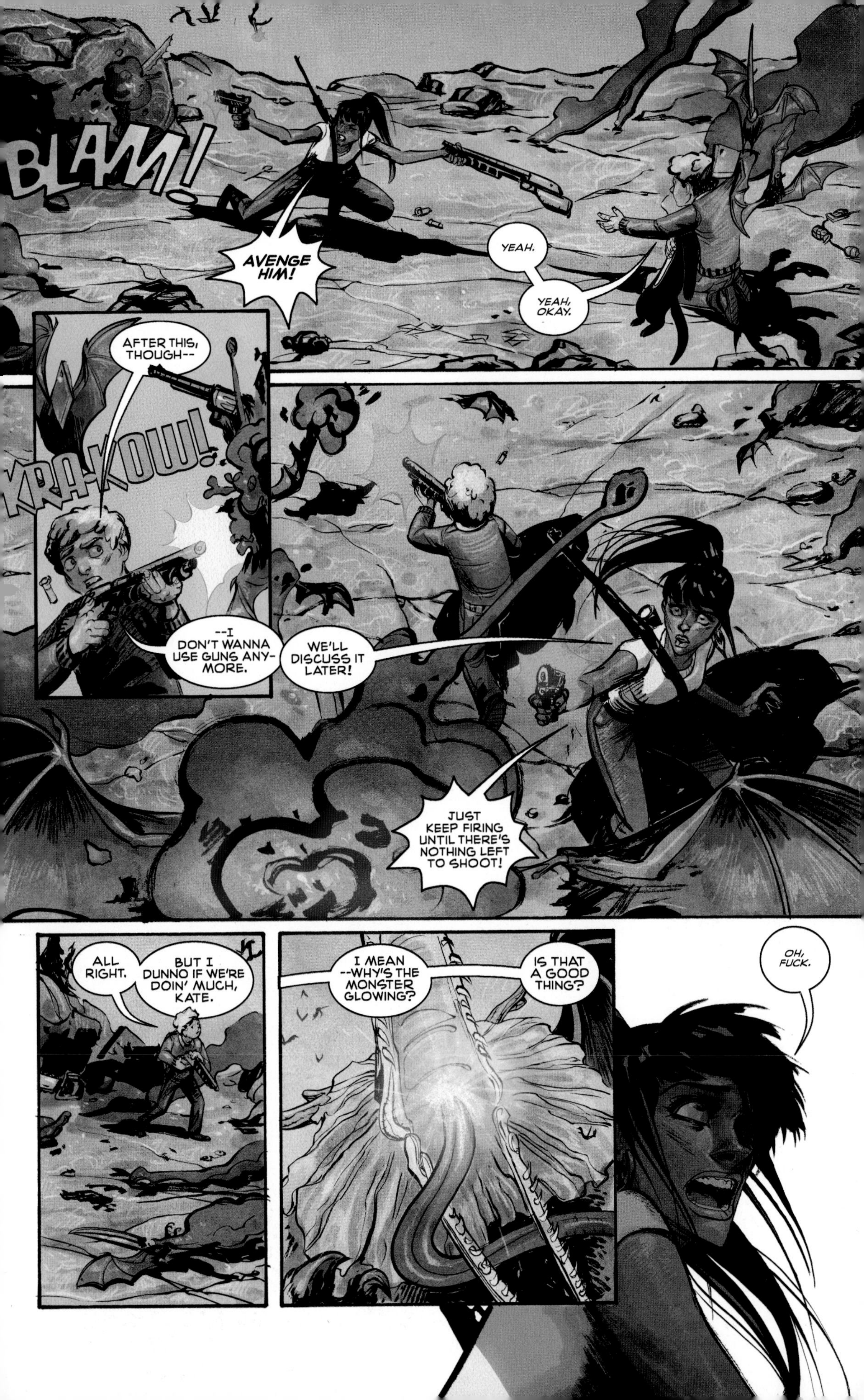
BLAM!
AVENGE HIM!
YEAH.
YEAH, OKAY.
AFTER THIS, THOUGH--
KRA-KOW!
--I DON'T WANNA USE GUNS ANYMORE.
WE'LL DISCUSS IT LATER!
JUST KEEP FIRING UNTIL THERE'S NOTHING LEFT TO SHOOT!
ALL RIGHT.
BUT I DUNNO IF WE'RE DOIN' MUCH, KATE.
I MEAN --WHY'S THE MONSTER GLOWING?
IS THAT A GOOD THING?
OH, FUCK.

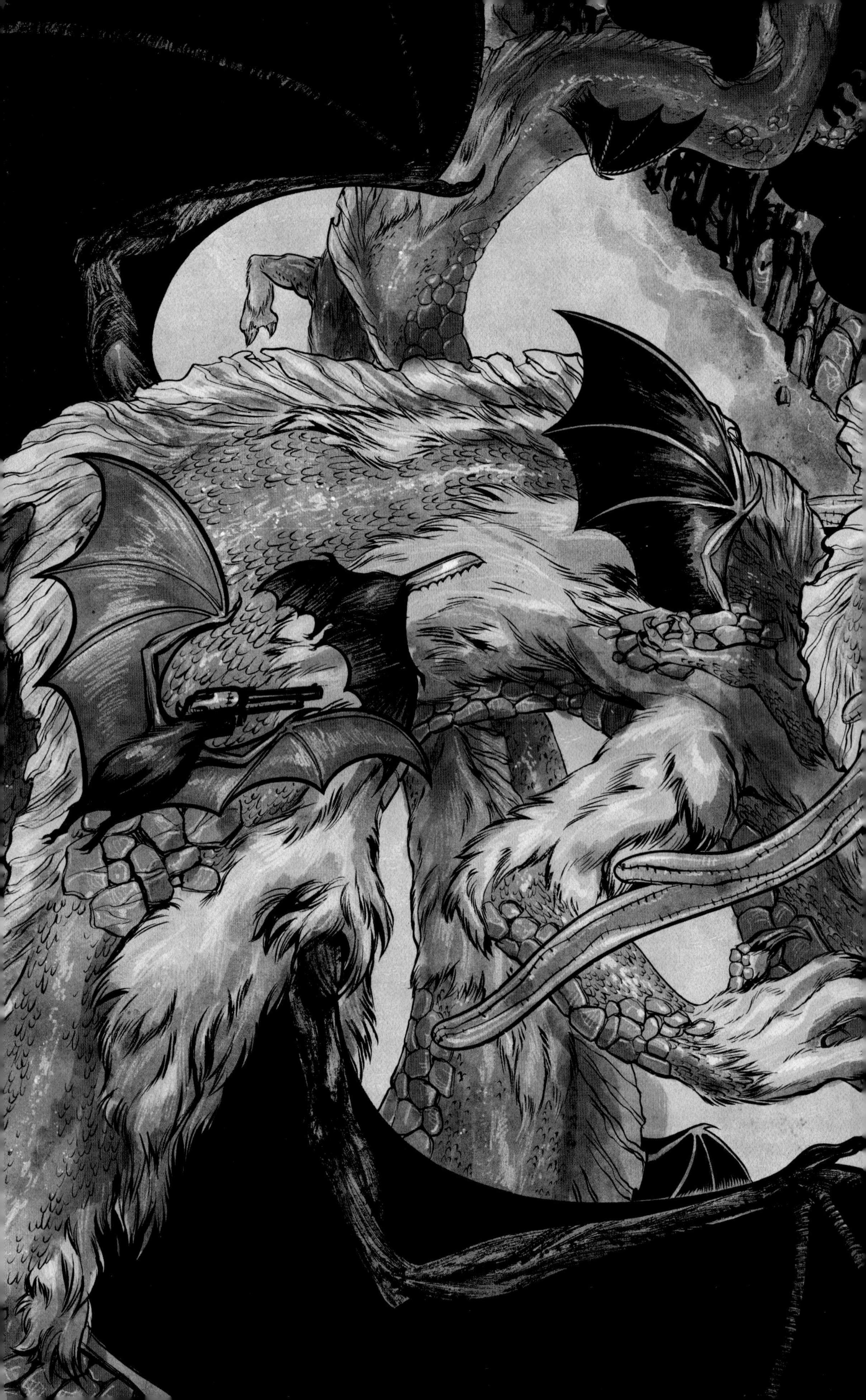

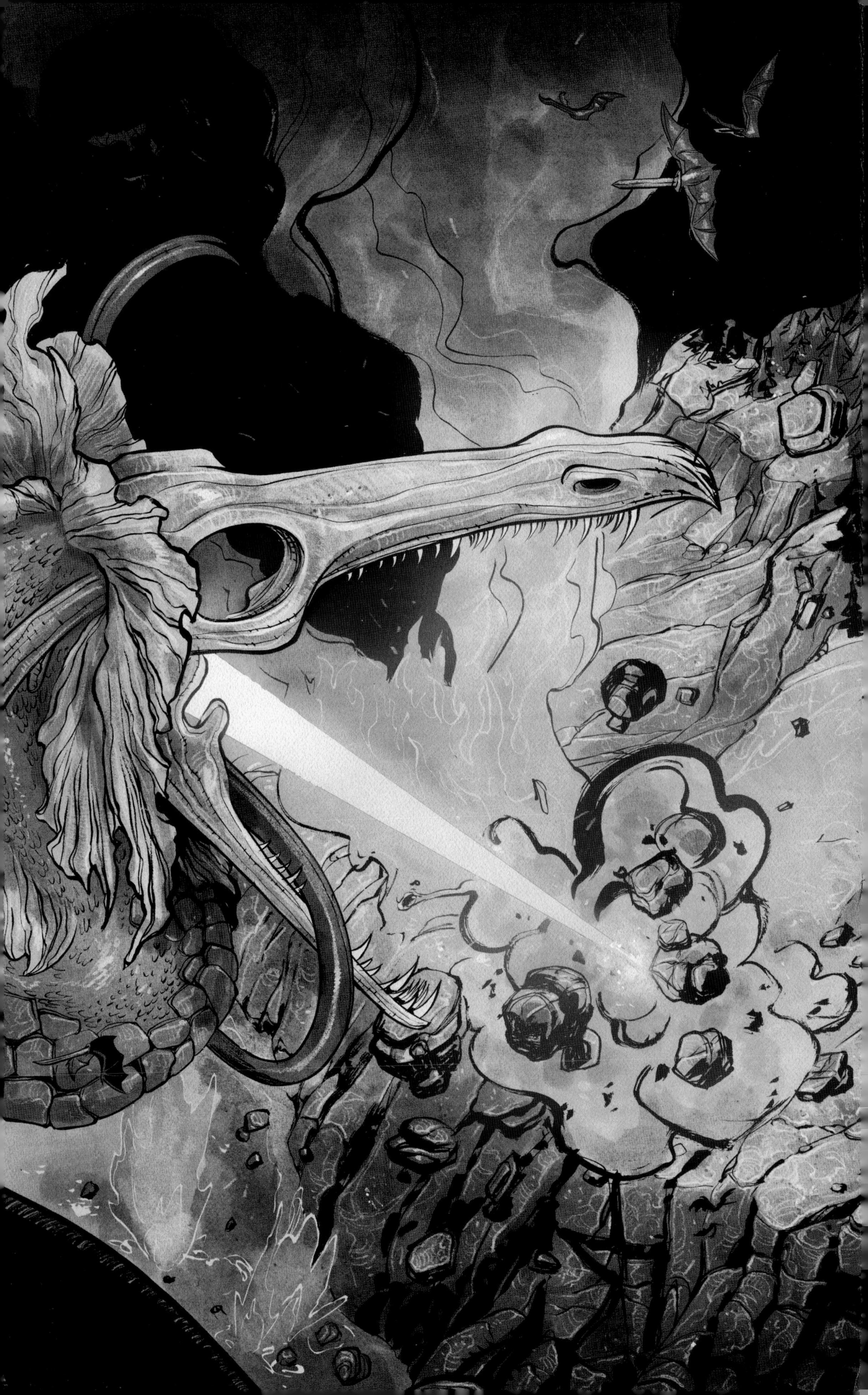

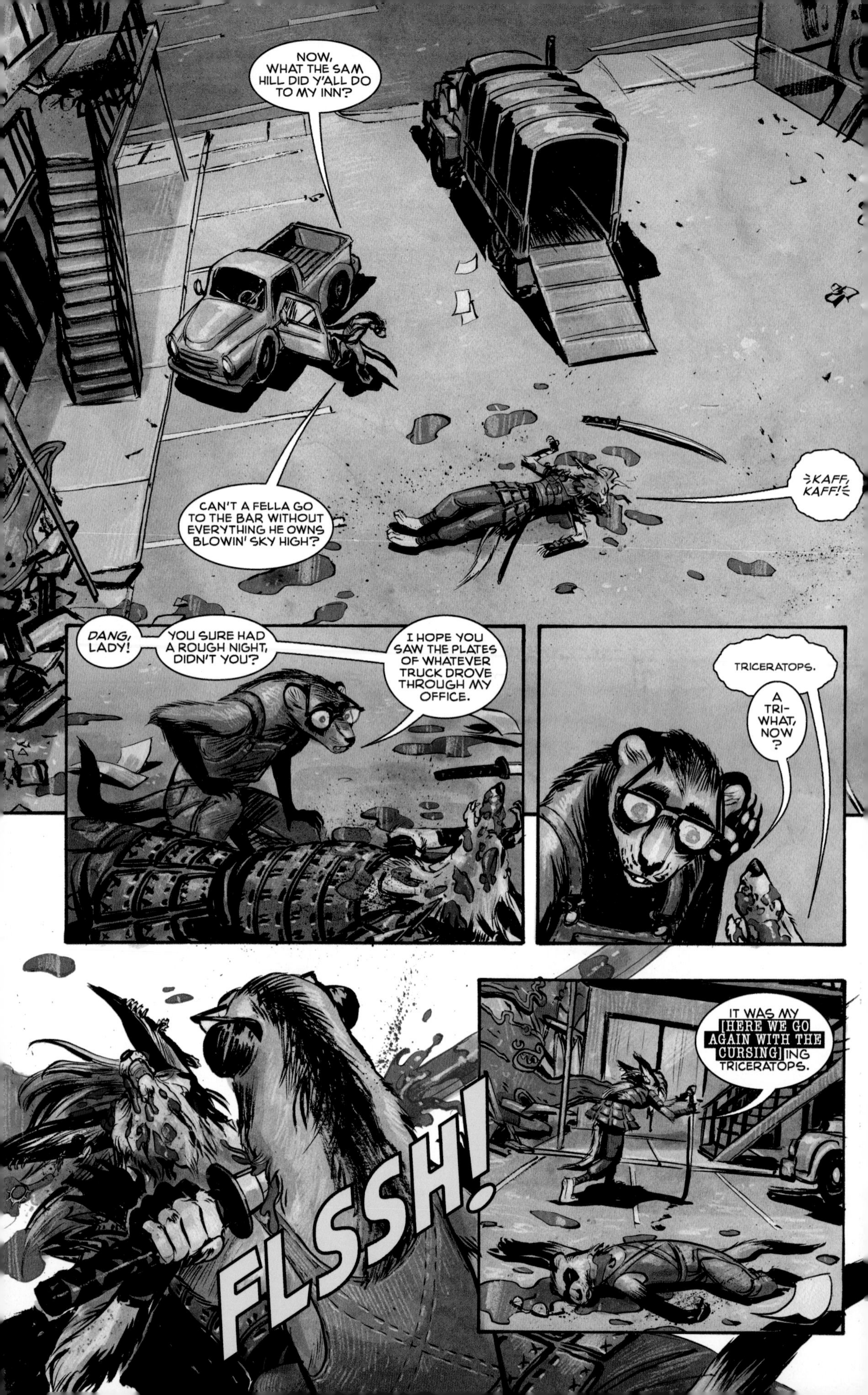
NOW, WHAT THE SAM HILL DID Y'ALL DO TO MY INN?
CAN'T A FELLA GO TO THE BAR WITHOUT EVERYTHING HE OWNS BLOWIN' SKY HIGH?
KAFF, KAFF!
DANG, LADY!
YOU SURE HAD A ROUGH NIGHT, DIDN'T YOU?
I HOPE YOU SAW THE PLATES OF WHATEVER TRUCK DROVE THROUGH MY OFFICE.
TRICERATOPS.
A TRI-WHAT, NOW?
FLSSH!
IT WAS MY [HERE WE GO AGAIN WITH THE CURSING] ING TRICERATOPS.

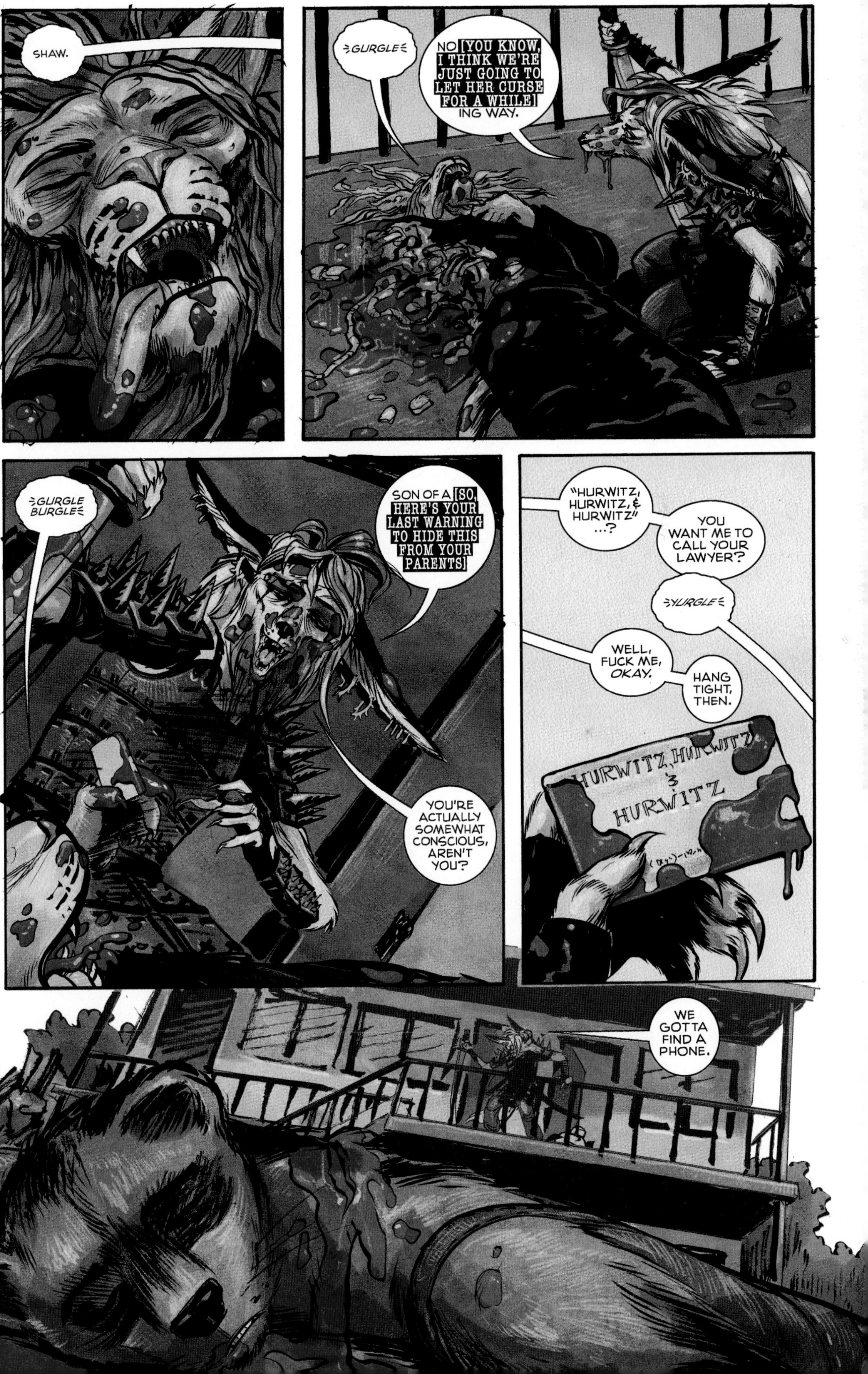
SHAW.
GURGLE
NO [YOU KNOW, I THINK WE'RE JUST GOING TO LET HER CURSE FOR A WHILE] ING WAY.
GURGLE BURGLE
SON OF A [SO, HERE'S YOUR LAST WARNING TO HIDE THIS FROM YOUR PARENTS]
YOU'RE ACTUALLY SOMEWHAT CONSCIOUS, AREN'T YOU?
"HURWITZ, HURWITZ, & HURWITZ" ...?
YOU WANT ME TO CALL YOUR LAWYER?
YURGLE
WELL, FUCK ME, OKAY.
HANG TIGHT, THEN.
HURWITZ, HURWITZ & HURWITZ
WE GOTTA FIND A PHONE.

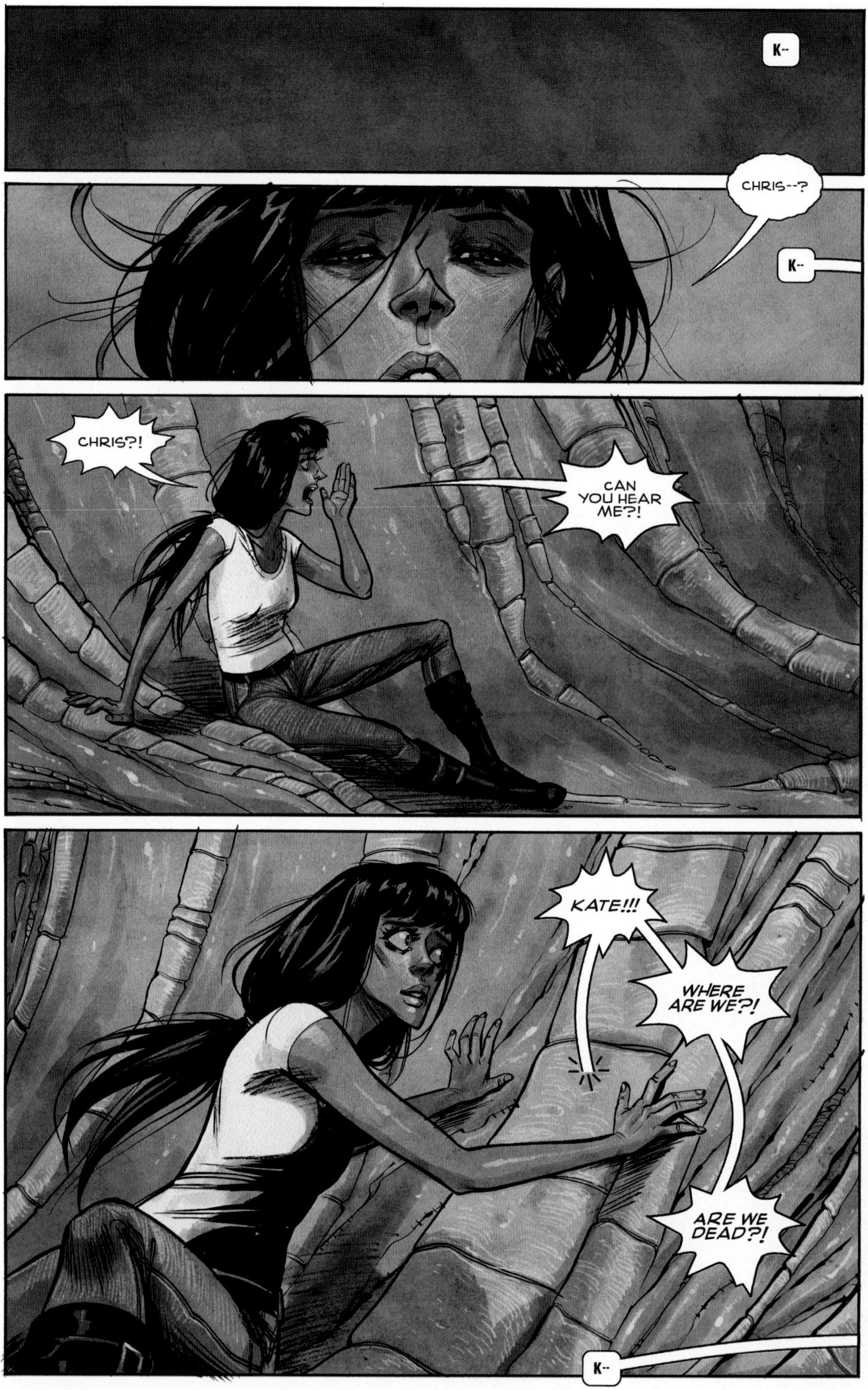

K--
CHRIS--?
K--
CHRIS?!
CAN YOU HEAR ME?!
KATE!!!
WHERE ARE WE?!
ARE WE DEAD?!
K--

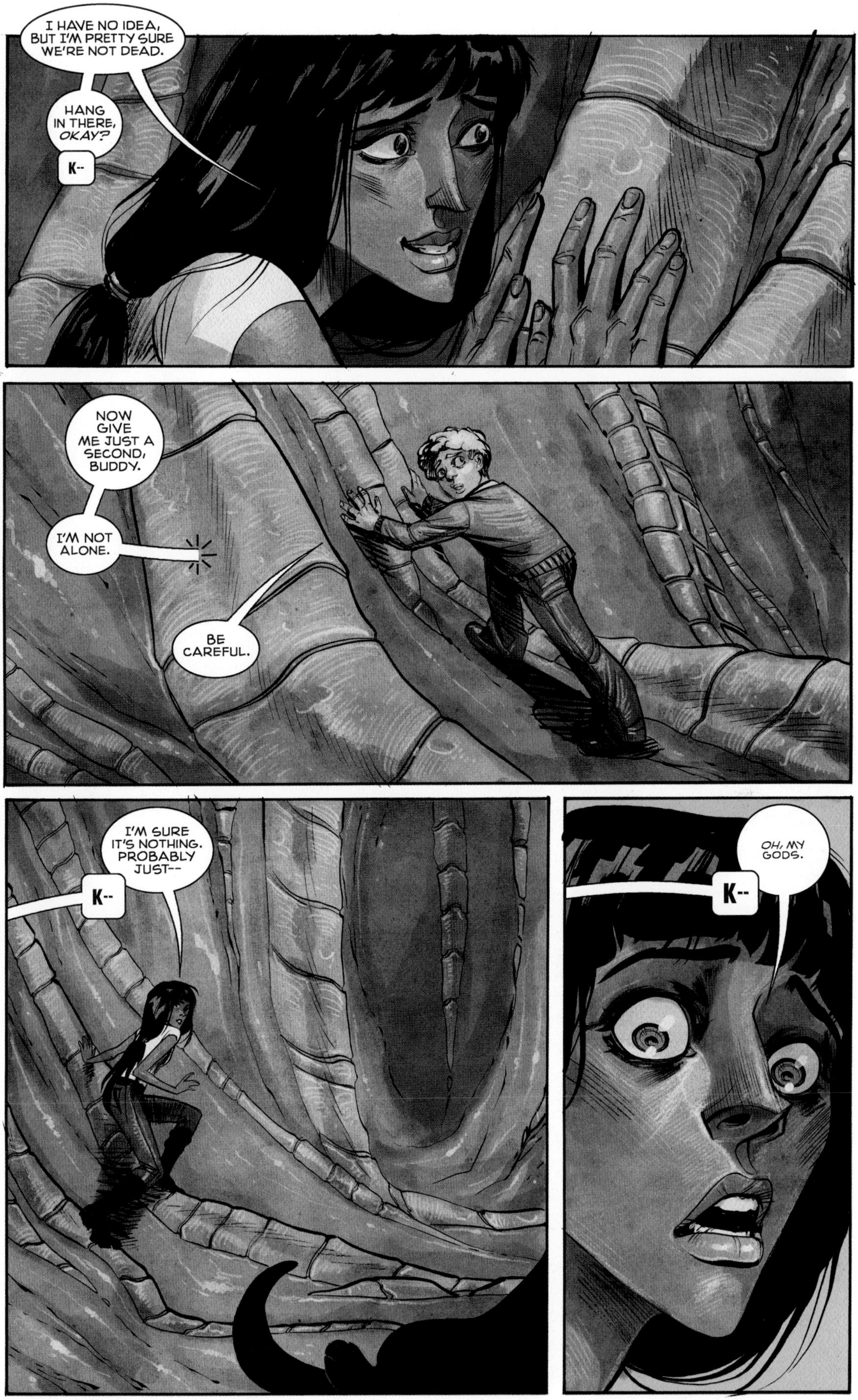
I HAVE NO IDEA, BUT I'M PRETTY SURE WE'RE NOT DEAD.
HANG IN THERE, OKAY?
K--
NOW GIVE ME JUST A SECOND, BUDDY.
I'M NOT ALONE.
BE CAREFUL.
I'M SURE IT'S NOTHING. PROBABLY JUST--
K--
OH, MY GODS.
K--

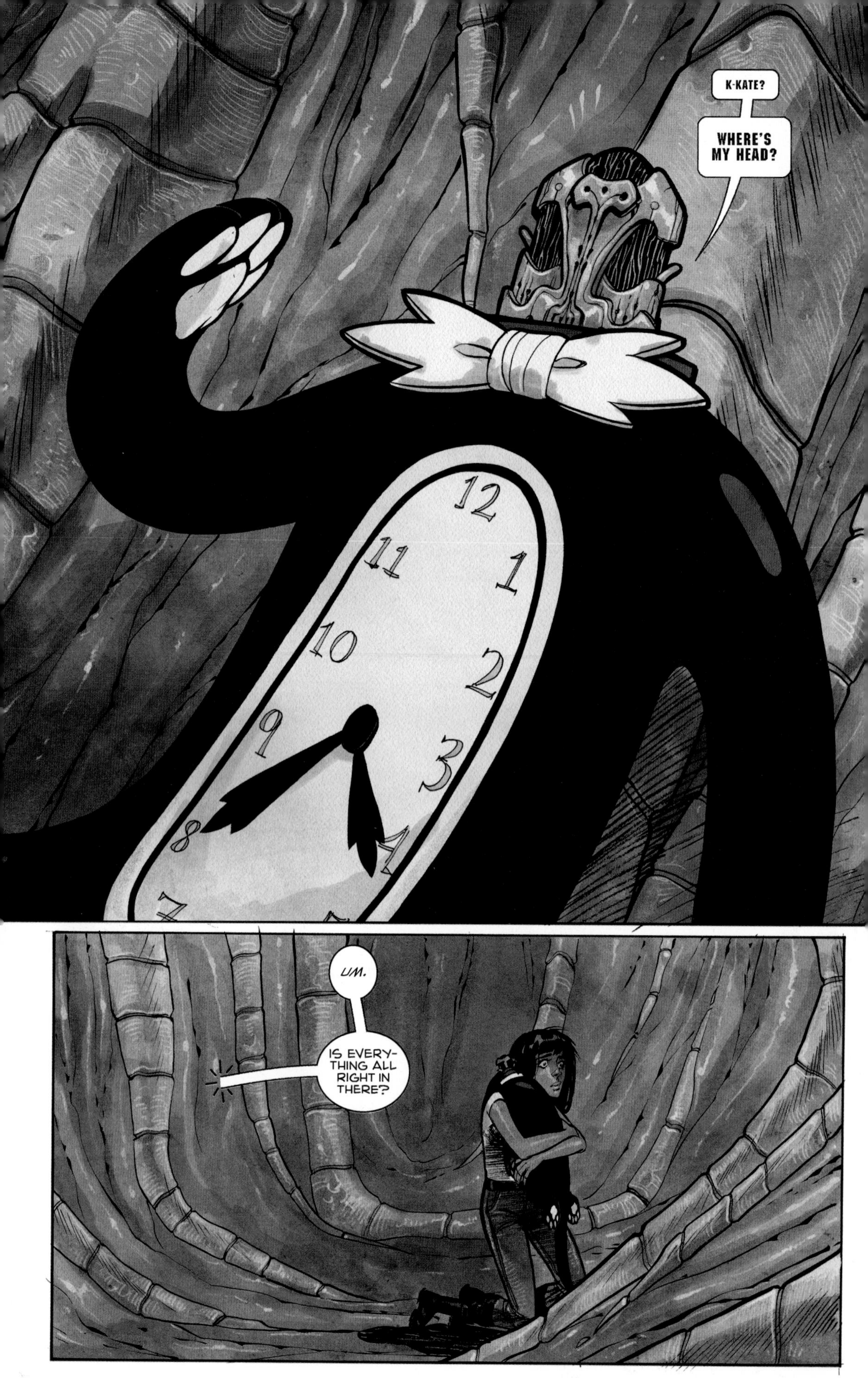
K-KATE?
WHERE'S MY HEAD?
UM.
IS EVERYTHING ALL RIGHT IN THERE?

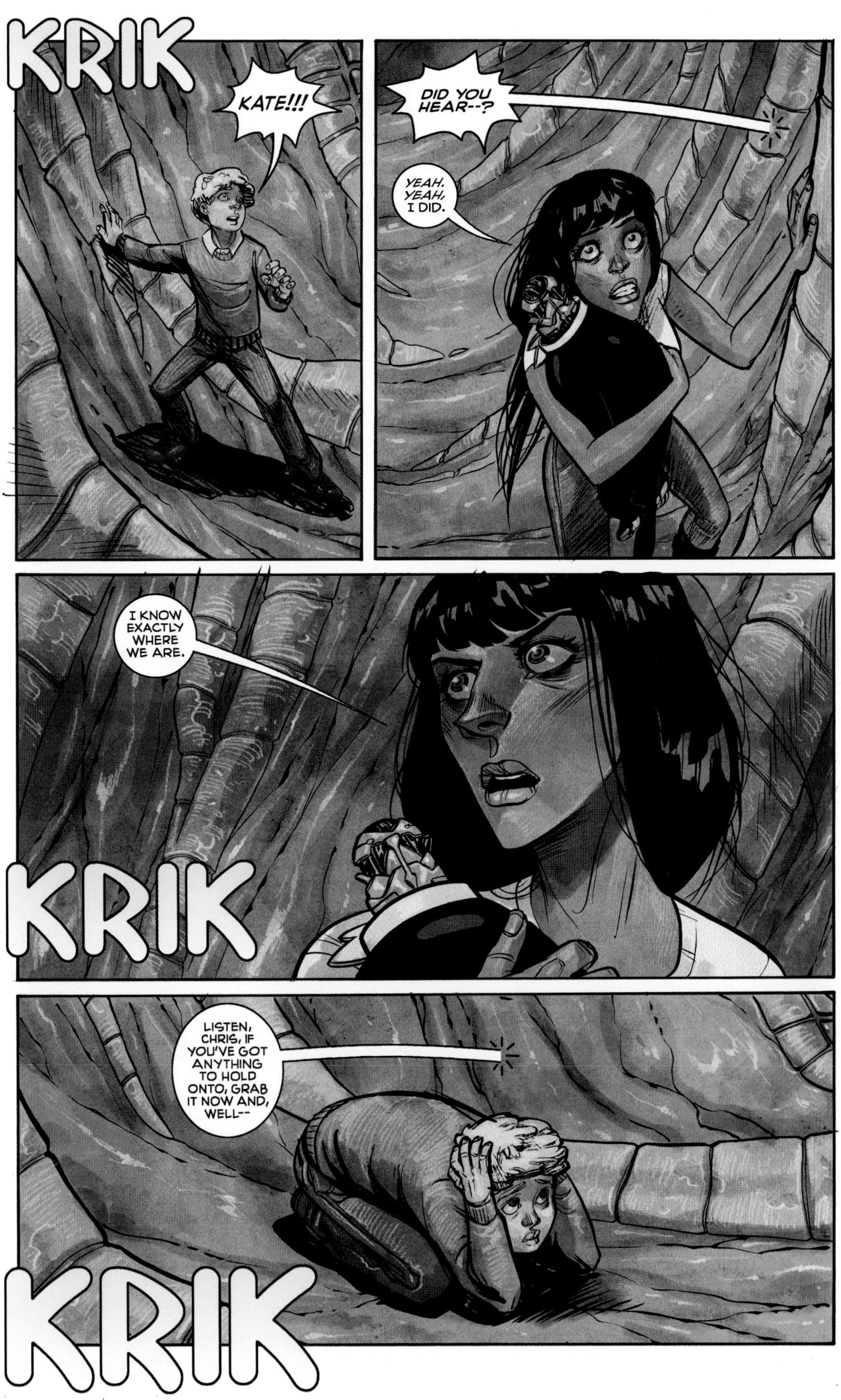
KRIK
KATE!!!
DID YOU HEAR--?
YEAH. YEAH, I DID.
I KNOW EXACTLY WHERE WE ARE.
KRIK
LISTEN, CHRIS, IF YOU'VE GOT ANYTHING TO HOLD ONTO, GRAB IT NOW AND, WELL--
KRIK

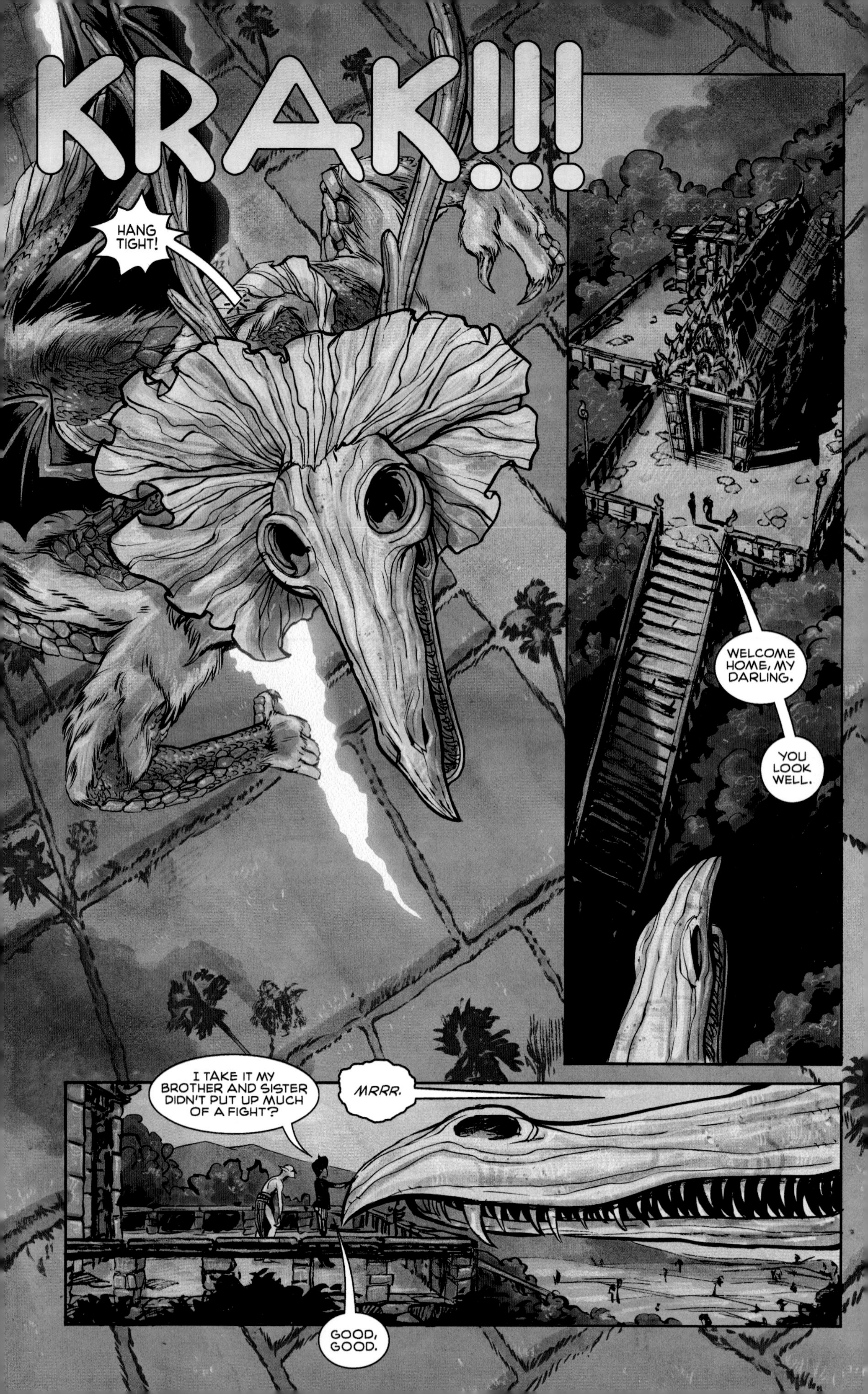
KRAK!!!
HANG TIGHT!
WELCOME HOME, MY DARLING.
YOU LOOK WELL.
I TAKE IT MY BROTHER AND SISTER DIDN'T PUT UP MUCH OF A FIGHT?
MRRR.
GOOD, GOOD.

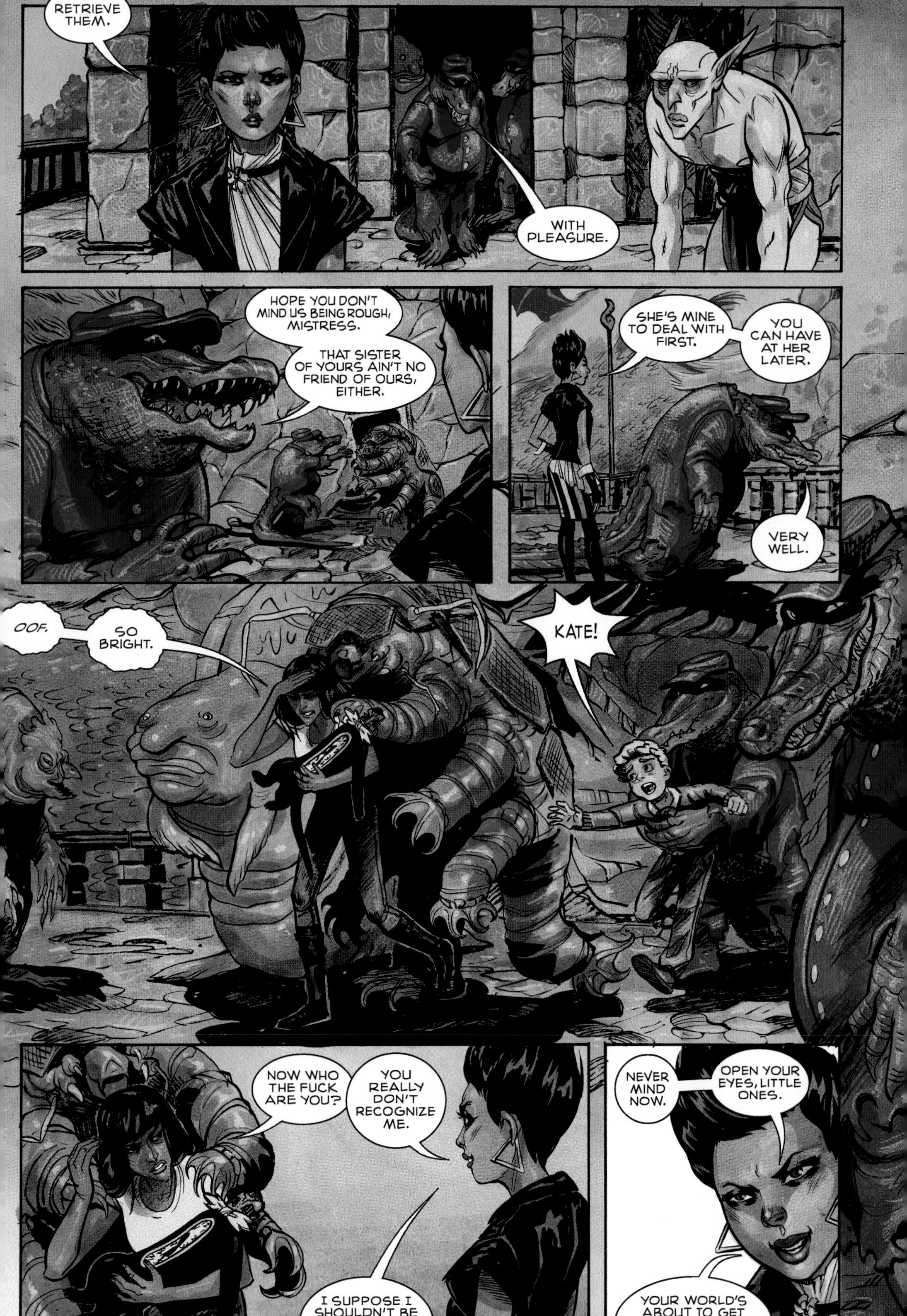
RETRIEVE THEM.
WITH PLEASURE.
HOPE YOU DON'T MIND US BEING ROUGH, MISTRESS.
THAT SISTER OF YOURS AIN'T NO FRIEND OF OURS, EITHER.
SHE'S MINE TO DEAL WITH FIRST.
YOU CAN HAVE AT HER LATER.
VERY WELL.
OOF.
SO BRIGHT.
KATE!
NOW WHO THE FUCK ARE YOU?
YOU REALLY DON'T RECOGNIZE ME.
I SUPPOSE I SHOULDN'T BE SURPRISED. YOU WERE SO YOUNG THEN.
NEVER MIND NOW.
OPEN YOUR EYES, LITTLE ONES.
YOUR WORLD'S ABOUT TO GET MUCH LARGER THAN YOU'VE EVER ANTICIPATED.

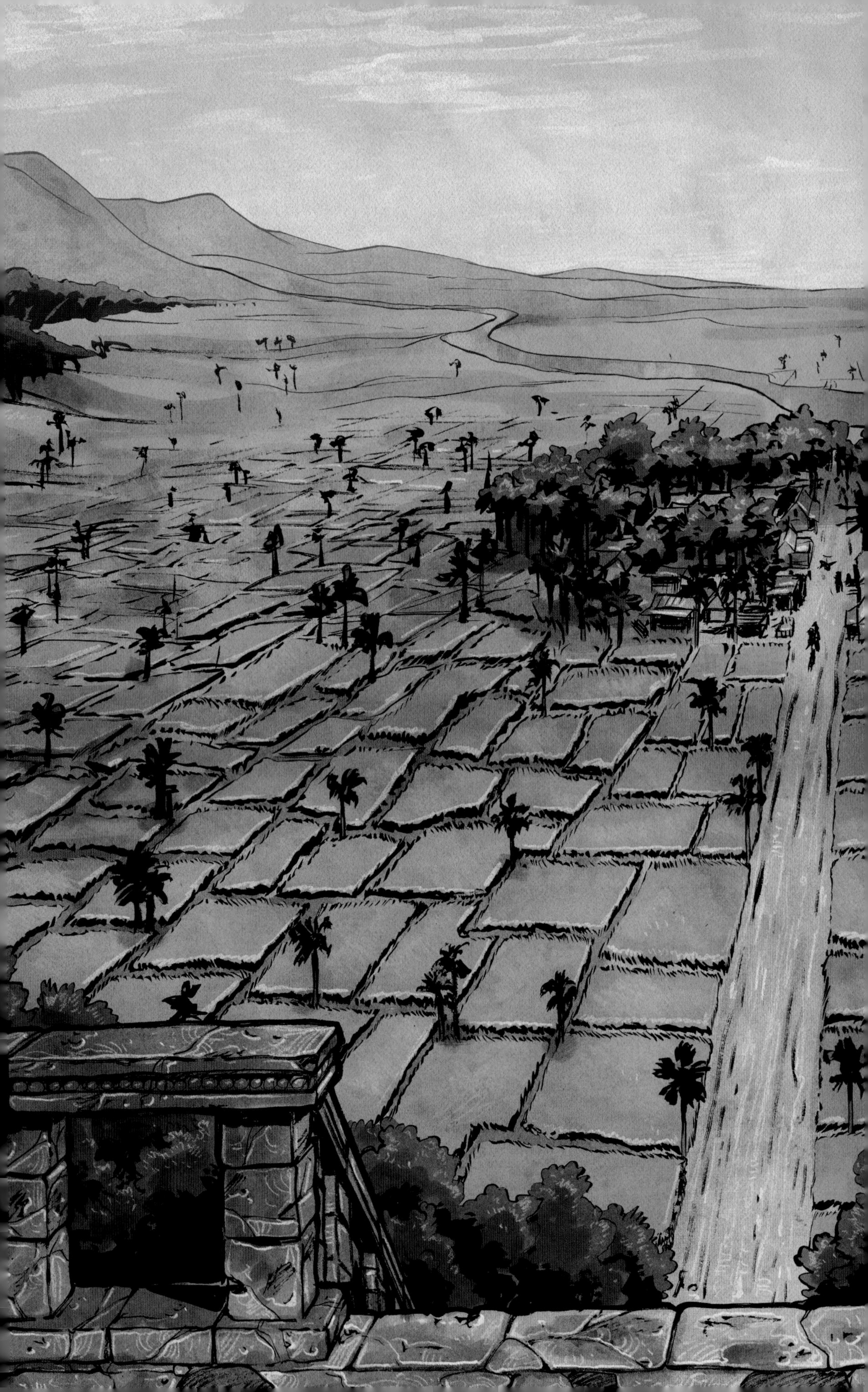

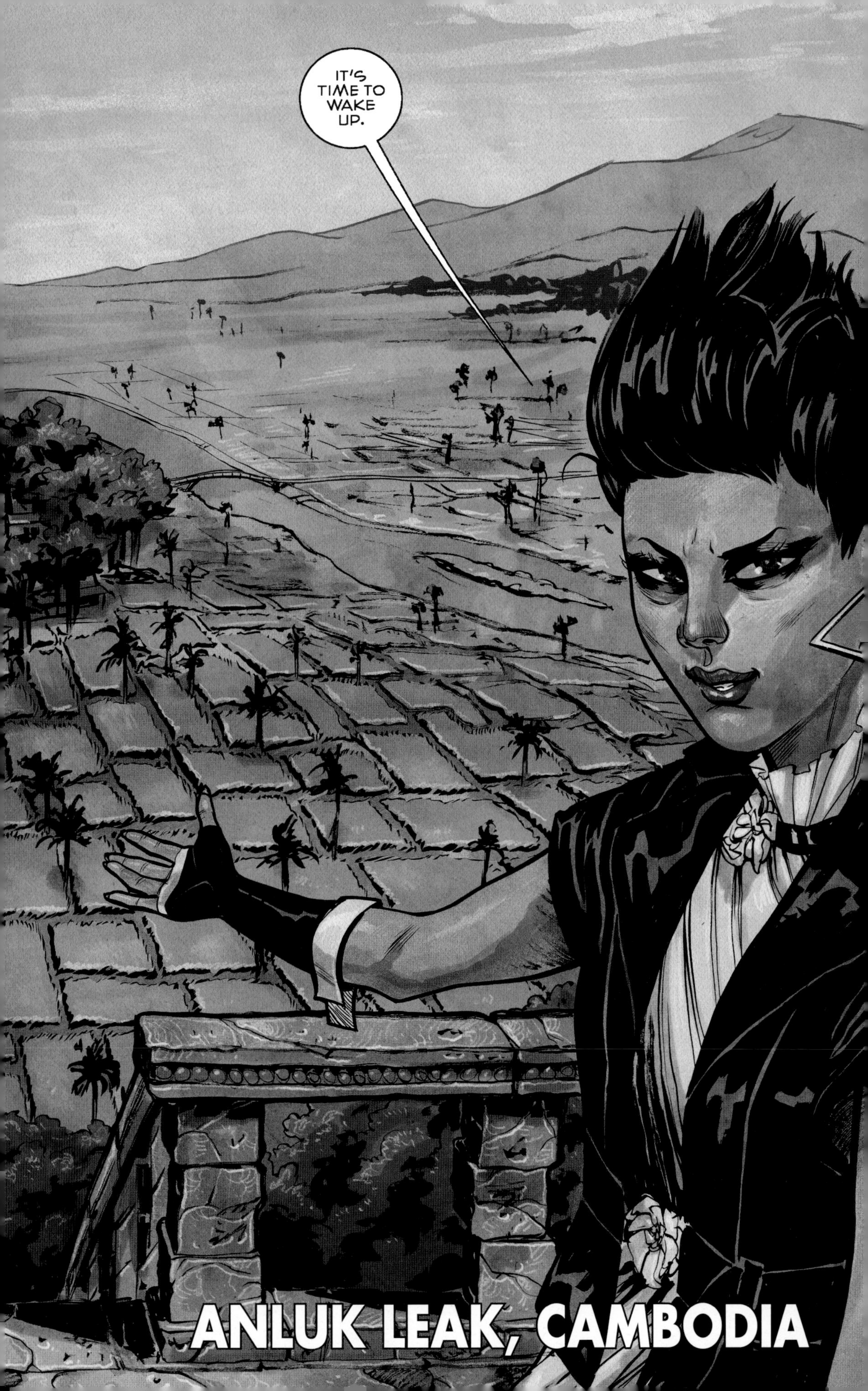
IT'S TIME TO WAKE UP.
ANLUK LEAK, CAMBODIA

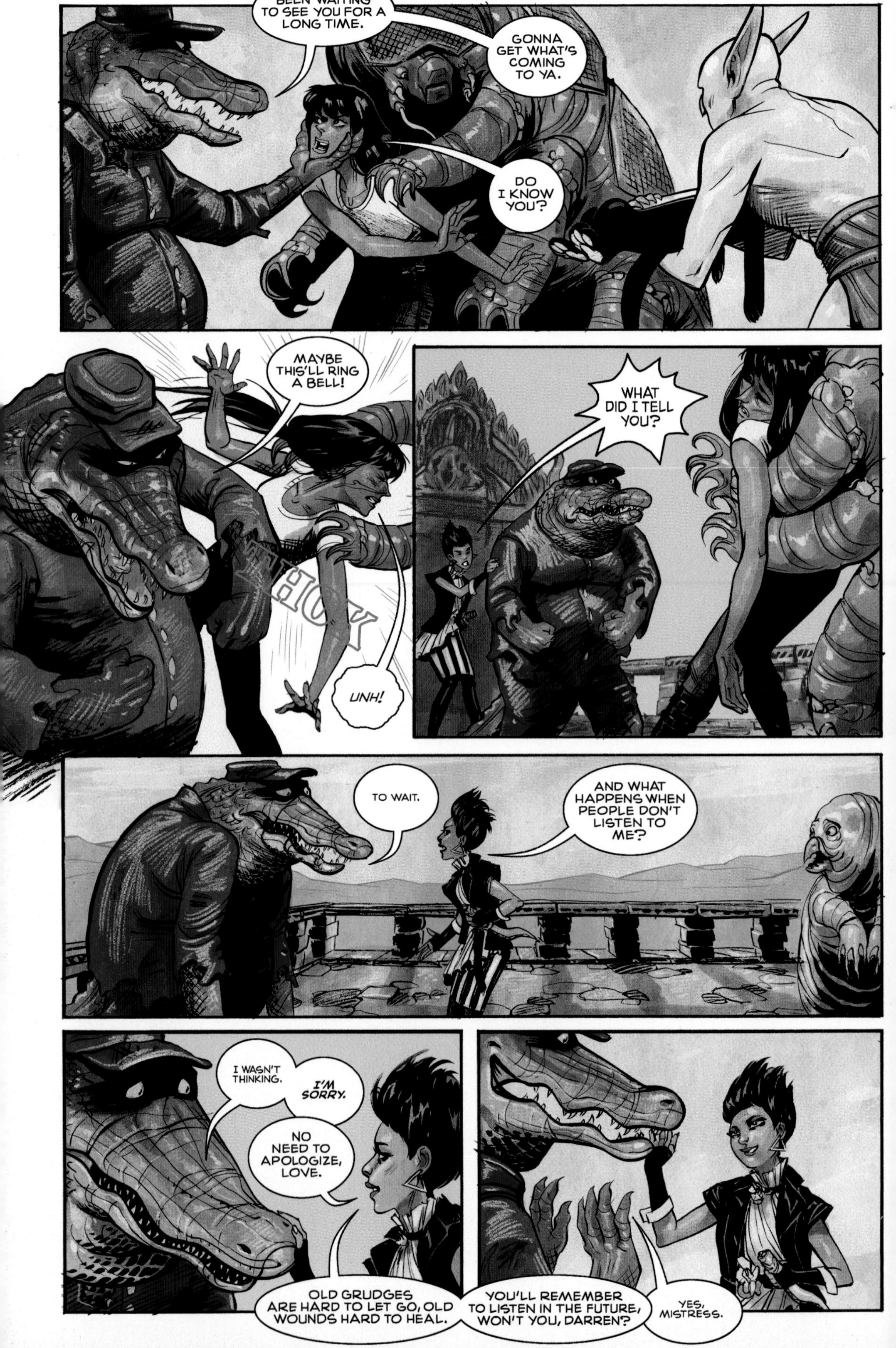
BEEN WAITING TO SEE YOU FOR A LONG TIME.
GONNA GET WHAT'S COMING TO YA.
DO I KNOW YOU?
MAYBE THIS'LL RING A BELL!
THOK
UNH!
WHAT DID I TELL YOU?
TO WAIT.
AND WHAT HAPPENS WHEN PEOPLE DON'T LISTEN TO ME?
I WASN'T THINKING.
I'M SORRY.
NO NEED TO APOLOGIZE, LOVE.
OLD GRUDGES ARE HARD TO LET GO, OLD WOUNDS HARD TO HEAL.
YOU'LL REMEMBER TO LISTEN IN THE FUTURE, WON'T YOU, DARREN?
YES, MISTRESS.

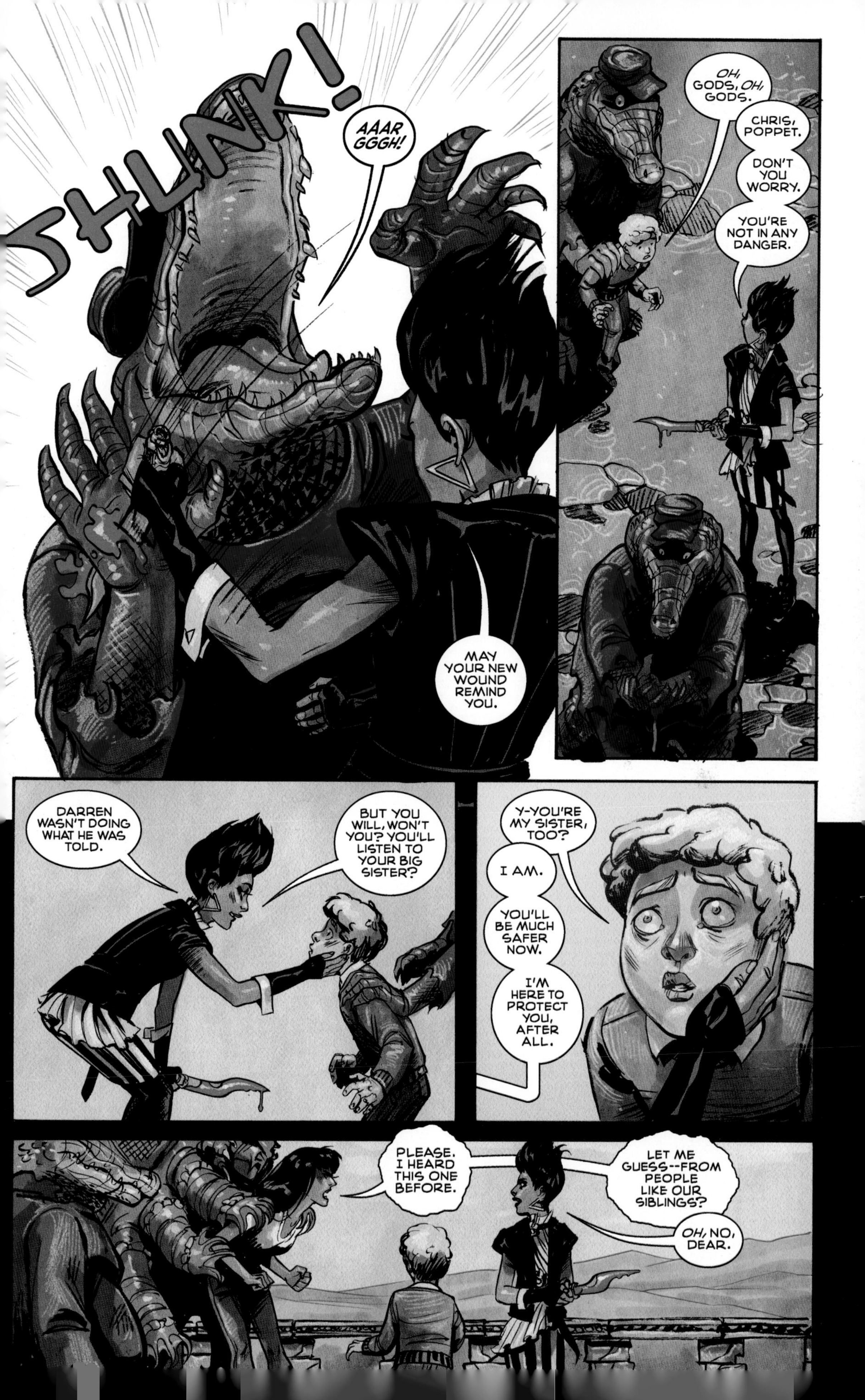
SHUNK!
AAARGGGH!
MAY YOUR NEW WOUND REMIND YOU.
OH, GODS, OH, GODS.
CHRIS, POPPET.
DON'T YOU WORRY.
YOU'RE NOT IN ANY DANGER.
DARREN WASN'T DOING WHAT HE WAS TOLD.
BUT YOU WILL, WON'T YOU? YOU'LL LISTEN TO YOUR BIG SISTER?
Y-YOU'RE MY SISTER, TOO?
I AM.
YOU'LL BE MUCH SAFER NOW.
I'M HERE TO PROTECT YOU, AFTER ALL.
PLEASE. I HEARD THIS ONE BEFORE.
LET ME GUESS--FROM PEOPLE LIKE OUR SIBLINGS?
OH, NO, DEAR.

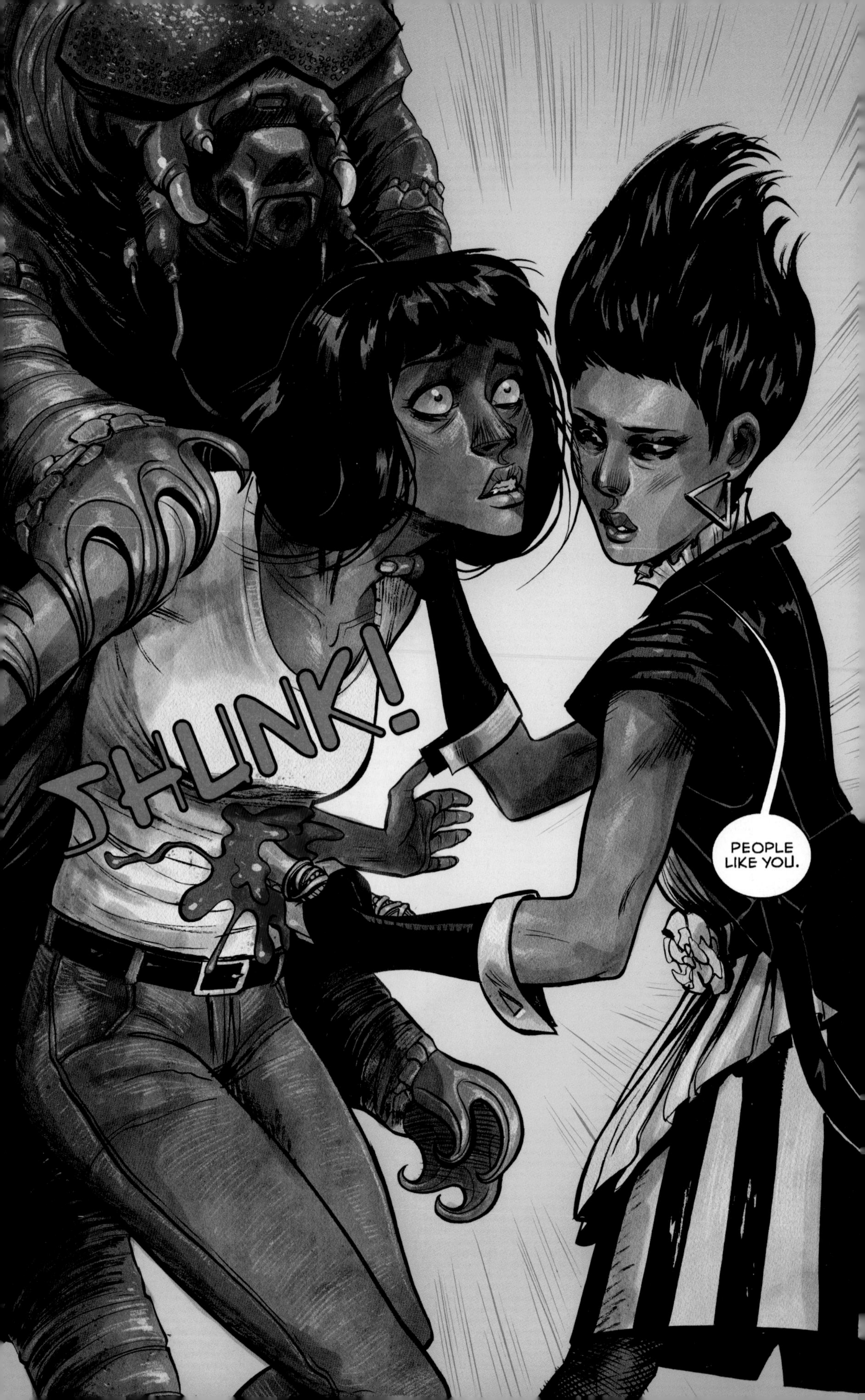
SHUNK!
PEOPLE LIKE YOU.

CHAPTER 8

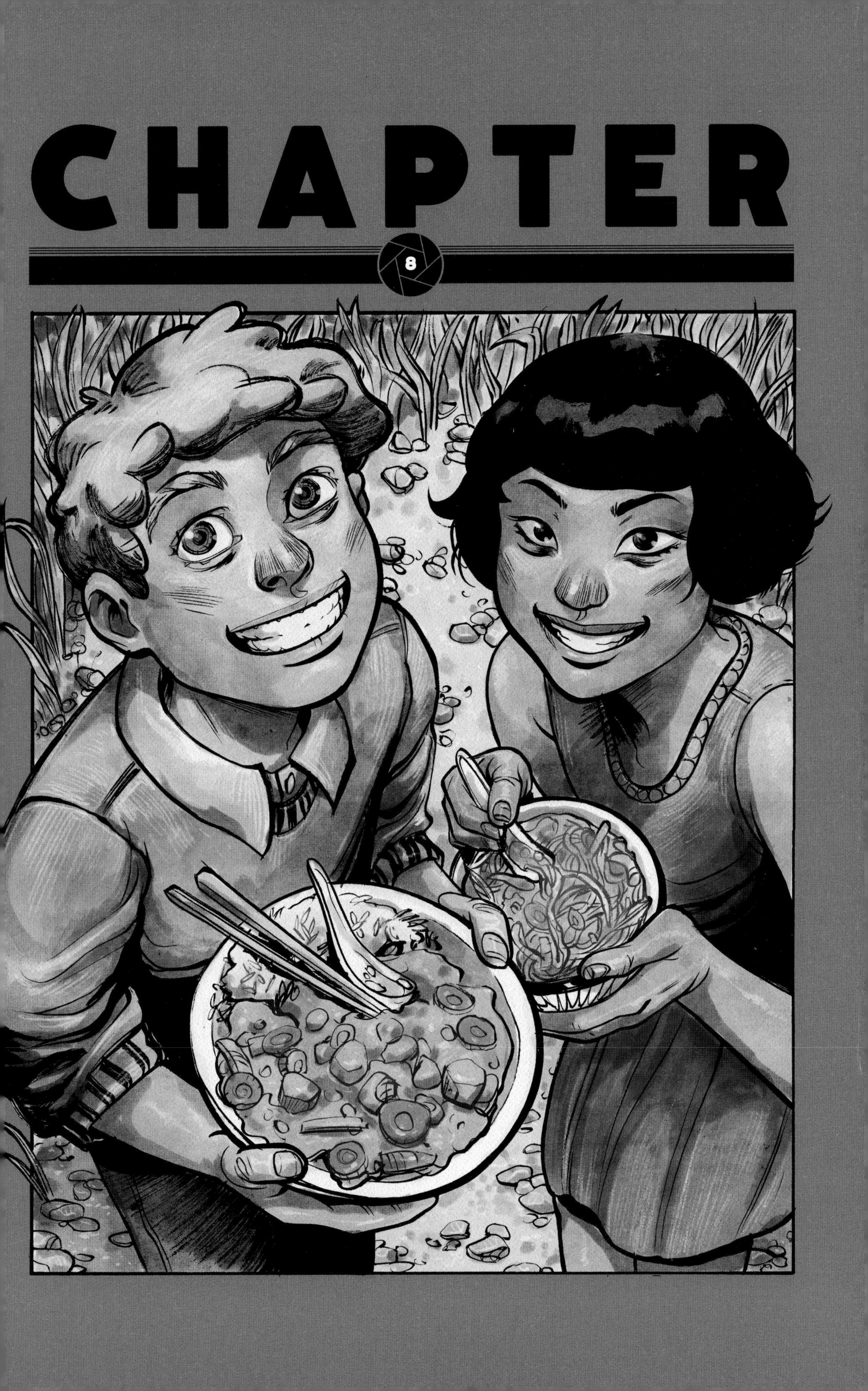

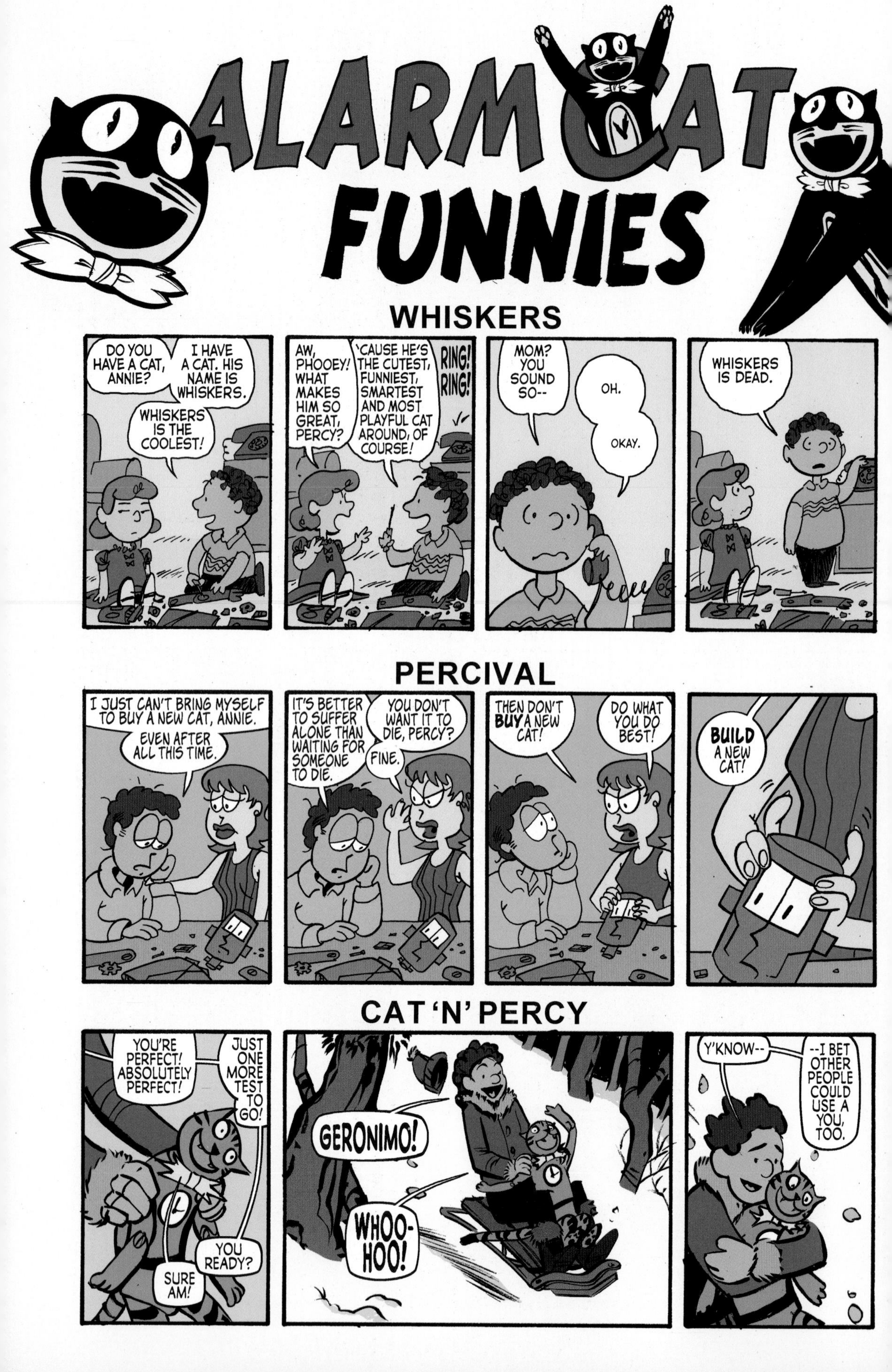

ALARM CAT FUNNIES
WHISKERS
DO YOU HAVE A CAT, ANNIE?
I HAVE A CAT. HIS NAME IS WHISKERS.
WHISKERS IS THE COOLEST!
AW, PHOOEY! WHAT MAKES HIM SO GREAT, PERCY?
'CAUSE HE'S THE CUTEST, FUNNIEST, SMARTEST AND MOST PLAYFUL CAT AROUND, OF COURSE!
RING! RING!
MOM? YOU SOUND SO--
OH.
OKAY.
WHISKERS IS DEAD.
PERCIVAL
I JUST CAN'T BRING MYSELF TO BUY A NEW CAT, ANNIE.
EVEN AFTER ALL THIS TIME.
IT'S BETTER TO SUFFER ALONE THAN WAITING FOR SOMEONE TO DIE.
YOU DON'T WANT IT TO DIE, PERCY?
FINE.
THEN DON'T BUY A NEW CAT!
DO WHAT YOU DO BEST!
BUILD A NEW CAT!
CAT 'N' PERCY
YOU'RE PERFECT! ABSOLUTELY PERFECT!
JUST ONE MORE TEST TO GO!
YOU READY?
SURE AM!
GERONIMO!
WHOO-HOO!
Y'KNOW--
--I BET OTHER PEOPLE COULD USE A YOU, TOO.

PRODUCTION CIRCUS

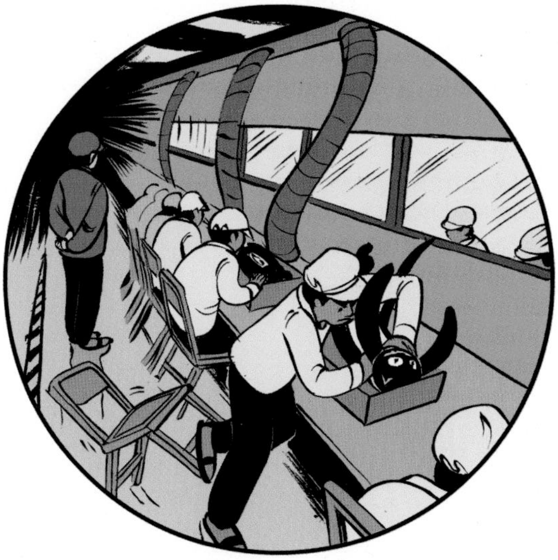

"Quit struggling! At least you get to leave!"

CAT-TROT

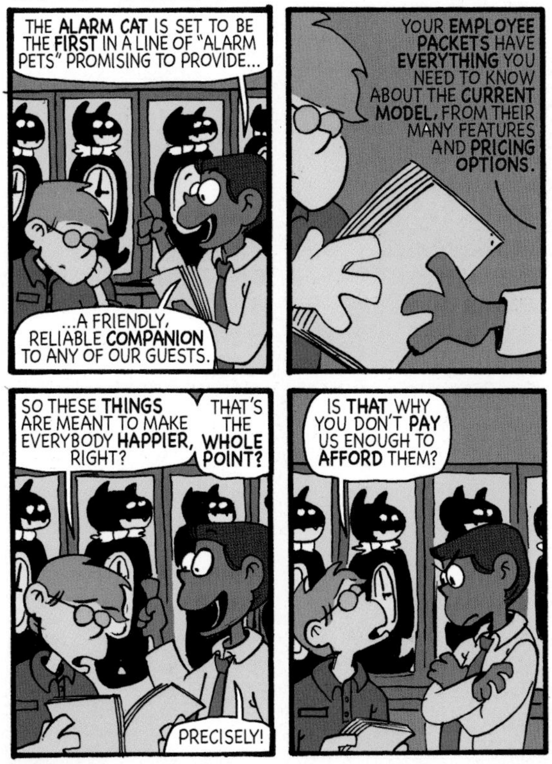
THE ALARM CAT IS SET TO BE THE FIRST IN A LINE OF "ALARM PETS" PROMISING TO PROVIDE...
...A FRIENDLY, RELIABLE COMPANION TO ANY OF OUR GUESTS.
YOUR EMPLOYEE PACKETS HAVE EVERYTHING YOU NEED TO KNOW ABOUT THE CURRENT MODEL, FROM THEIR MANY FEATURES AND PRICING OPTIONS.
SO THESE THINGS ARE MEANT TO MAKE EVERYBODY HAPPIER, RIGHT?
THAT'S THE WHOLE POINT?
PRECISELY!
IS THAT WHY YOU DON'T PAY US ENOUGH TO AFFORD THEM?

MOOGIES

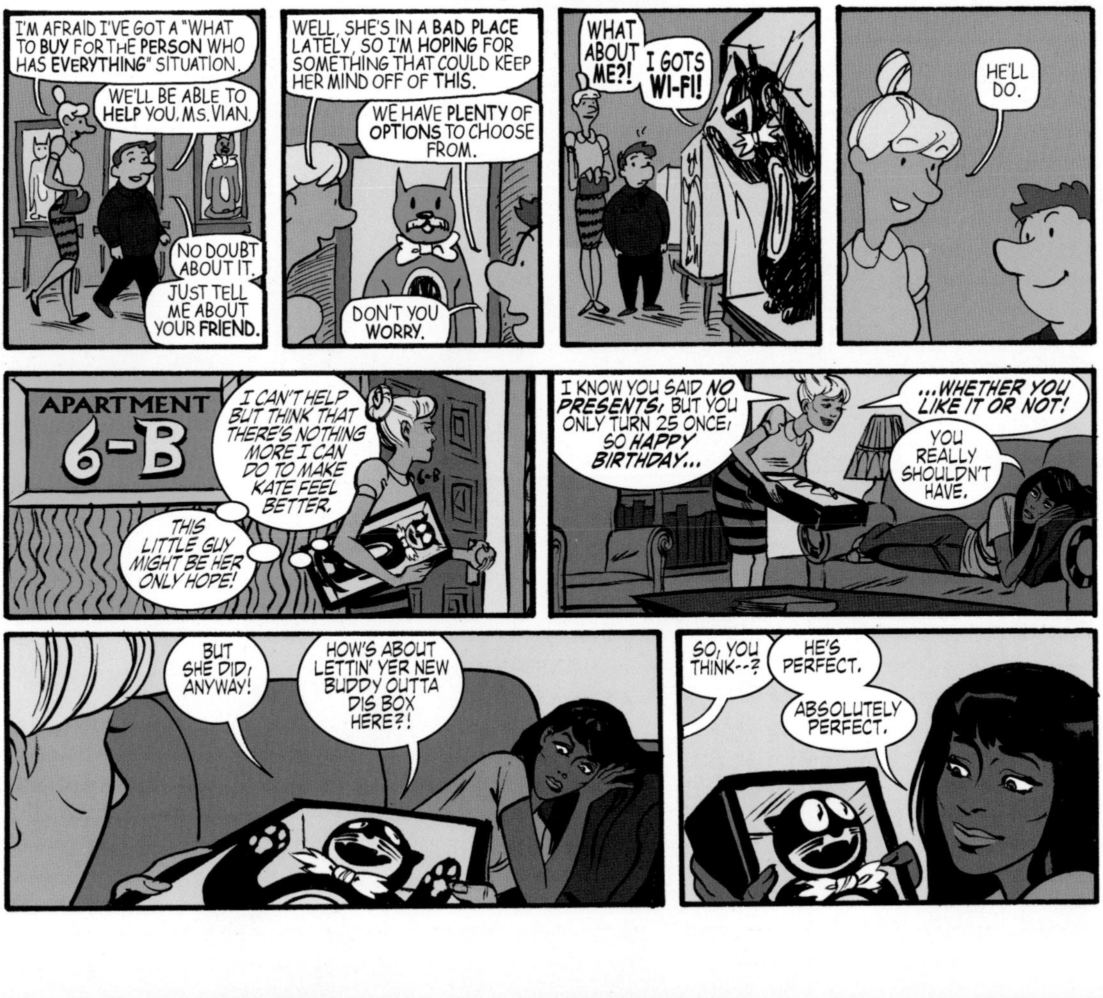
I'M AFRAID I'VE GOT A "WHAT TO BUY FOR THE PERSON WHO HAS EVERYTHING" SITUATION.
WE'LL BE ABLE TO HELP YOU, MS. VIAN.
NO DOUBT ABOUT IT.
JUST TELL ME ABOUT YOUR FRIEND.
WELL, SHE'S IN A BAD PLACE LATELY, SO I'M HOPING FOR SOMETHING THAT COULD KEEP HER MIND OFF OF THIS.
WE HAVE PLENTY OF OPTIONS TO CHOOSE FROM.
DON'T YOU WORRY.
WHAT ABOUT ME?!
I GOTS WI-FI!
HE'LL DO.
APARTMENT
6-B
I CAN'T HELP BUT THINK THAT THERE'S NOTHING MORE I CAN DO TO MAKE KATE FEEL BETTER.
THIS LITTLE GUY MIGHT BE HER ONLY HOPE!
I KNOW YOU SAID NO PRESENTS, BUT YOU ONLY TURN 25 ONCE, SO HAPPY BIRTHDAY...
...WHETHER YOU LIKE IT OR NOT!
YOU REALLY SHOULDN'T HAVE.
BUT SHE DID, ANYWAY!
HOW'S ABOUT LETTIN' YER NEW BUDDY OUTTA DIS BOX HERE?!
SO, YOU THINK--?
HE'S PERFECT.
ABSOLUTELY PERFECT.

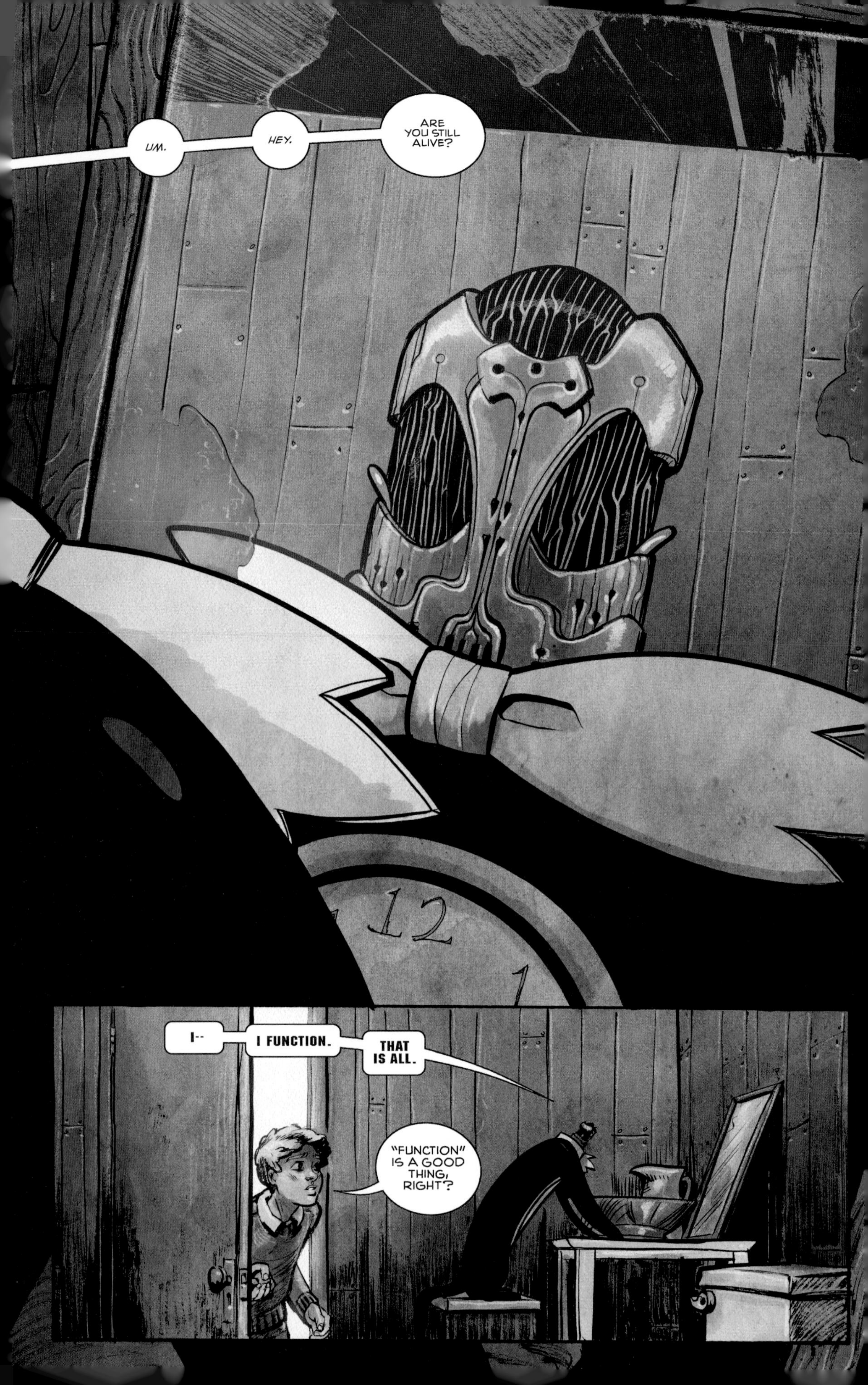
UM.
HEY.
ARE YOU STILL ALIVE?
12
1
I--
I FUNCTION.
THAT IS ALL.
"FUNCTION" IS A GOOD THING, RIGHT?

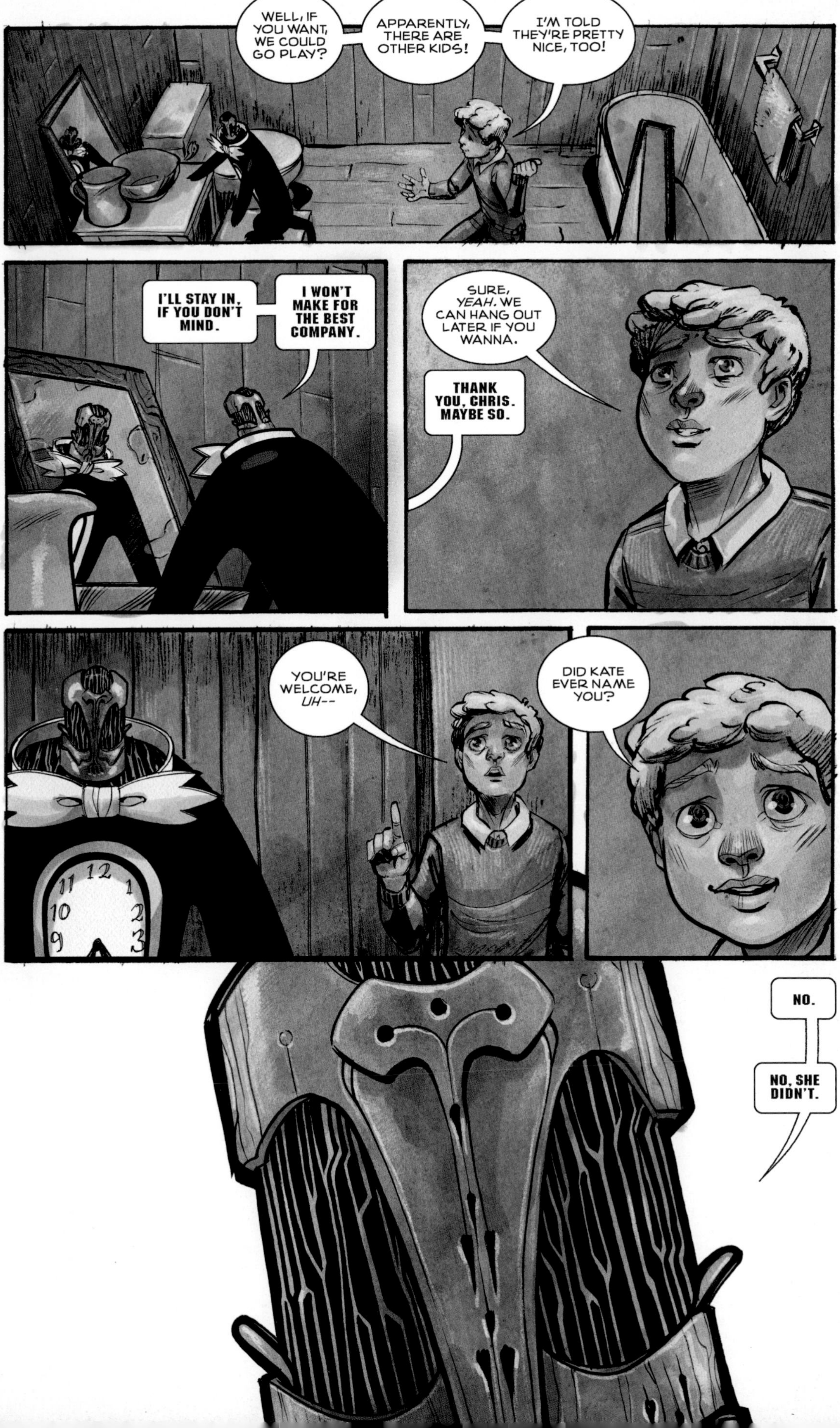
WELL, IF YOU WANT, WE COULD GO PLAY?
APPARENTLY, THERE ARE OTHER KIDS!
I'M TOLD THEY'RE PRETTY NICE, TOO!
I'LL STAY IN, IF YOU DON'T MIND.
I WON'T MAKE FOR THE BEST COMPANY.
SURE, *YEAH.* WE CAN HANG OUT LATER IF YOU WANNA.
THANK YOU, CHRIS. MAYBE SO.
YOU'RE WELCOME, *UH--*
DID KATE EVER NAME YOU?
NO.
NO, SHE DIDN'T.

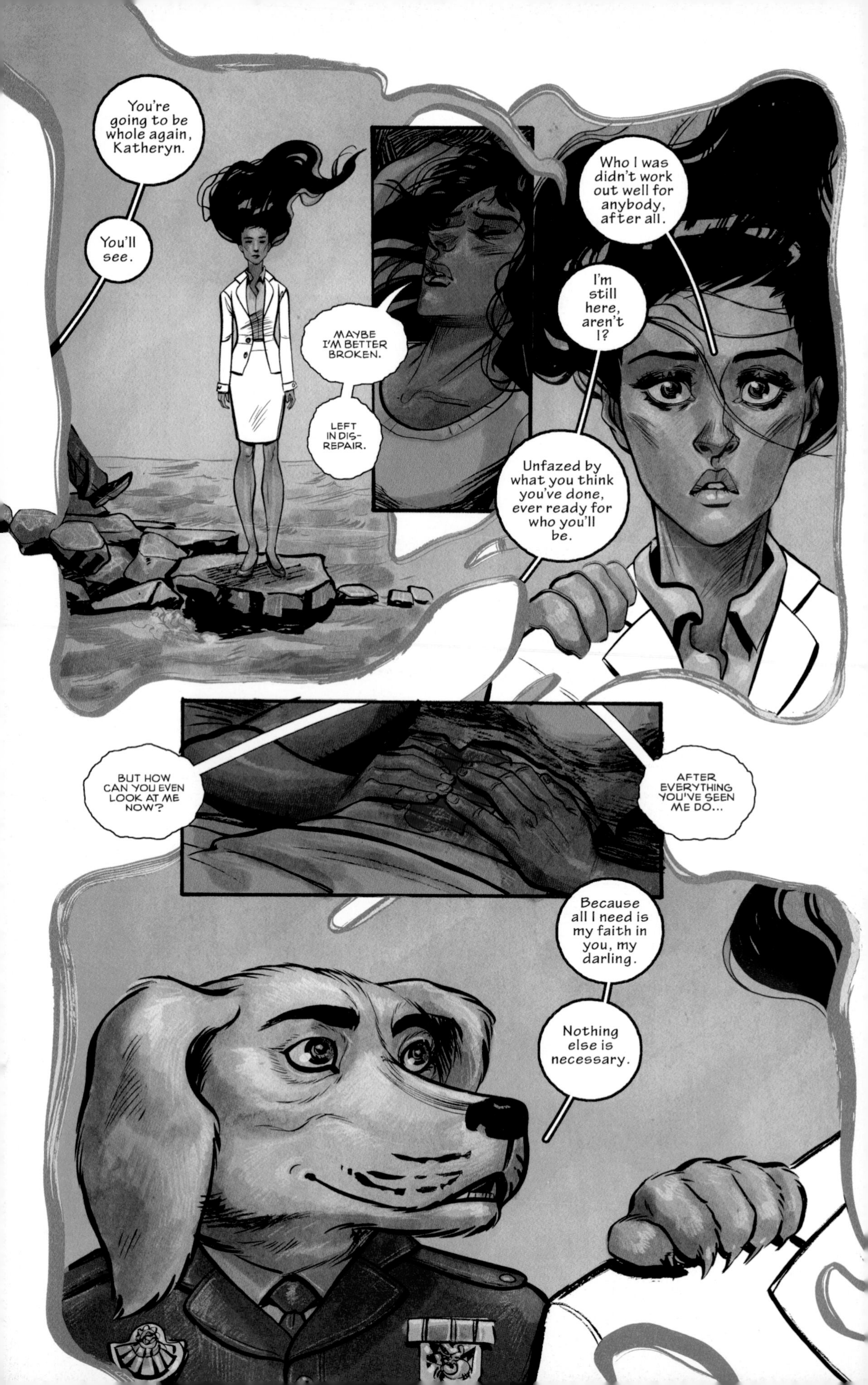
You're going to be whole again, Katheryn.
You'll see.
MAYBE I'M BETTER BROKEN.
LEFT IN DIS-REPAIR.
Who I was didn't work out well for anybody, after all.
I'm still here, aren't I?
Unfazed by what you think you've done, ever ready for who you'll be.
BUT HOW CAN YOU EVEN LOOK AT ME NOW?
AFTER EVERYTHING YOU'VE SEEN ME DO...
Because all I need is my faith in you, my darling.
Nothing else is necessary.

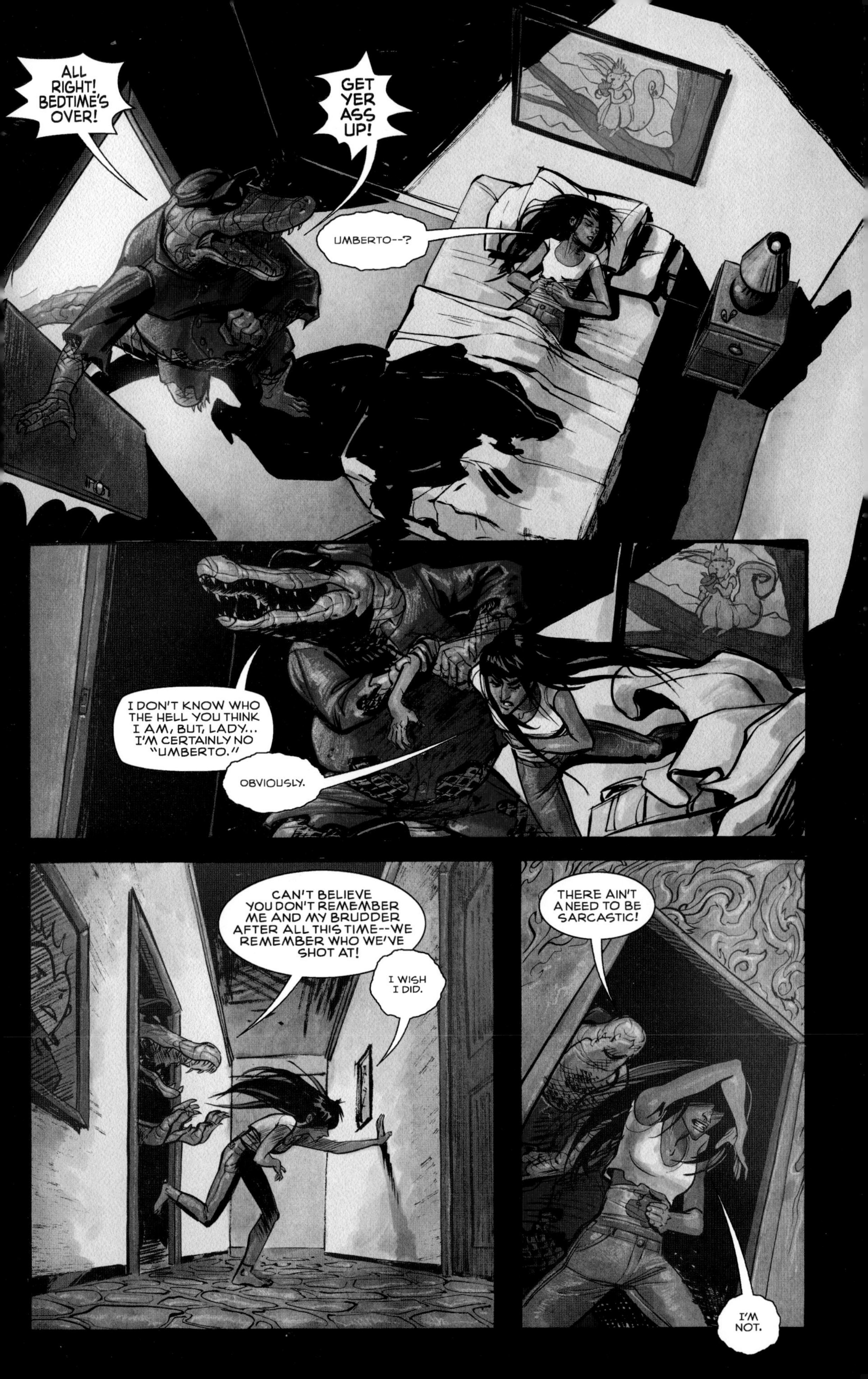
ALL RIGHT! BEDTIME'S OVER!
GET YER ASS UP!
UMBERTO--?
I DON'T KNOW WHO THE HELL YOU THINK I AM, BUT, LADY... I'M CERTAINLY NO "UMBERTO."
OBVIOUSLY.
CAN'T BELIEVE YOU DON'T REMEMBER ME AND MY BRUDDER AFTER ALL THIS TIME--WE REMEMBER WHO WE'VE SHOT AT!
I WISH I DID.
THERE AIN'T A NEED TO BE SARCASTIC!
I'M NOT.

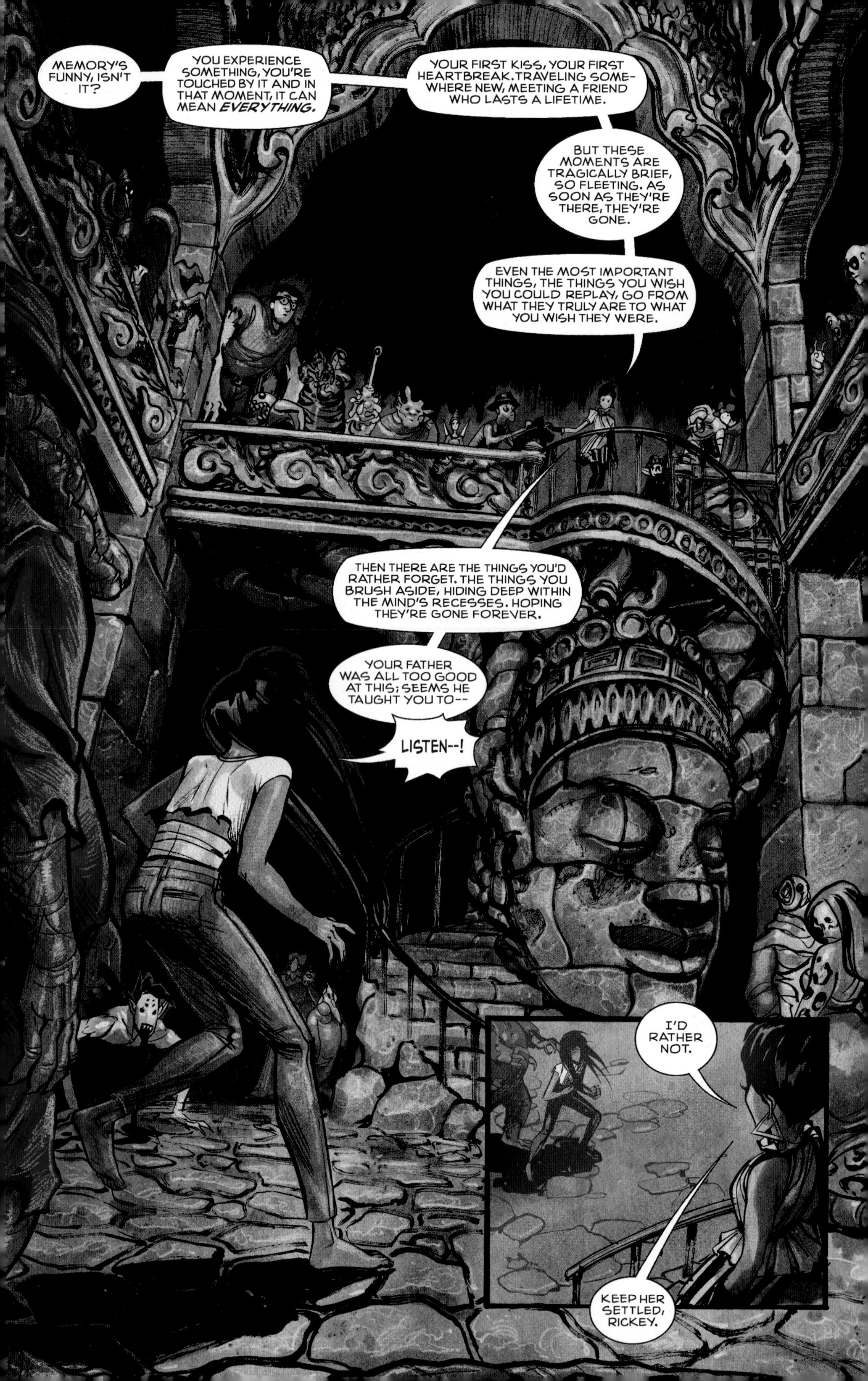

MEMORY'S FUNNY, ISN'T IT?
YOU EXPERIENCE SOMETHING, YOU'RE TOUCHED BY IT AND IN THAT MOMENT, IT CAN MEAN *EVERYTHING.*
YOUR FIRST KISS, YOUR FIRST HEARTBREAK. TRAVELING SOMEWHERE NEW, MEETING A FRIEND WHO LASTS A LIFETIME.
BUT THESE MOMENTS ARE TRAGICALLY BRIEF, SO FLEETING. AS SOON AS THEY'RE THERE, THEY'RE GONE.
EVEN THE MOST IMPORTANT THINGS, THE THINGS YOU WISH YOU COULD REPLAY, GO FROM WHAT THEY TRULY ARE TO WHAT YOU WISH THEY WERE.
THEN THERE ARE THE THINGS YOU'D RATHER FORGET. THE THINGS YOU BRUSH ASIDE, HIDING DEEP WITHIN THE MIND'S RECESSES. HOPING THEY'RE GONE FOREVER.
YOUR FATHER WAS ALL TOO GOOD AT THIS; SEEMS HE TAUGHT YOU TO--
LISTEN--!
I'D RATHER NOT.
KEEP HER SETTLED, RICKEY.

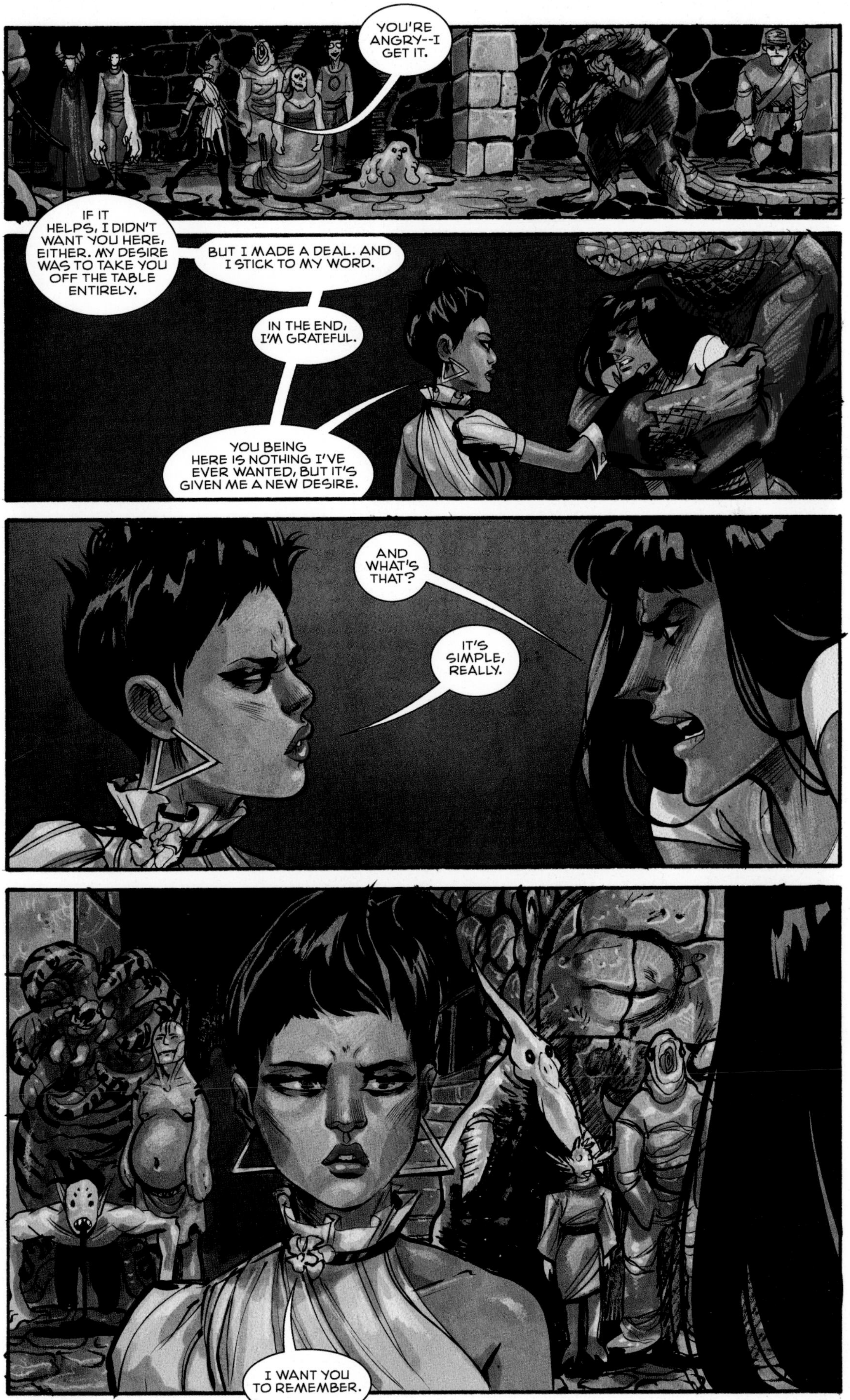
YOU'RE ANGRY--I GET IT.
IF IT HELPS, I DIDN'T WANT YOU HERE, EITHER. MY DESIRE WAS TO TAKE YOU OFF THE TABLE ENTIRELY.
BUT I MADE A DEAL. AND I STICK TO MY WORD.
IN THE END, I'M GRATEFUL.
YOU BEING HERE IS NOTHING I'VE EVER WANTED, BUT IT'S GIVEN ME A NEW DESIRE.
AND WHAT'S THAT?
IT'S SIMPLE, REALLY.
I WANT YOU TO REMEMBER.

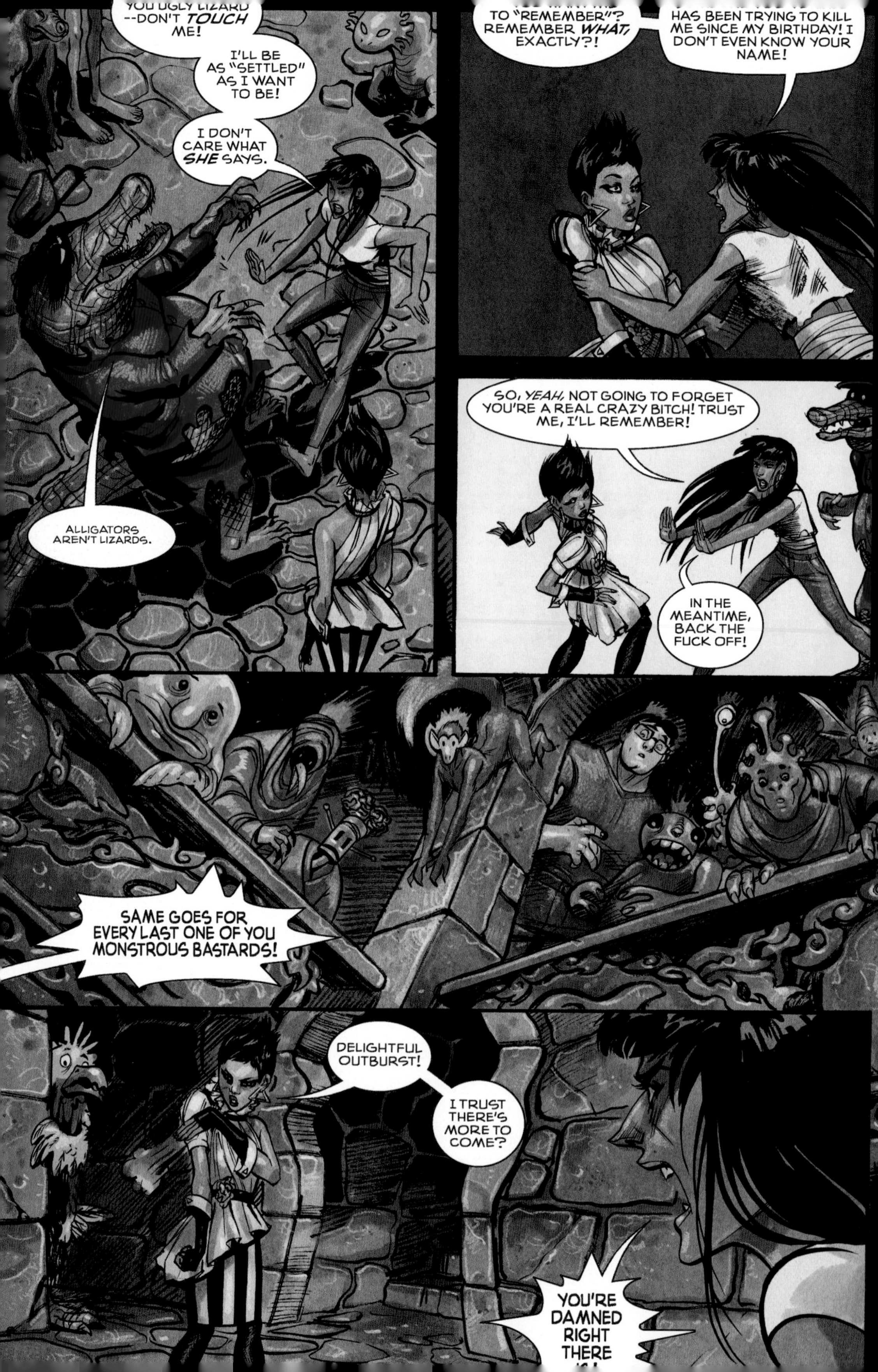
YOU UGLY LIZARD --DON'T TOUCH ME!
I'LL BE AS "SETTLED" AS I WANT TO BE!
I DON'T CARE WHAT SHE SAYS.
ALLIGATORS AREN'T LIZARDS.
TO "REMEMBER"? REMEMBER WHAT, EXACTLY?!
HAS BEEN TRYING TO KILL ME SINCE MY BIRTHDAY! I DON'T EVEN KNOW YOUR NAME!
SO, YEAH, NOT GOING TO FORGET YOU'RE A REAL CRAZY BITCH! TRUST ME, I'LL REMEMBER!
IN THE MEANTIME, BACK THE FUCK OFF!
SAME GOES FOR EVERY LAST ONE OF YOU MONSTROUS BASTARDS!
DELIGHTFUL OUTBURST!
I TRUST THERE'S MORE TO COME?
YOU'RE DAMNED RIGHT THERE

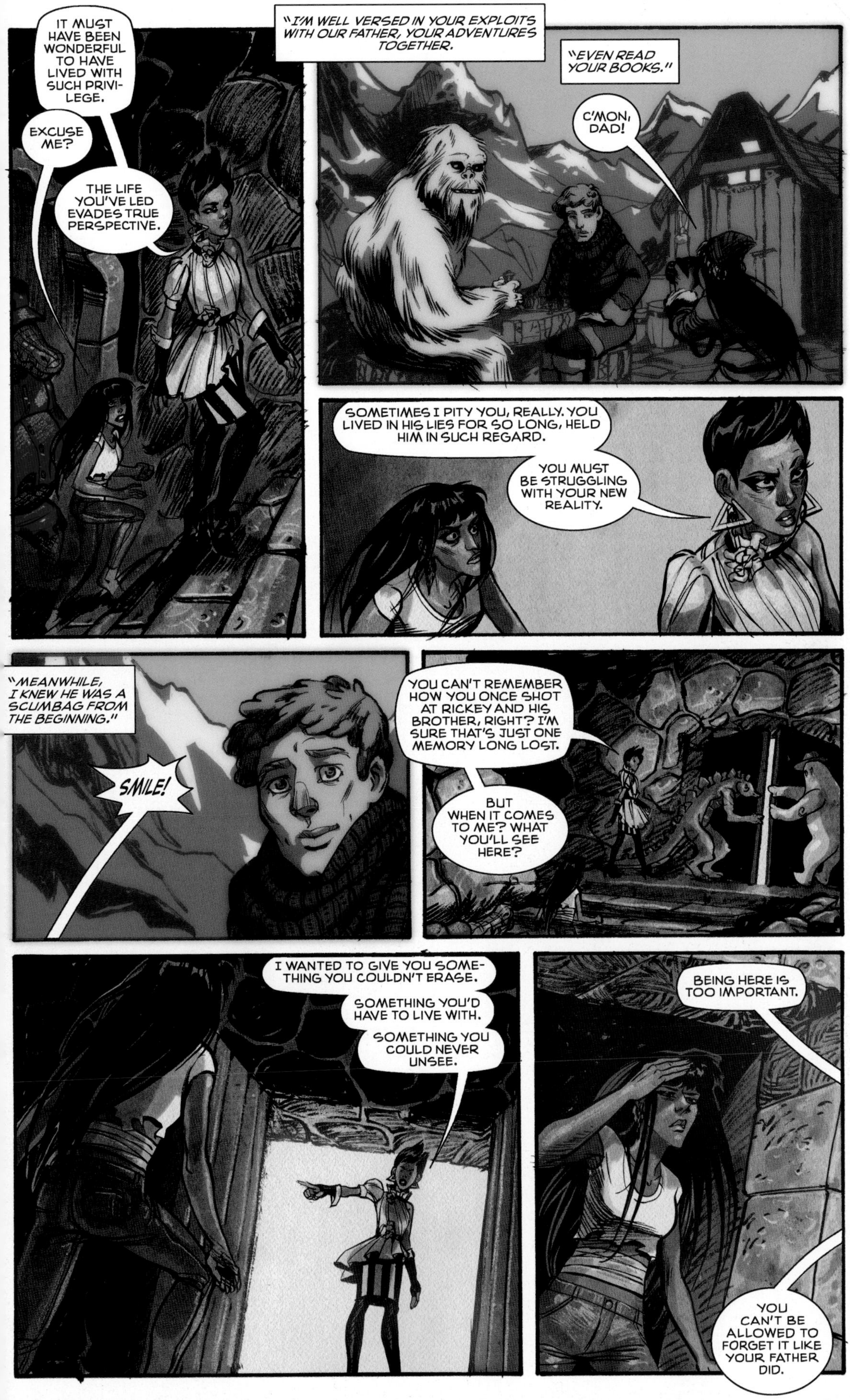
IT MUST HAVE BEEN WONDERFUL TO HAVE LIVED WITH SUCH PRIVI-LEGE.
EXCUSE ME?
THE LIFE YOU'VE LED EVADES TRUE PERSPECTIVE.
"I'M WELL VERSED IN YOUR EXPLOITS WITH OUR FATHER, YOUR ADVENTURES TOGETHER.
"EVEN READ YOUR BOOKS."
C'MON, DAD!
SOMETIMES I PITY YOU, REALLY. YOU LIVED IN HIS LIES FOR SO LONG, HELD HIM IN SUCH REGARD.
YOU MUST BE STRUGGLING WITH YOUR NEW REALITY.
"MEANWHILE, I KNEW HE WAS A SCUMBAG FROM THE BEGINNING."
SMILE!
YOU CAN'T REMEMBER HOW YOU ONCE SHOT AT RICKEY AND HIS BROTHER, RIGHT? I'M SURE THAT'S JUST ONE MEMORY LONG LOST.
BUT WHEN IT COMES TO ME? WHAT YOU'LL SEE HERE?
I WANTED TO GIVE YOU SOME-THING YOU COULDN'T ERASE.
SOMETHING YOU'D HAVE TO LIVE WITH.
SOMETHING YOU COULD NEVER UNSEE.
BEING HERE IS TOO IMPORTANT.
YOU CAN'T BE ALLOWED TO FORGET IT LIKE YOUR FATHER DID.

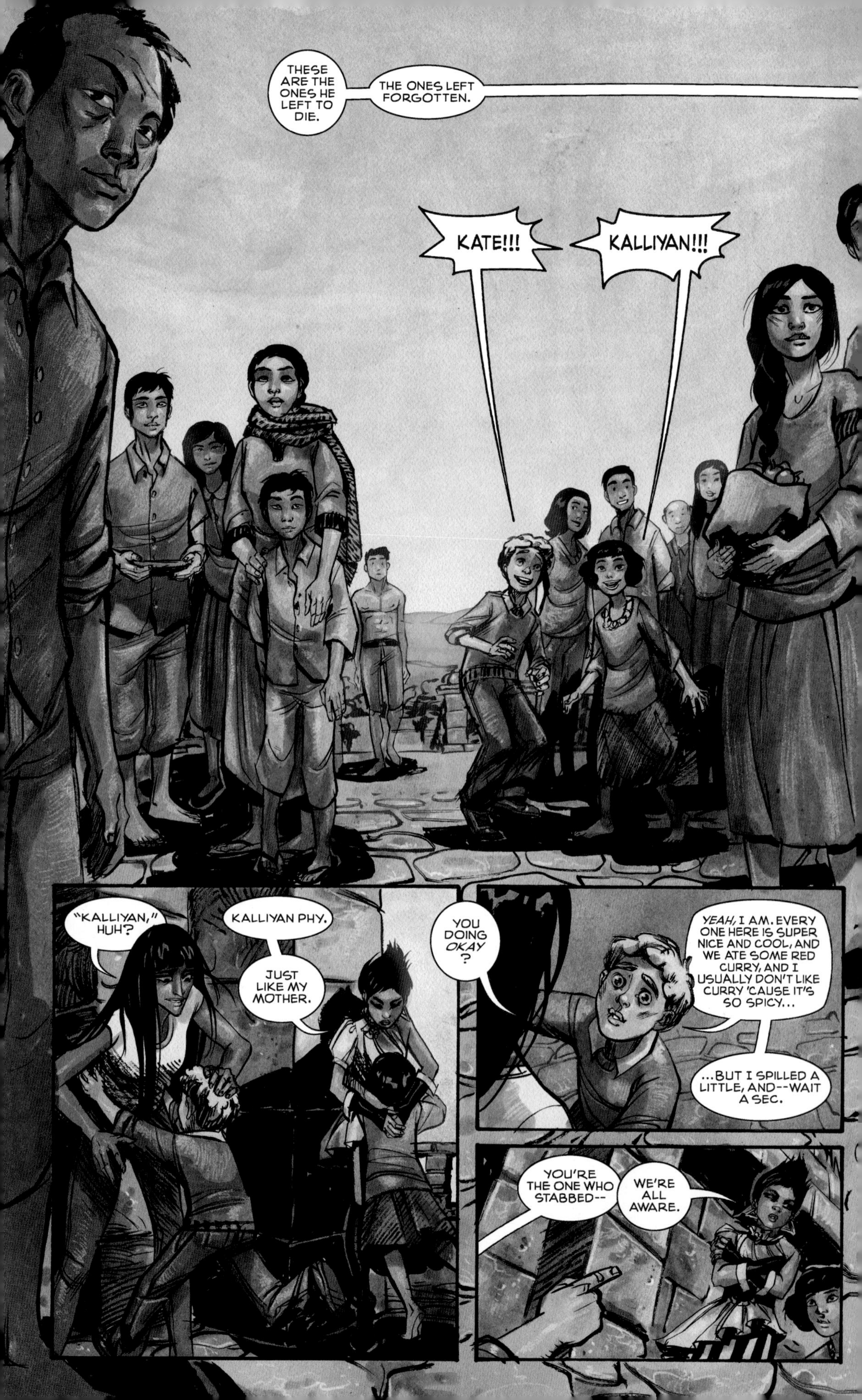
THESE ARE THE ONES HE LEFT TO DIE.
THE ONES LEFT FORGOTTEN.
KATE!!!
KALLIYAN!!!
"KALLIYAN," HUH?
KALLIYAN PHY.
JUST LIKE MY MOTHER.
YOU DOING *OKAY*?
YEAH, I AM. EVERY ONE HERE IS SUPER NICE AND COOL, AND WE ATE SOME RED CURRY, AND I USUALLY DON'T LIKE CURRY 'CAUSE IT'S SO SPICY...
...BUT I SPILLED A LITTLE, AND--WAIT A SEC.
YOU'RE THE ONE WHO STABBED--
WE'RE ALL AWARE.

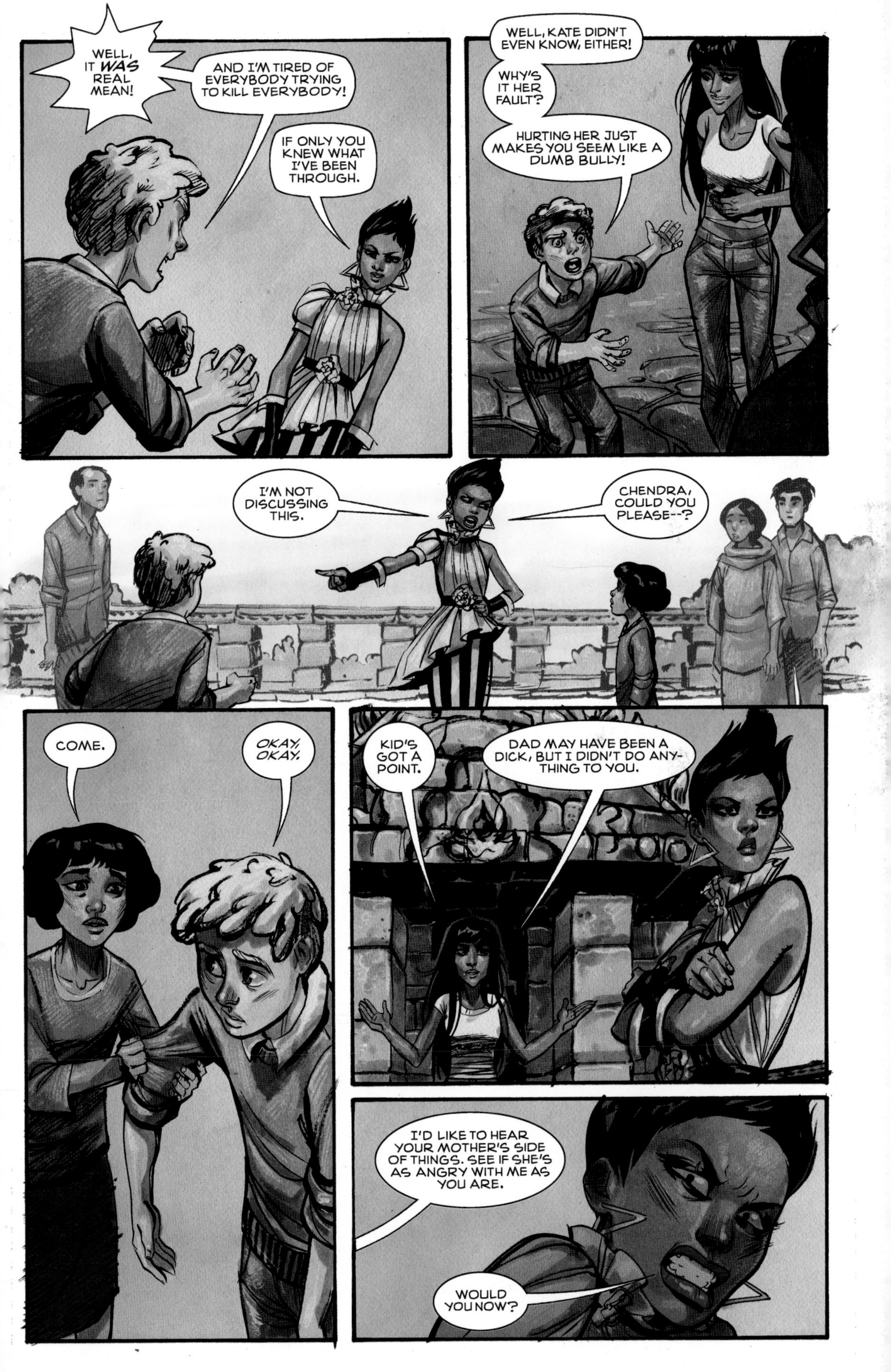

WELL, IT *WAS* REAL MEAN!
AND I'M TIRED OF EVERYBODY TRYING TO KILL EVERYBODY!
IF ONLY YOU KNEW WHAT I'VE BEEN THROUGH.
WELL, KATE DIDN'T EVEN KNOW, EITHER!
WHY'S IT HER FAULT?
HURTING HER JUST MAKES YOU SEEM LIKE A DUMB BULLY!
I'M NOT DISCUSSING THIS.
CHENDRA, COULD YOU PLEASE--?
COME.
OKAY, OKAY.
KID'S GOT A POINT.
DAD MAY HAVE BEEN A DICK, BUT I DIDN'T DO ANY-THING TO YOU.
I'D LIKE TO HEAR YOUR MOTHER'S SIDE OF THINGS. SEE IF SHE'S AS ANGRY WITH ME AS YOU ARE.
WOULD YOU NOW?

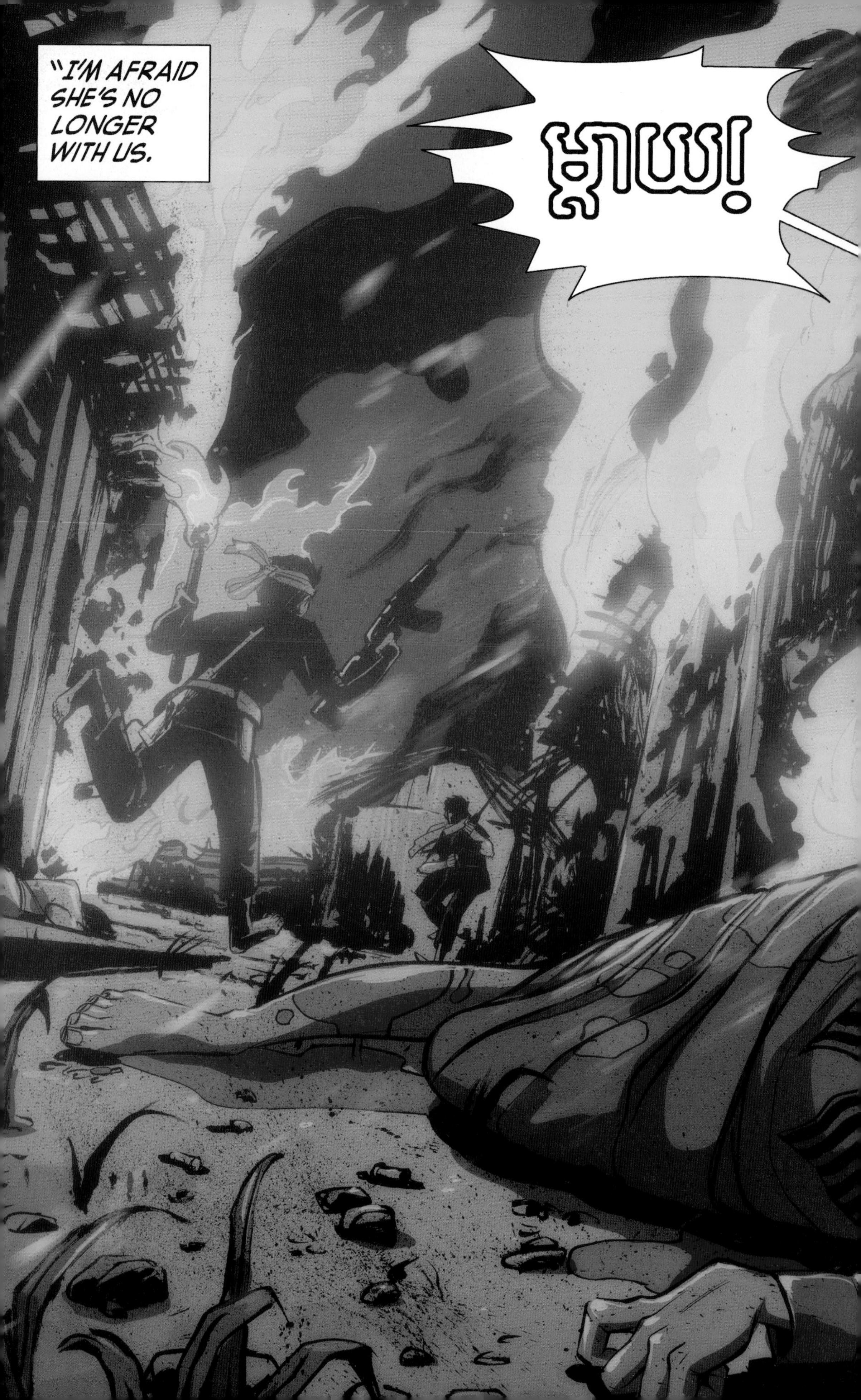
"I'M AFRAID SHE'S NO LONGER WITH US.
ម្តាយ!

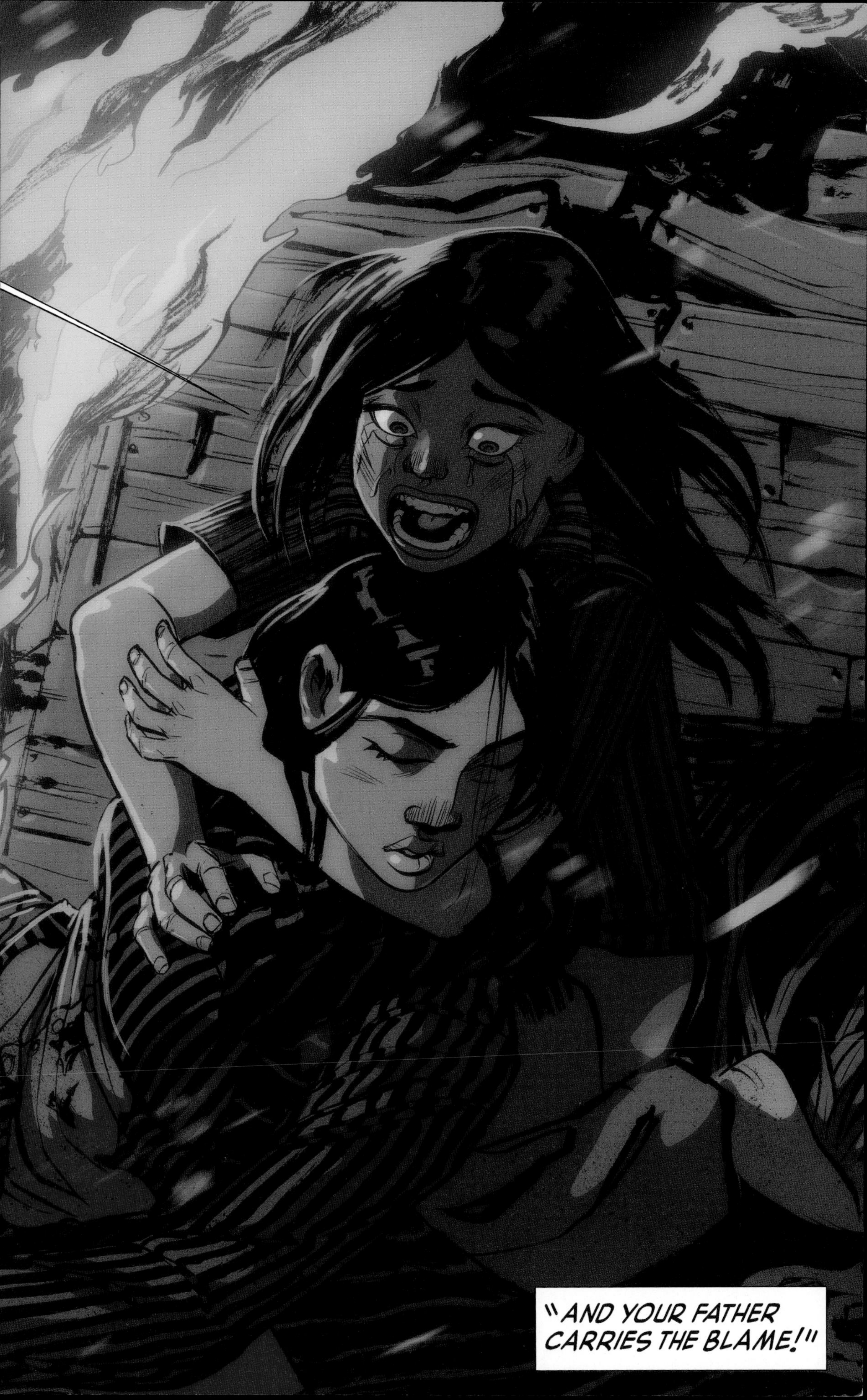
"AND YOUR FATHER CARRIES THE BLAME!"

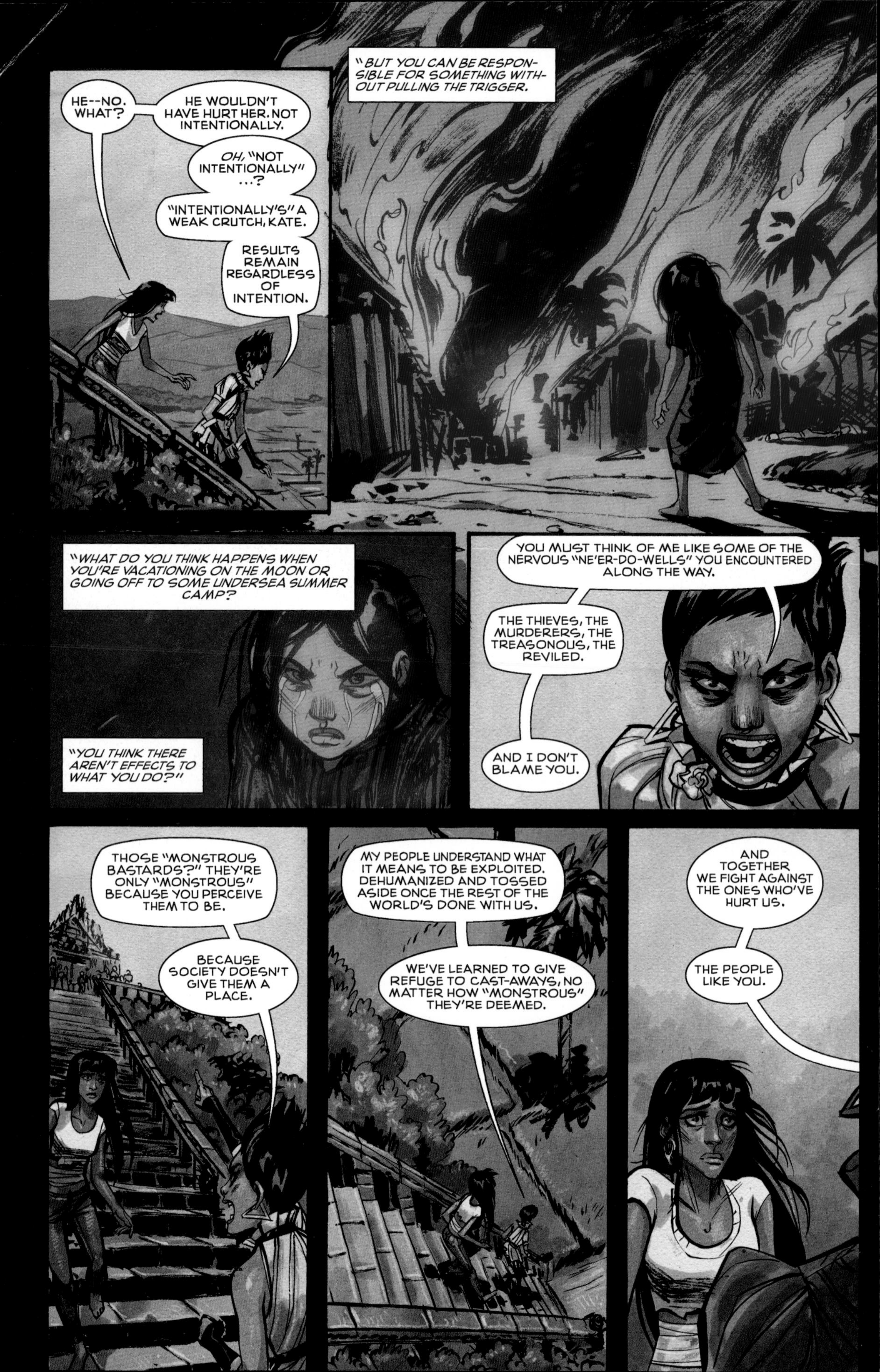
"BUT YOU CAN BE RESPONSIBLE FOR SOMETHING WITHOUT PULLING THE TRIGGER.
HE--NO. WHAT?
HE WOULDN'T HAVE HURT HER. NOT INTENTIONALLY.
OH, "NOT INTENTIONALLY" ...?
"INTENTIONALLY'S" A WEAK CRUTCH, KATE.
RESULTS REMAIN REGARDLESS OF INTENTION.
"WHAT DO YOU THINK HAPPENS WHEN YOU'RE VACATIONING ON THE MOON OR GOING OFF TO SOME UNDERSEA SUMMER CAMP?
"YOU THINK THERE AREN'T EFFECTS TO WHAT YOU DO?"
YOU MUST THINK OF ME LIKE SOME OF THE NERVOUS "NE'ER-DO-WELLS" YOU ENCOUNTERED ALONG THE WAY.
THE THIEVES, THE MURDERERS, THE TREASONOUS, THE REVILED.
AND I DON'T BLAME YOU.
THOSE "MONSTROUS BASTARDS?" THEY'RE ONLY "MONSTROUS" BECAUSE YOU PERCEIVE THEM TO BE.
BECAUSE SOCIETY DOESN'T GIVE THEM A PLACE.
MY PEOPLE UNDERSTAND WHAT IT MEANS TO BE EXPLOITED. DEHUMANIZED AND TOSSED ASIDE ONCE THE REST OF THE WORLD'S DONE WITH US.
WE'VE LEARNED TO GIVE REFUGE TO CAST-AWAYS, NO MATTER HOW "MONSTROUS" THEY'RE DEEMED.
AND TOGETHER WE FIGHT AGAINST THE ONES WHO'VE HURT US.
THE PEOPLE LIKE YOU.

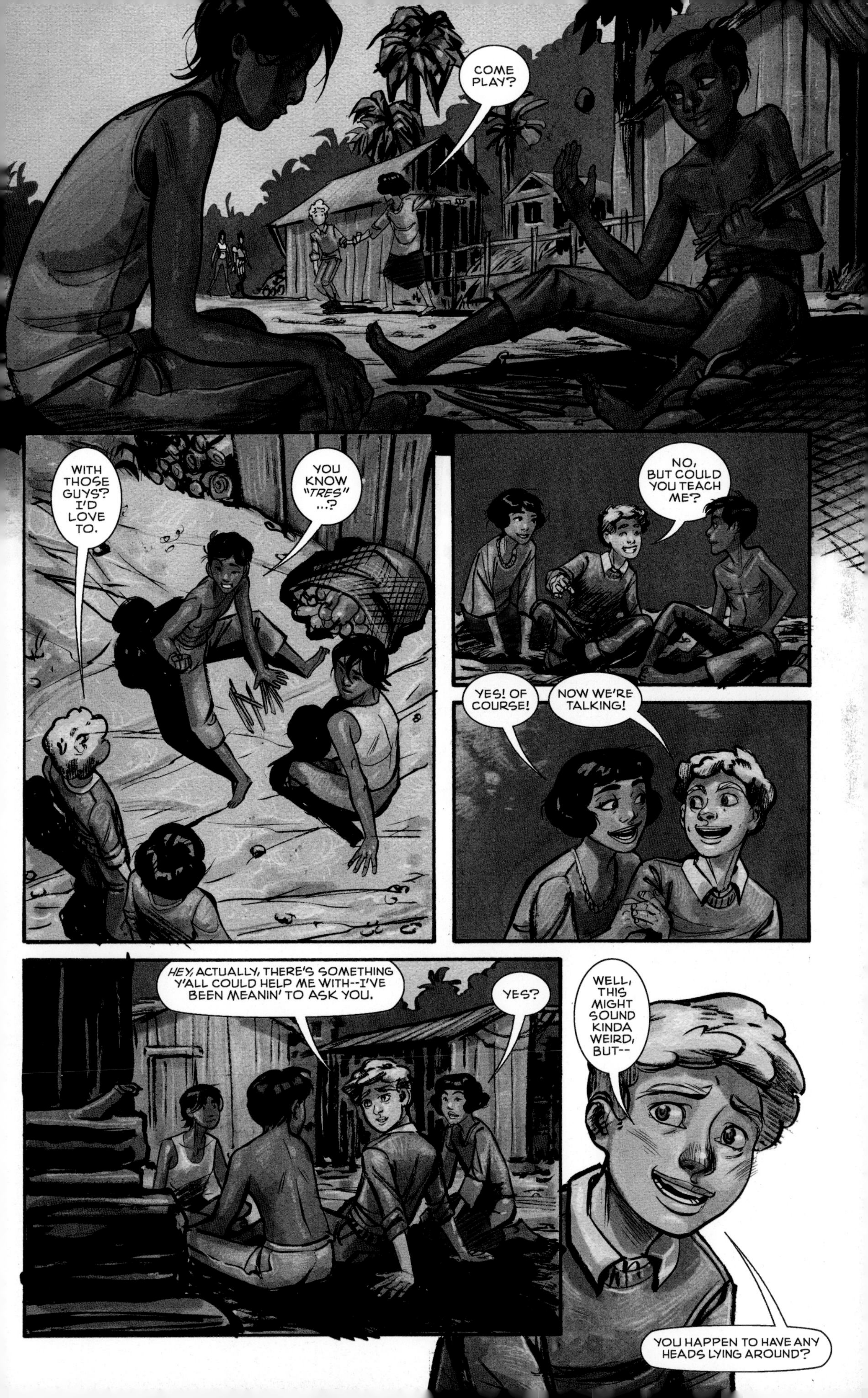

COME PLAY?
WITH THOSE GUYS? I'D LOVE TO.
YOU KNOW "*TRES*"...?
NO, BUT COULD YOU TEACH ME?
YES! OF COURSE!
NOW WE'RE TALKING!
HEY, ACTUALLY, THERE'S SOMETHING Y'ALL COULD HELP ME WITH--I'VE BEEN MEANIN' TO ASK YOU.
YES?
WELL, THIS MIGHT SOUND KINDA WEIRD, BUT--
YOU HAPPEN TO HAVE ANY HEADS LYING AROUND?

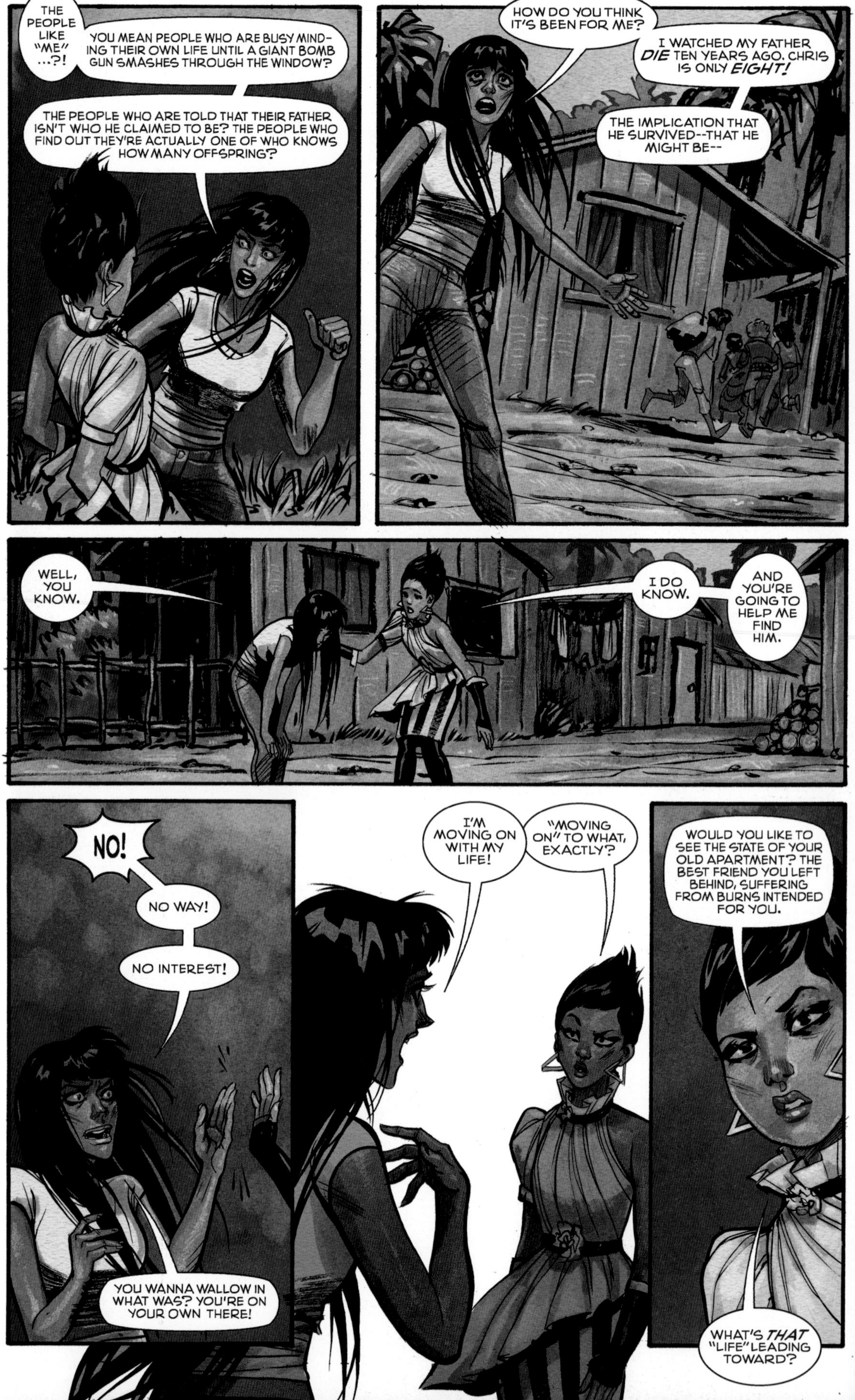
THE PEOPLE LIKE "ME" ...?!
YOU MEAN PEOPLE WHO ARE BUSY MINDING THEIR OWN LIFE UNTIL A GIANT BOMB GUN SMASHES THROUGH THE WINDOW?
THE PEOPLE WHO ARE TOLD THAT THEIR FATHER ISN'T WHO HE CLAIMED TO BE? THE PEOPLE WHO FIND OUT THEY'RE ACTUALLY ONE OF WHO KNOWS HOW MANY OFFSPRING?
HOW DO YOU THINK IT'S BEEN FOR ME?
I WATCHED MY FATHER *DIE* TEN YEARS AGO. CHRIS IS ONLY *EIGHT!*
THE IMPLICATION THAT HE SURVIVED--THAT HE MIGHT BE--
WELL, YOU KNOW.
I DO KNOW.
AND YOU'RE GOING TO HELP ME FIND HIM.
NO!
NO WAY!
NO INTEREST!
YOU WANNA WALLOW IN WHAT WAS? YOU'RE ON YOUR OWN THERE!
I'M MOVING ON WITH MY LIFE!
"MOVING ON" TO WHAT, EXACTLY?
WOULD YOU LIKE TO SEE THE STATE OF YOUR OLD APARTMENT? THE BEST FRIEND YOU LEFT BEHIND, SUFFERING FROM BURNS INTENDED FOR YOU.
WHAT'S *THAT* "LIFE" LEADING TOWARD?

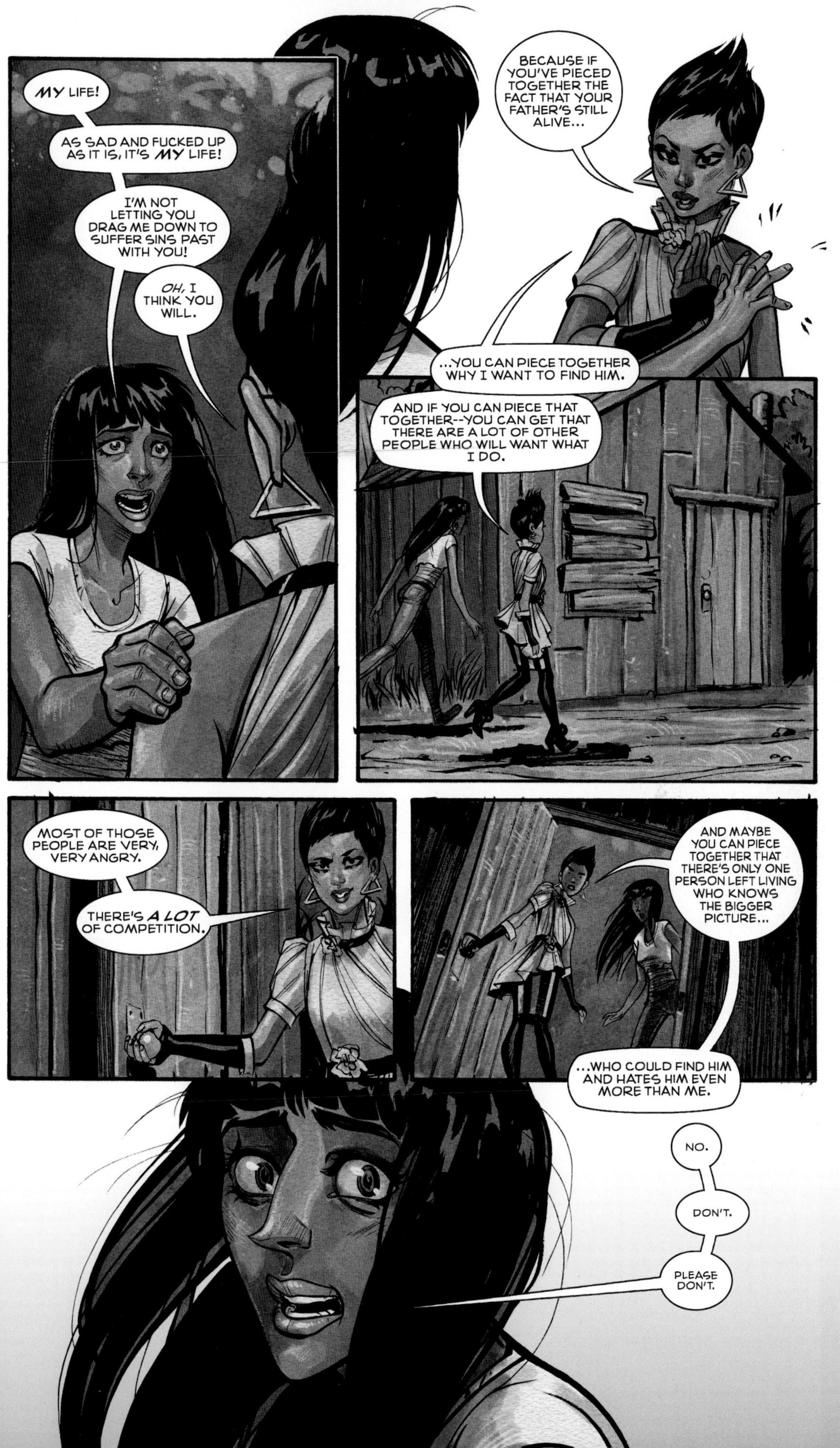
MY LIFE!
AS SAD AND FUCKED UP AS IT IS, IT'S MY LIFE!
I'M NOT LETTING YOU DRAG ME DOWN TO SUFFER SINS PAST WITH YOU!
OH, I THINK YOU WILL.
BECAUSE IF YOU'VE PIECED TOGETHER THE FACT THAT YOUR FATHER'S STILL ALIVE...
...YOU CAN PIECE TOGETHER WHY I WANT TO FIND HIM.
AND IF YOU CAN PIECE THAT TOGETHER--YOU CAN GET THAT THERE ARE A LOT OF OTHER PEOPLE WHO WILL WANT WHAT I DO.
MOST OF THOSE PEOPLE ARE VERY, VERY ANGRY.
THERE'S A LOT OF COMPETITION.
AND MAYBE YOU CAN PIECE TOGETHER THAT THERE'S ONLY ONE PERSON LEFT LIVING WHO KNOWS THE BIGGER PICTURE...
...WHO COULD FIND HIM AND HATES HIM EVEN MORE THAN ME.
NO.
DON'T.
PLEASE DON'T.

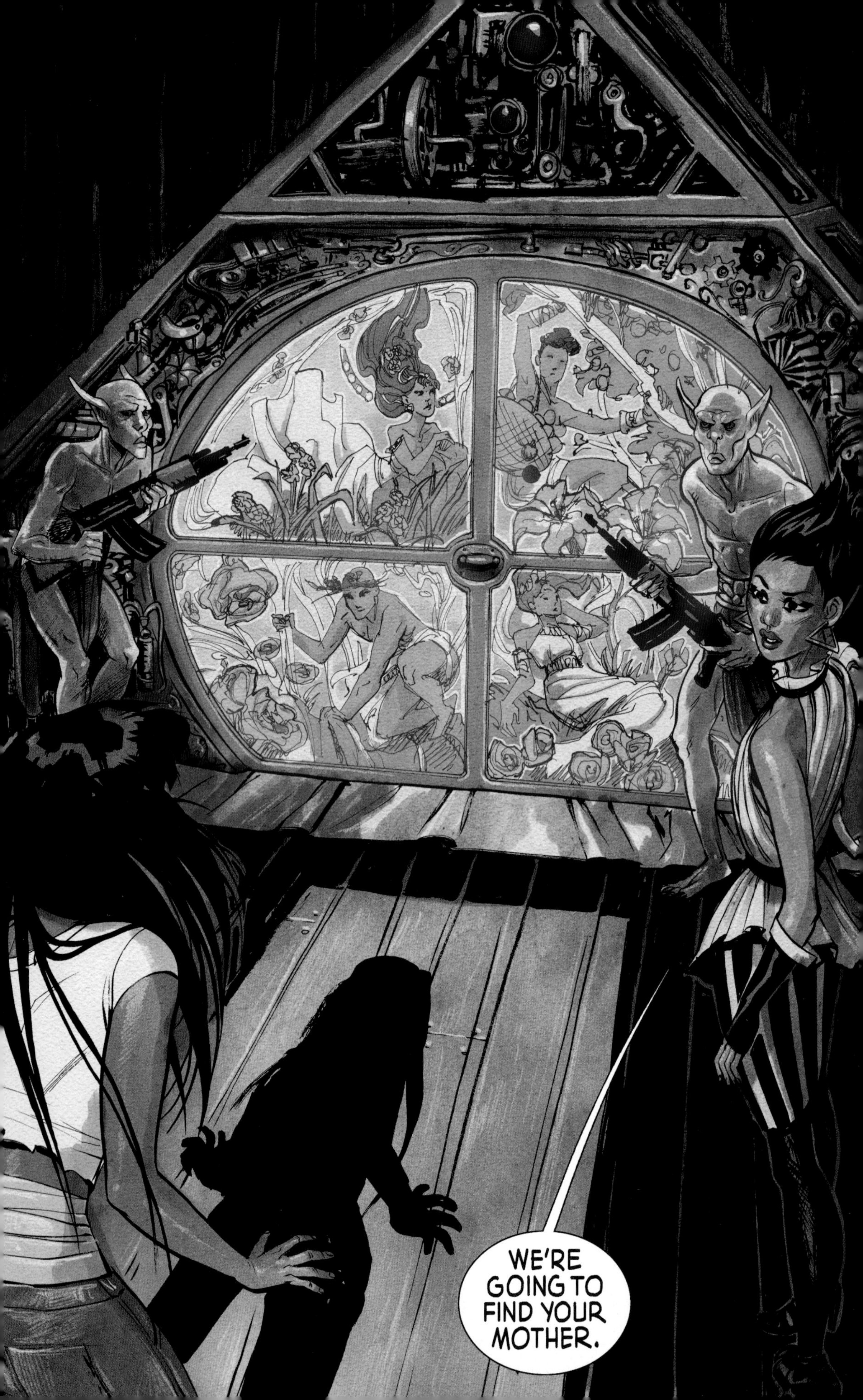
WE'RE GOING TO FIND YOUR MOTHER.

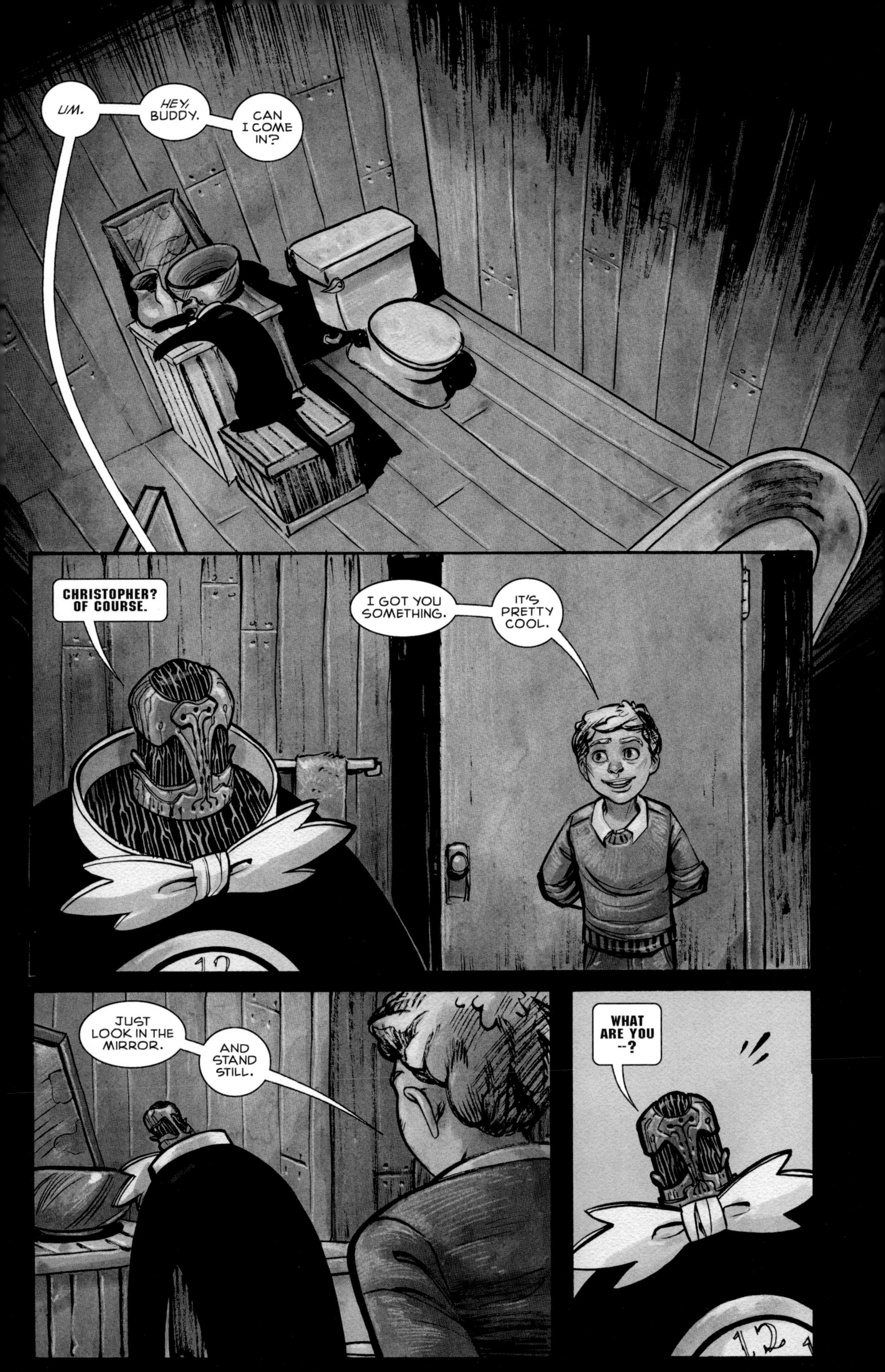
UM.
HEY, BUDDY.
CAN I COME IN?
CHRISTOPHER? OF COURSE.
I GOT YOU SOMETHING.
IT'S PRETTY COOL.
JUST LOOK IN THE MIRROR.
AND STAND STILL.
WHAT ARE YOU --?

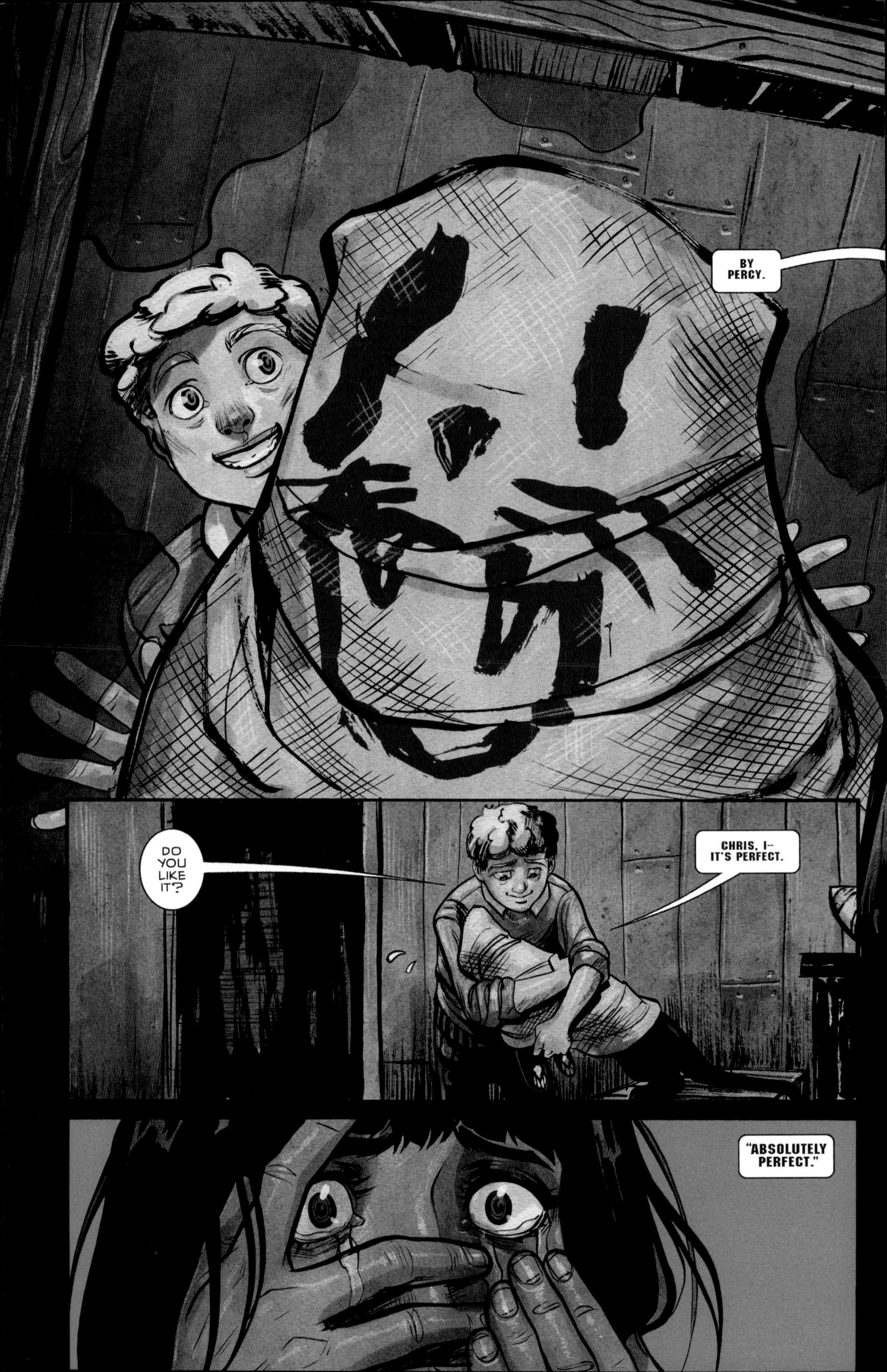
BY PERCY.
DO YOU LIKE IT?
CHRIS, I-- IT'S PERFECT.
"ABSOLUTELY PERFECT."

CHAPTER 9

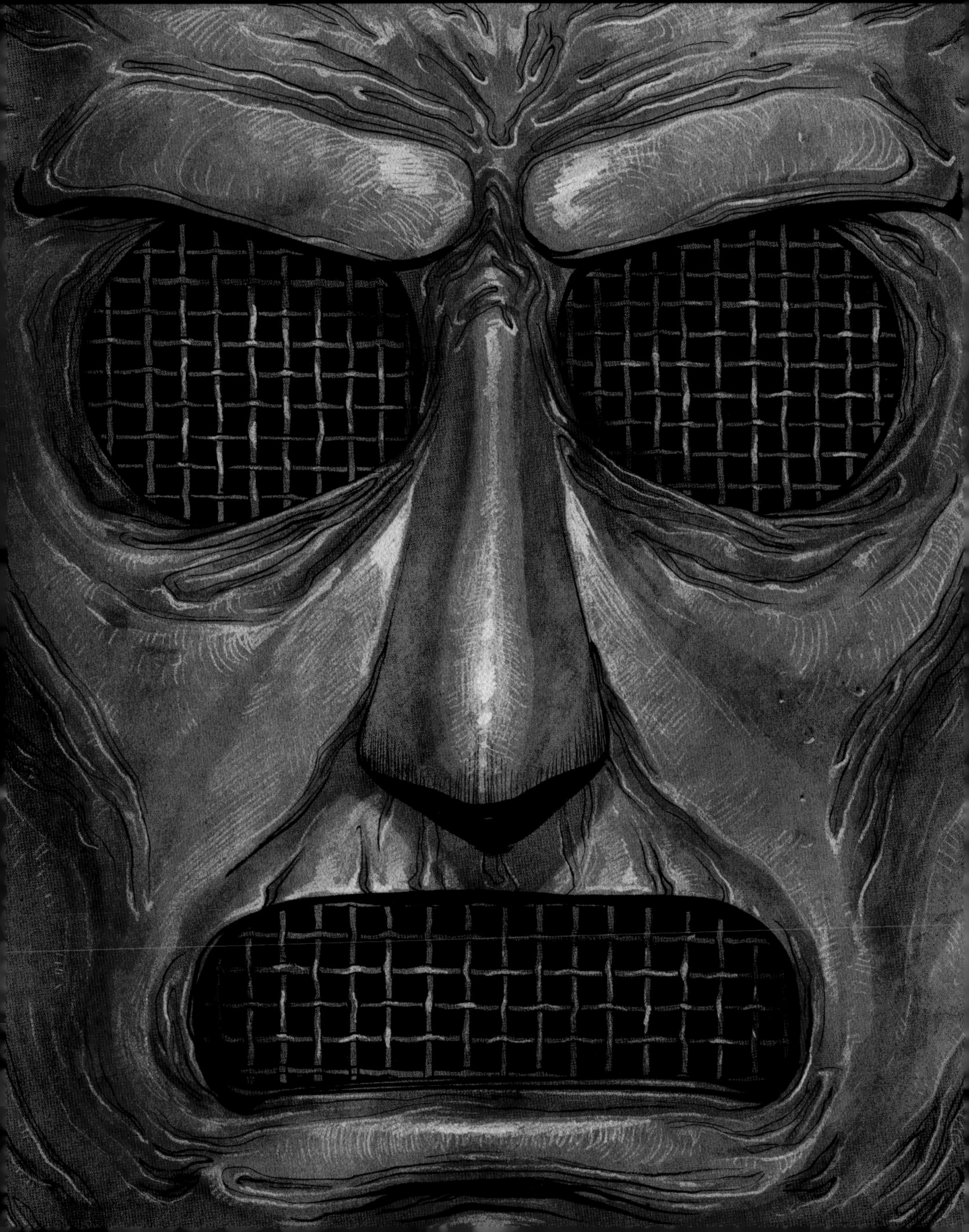

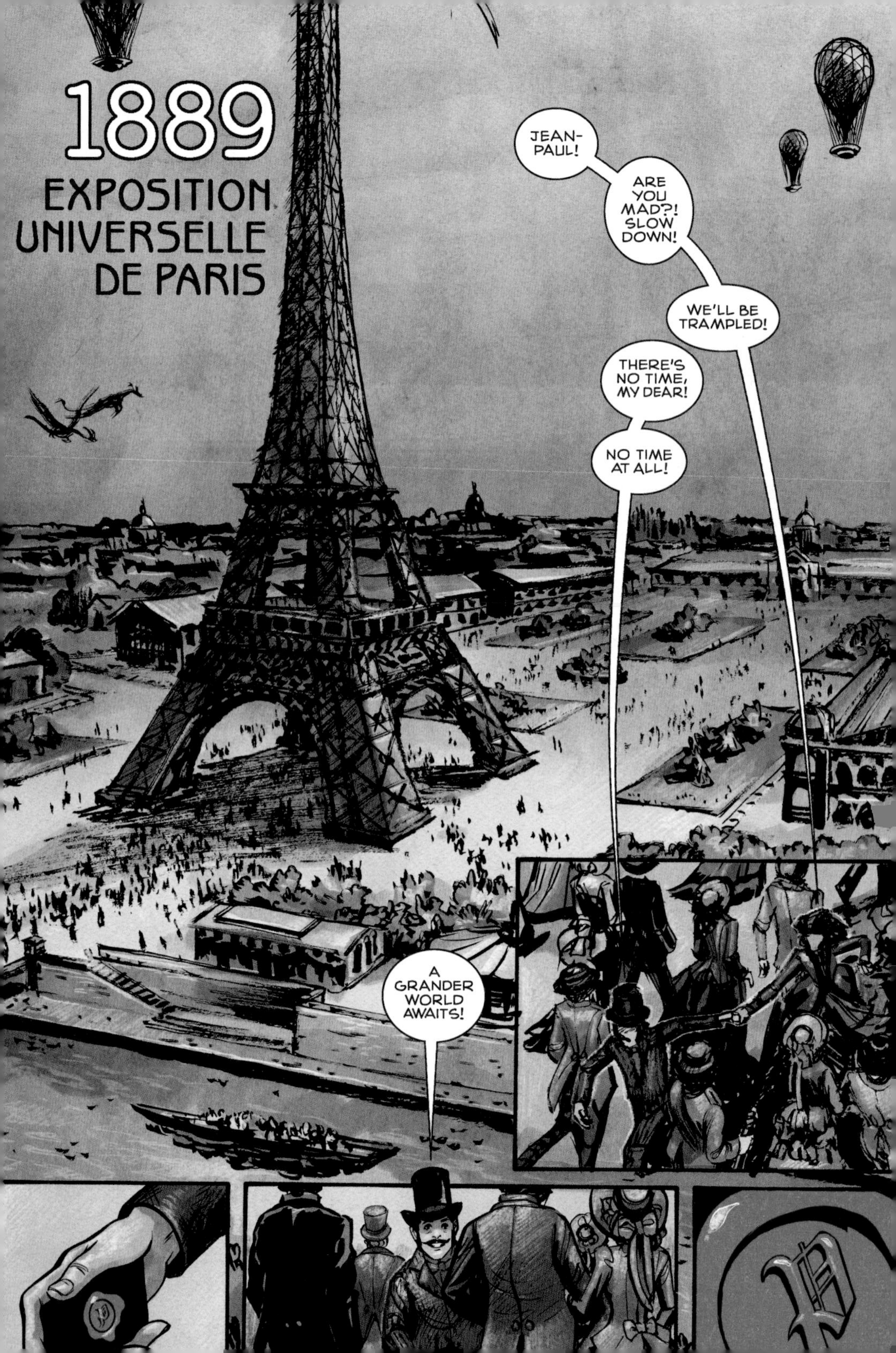
1889
EXPOSITION UNIVERSELLE DE PARIS
JEAN-PAUL!
ARE YOU MAD?! SLOW DOWN!
WE'LL BE TRAMPLED!
THERE'S NO TIME, MY DEAR!
NO TIME AT ALL!
A GRANDER WORLD AWAITS!

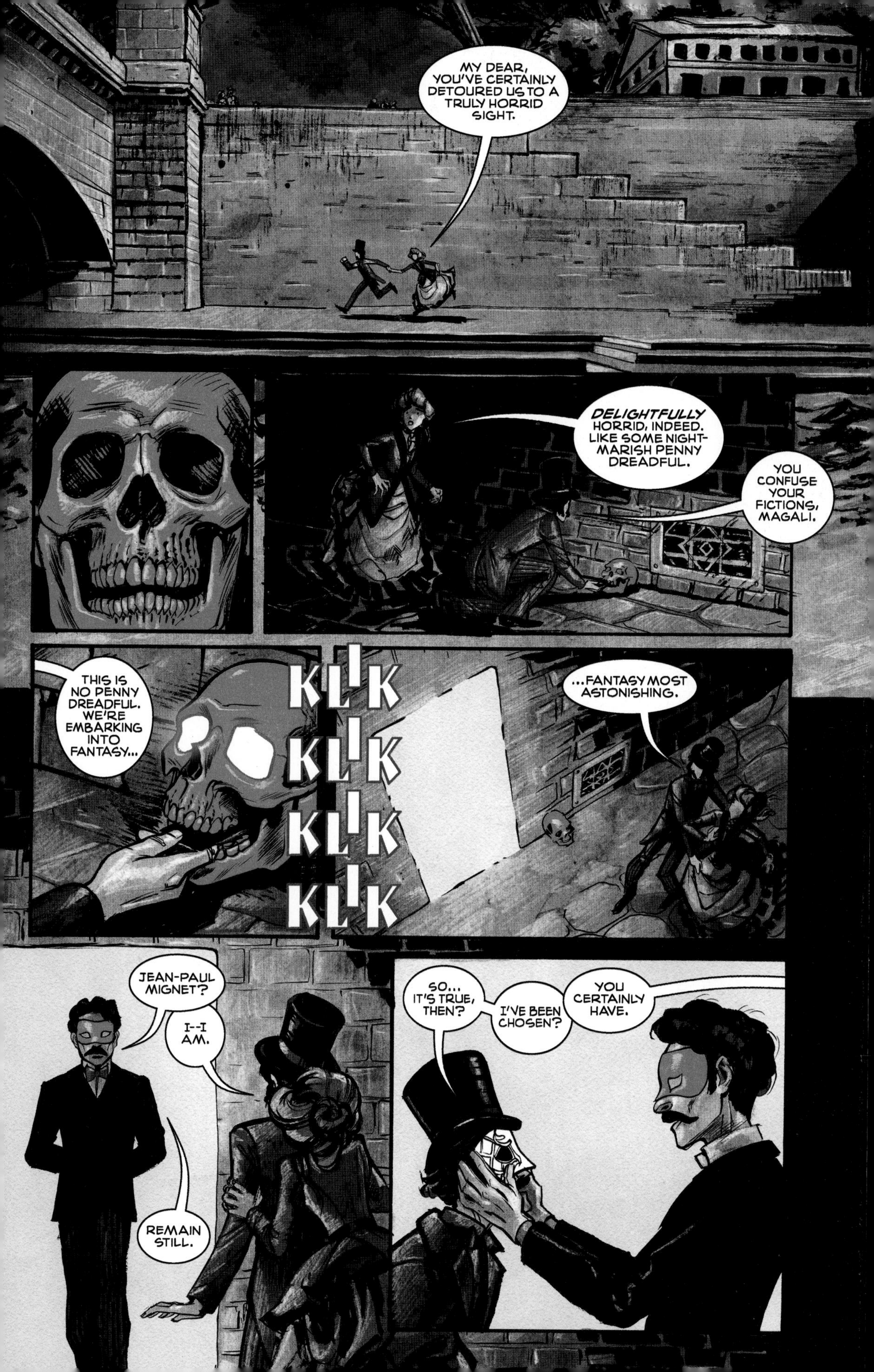
MY DEAR, YOU'VE CERTAINLY DETOURED US TO A TRULY HORRID SIGHT.
DELIGHTFULLY HORRID, INDEED. LIKE SOME NIGHT-MARISH PENNY DREADFUL.
YOU CONFUSE YOUR FICTIONS, MAGALI.
THIS IS NO PENNY DREADFUL. WE'RE EMBARKING INTO FANTASY...
KLIK
KLIK
KLIK
KLIK
...FANTASY MOST ASTONISHING.
JEAN-PAUL MIGNET?
I--I AM.
REMAIN STILL.
SO... IT'S TRUE, THEN?
I'VE BEEN CHOSEN?
YOU CERTAINLY HAVE.

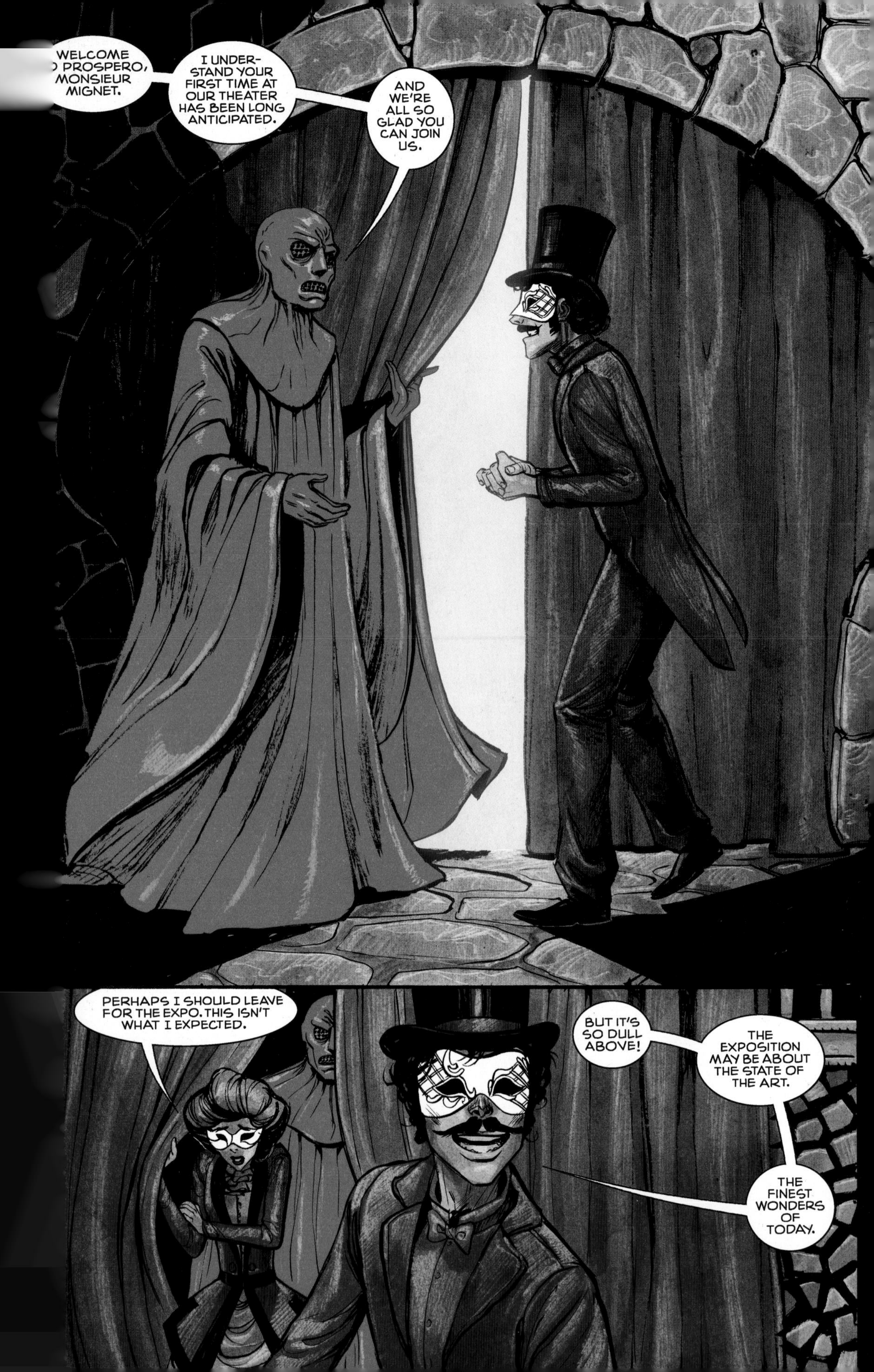
WELCOME O PROSPERO, MONSIEUR MIGNET.
I UNDER-STAND YOUR FIRST TIME AT OUR THEATER HAS BEEN LONG ANTICIPATED.
AND WE'RE ALL SO GLAD YOU CAN JOIN US.
PERHAPS I SHOULD LEAVE FOR THE EXPO. THIS ISN'T WHAT I EXPECTED.
BUT IT'S SO DULL ABOVE!
THE EXPOSITION MAY BE ABOUT THE STATE OF THE ART.
THE FINEST WONDERS OF TODAY.

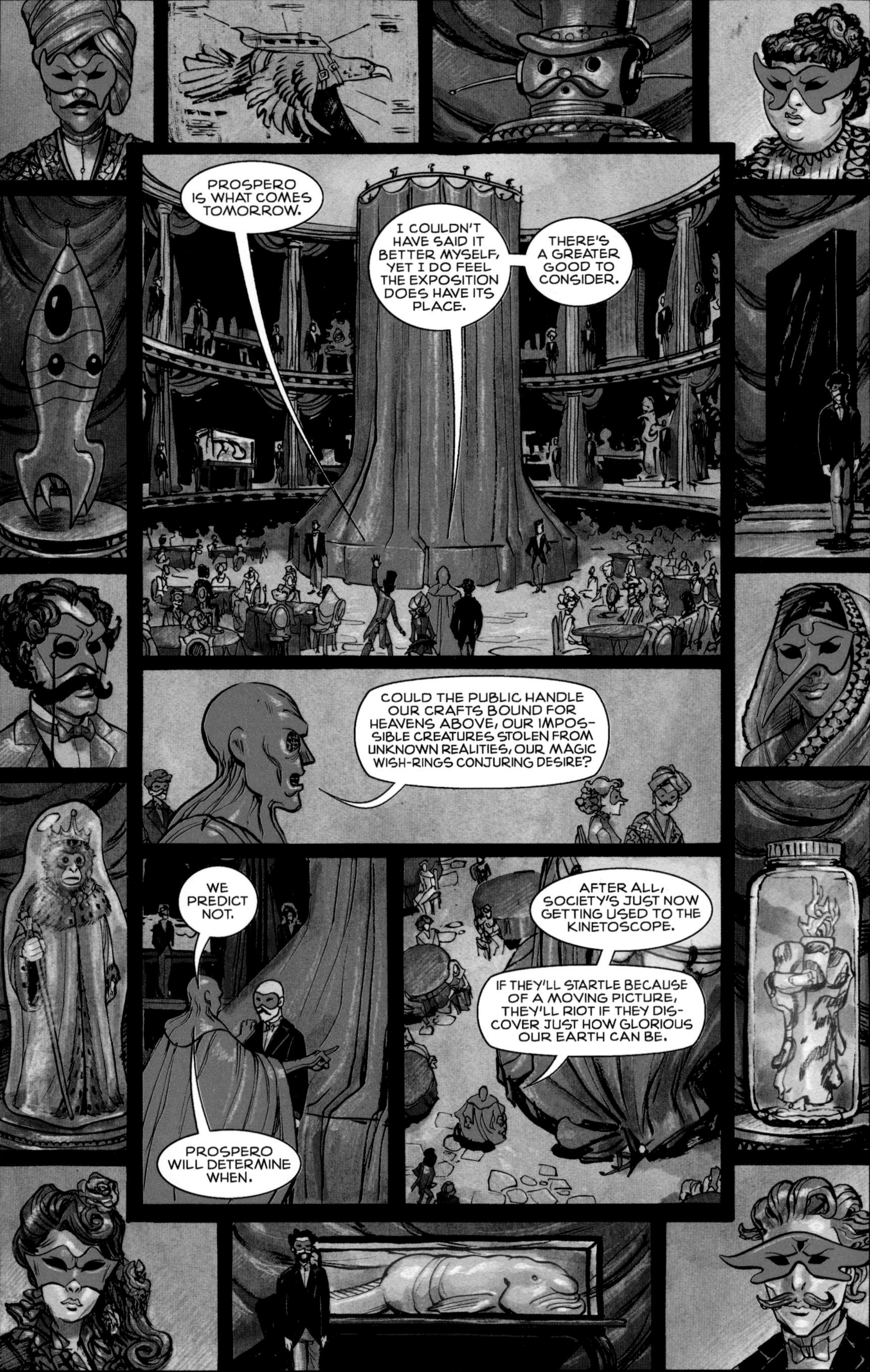

PROSPERO IS WHAT COMES TOMORROW.
I COULDN'T HAVE SAID IT BETTER MYSELF, YET I DO FEEL THE EXPOSITION DOES HAVE ITS PLACE.
THERE'S A GREATER GOOD TO CONSIDER.
COULD THE PUBLIC HANDLE OUR CRAFTS BOUND FOR HEAVENS ABOVE, OUR IMPOS-SIBLE CREATURES STOLEN FROM UNKNOWN REALITIES, OUR MAGIC WISH-RINGS CONJURING DESIRE?
WE PREDICT NOT.
PROSPERO WILL DETERMINE WHEN.
AFTER ALL, SOCIETY'S JUST NOW GETTING USED TO THE KINETOSCOPE.
IF THEY'LL STARTLE BECAUSE OF A MOVING PICTURE, THEY'LL RIOT IF THEY DIS-COVER JUST HOW GLORIOUS OUR EARTH CAN BE.

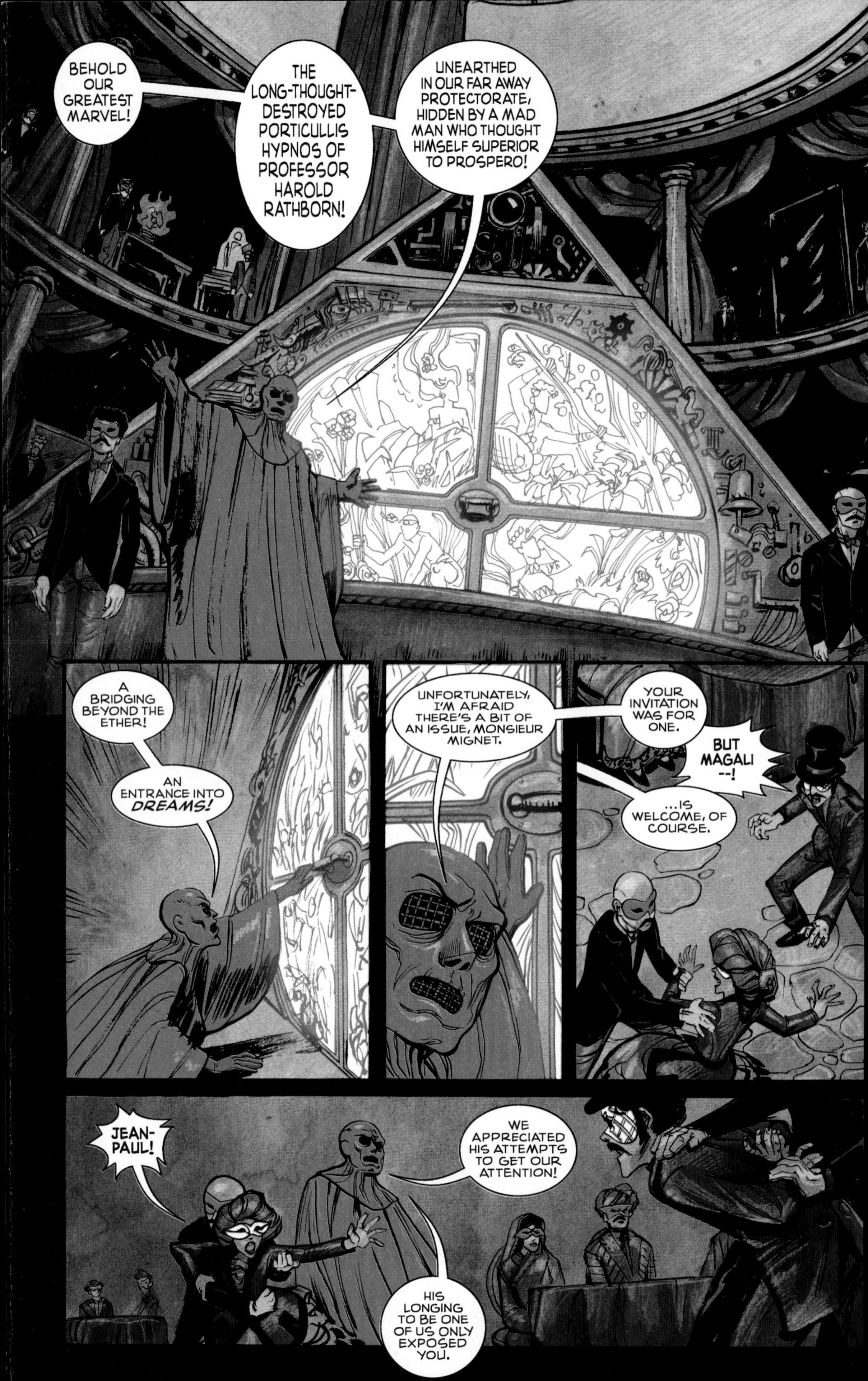
BEHOLD OUR GREATEST MARVEL!
THE LONG-THOUGHT-DESTROYED PORTICULLIS HYPNOS OF PROFESSOR HAROLD RATHBORN!
UNEARTHED IN OUR FAR AWAY PROTECTORATE, HIDDEN BY A MAD MAN WHO THOUGHT HIMSELF SUPERIOR TO PROSPERO!
A BRIDGING BEYOND THE ETHER!
AN ENTRANCE INTO *DREAMS!*
UNFORTUNATELY, I'M AFRAID THERE'S A BIT OF AN ISSUE, MONSIEUR MIGNET.
YOUR INVITATION WAS FOR ONE.
BUT MAGALI --!
...IS WELCOME, OF COURSE.
JEAN-PAUL!
WE APPRECIATED HIS ATTEMPTS TO GET OUR ATTENTION!
HIS LONGING TO BE ONE OF US ONLY EXPOSED YOU.

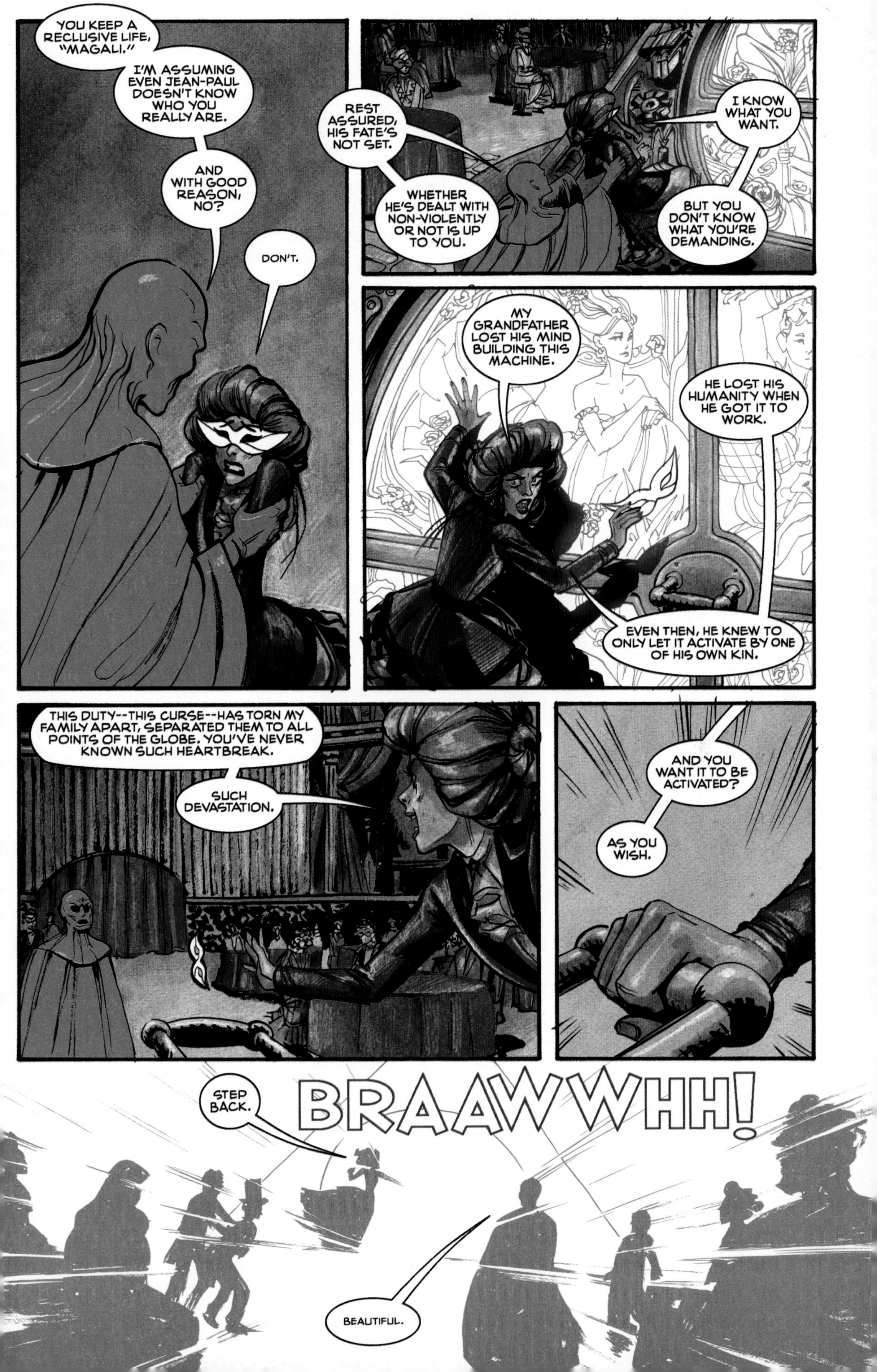

YOU KEEP A RECLUSIVE LIFE, "MAGALI."
I'M ASSUMING EVEN JEAN-PAUL DOESN'T KNOW WHO YOU REALLY ARE.
AND WITH GOOD REASON, NO?
DON'T.
REST ASSURED, HIS FATE'S NOT SET.
WHETHER HE'S DEALT WITH NON-VIOLENTLY OR NOT IS UP TO YOU.
I KNOW WHAT YOU WANT.
BUT YOU DON'T KNOW WHAT YOU'RE DEMANDING.
MY GRANDFATHER LOST HIS MIND BUILDING THIS MACHINE.
HE LOST HIS HUMANITY WHEN HE GOT IT TO WORK.
EVEN THEN, HE KNEW TO ONLY LET IT ACTIVATE BY ONE OF HIS OWN KIN.
THIS DUTY--THIS CURSE--HAS TORN MY FAMILY APART, SEPARATED THEM TO ALL POINTS OF THE GLOBE. YOU'VE NEVER KNOWN SUCH HEARTBREAK.
SUCH DEVASTATION.
AND YOU WANT IT TO BE ACTIVATED?
AS YOU WISH.
STEP BACK.
BRAAWWHH!
BEAUTIFUL.

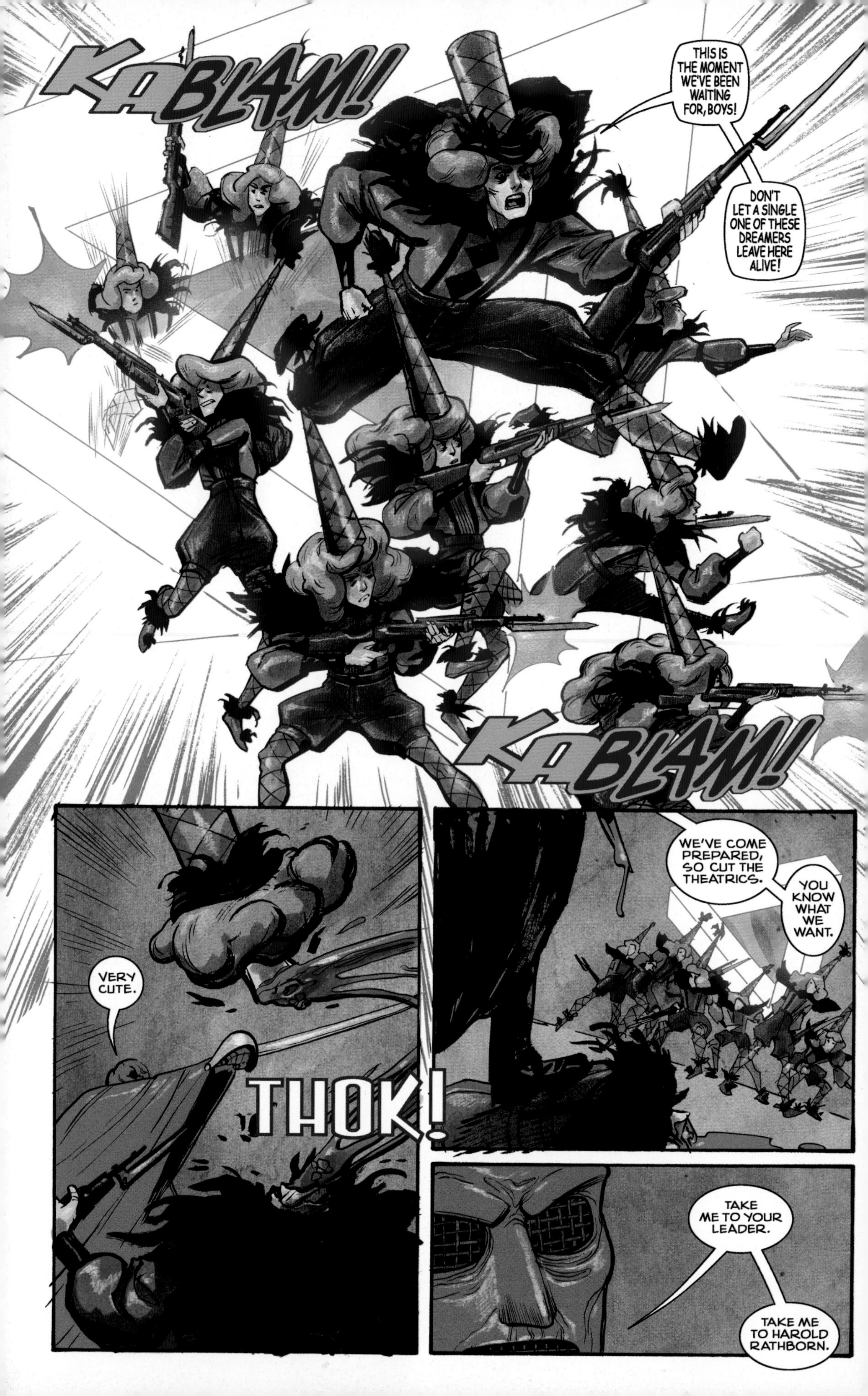
KABLAM!
THIS IS THE MOMENT WE'VE BEEN WAITING FOR, BOYS!
DON'T LET A SINGLE ONE OF THESE DREAMERS LEAVE HERE ALIVE!
KABLAM!
VERY CUTE.
THOK!
WE'VE COME PREPARED, SO CUT THE THEATRICS.
YOU KNOW WHAT WE WANT.
TAKE ME TO YOUR LEADER.
TAKE ME TO HAROLD RATHBORN.

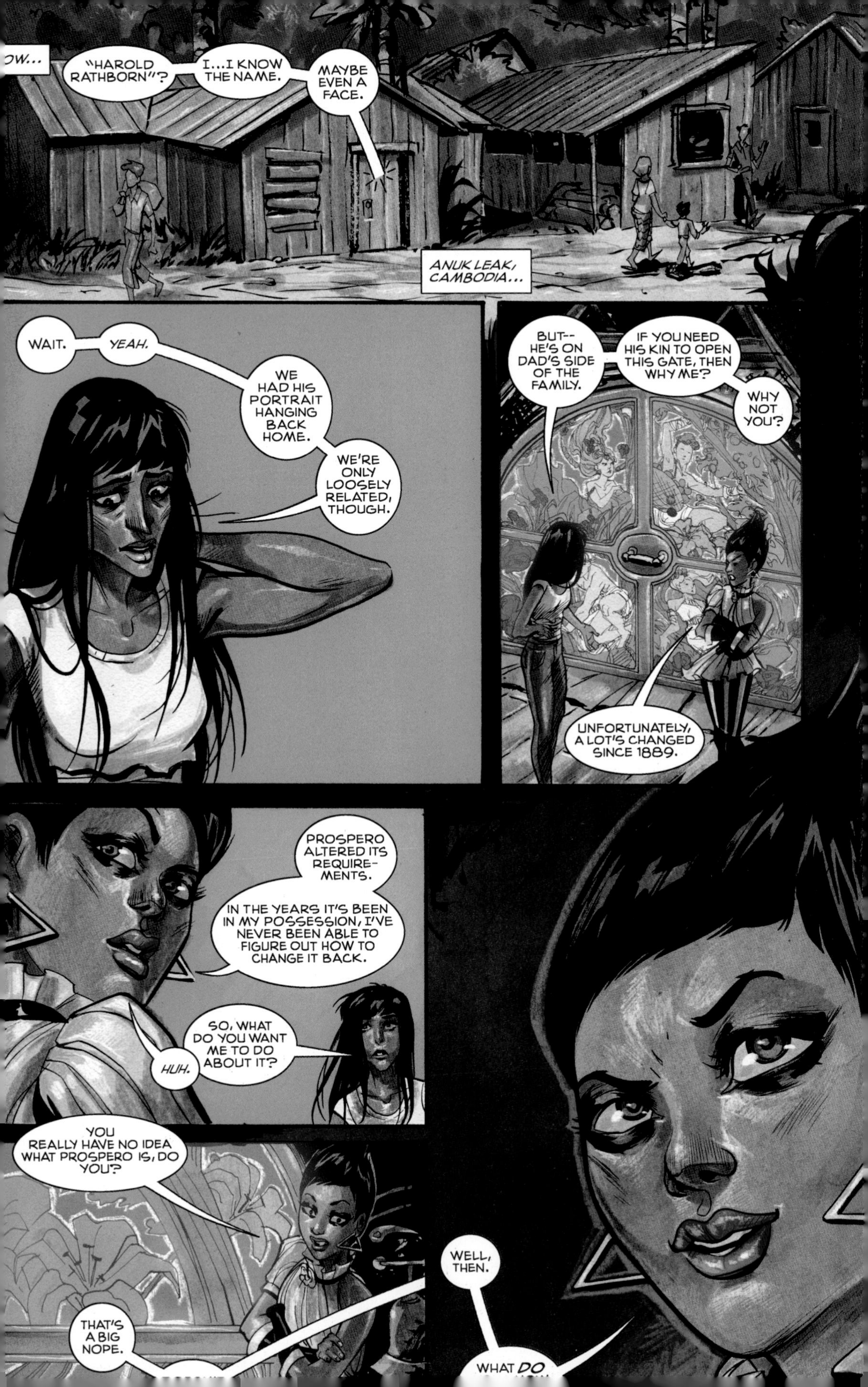
...OW...
"HAROLD RATHBORN"?
I...I KNOW THE NAME.
MAYBE EVEN A FACE.
ANUK LEAK, CAMBODIA...
WAIT.
YEAH.
WE HAD HIS PORTRAIT HANGING BACK HOME.
WE'RE ONLY LOOSELY RELATED, THOUGH.
BUT-- HE'S ON DAD'S SIDE OF THE FAMILY.
IF YOU NEED HIS KIN TO OPEN THIS GATE, THEN WHY ME?
WHY NOT YOU?
UNFORTUNATELY, A LOT'S CHANGED SINCE 1889.
PROSPERO ALTERED ITS REQUIRE- MENTS.
IN THE YEARS IT'S BEEN IN MY POSSESSION, I'VE NEVER BEEN ABLE TO FIGURE OUT HOW TO CHANGE IT BACK.
HUH.
SO, WHAT DO YOU WANT ME TO DO ABOUT IT?
YOU REALLY HAVE NO IDEA WHAT PROSPERO IS, DO YOU?
THAT'S A BIG NOPE.
WELL, THEN.

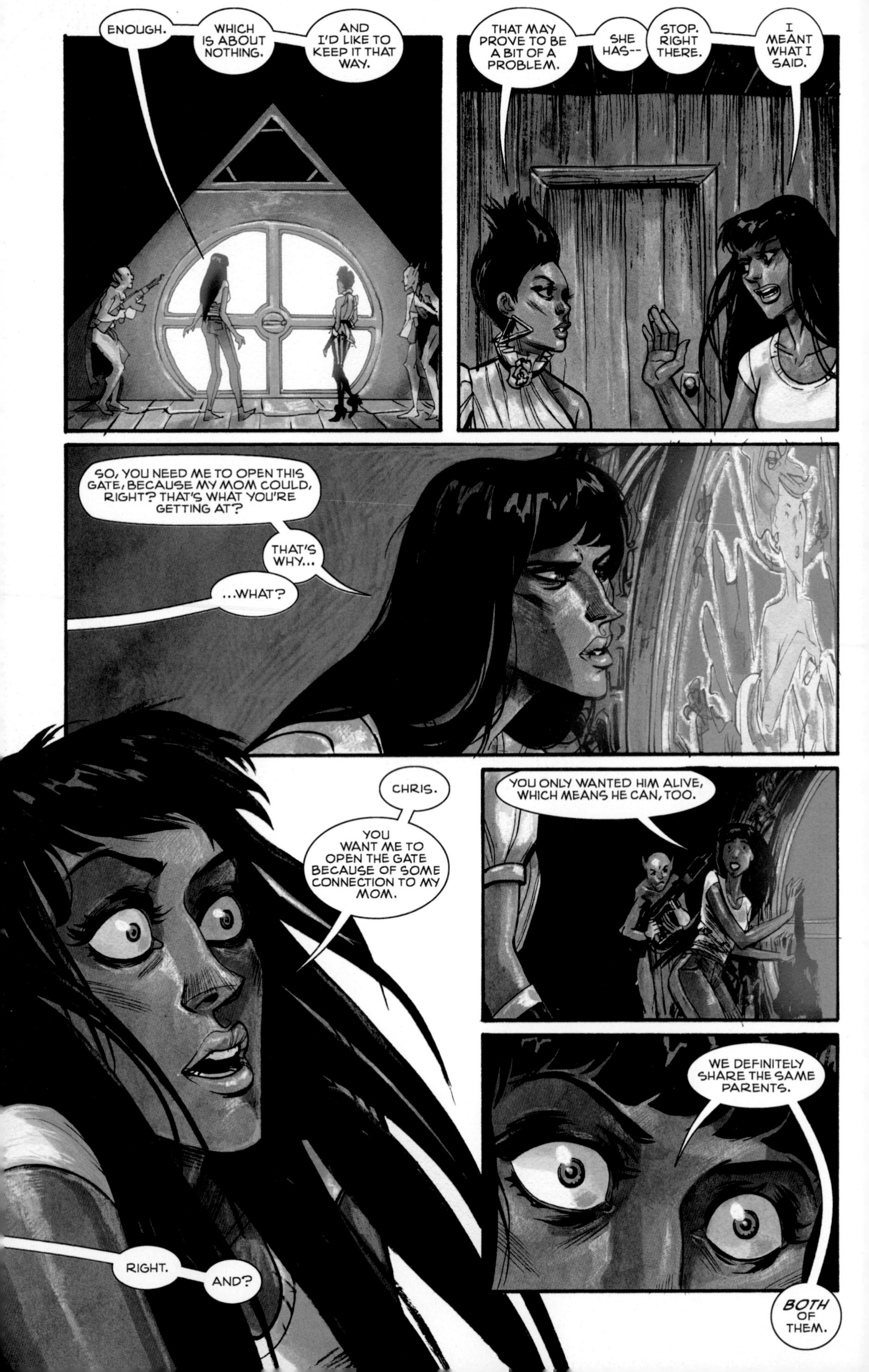
ENOUGH.
WHICH IS ABOUT NOTHING.
AND I'D LIKE TO KEEP IT THAT WAY.
THAT MAY PROVE TO BE A BIT OF A PROBLEM.
SHE HAS--
STOP. RIGHT THERE.
I MEANT WHAT I SAID.
SO, YOU NEED ME TO OPEN THIS GATE, BECAUSE MY MOM COULD, RIGHT? THAT'S WHAT YOU'RE GETTING AT?
THAT'S WHY...
...WHAT?
CHRIS.
YOU WANT ME TO OPEN THE GATE BECAUSE OF SOME CONNECTION TO MY MOM.
RIGHT.
AND?
YOU ONLY WANTED HIM ALIVE, WHICH MEANS HE CAN, TOO.
WE DEFINITELY SHARE THE SAME PARENTS.
BOTH OF THEM.

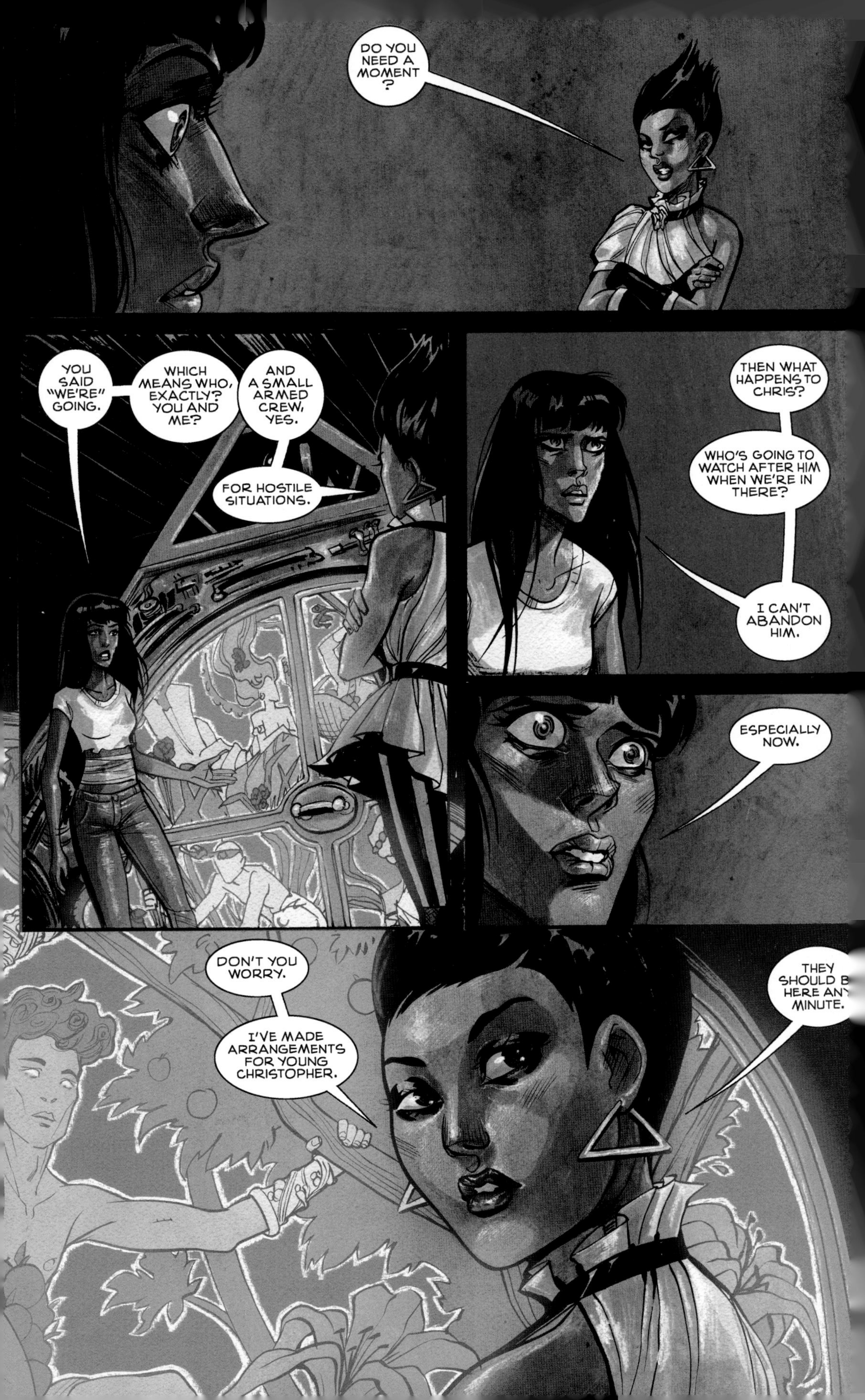
DO YOU NEED A MOMENT ?
YOU SAID "WE'RE" GOING.
WHICH MEANS WHO, EXACTLY? YOU AND ME?
AND A SMALL ARMED CREW, YES.
FOR HOSTILE SITUATIONS.
THEN WHAT HAPPENS TO CHRIS?
WHO'S GOING TO WATCH AFTER HIM WHEN WE'RE IN THERE?
I CAN'T ABANDON HIM.
ESPECIALLY NOW.
DON'T YOU WORRY.
I'VE MADE ARRANGEMENTS FOR YOUNG CHRISTOPHER.
THEY SHOULD B HERE ANY MINUTE.

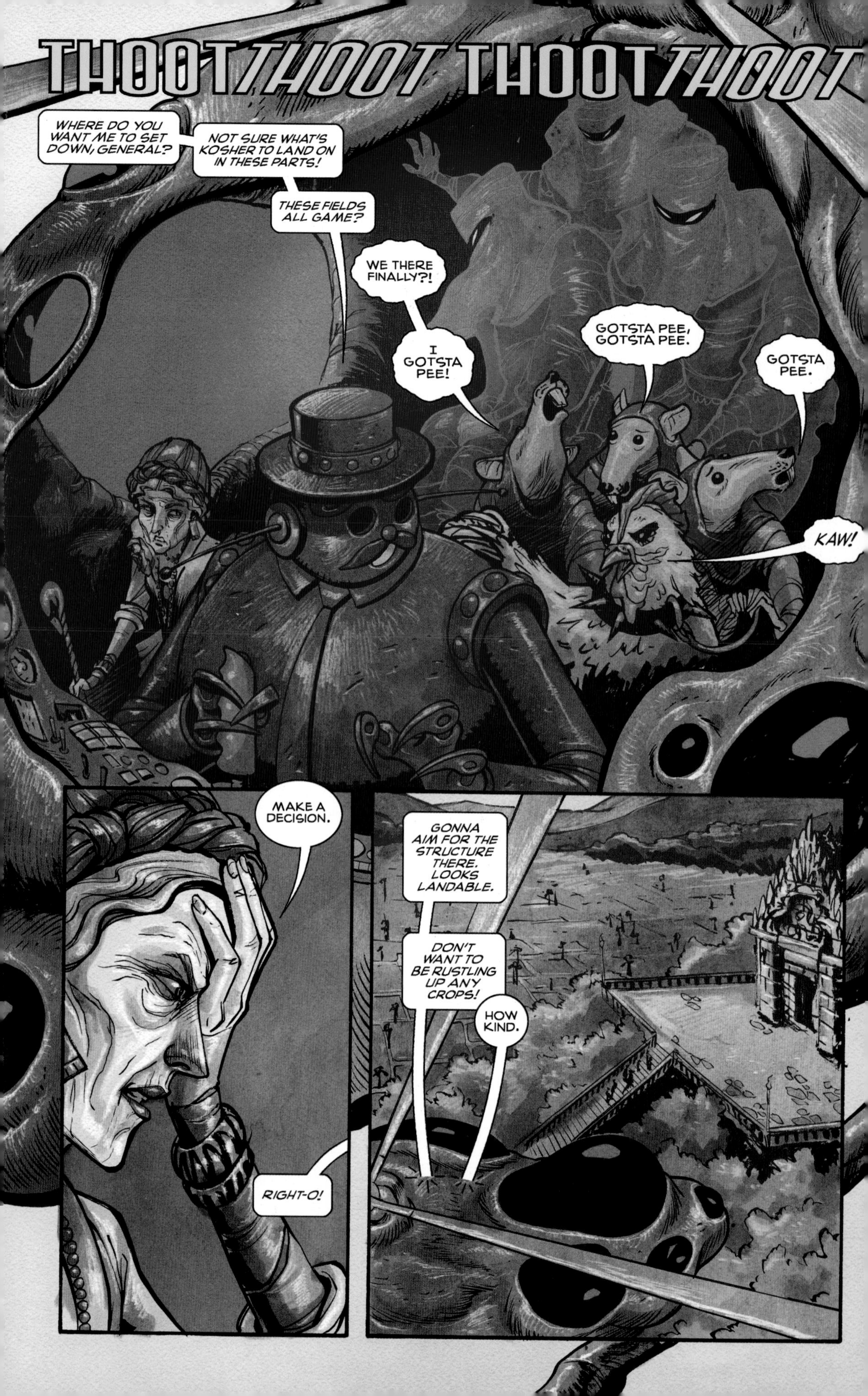
THOOT THOOT THOOT THOOT
WHERE DO YOU WANT ME TO SET DOWN, GENERAL?
NOT SURE WHAT'S KOSHER TO LAND ON IN THESE PARTS!
THESE FIELDS ALL GAME?
WE THERE FINALLY?!
I GOTSTA PEE!
GOTSTA PEE, GOTSTA PEE.
GOTSTA PEE.
KAW!
MAKE A DECISION.
RIGHT-O!
GONNA AIM FOR THE STRUCTURE THERE. LOOKS LANDABLE.
DON'T WANT TO BE RUSTLING UP ANY CROPS!
HOW KIND.

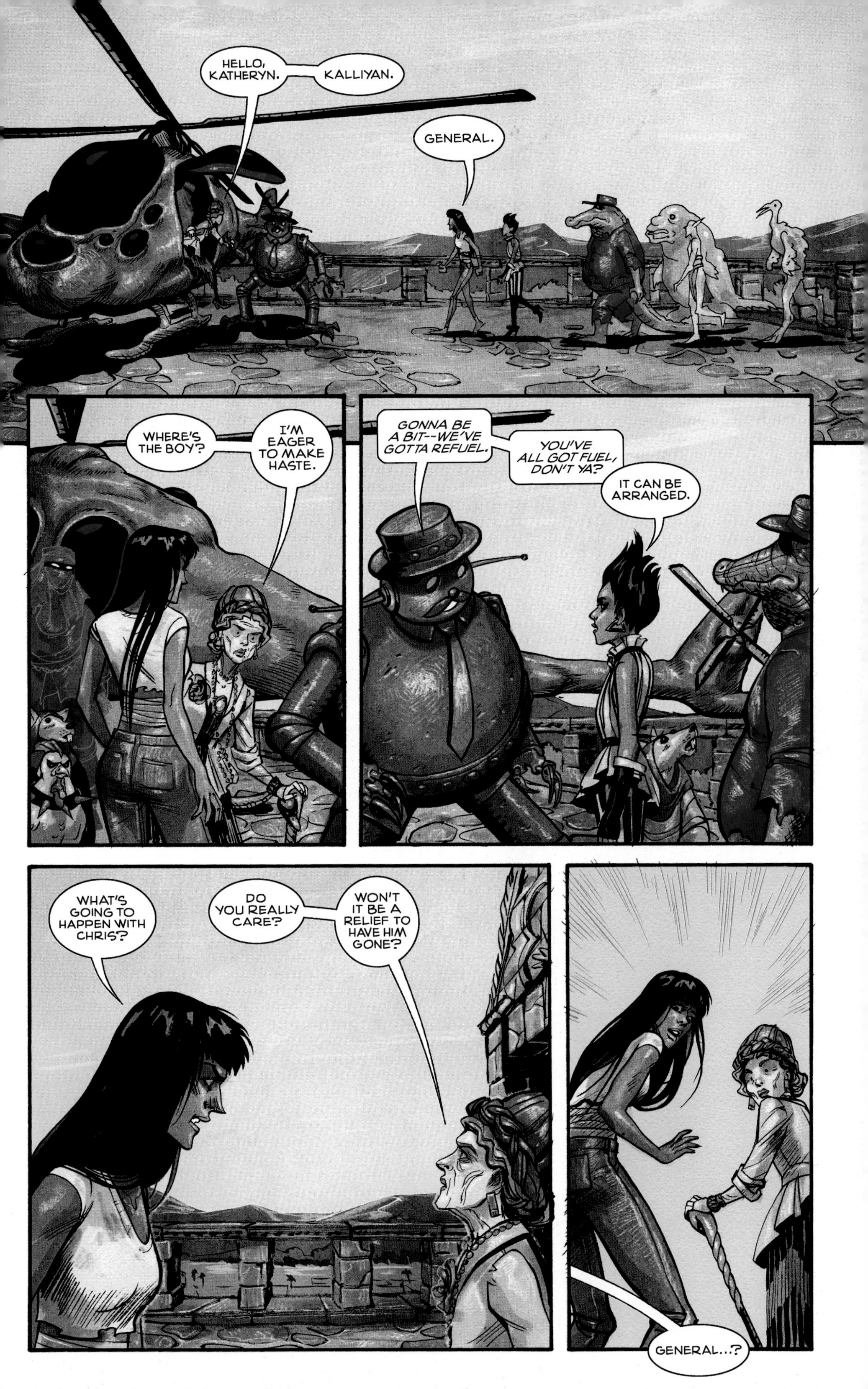
HELLO, KATHERYN.
KALLIYAN.
GENERAL.
WHERE'S THE BOY?
I'M EAGER TO MAKE HASTE.
GONNA BE A BIT--WE'VE GOTTA REFUEL.
YOU'VE ALL GOT FUEL, DON'T YA?
IT CAN BE ARRANGED.
WHAT'S GOING TO HAPPEN WITH CHRIS?
DO YOU REALLY CARE?
WON'T IT BE A RELIEF TO HAVE HIM GONE?
GENERAL...?

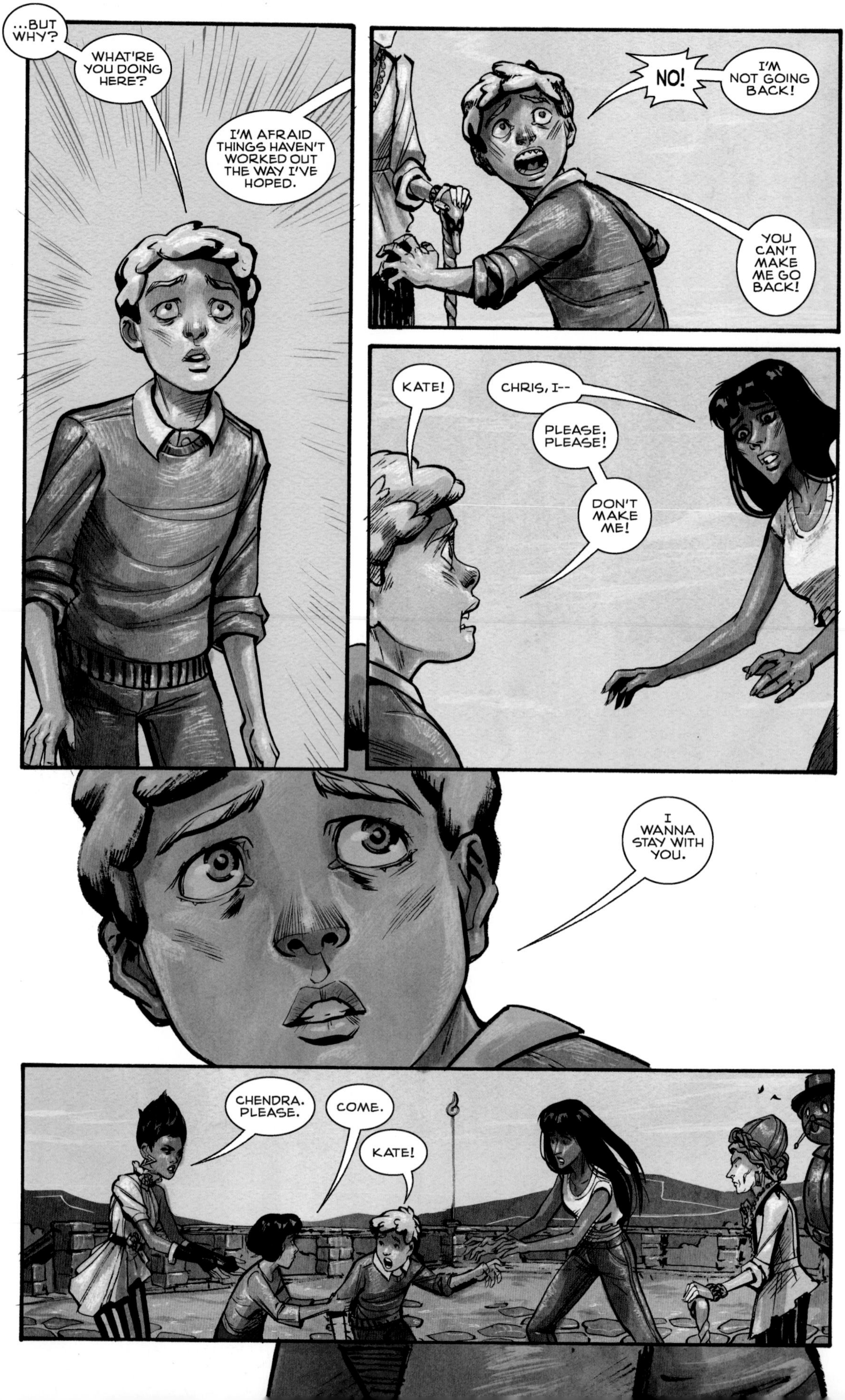
...BUT WHY?
WHAT'RE YOU DOING HERE?
I'M AFRAID THINGS HAVEN'T WORKED OUT THE WAY I'VE HOPED.
NO!
I'M NOT GOING BACK!
YOU CAN'T MAKE ME GO BACK!
KATE!
CHRIS, I--
PLEASE. PLEASE!
DON'T MAKE ME!
I WANNA STAY WITH YOU.
CHENDRA. PLEASE.
COME.
KATE!

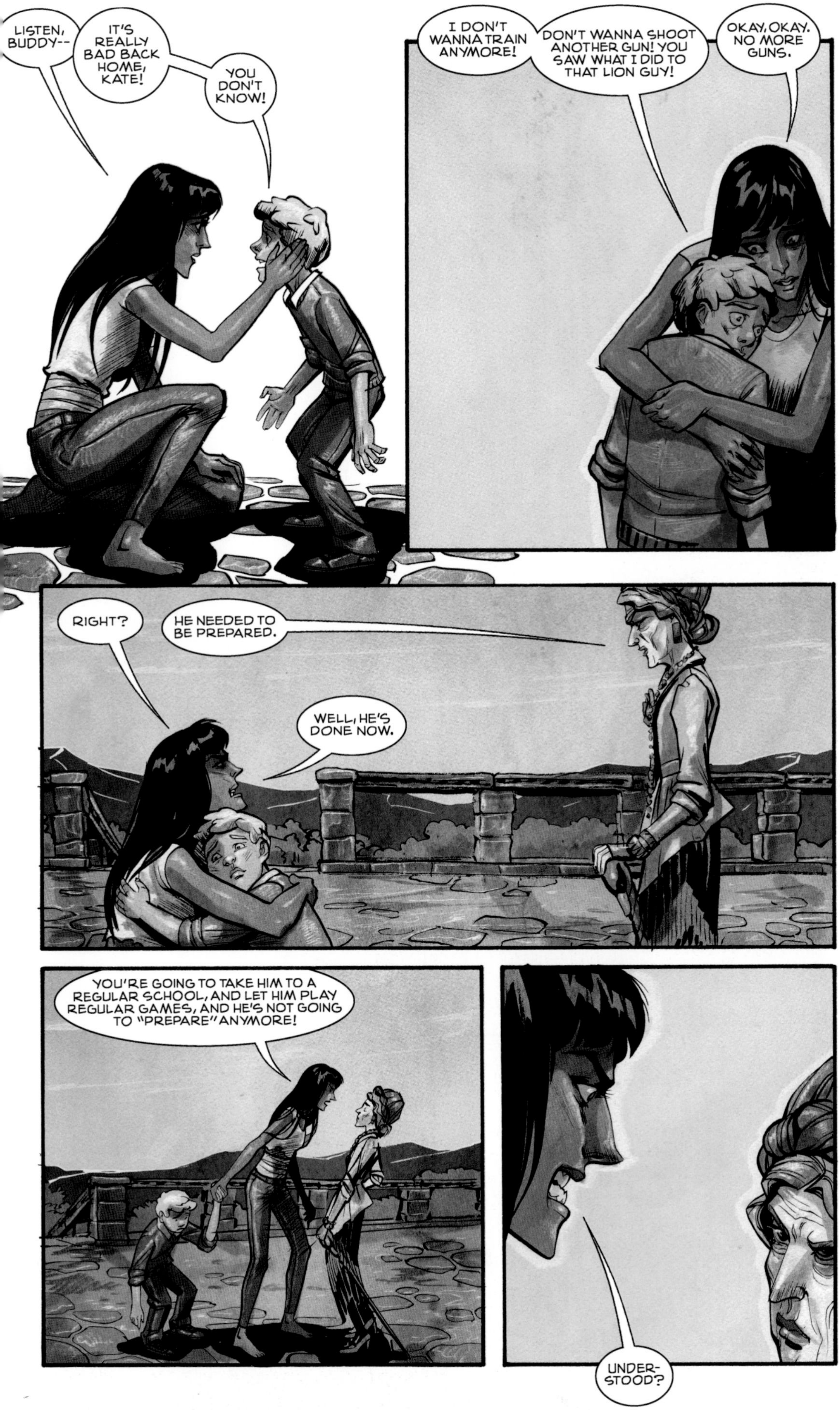
LISTEN, BUDDY--
IT'S REALLY BAD BACK HOME, KATE!
YOU DON'T KNOW!
I DON'T WANNA TRAIN ANYMORE!
DON'T WANNA SHOOT ANOTHER GUN! YOU SAW WHAT I DID TO THAT LION GUY!
OKAY, OKAY. NO MORE GUNS.
RIGHT?
HE NEEDED TO BE PREPARED.
WELL, HE'S DONE NOW.
YOU'RE GOING TO TAKE HIM TO A REGULAR SCHOOL, AND LET HIM PLAY REGULAR GAMES, AND HE'S NOT GOING TO "PREPARE" ANYMORE!
UNDER-STOOD?

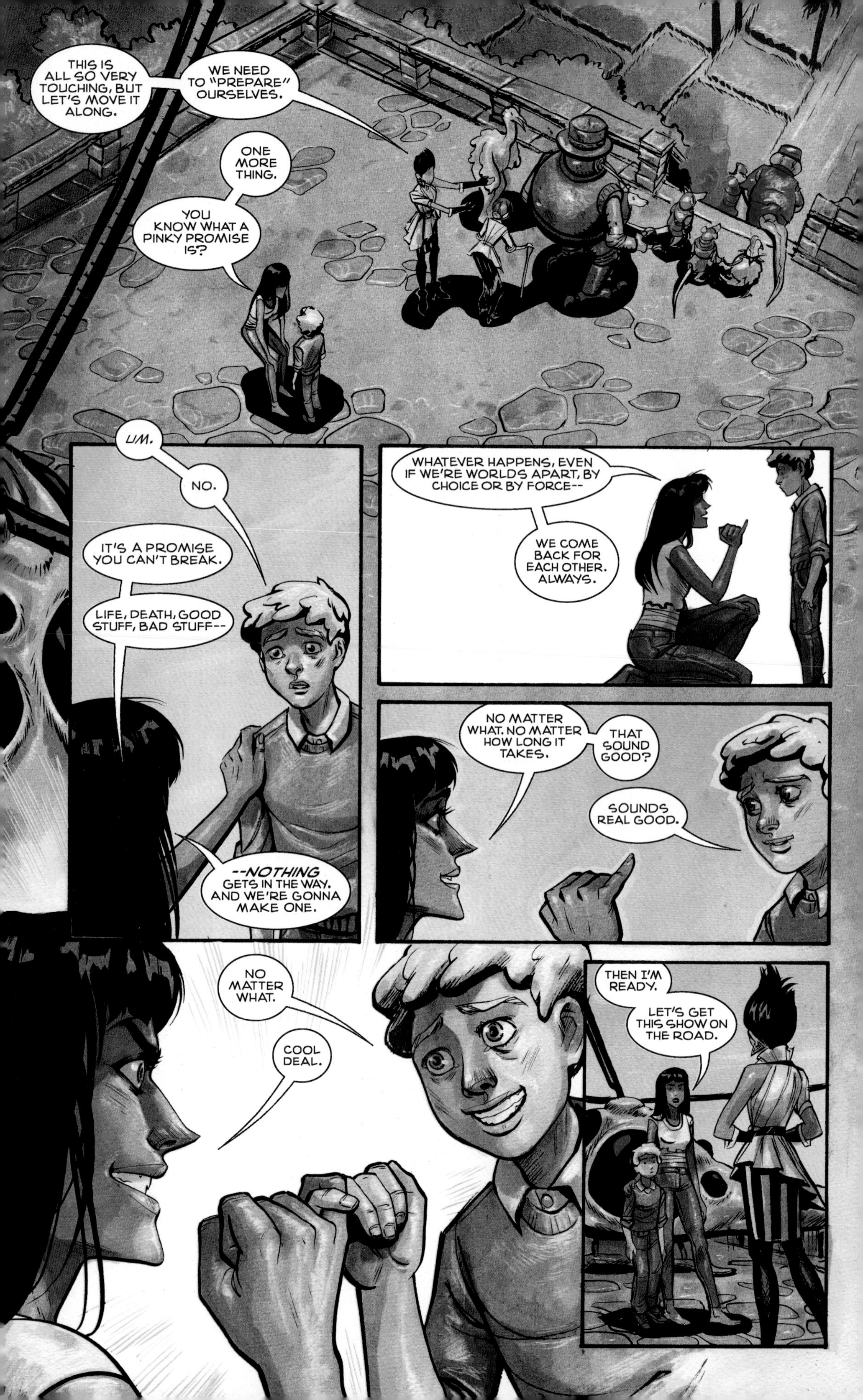

THIS IS ALL SO VERY TOUCHING, BUT LET'S MOVE IT ALONG.
WE NEED TO "PREPARE" OURSELVES.
ONE MORE THING.
YOU KNOW WHAT A PINKY PROMISE IS?
UM.
NO.
IT'S A PROMISE YOU CAN'T BREAK.
LIFE, DEATH, GOOD STUFF, BAD STUFF--
--NOTHING GETS IN THE WAY. AND WE'RE GONNA MAKE ONE.
WHATEVER HAPPENS, EVEN IF WE'RE WORLDS APART, BY CHOICE OR BY FORCE--
WE COME BACK FOR EACH OTHER. ALWAYS.
NO MATTER WHAT. NO MATTER HOW LONG IT TAKES.
THAT SOUND GOOD?
SOUNDS REAL GOOD.
NO MATTER WHAT.
COOL DEAL.
THEN I'M READY.
LET'S GET THIS SHOW ON THE ROAD.

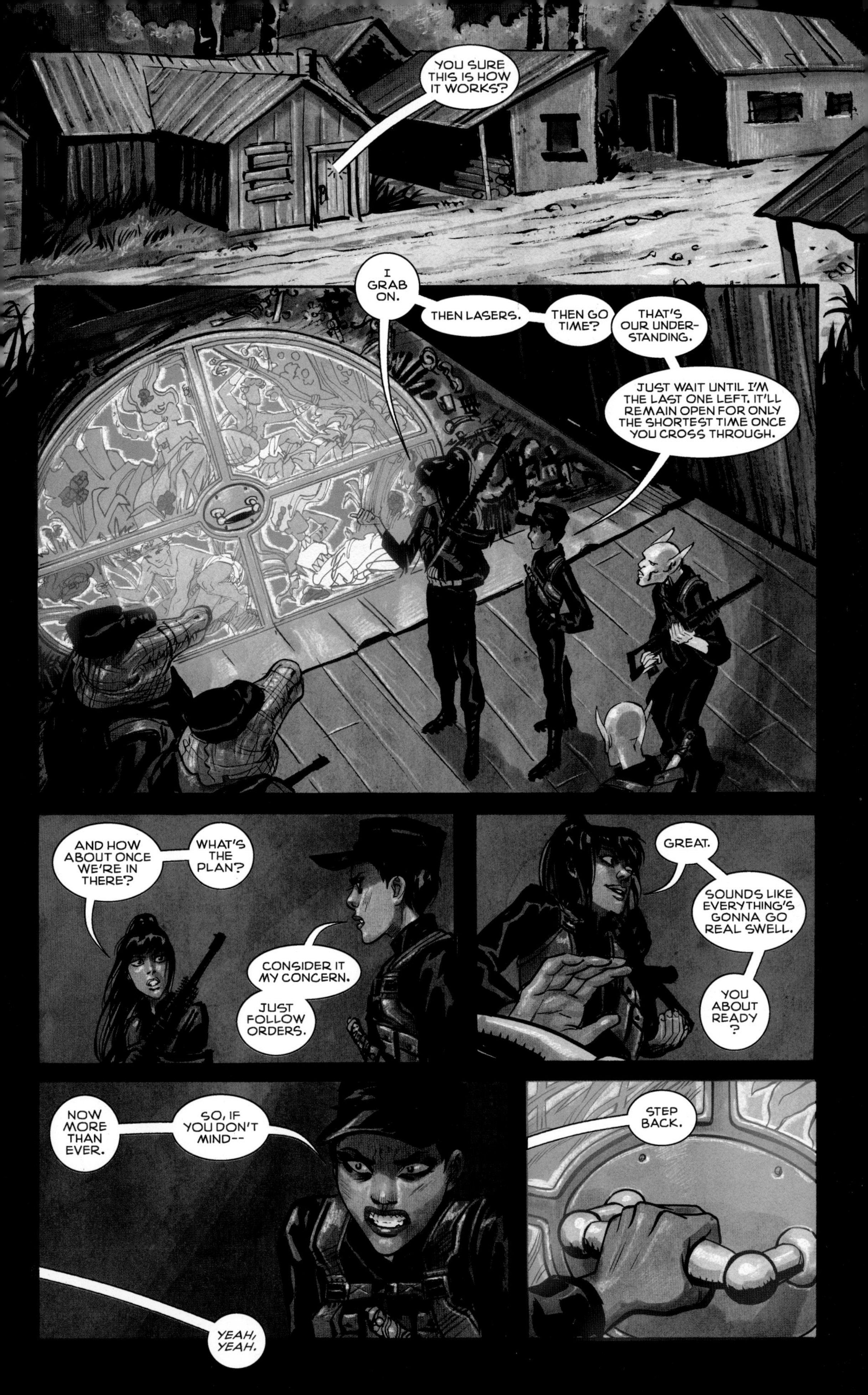
YOU SURE THIS IS HOW IT WORKS?
I GRAB ON.
THEN LASERS.
THEN GO TIME?
THAT'S OUR UNDER-STANDING.
JUST WAIT UNTIL I'M THE LAST ONE LEFT. IT'LL REMAIN OPEN FOR ONLY THE SHORTEST TIME ONCE YOU CROSS THROUGH.
AND HOW ABOUT ONCE WE'RE IN THERE?
WHAT'S THE PLAN?
CONSIDER IT MY CONCERN.
JUST FOLLOW ORDERS.
GREAT.
SOUNDS LIKE EVERYTHING'S GONNA GO REAL SWELL.
YOU ABOUT READY?
NOW MORE THAN EVER.
SO, IF YOU DON'T MIND--
YEAH, YEAH.
STEP BACK.

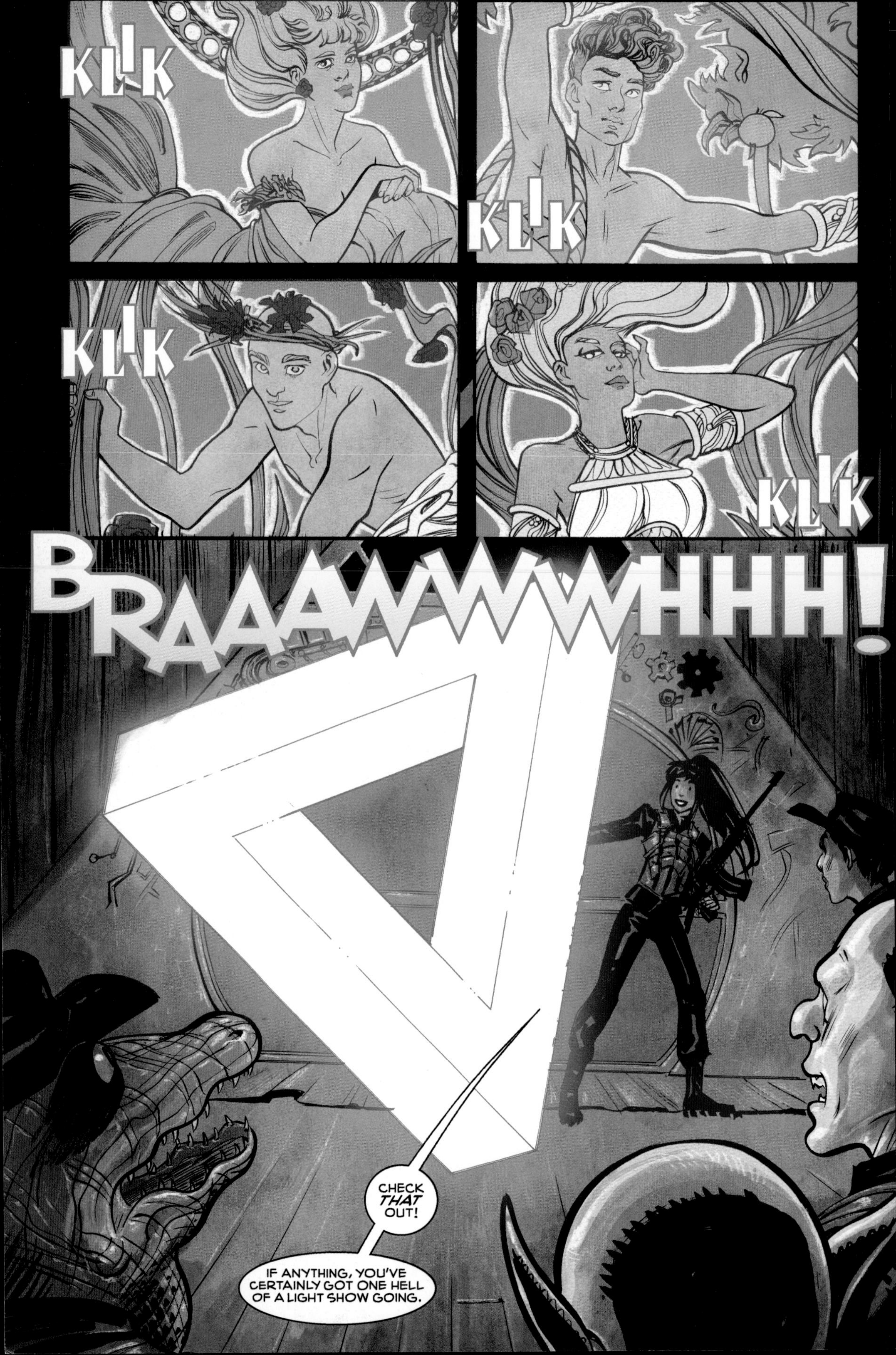
KLIK
KLIK
KLIK
KLIK
BRAAAWWWHHH!
CHECK *THAT* OUT!
IF ANYTHING, YOU'VE CERTAINLY GOT ONE HELL OF A LIGHT SHOW GOING.

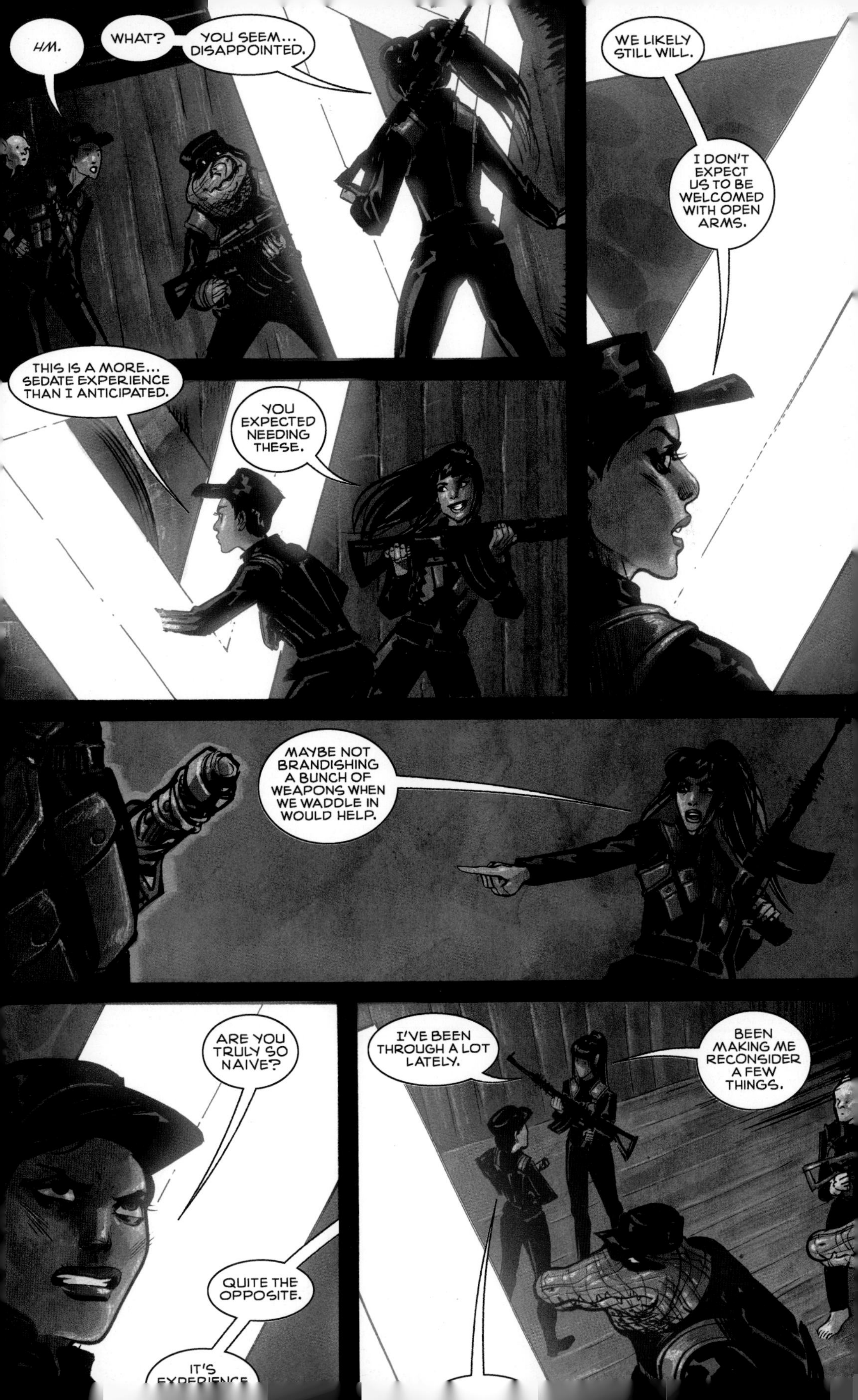
HM.
WHAT?
YOU SEEM... DISAPPOINTED.
WE LIKELY STILL WILL.
I DON'T EXPECT US TO BE WELCOMED WITH OPEN ARMS.
THIS IS A MORE... SEDATE EXPERIENCE THAN I ANTICIPATED.
YOU EXPECTED NEEDING THESE.
MAYBE NOT BRANDISHING A BUNCH OF WEAPONS WHEN WE WADDLE IN WOULD HELP.
ARE YOU TRULY SO NAIVE?
QUITE THE OPPOSITE.
I'VE BEEN THROUGH A LOT LATELY.
BEEN MAKING ME RECONSIDER A FEW THINGS.

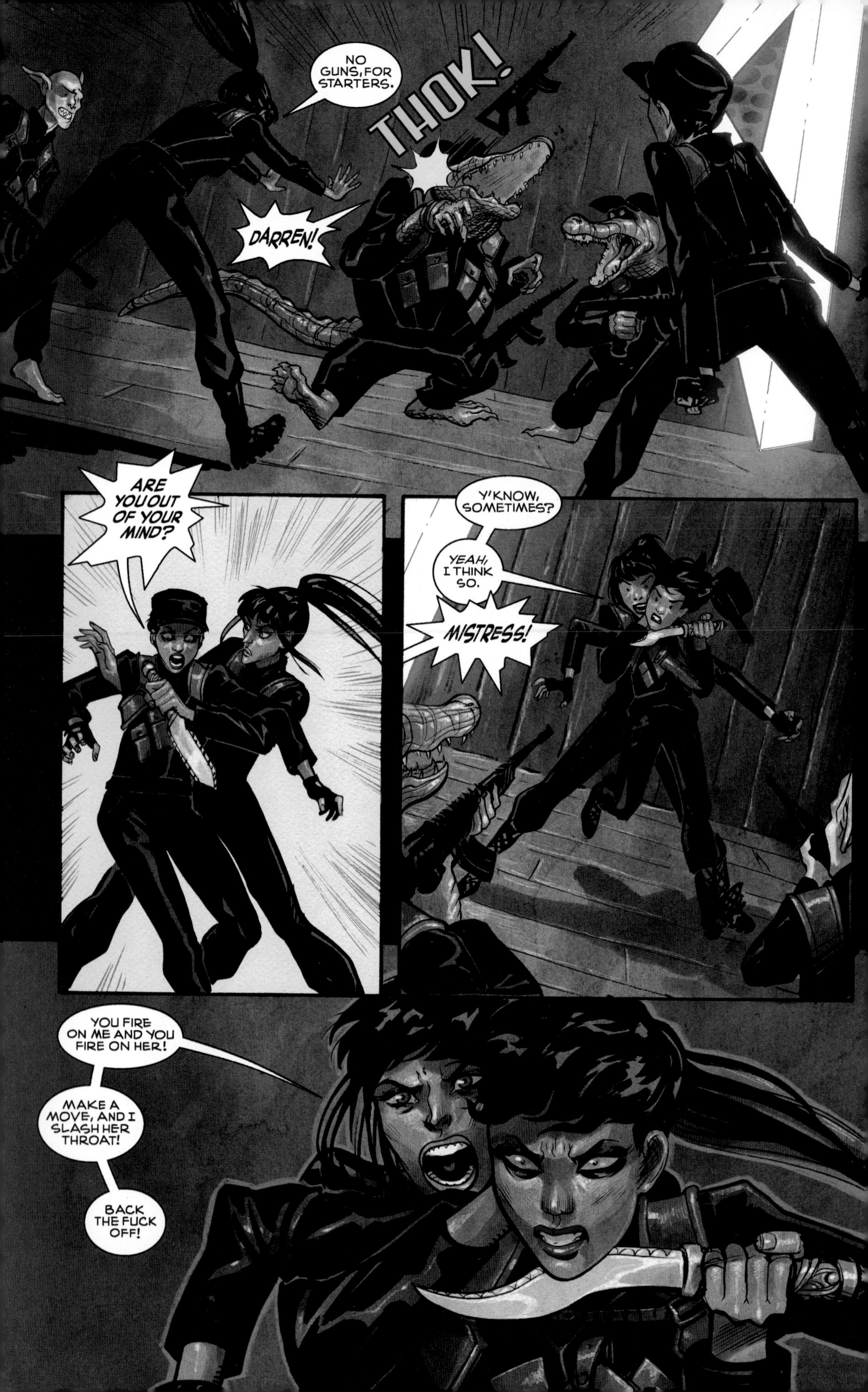
NO GUNS, FOR STARTERS.
THOK!
DARREN!
ARE YOU OUT OF YOUR MIND?
Y'KNOW, SOMETIMES?
YEAH, I THINK SO.
MISTRESS!
YOU FIRE ON ME AND YOU FIRE ON HER!
MAKE A MOVE, AND I SLASH HER THROAT!
BACK THE FUCK OFF!

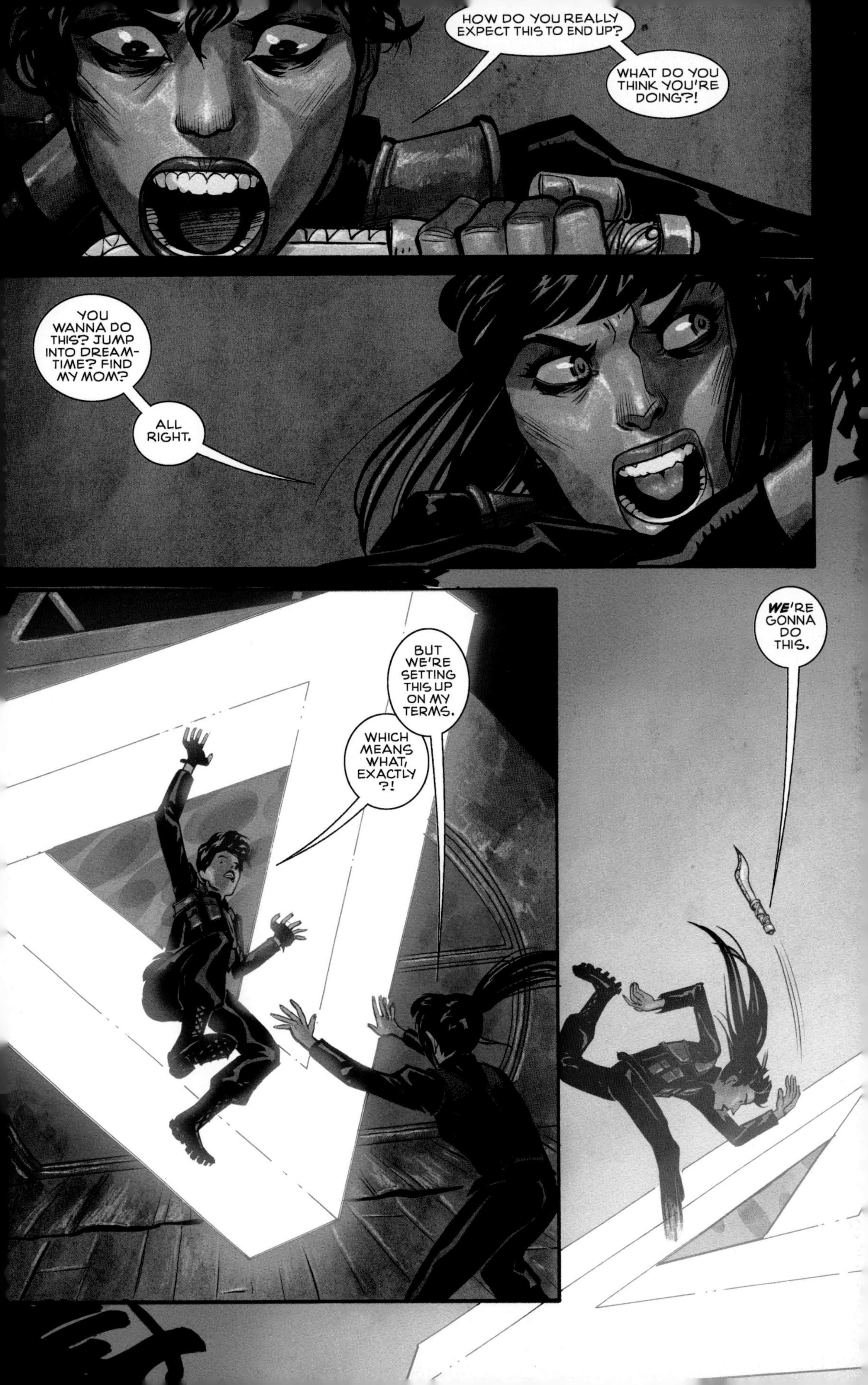
HOW DO YOU REALLY EXPECT THIS TO END UP?
WHAT DO YOU THINK YOU'RE DOING?!
YOU WANNA DO THIS? JUMP INTO DREAM-TIME? FIND MY MOM?
ALL RIGHT.
WE'RE GONNA DO THIS.
BUT WE'RE SETTING THIS UP ON MY TERMS.
WHICH MEANS WHAT, EXACTLY ?!

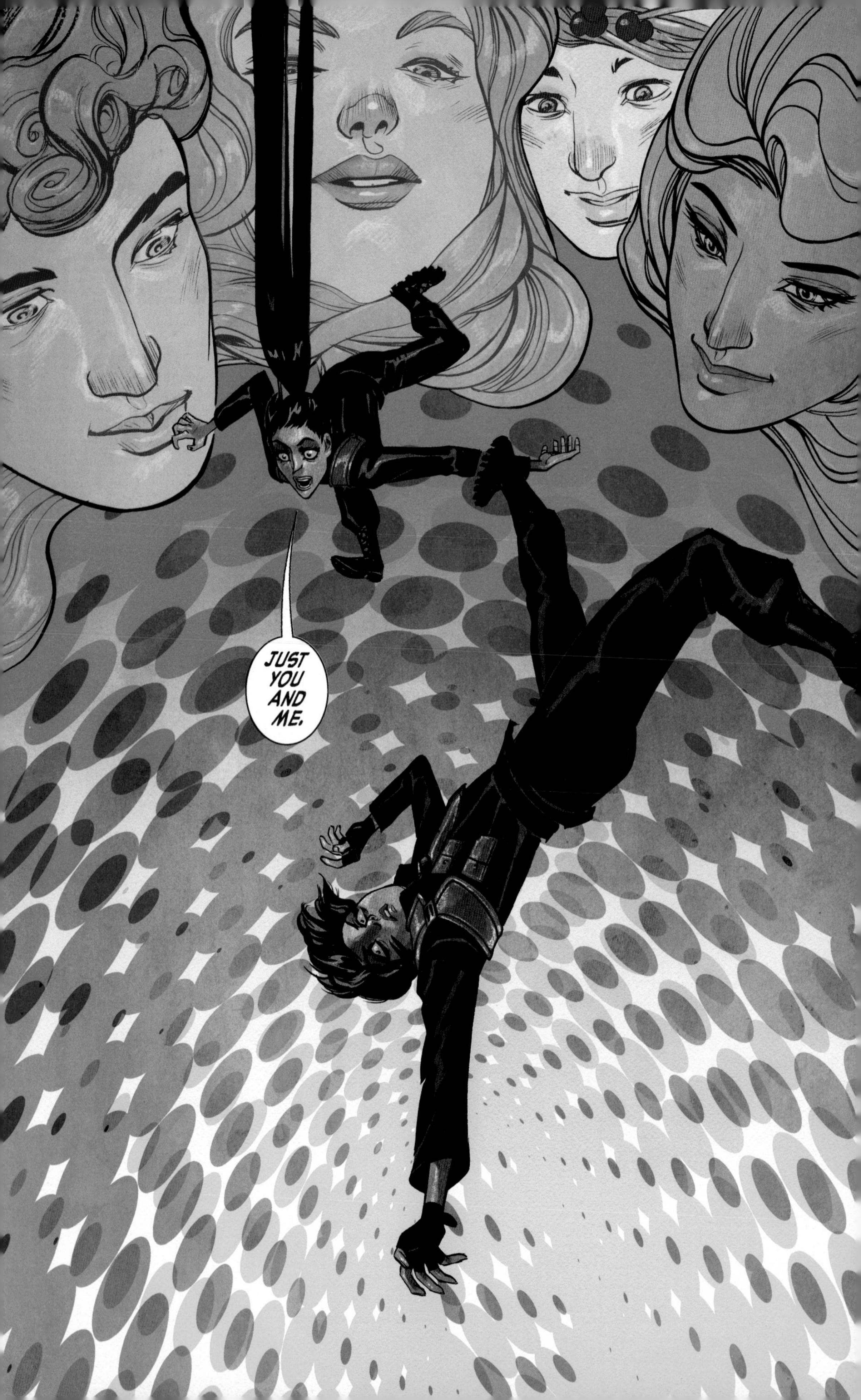
JUST YOU AND ME.

CHAPTER 10

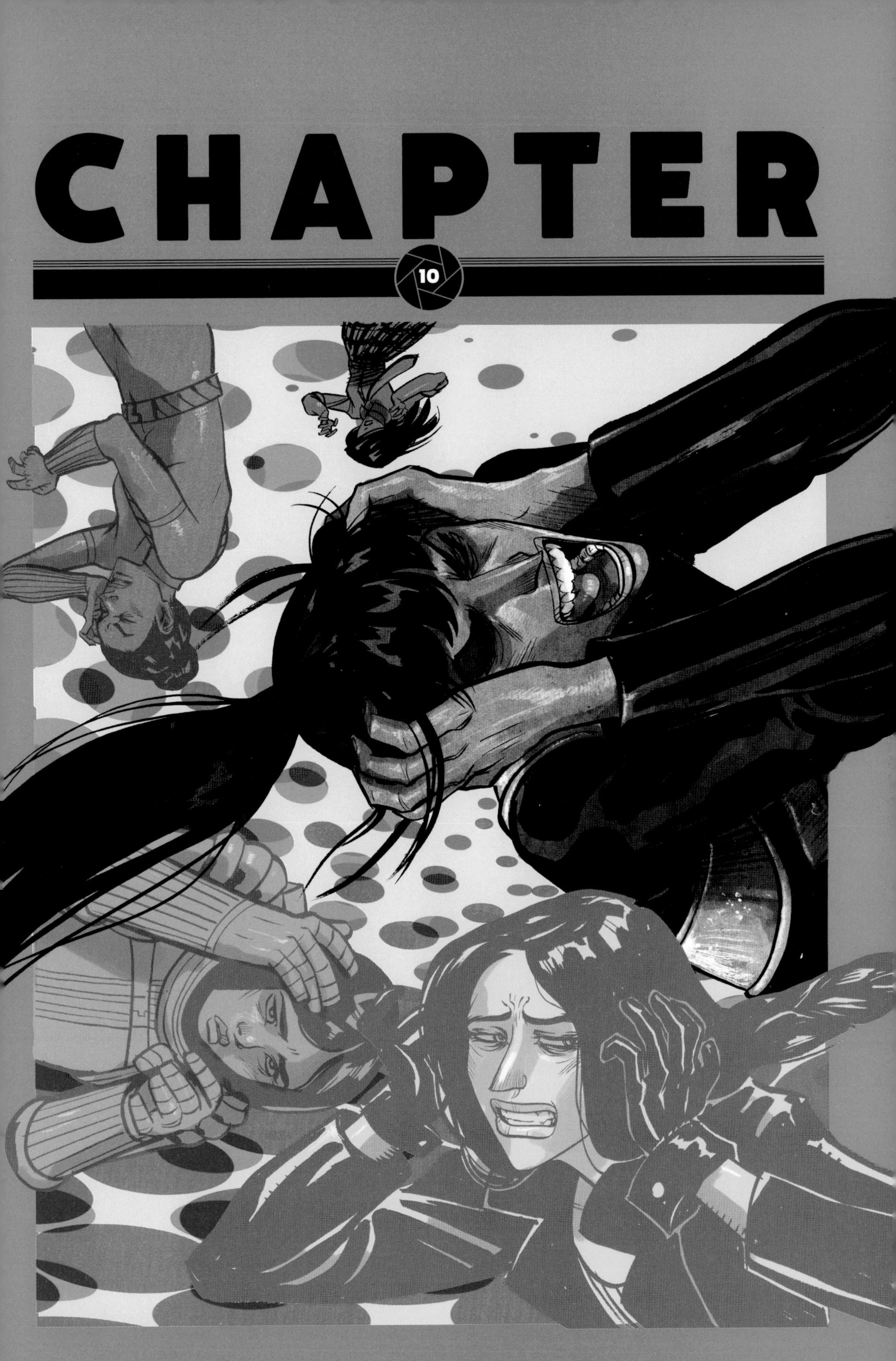

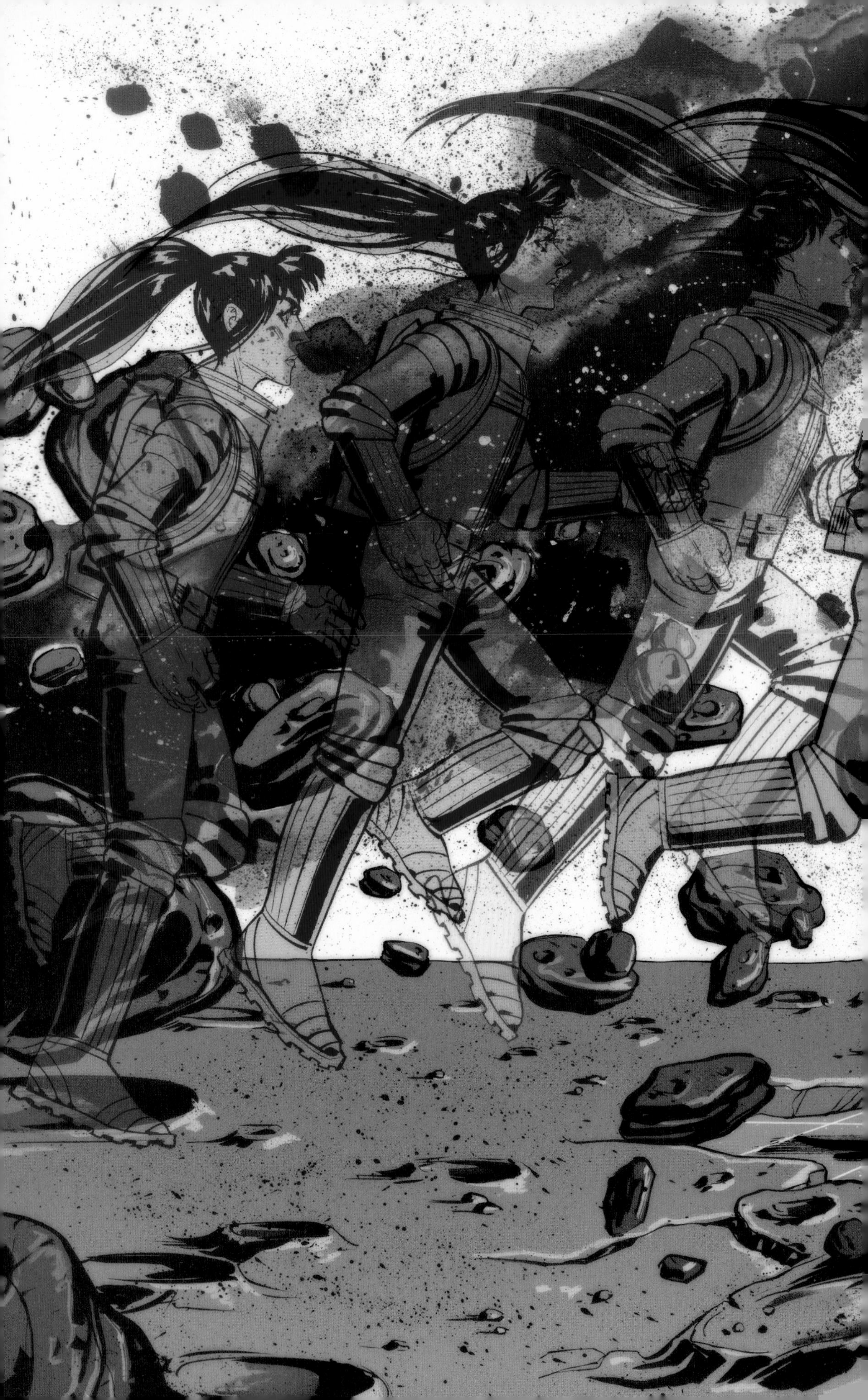

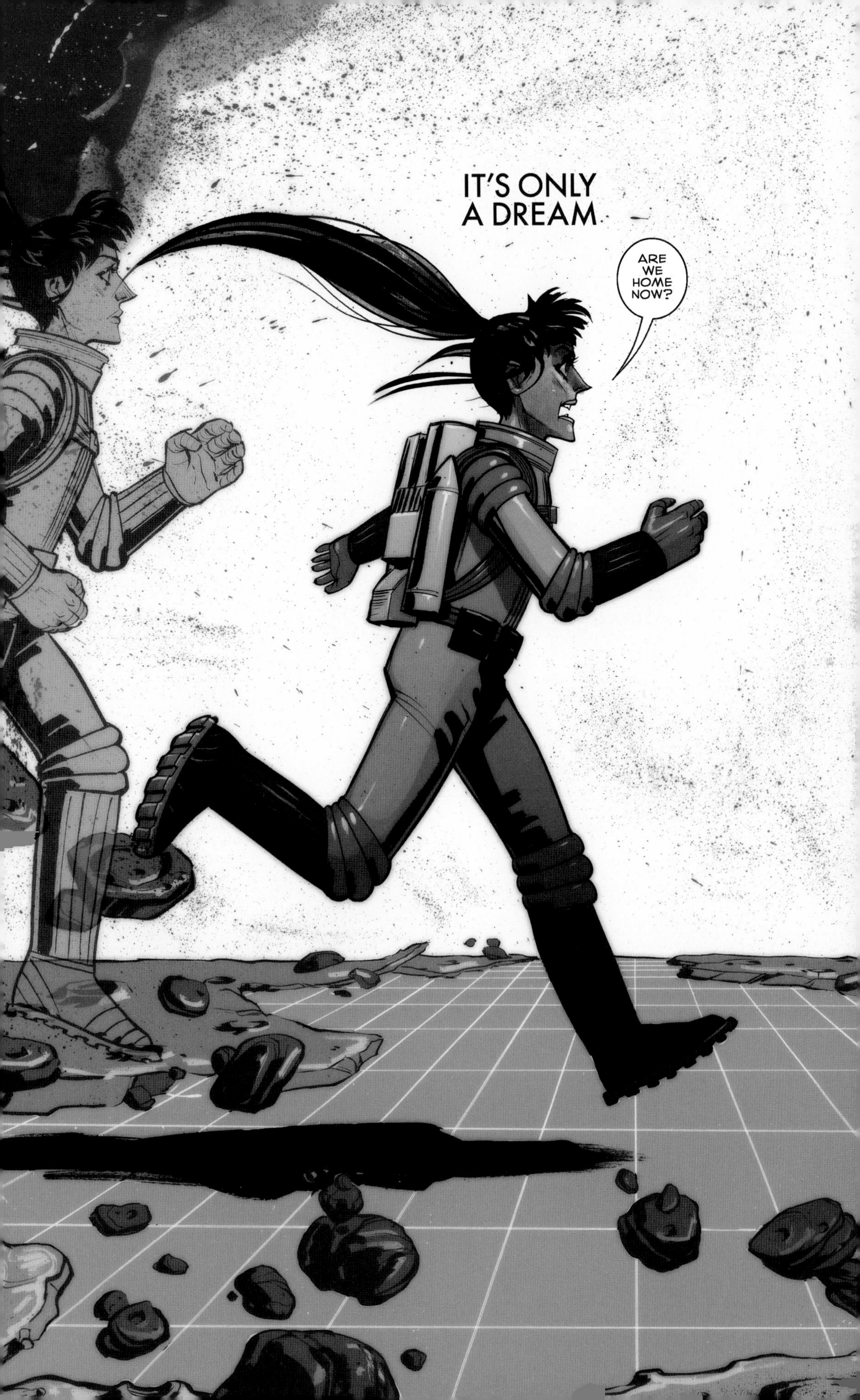
IT'S ONLY A DREAM
ARE WE HOME NOW?

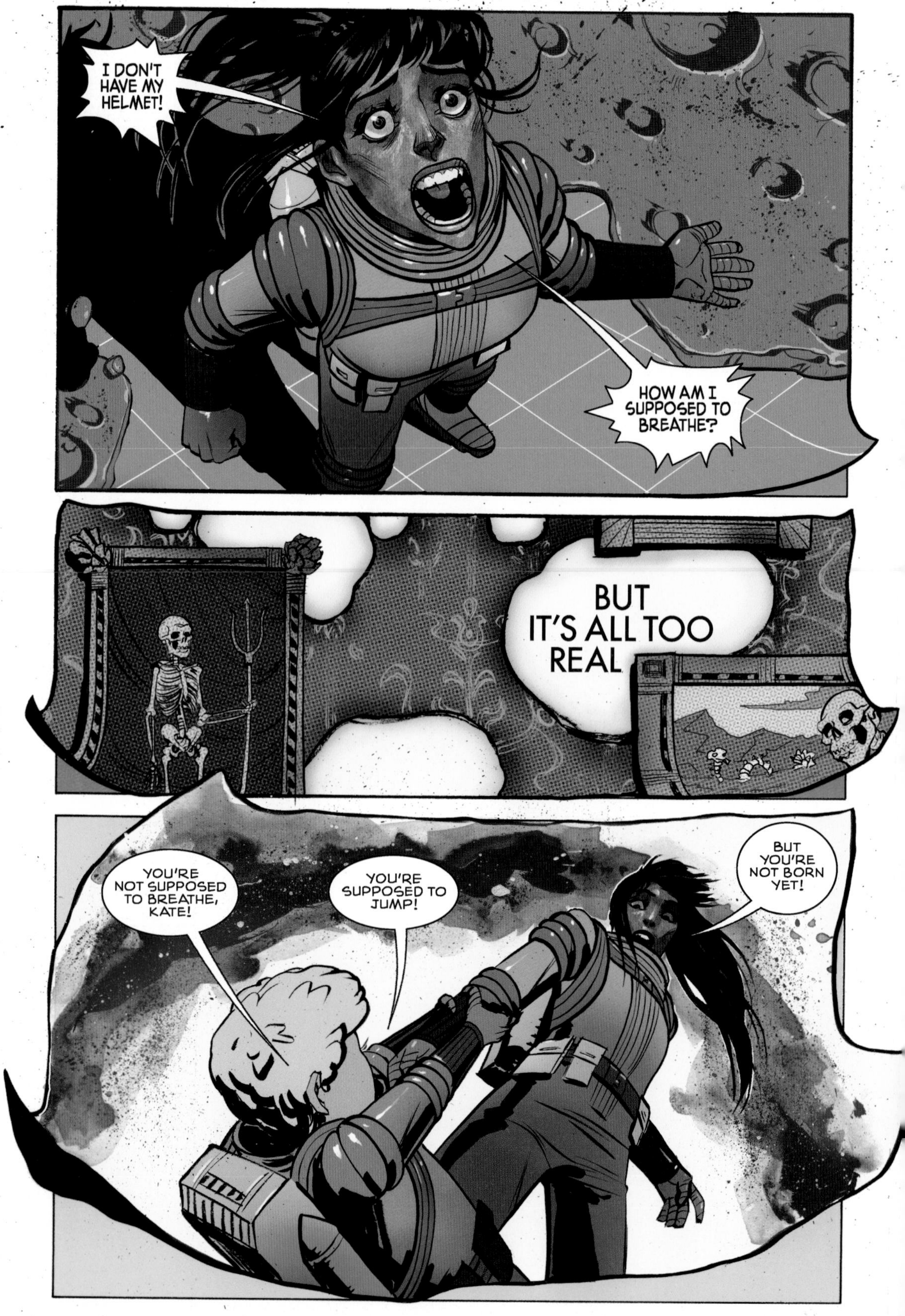
I DON'T HAVE MY HELMET!
HOW AM I SUPPOSED TO BREATHE?
BUT IT'S ALL TOO REAL
YOU'RE NOT SUPPOSED TO BREATHE, KATE!
YOU'RE SUPPOSED TO JUMP!
BUT YOU'RE NOT BORN YET!

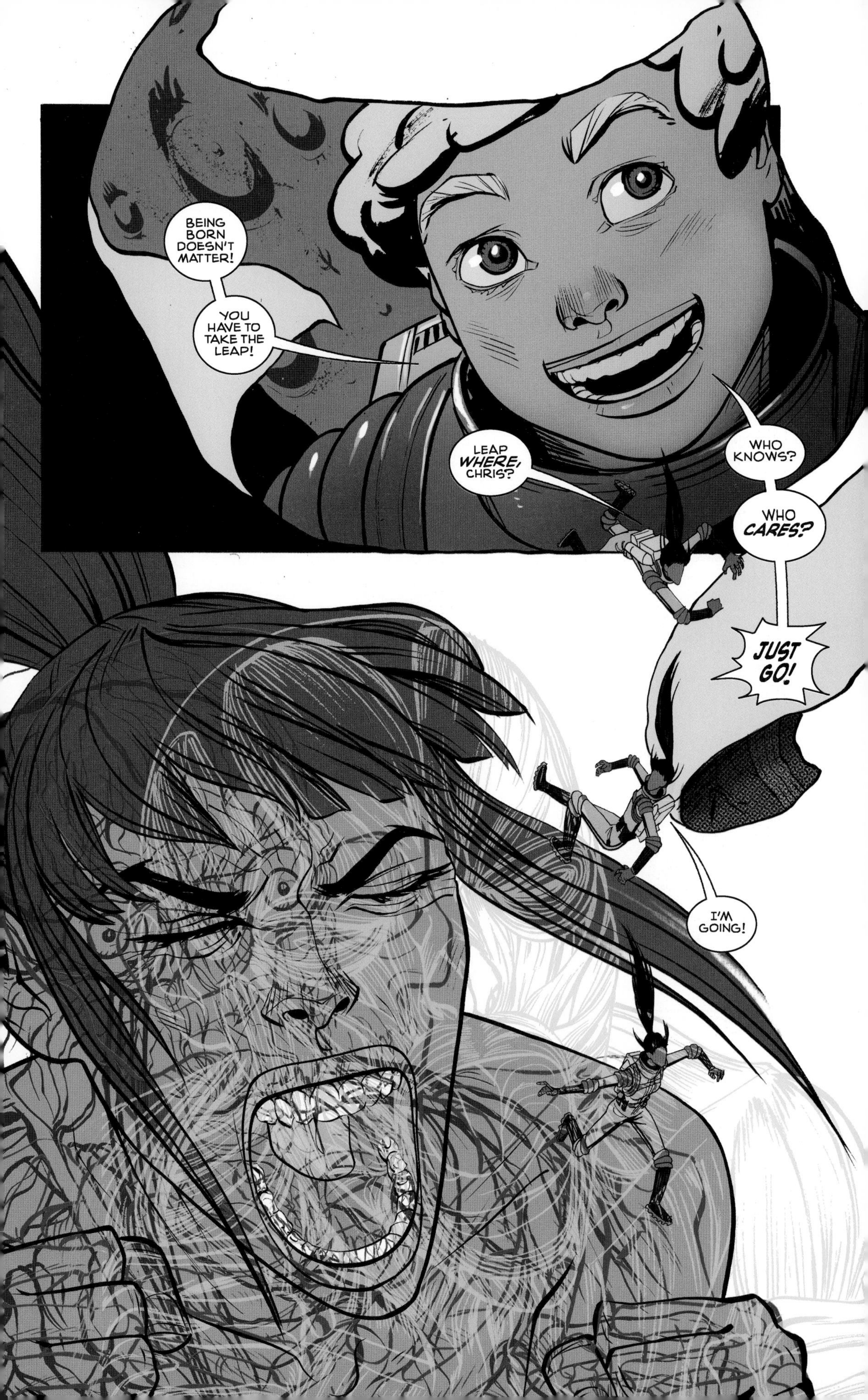
BEING BORN DOESN'T MATTER!
YOU HAVE TO TAKE THE LEAP!
LEAP WHERE, CHRIS?
WHO KNOWS?
WHO CARES?
JUST GO!
I'M GOING!

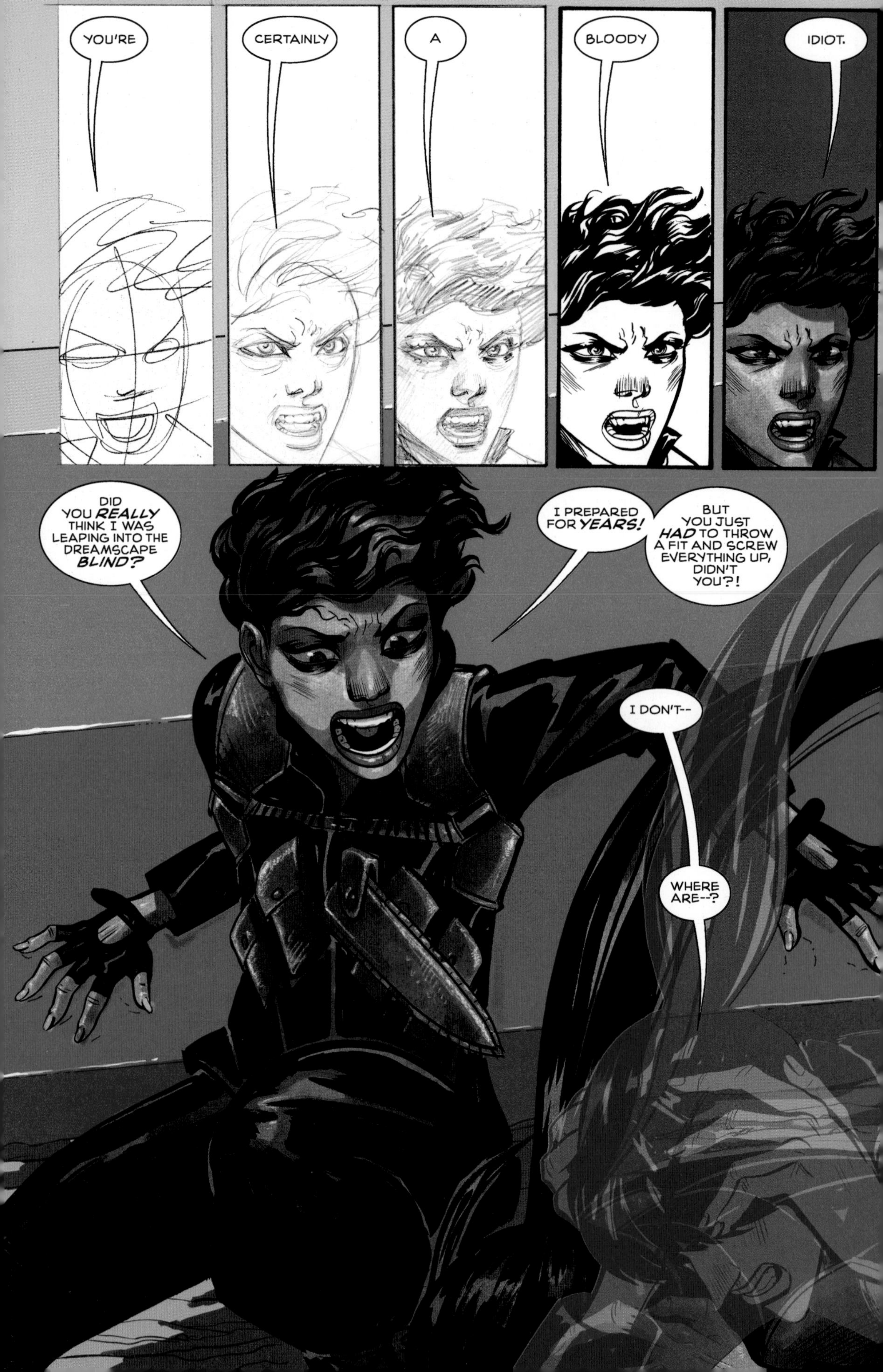
YOU'RE
CERTAINLY
A
BLOODY
IDIOT.
DID YOU *REALLY* THINK I WAS LEAPING INTO THE DREAMSCAPE *BLIND?*
I PREPARED FOR *YEARS!*
BUT YOU JUST *HAD* TO THROW A FIT AND SCREW EVERYTHING UP, DIDN'T YOU?!
I DON'T--
WHERE ARE--?

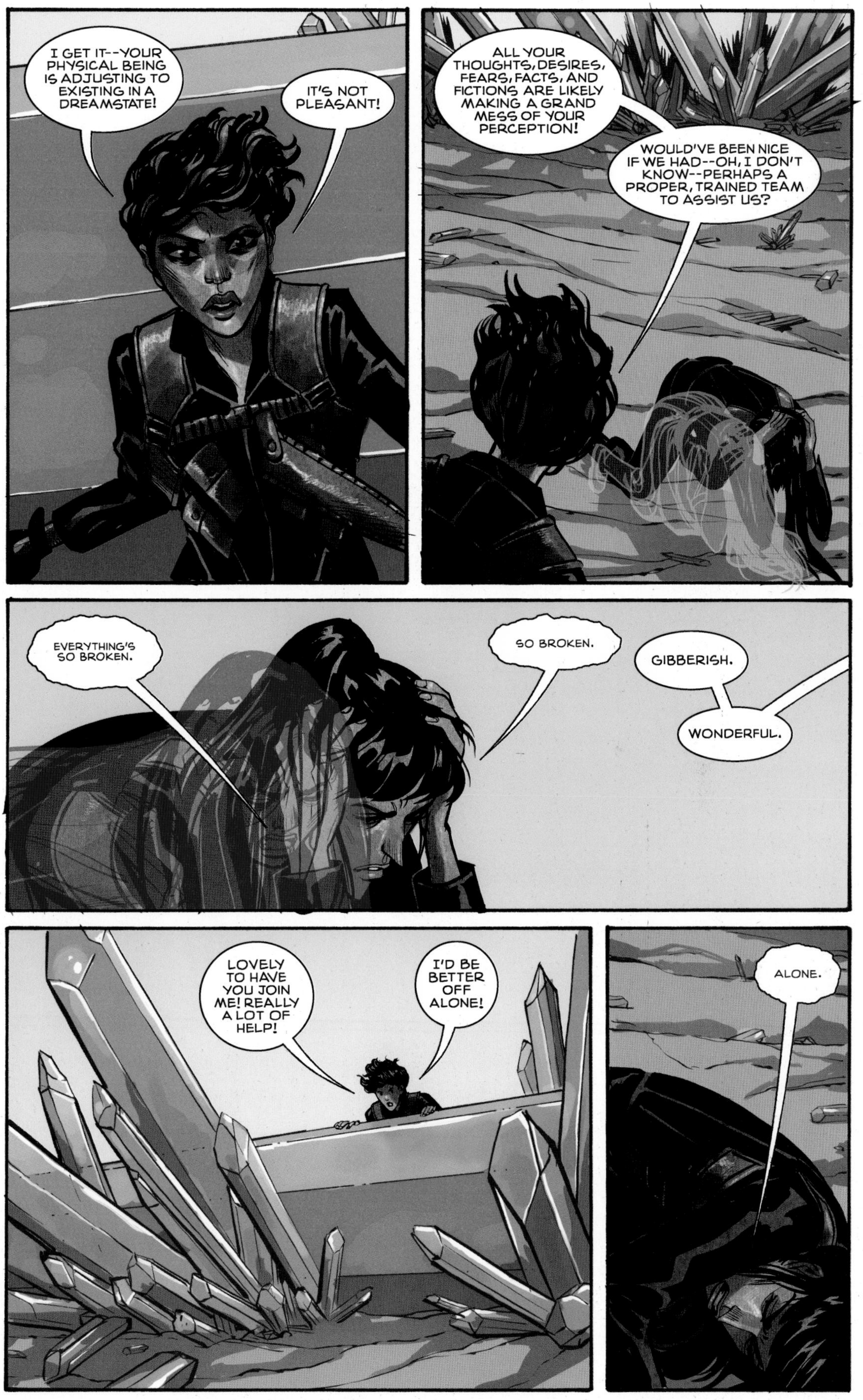
I GET IT--YOUR PHYSICAL BEING IS ADJUSTING TO EXISTING IN A DREAMSTATE!
IT'S NOT PLEASANT!
ALL YOUR THOUGHTS, DESIRES, FEARS, FACTS, AND FICTIONS ARE LIKELY MAKING A GRAND MESS OF YOUR PERCEPTION!
WOULD'VE BEEN NICE IF WE HAD--OH, I DON'T KNOW--PERHAPS A PROPER, TRAINED TEAM TO ASSIST US?
EVERYTHING'S SO BROKEN.
SO BROKEN.
GIBBERISH.
WONDERFUL.
LOVELY TO HAVE YOU JOIN ME! REALLY A LOT OF HELP!
I'D BE BETTER OFF ALONE!
ALONE.

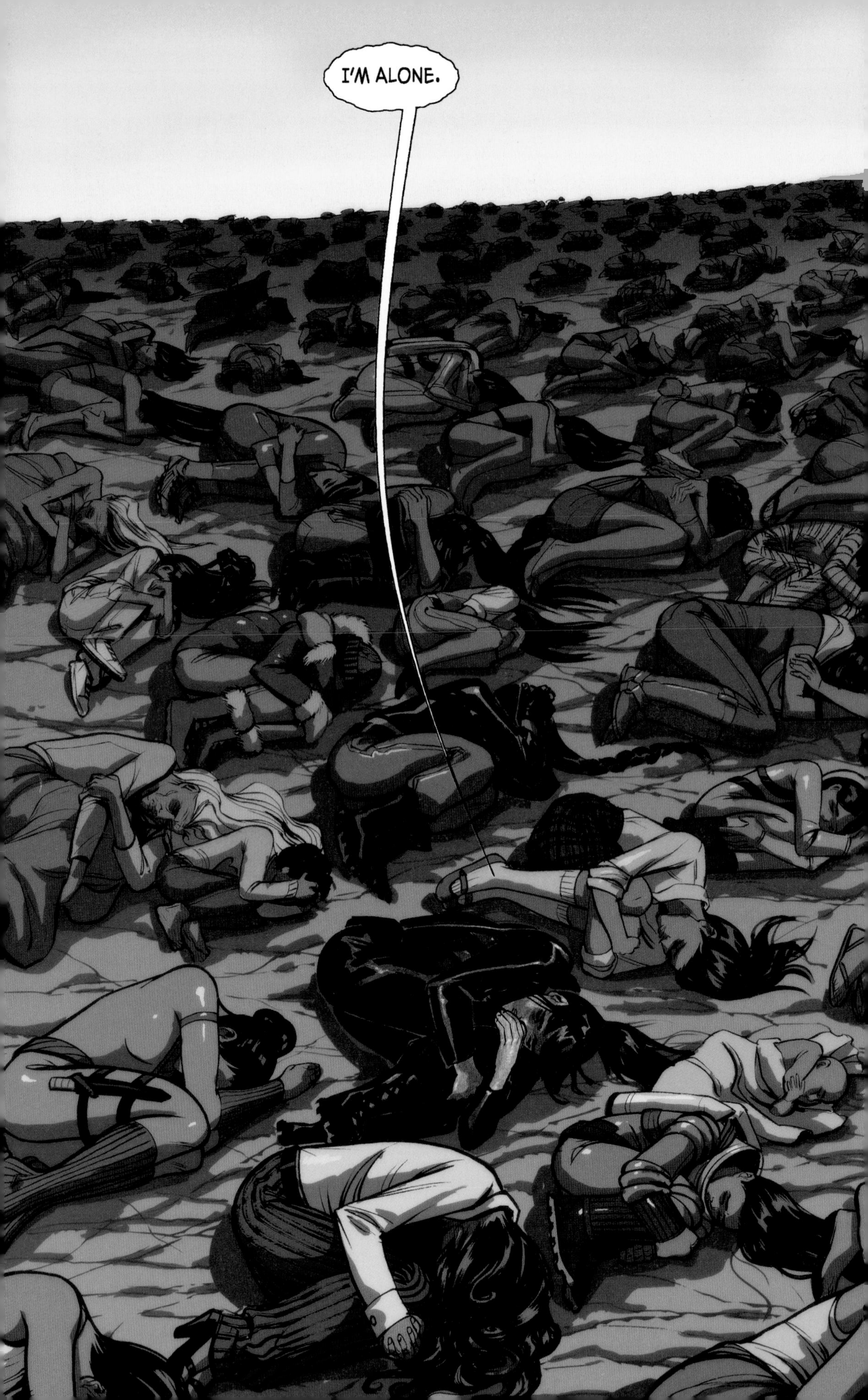
I'M ALONE.

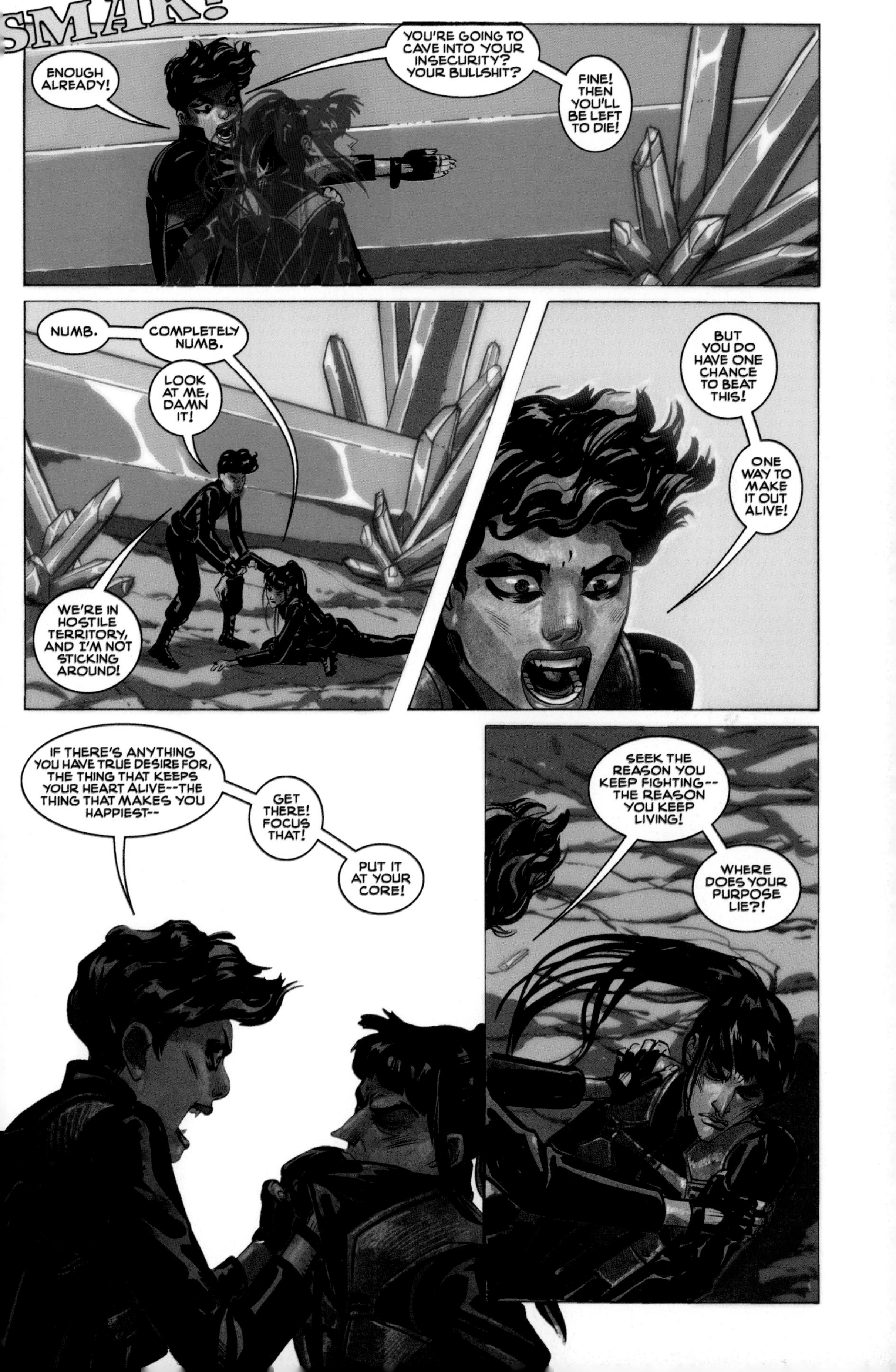
SMAK!
ENOUGH ALREADY!
YOU'RE GOING TO CAVE INTO YOUR INSECURITY? YOUR BULLSHIT?
FINE! THEN YOU'LL BE LEFT TO DIE!
NUMB.
COMPLETELY NUMB.
LOOK AT ME, DAMN IT!
WE'RE IN HOSTILE TERRITORY, AND I'M NOT STICKING AROUND!
BUT YOU DO HAVE ONE CHANCE TO BEAT THIS!
ONE WAY TO MAKE IT OUT ALIVE!
IF THERE'S ANYTHING YOU HAVE TRUE DESIRE FOR, THE THING THAT KEEPS YOUR HEART ALIVE--THE THING THAT MAKES YOU HAPPIEST--
GET THERE! FOCUS THAT!
PUT IT AT YOUR CORE!
SEEK THE REASON YOU KEEP FIGHTING-- THE REASON YOU KEEP LIVING!
WHERE DOES YOUR PURPOSE LIE?!

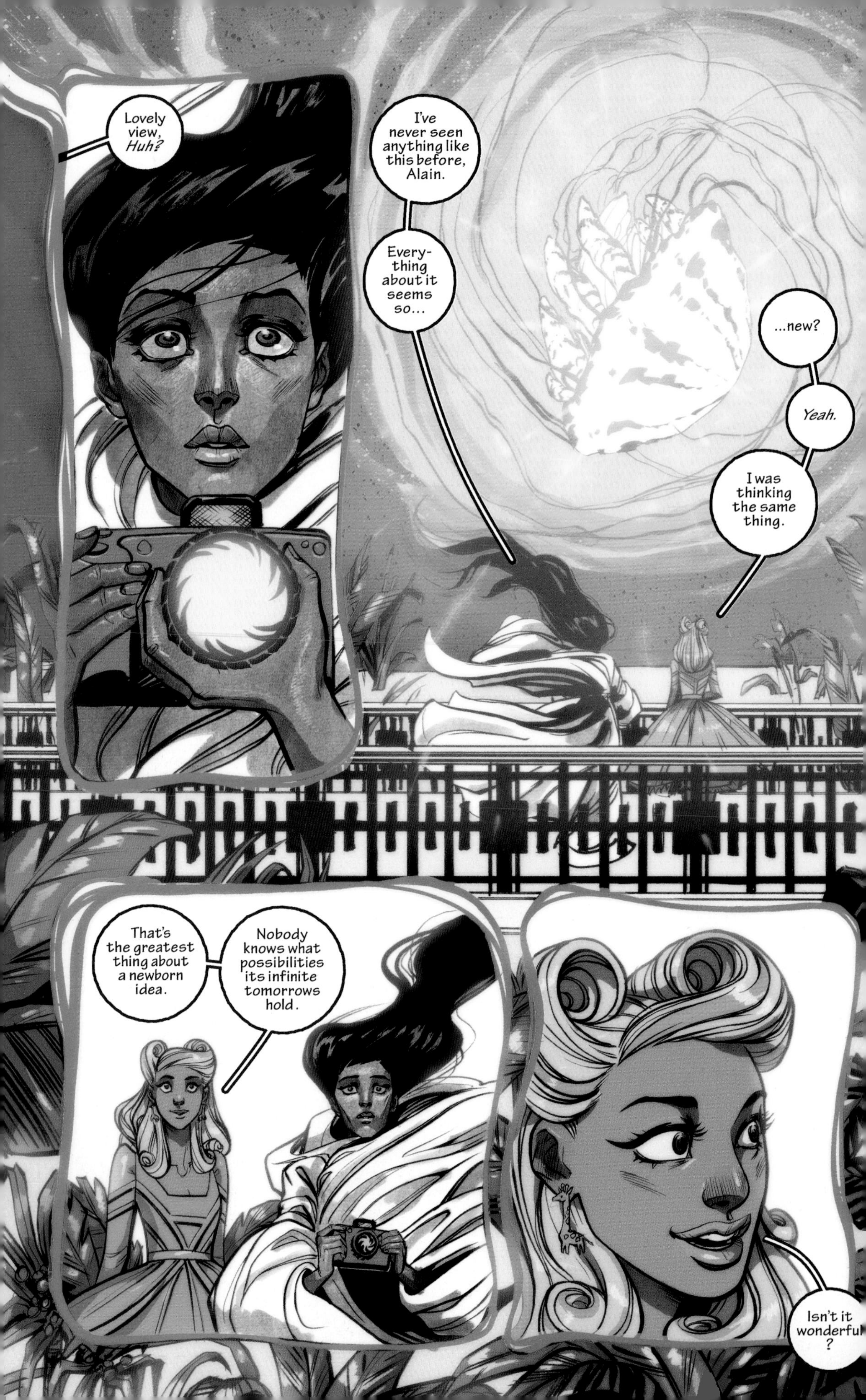

Lovely view, *Huh?*
I've never seen anything like this before, Alain.
Every-thing about it seems so...
...new?
Yeah.
I was thinking the same thing.
That's the greatest thing about a newborn idea.
Nobody knows what possibilities its infinite tomorrows hold.
Isn't it wonderful?

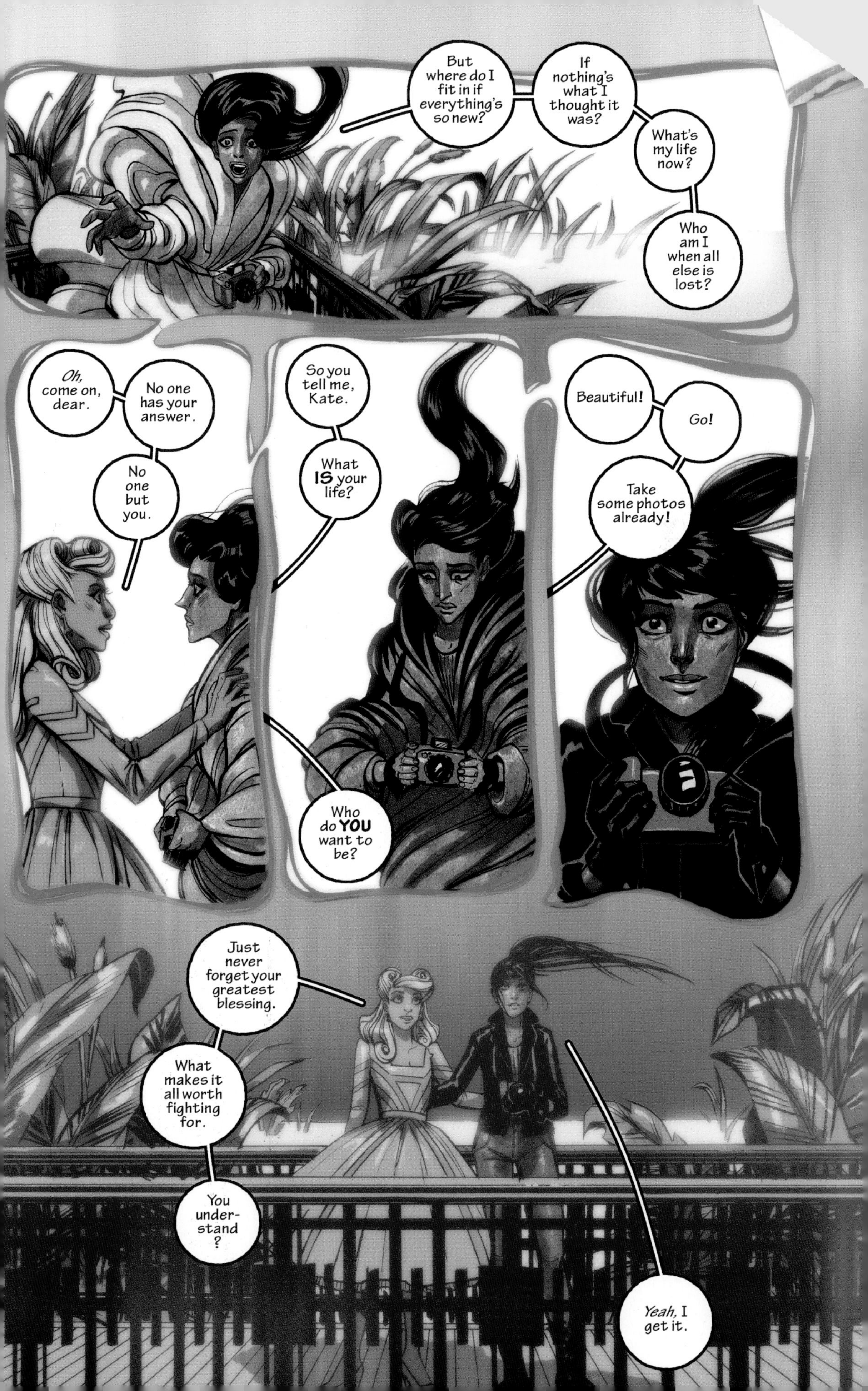
But where do I fit in if everything's so new?
If nothing's what I thought it was?
What's my life now?
Who am I when all else is lost?
Oh, come on, dear.
No one has your answer.
No one but you.
So you tell me, Kate.
What **IS** your life?
Who do **YOU** want to be?
Beautiful!
Go!
Take some photos already!
Just never forget your greatest blessing.
What makes it all worth fighting for.
You under-stand?
Yeah, I get it.

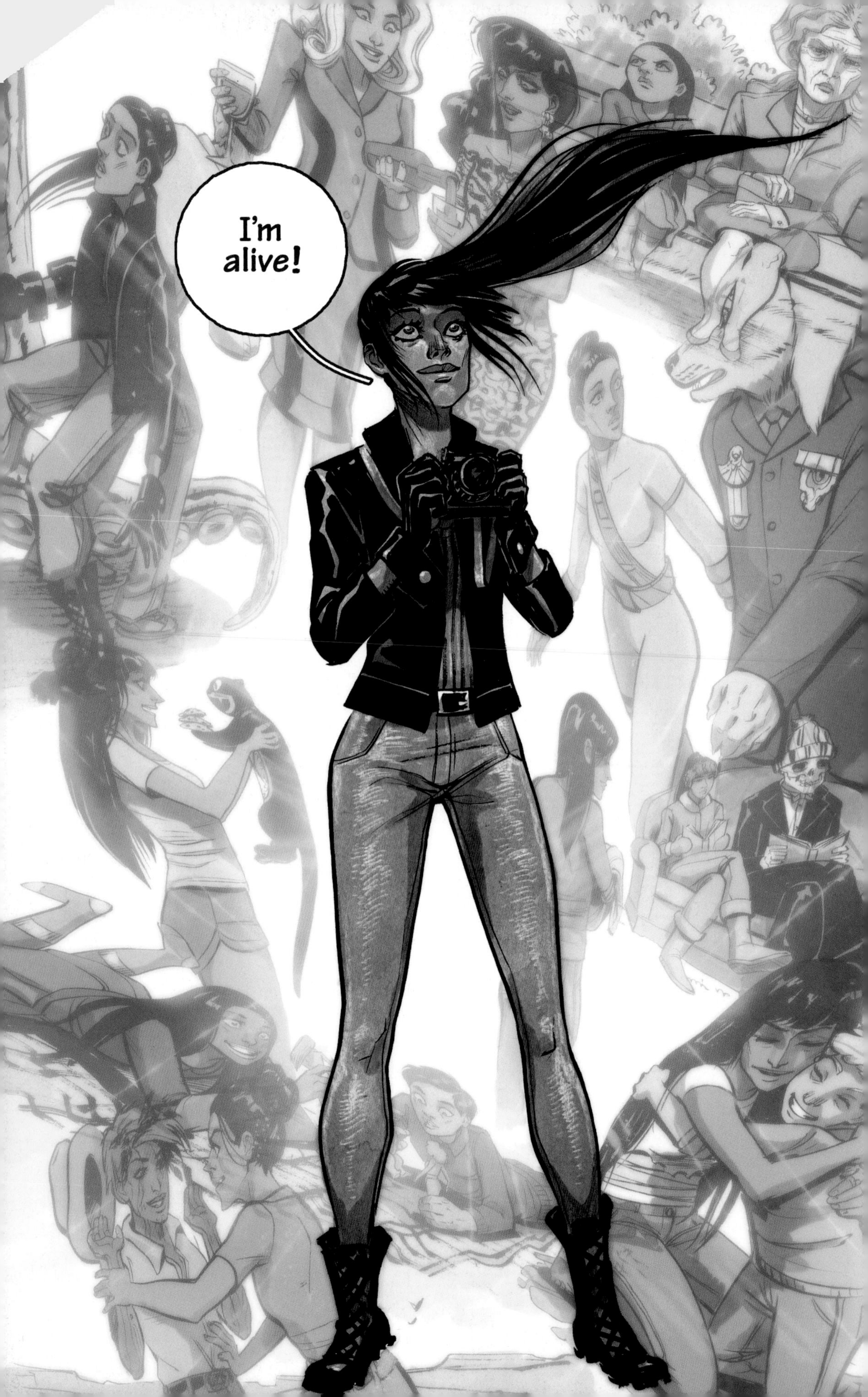
I'm alive!

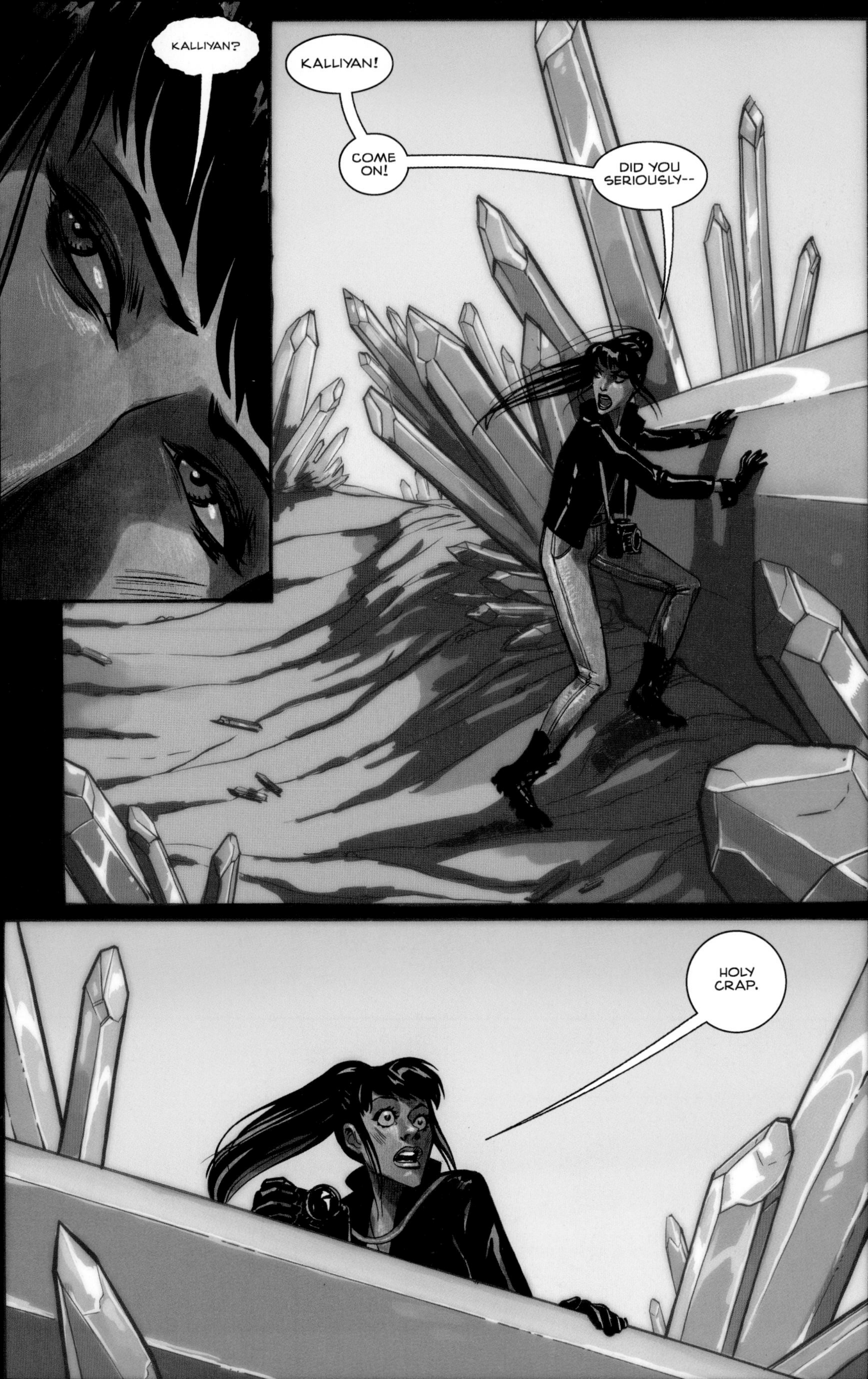
KALLIYAN?
KALLIYAN!
COME ON!
DID YOU SERIOUSLY--
HOLY CRAP.

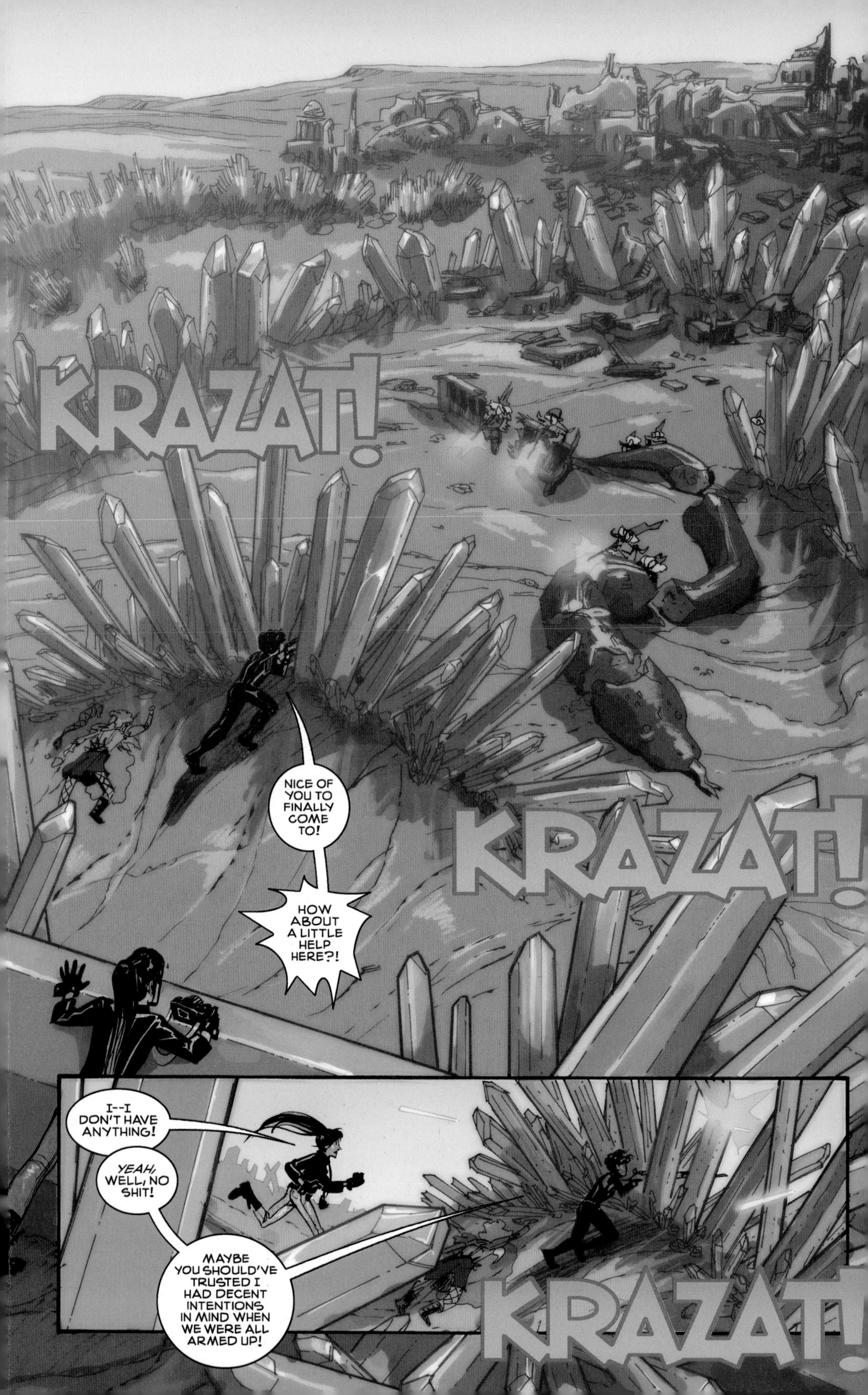
KRAZAT!
NICE OF YOU TO FINALLY COME TO!
HOW ABOUT A LITTLE HELP HERE?!
KRAZAT!
I--I DON'T HAVE ANYTHING!
YEAH, WELL, NO SHIT!
MAYBE YOU SHOULD'VE TRUSTED I HAD DECENT INTENTIONS IN MIND WHEN WE WERE ALL ARMED UP!
KRAZAT!

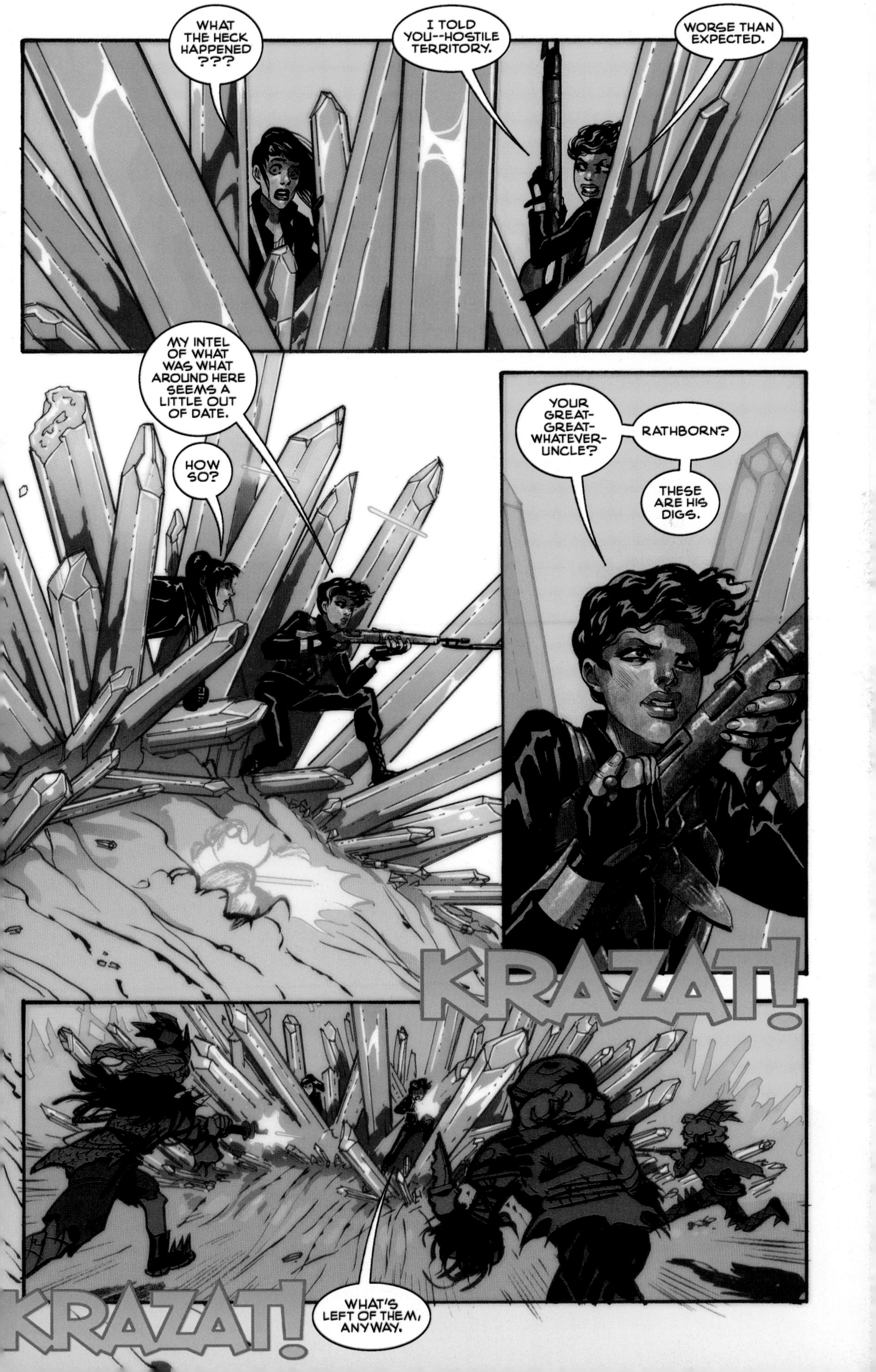
WHAT THE HECK HAPPENED ???
I TOLD YOU--HOSTILE TERRITORY.
WORSE THAN EXPECTED.
MY INTEL OF WHAT WAS WHAT AROUND HERE SEEMS A LITTLE OUT OF DATE.
HOW SO?
YOUR GREAT-GREAT-WHATEVER-UNCLE?
RATHBORN?
THESE ARE HIS DIGS.
KRAZAT!
KRAZAT!
WHAT'S LEFT OF THEM, ANYWAY.

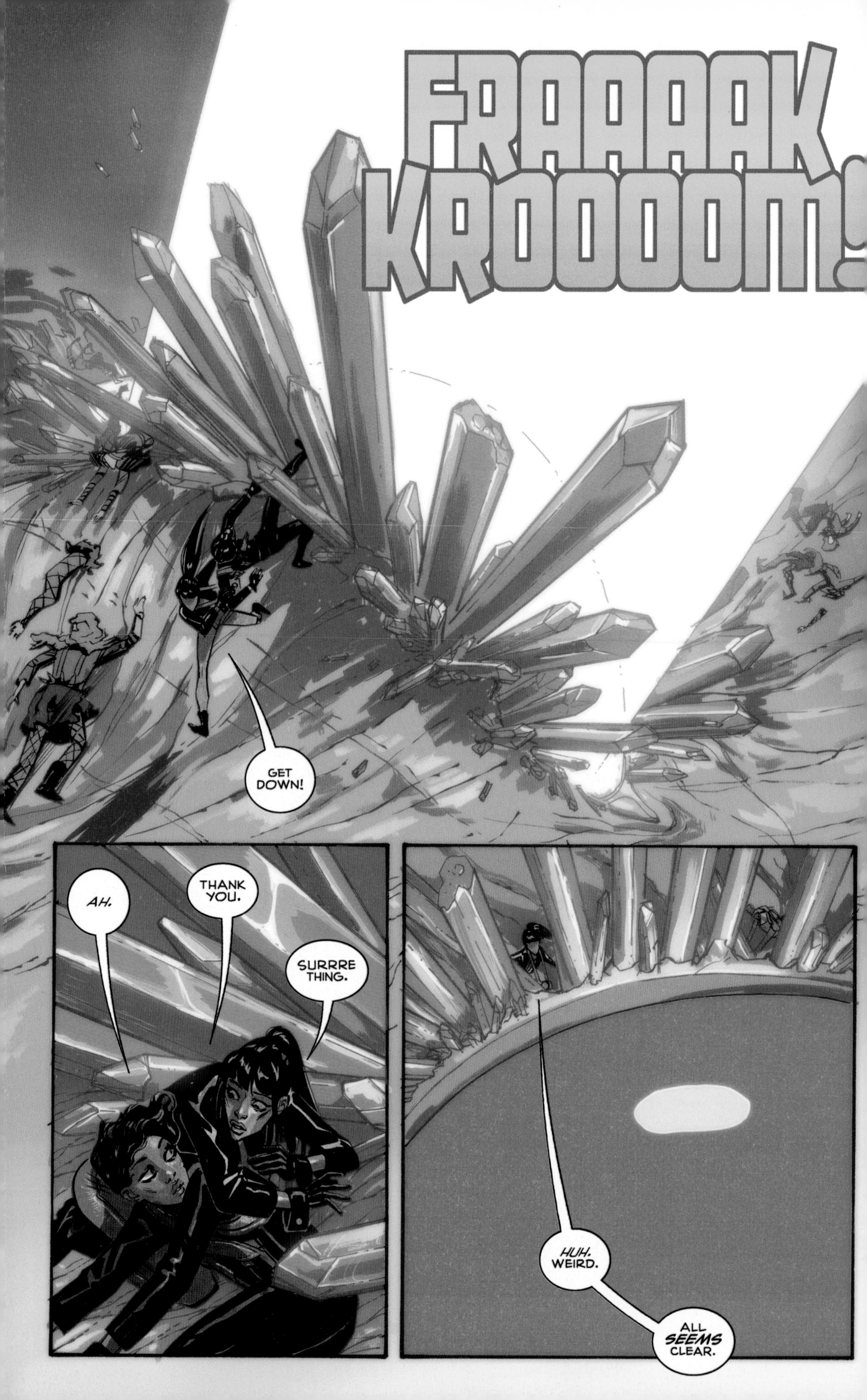
FRAAAAK KROOOOM!
GET DOWN!
AH.
THANK YOU.
SURRRE THING.
HUH. WEIRD.
ALL SEEMS CLEAR.

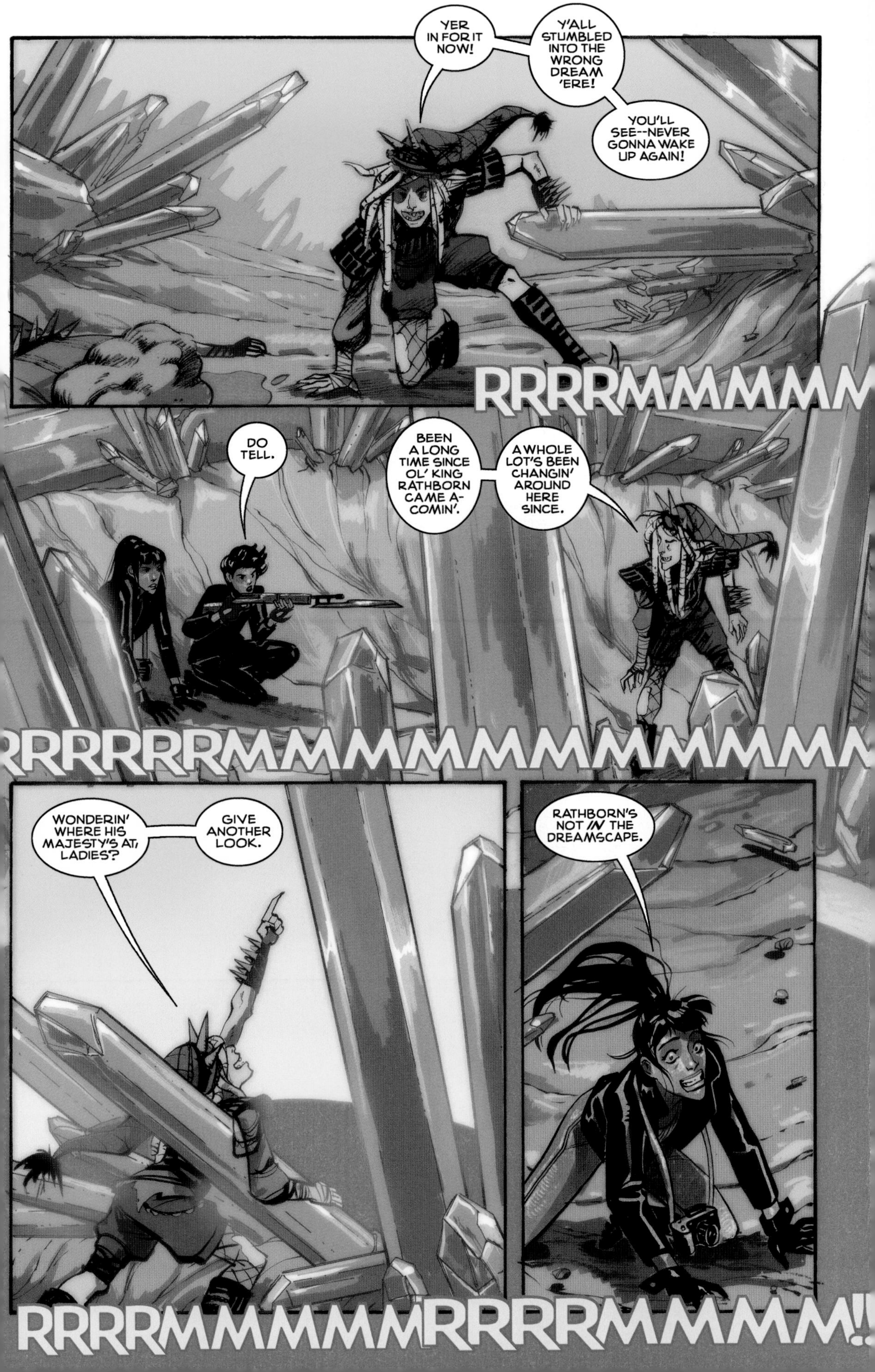
YER IN FOR IT NOW!
Y'ALL STUMBLED INTO THE WRONG DREAM 'ERE!
YOU'LL SEE--NEVER GONNA WAKE UP AGAIN!
RRRRMMMMM
DO TELL.
BEEN A LONG TIME SINCE OL' KING RATHBORN CAME A-COMIN'.
A WHOLE LOT'S BEEN CHANGIN' AROUND HERE SINCE.
RRRRRRMMMMMMMMMMMM
WONDERIN' WHERE HIS MAJESTY'S AT, LADIES?
GIVE ANOTHER LOOK.
RATHBORN'S NOT IN THE DREAMSCAPE.
RRRRMMMMMRRRRRMMMMM!!

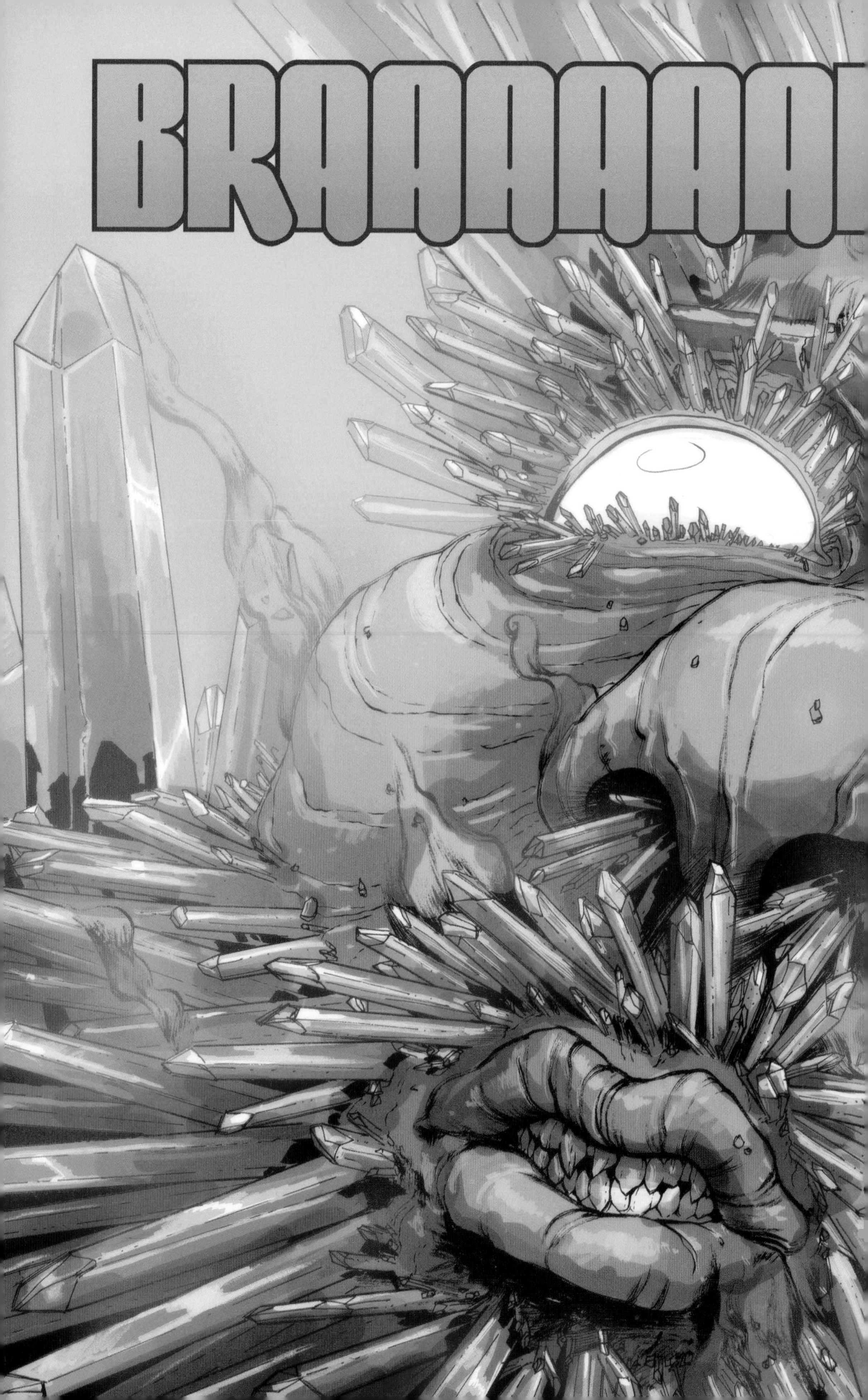
BRAAAAAAAA

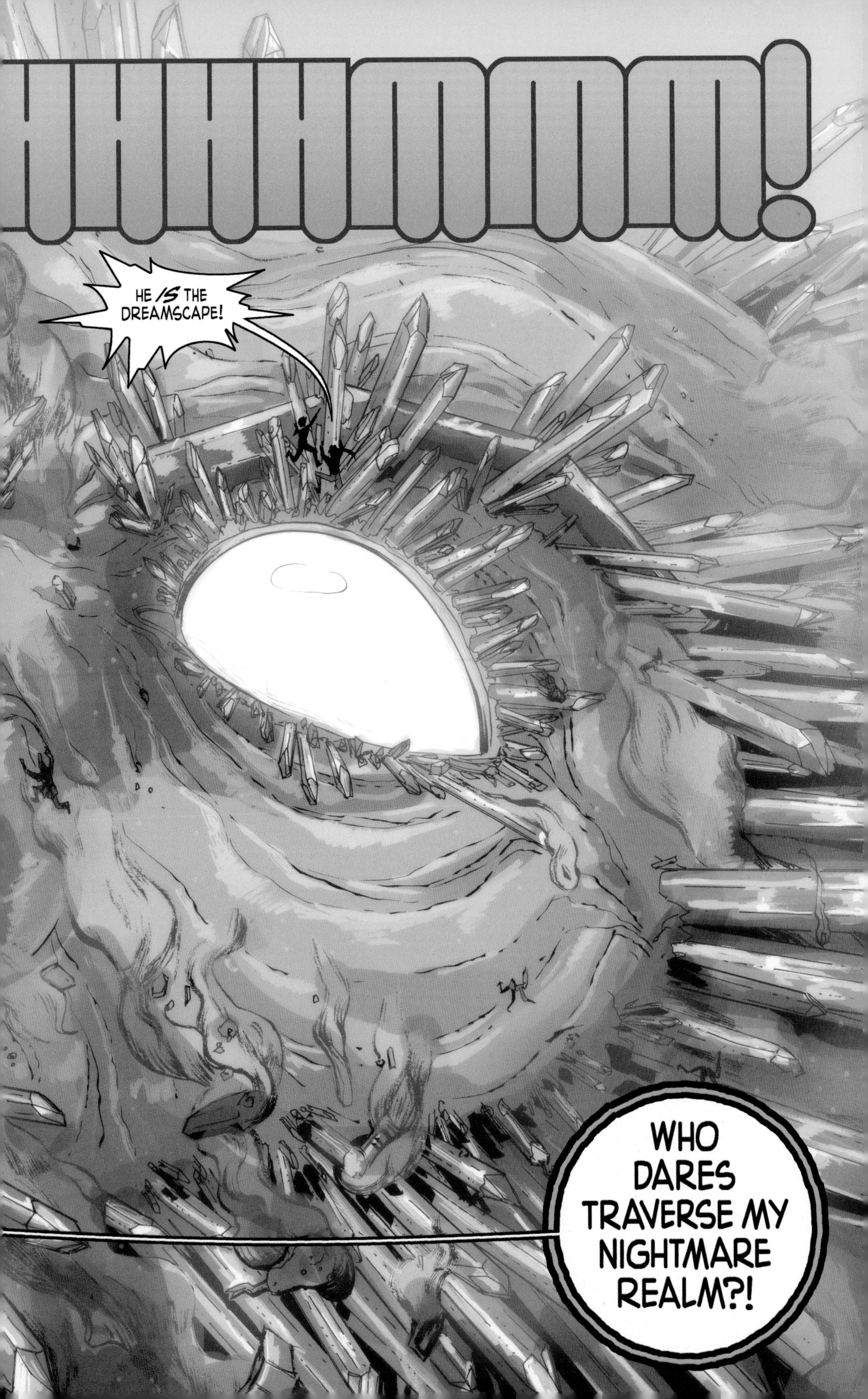
HHHHMMMM!
HE IS THE DREAMSCAPE!
WHO DARES TRAVERSE MY NIGHTMARE REALM?!

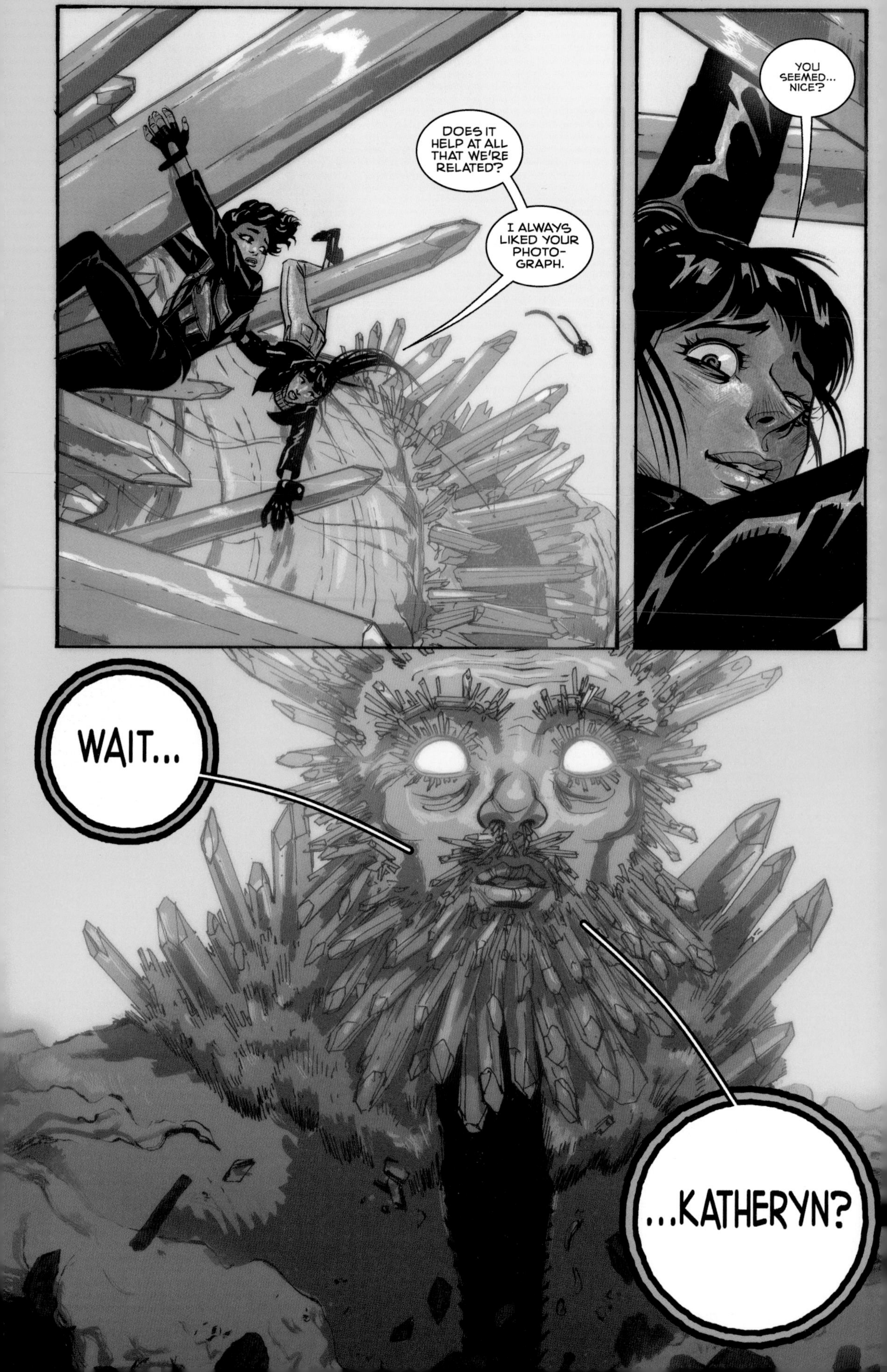
DOES IT HELP AT ALL THAT WE'RE RELATED?
I ALWAYS LIKED YOUR PHOTO-GRAPH.
YOU SEEMED... NICE?
WAIT...
...KATHERYN?

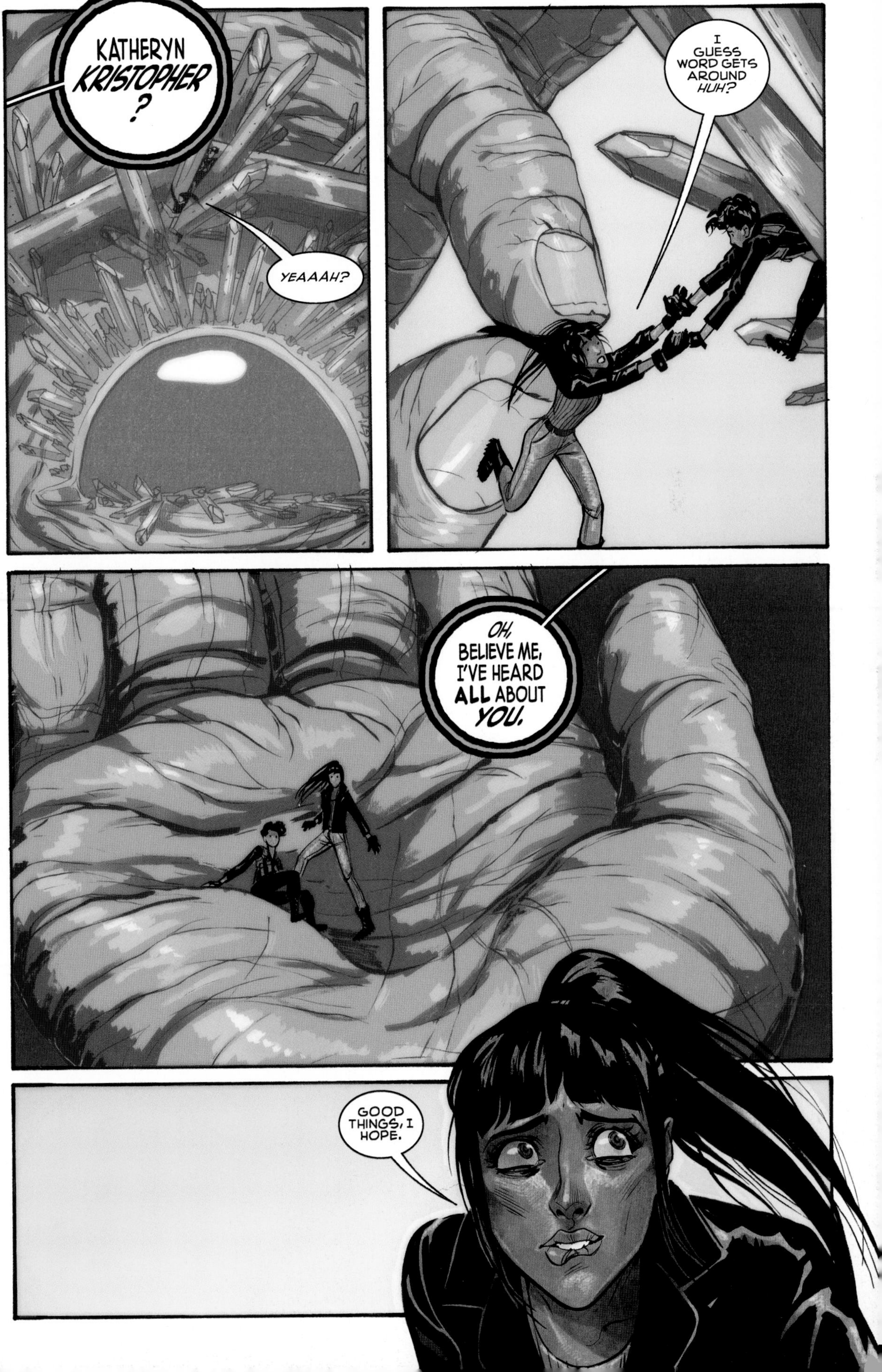
KATHERYN KRISTOPHER ?
YEAAAH?
I GUESS WORD GETS AROUND HUH?
OH, BELIEVE ME, I'VE HEARD ALL ABOUT YOU.
GOOD THINGS, I HOPE.

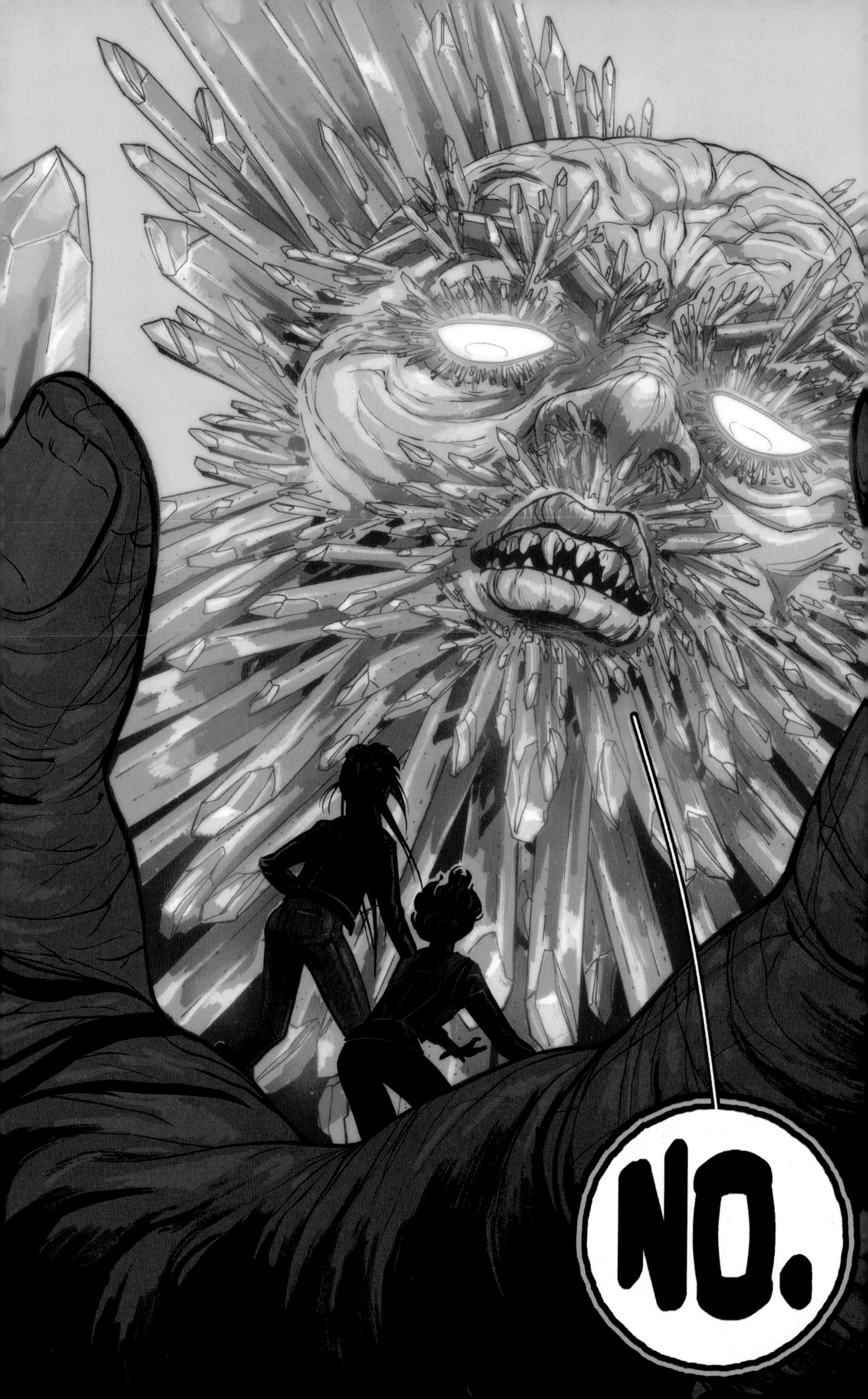
NO.

CHAPTER 11

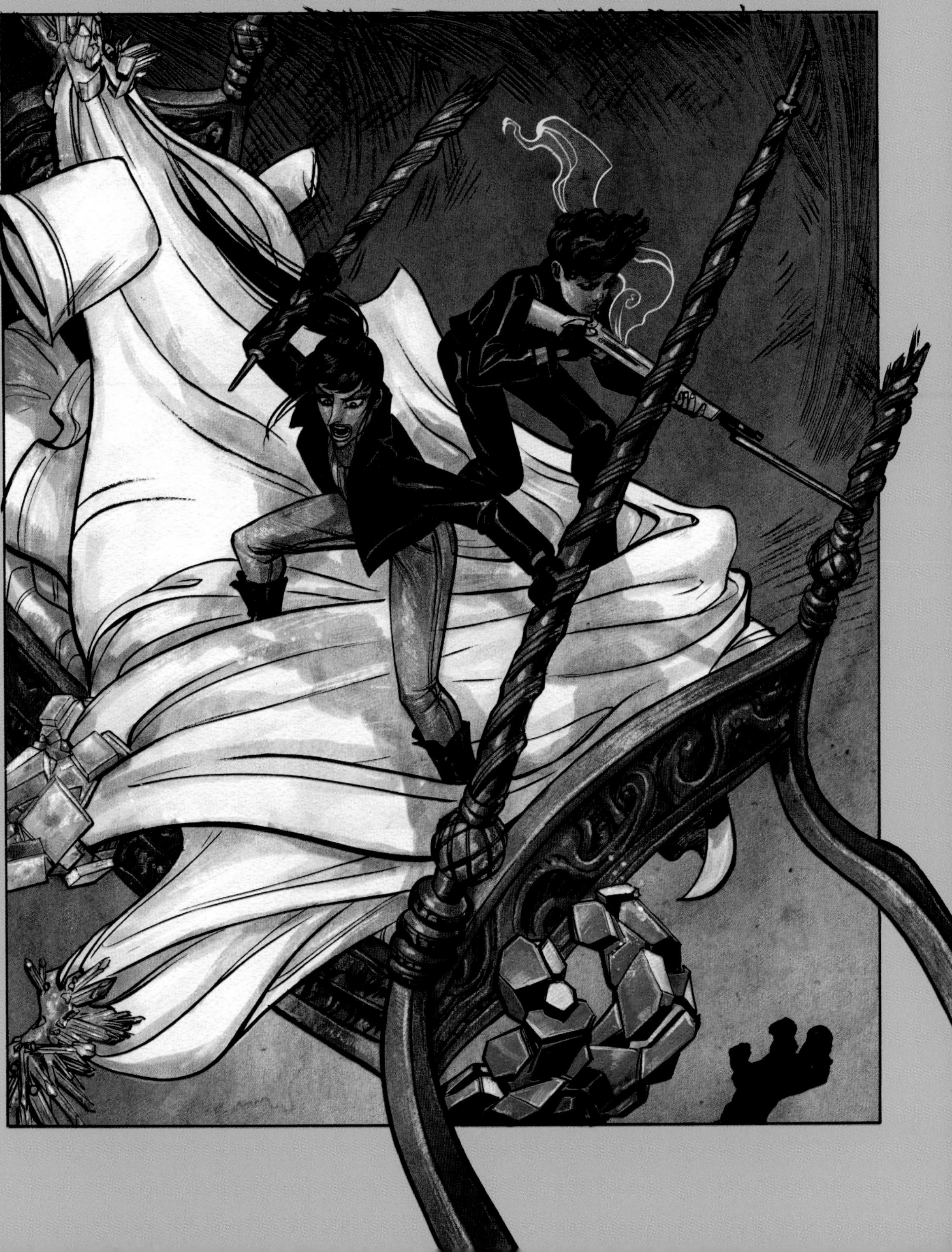

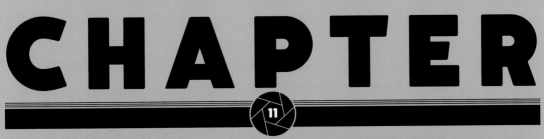

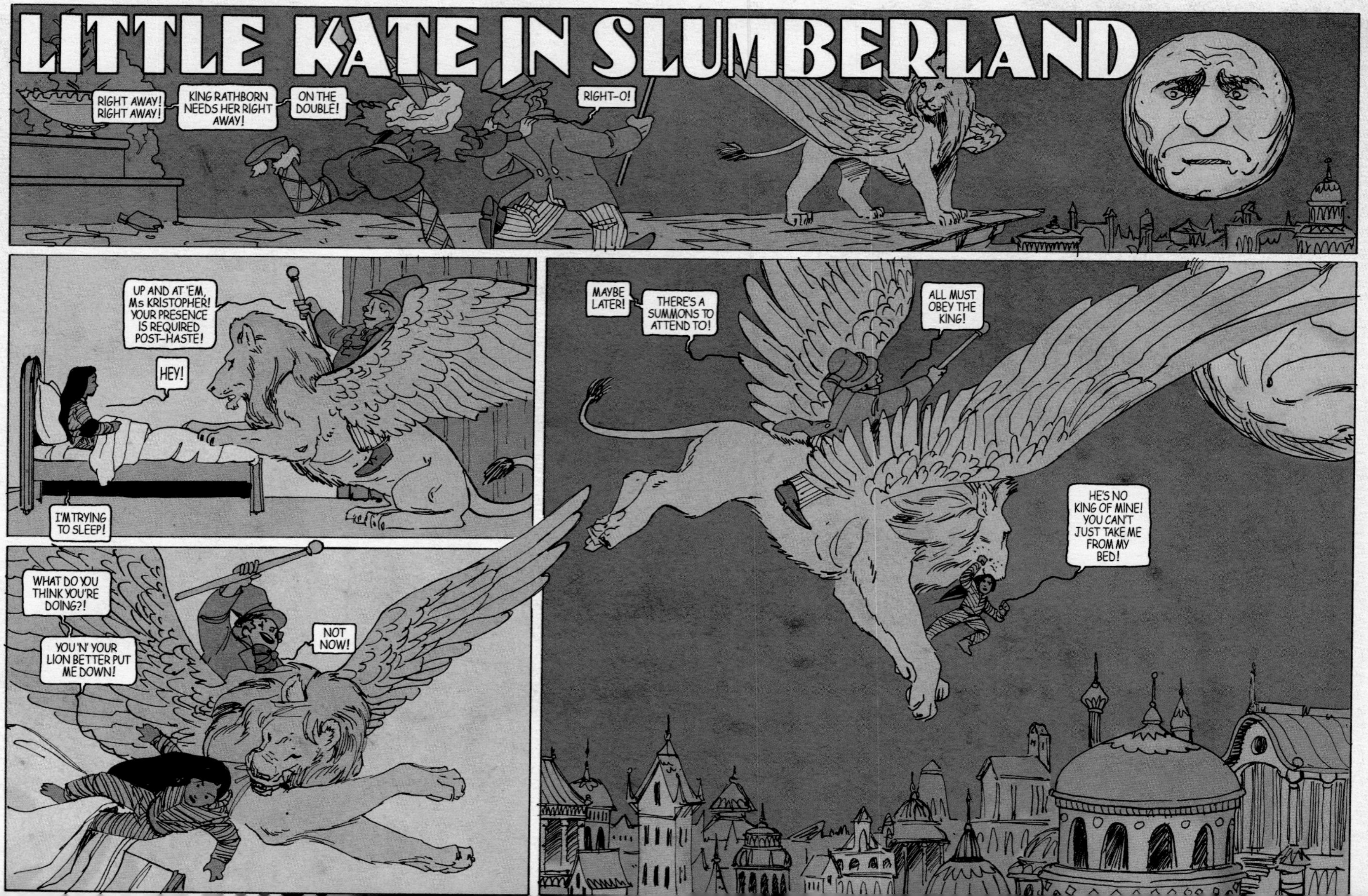
LITTLE KATE IN SLUMBERLAND
RIGHT AWAY! RIGHT AWAY!
KING RATHBORN NEEDS HER RIGHT AWAY!
ON THE DOUBLE!
RIGHT-O!
UP AND AT 'EM, Ms KRISTOPHER! YOUR PRESENCE IS REQUIRED POST-HASTE!
HEY!
I'M TRYING TO SLEEP!
WHAT DO YOU THINK YOU'RE DOING?!
YOU 'N' YOUR LION BETTER PUT ME DOWN!
NOT NOW!
MAYBE LATER!
THERE'S A SUMMONS TO ATTEND TO!
ALL MUST OBEY THE KING!
HE'S NO KING OF MINE! YOU CAN'T JUST TAKE ME FROM MY BED!

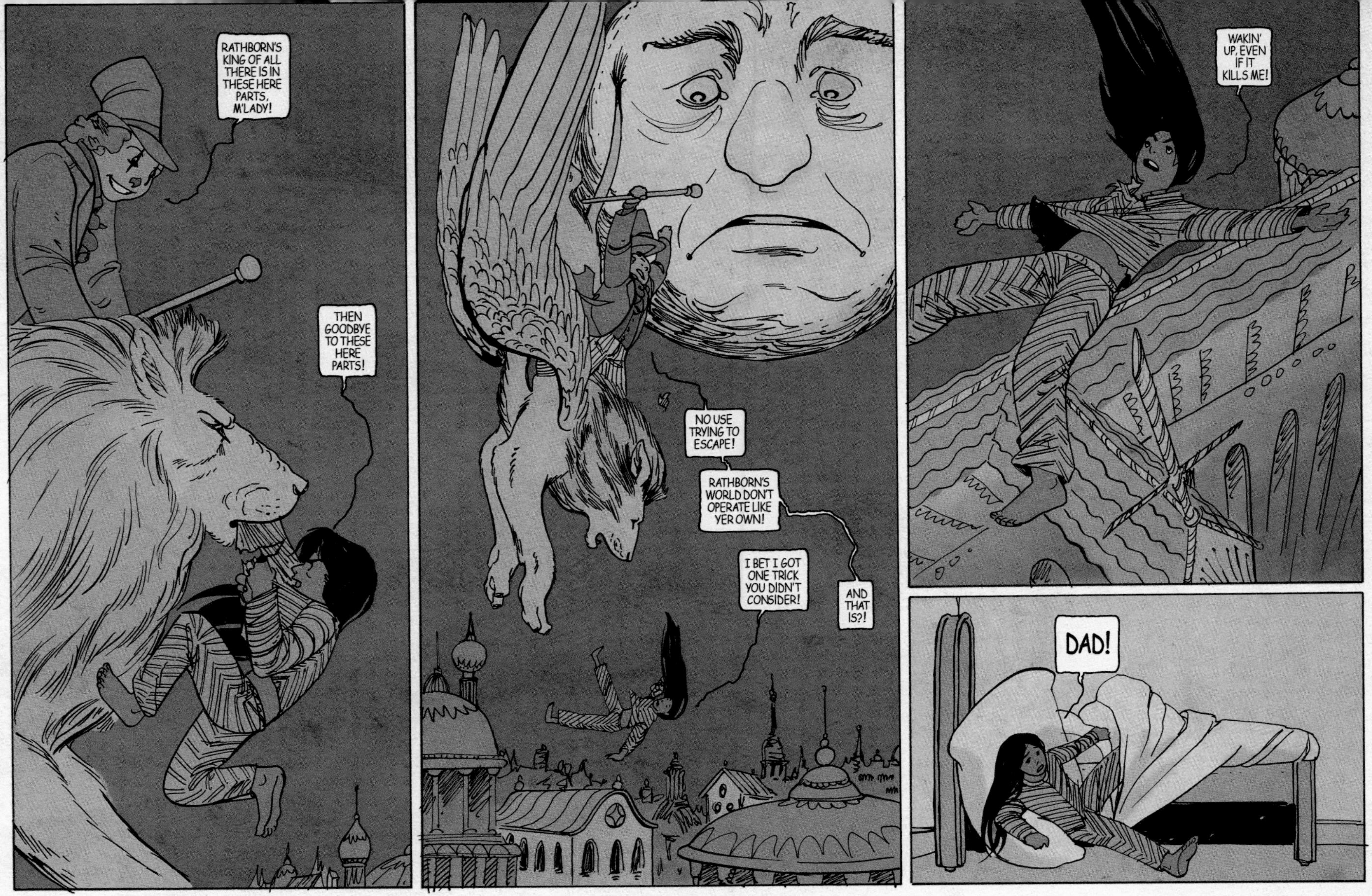
RATHBORN'S KING OF ALL THERE IS IN THESE HERE PARTS, M'LADY!
THEN GOODBYE TO THESE HERE PARTS!
NO USE TRYING TO ESCAPE!
RATHBORN'S WORLD DON'T OPERATE LIKE YER OWN!
I BET I GOT ONE TRICK YOU DIDN'T CONSIDER!
AND THAT IS?!
WAKIN' UP, EVEN IF IT KILLS ME!
DAD!

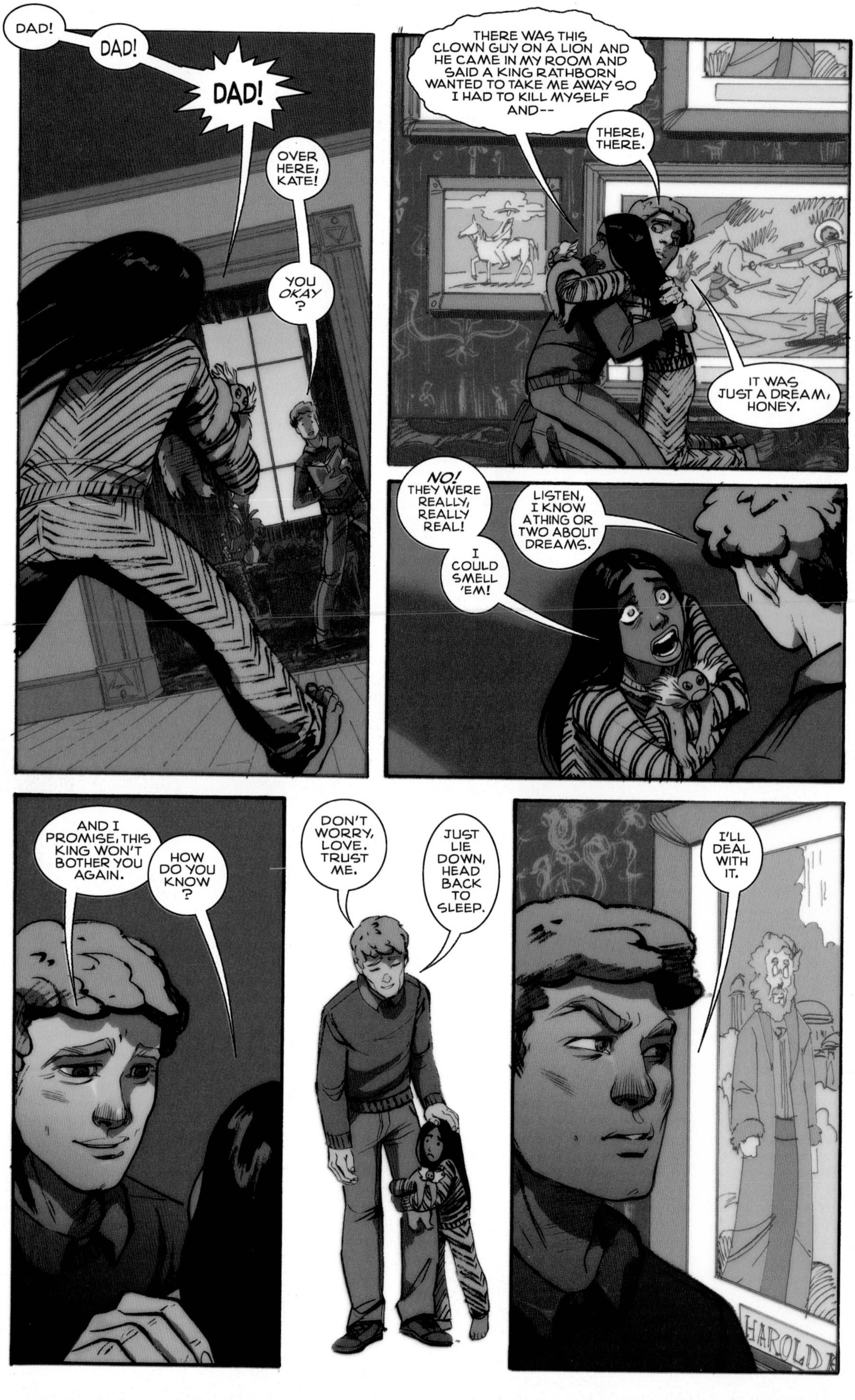
DAD!
DAD!
DAD!
OVER HERE, KATE!
YOU *OKAY*?
THERE WAS THIS CLOWN GUY ON A LION AND HE CAME IN MY ROOM AND SAID A KING RATHBORN WANTED TO TAKE ME AWAY SO I HAD TO KILL MYSELF AND--
THERE, THERE.
IT WAS JUST A DREAM, HONEY.
NO! THEY WERE REALLY, REALLY REAL!
I COULD SMELL 'EM!
LISTEN, I KNOW A THING OR TWO ABOUT DREAMS.
AND I PROMISE, THIS KING WON'T BOTHER YOU AGAIN.
HOW DO YOU KNOW?
DON'T WORRY, LOVE. TRUST ME.
JUST LIE DOWN, HEAD BACK TO SLEEP.
I'LL DEAL WITH IT.
HAROLD

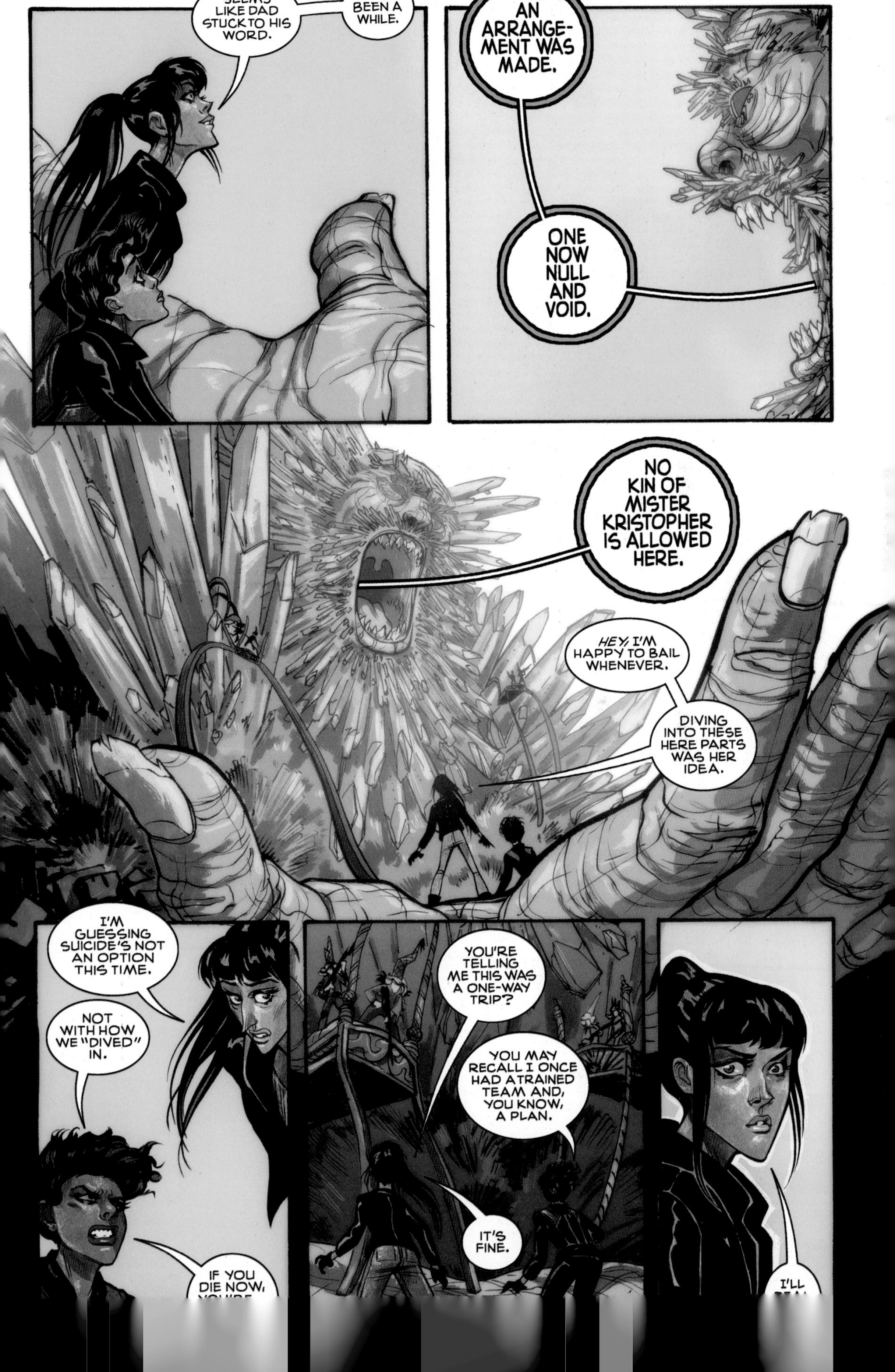
SEEMS LIKE DAD STUCK TO HIS WORD.
IT'S BEEN A WHILE.
AN ARRANGE-MENT WAS MADE.
ONE NOW NULL AND VOID.
NO KIN OF MISTER KRISTOPHER IS ALLOWED HERE.
HEY, I'M HAPPY TO BAIL WHENEVER.
DIVING INTO THESE HERE PARTS WAS HER IDEA.
I'M GUESSING SUICIDE'S NOT AN OPTION THIS TIME.
NOT WITH HOW WE "DIVED" IN.
IF YOU DIE NOW,
YOU'RE TELLING ME THIS WAS A ONE-WAY TRIP?
YOU MAY RECALL I ONCE HAD A TRAINED TEAM AND, YOU KNOW, A PLAN.
IT'S FINE.
I'LL

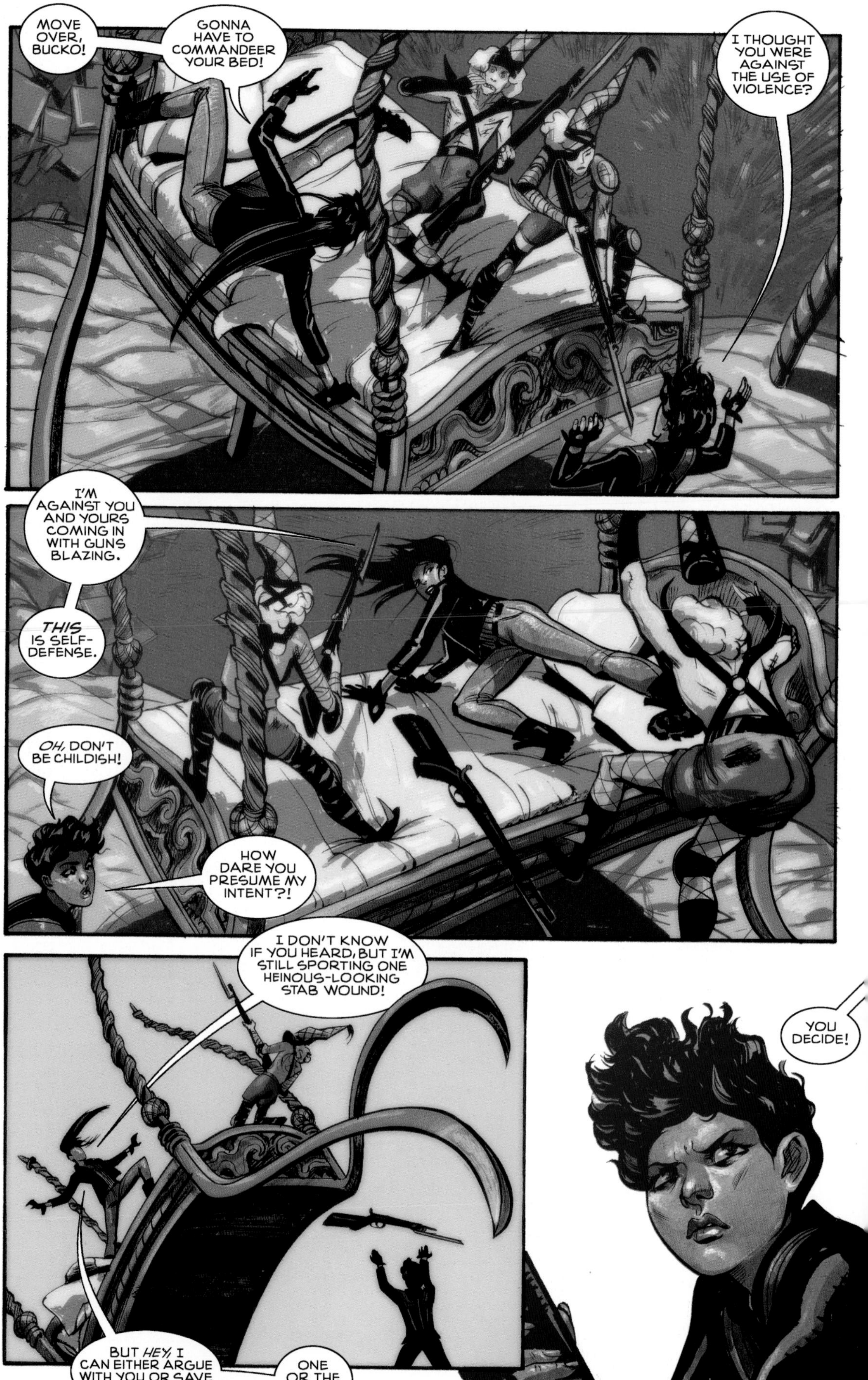
MOVE OVER, BUCKO!
GONNA HAVE TO COMMANDEER YOUR BED!
I THOUGHT YOU WERE AGAINST THE USE OF VIOLENCE?
I'M AGAINST YOU AND YOURS COMING IN WITH GUNS BLAZING.
THIS IS SELF-DEFENSE.
OH, DON'T BE CHILDISH!
HOW DARE YOU PRESUME MY INTENT?!
I DON'T KNOW IF YOU HEARD, BUT I'M STILL SPORTING ONE HEINOUS-LOOKING STAB WOUND!
BUT HEY, I CAN EITHER ARGUE WITH YOU OR SAVE YOUR ASS!
ONE OR THE OTHER!
YOU DECIDE!

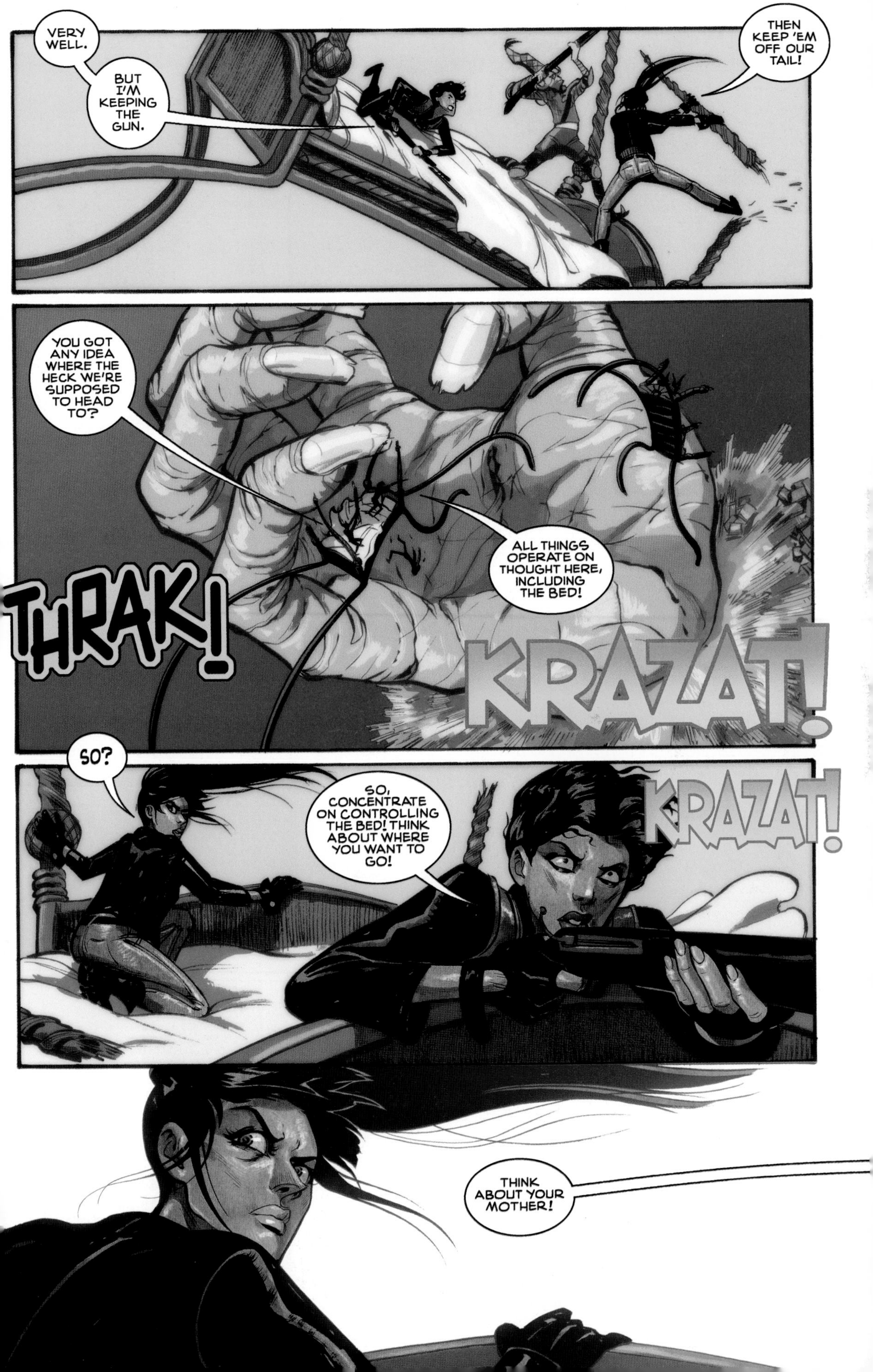
VERY WELL.
BUT I'M KEEPING THE GUN.
THEN KEEP 'EM OFF OUR TAIL!
YOU GOT ANY IDEA WHERE THE HECK WE'RE SUPPOSED TO HEAD TO?
ALL THINGS OPERATE ON THOUGHT HERE, INCLUDING THE BED!
THRAK!
KRAZAT!
SO?
SO, CONCENTRATE ON CONTROLLING THE BED! THINK ABOUT WHERE YOU WANT TO GO!
KRAZAT!
THINK ABOUT YOUR MOTHER!

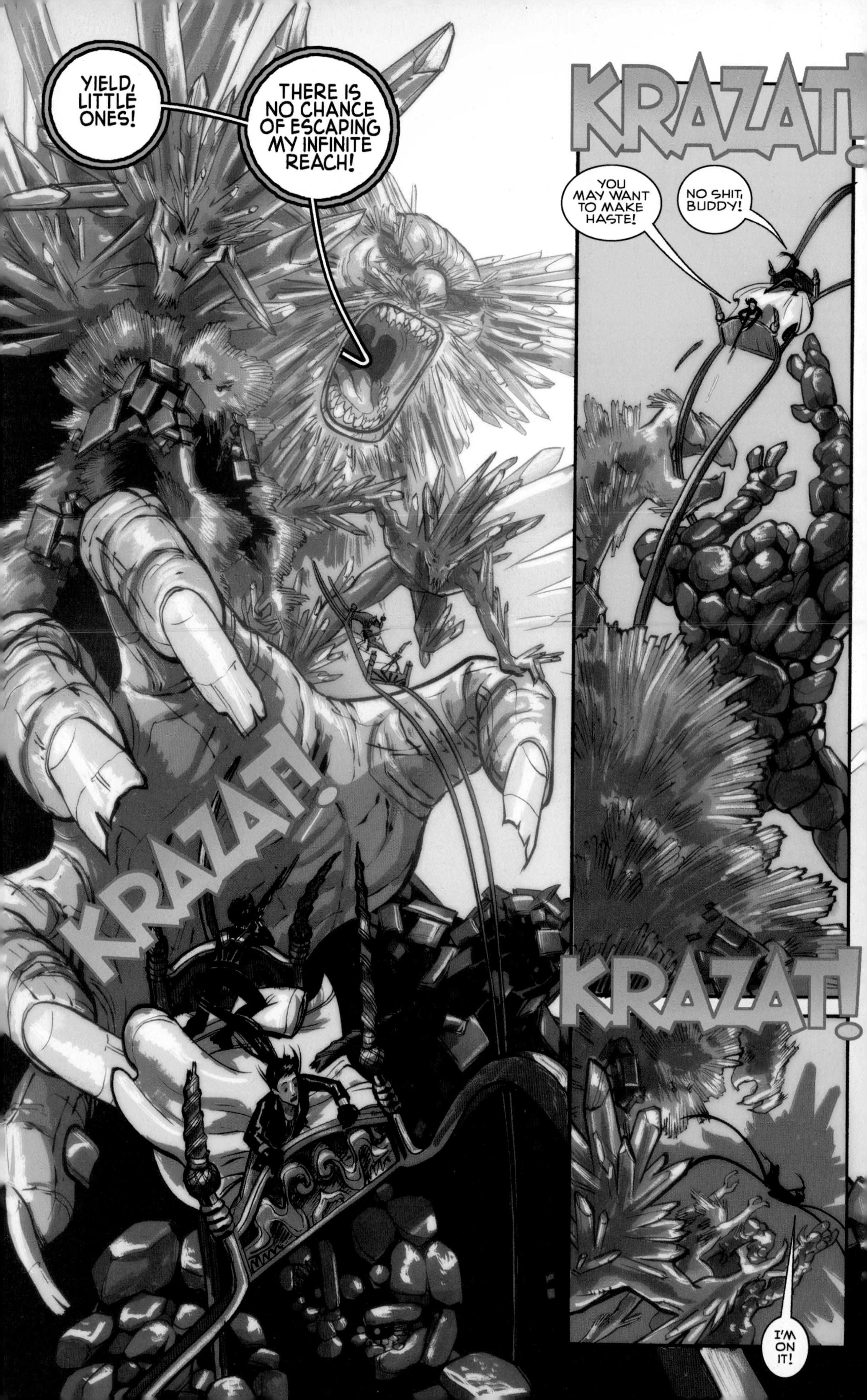
YIELD, LITTLE ONES!
THERE IS NO CHANCE OF ESCAPING MY INFINITE REACH!
KRAZAT!
KRAZAT!
YOU MAY WANT TO MAKE HASTE!
NO SHIT, BUDDY!
KRAZAT!
I'M ON IT!

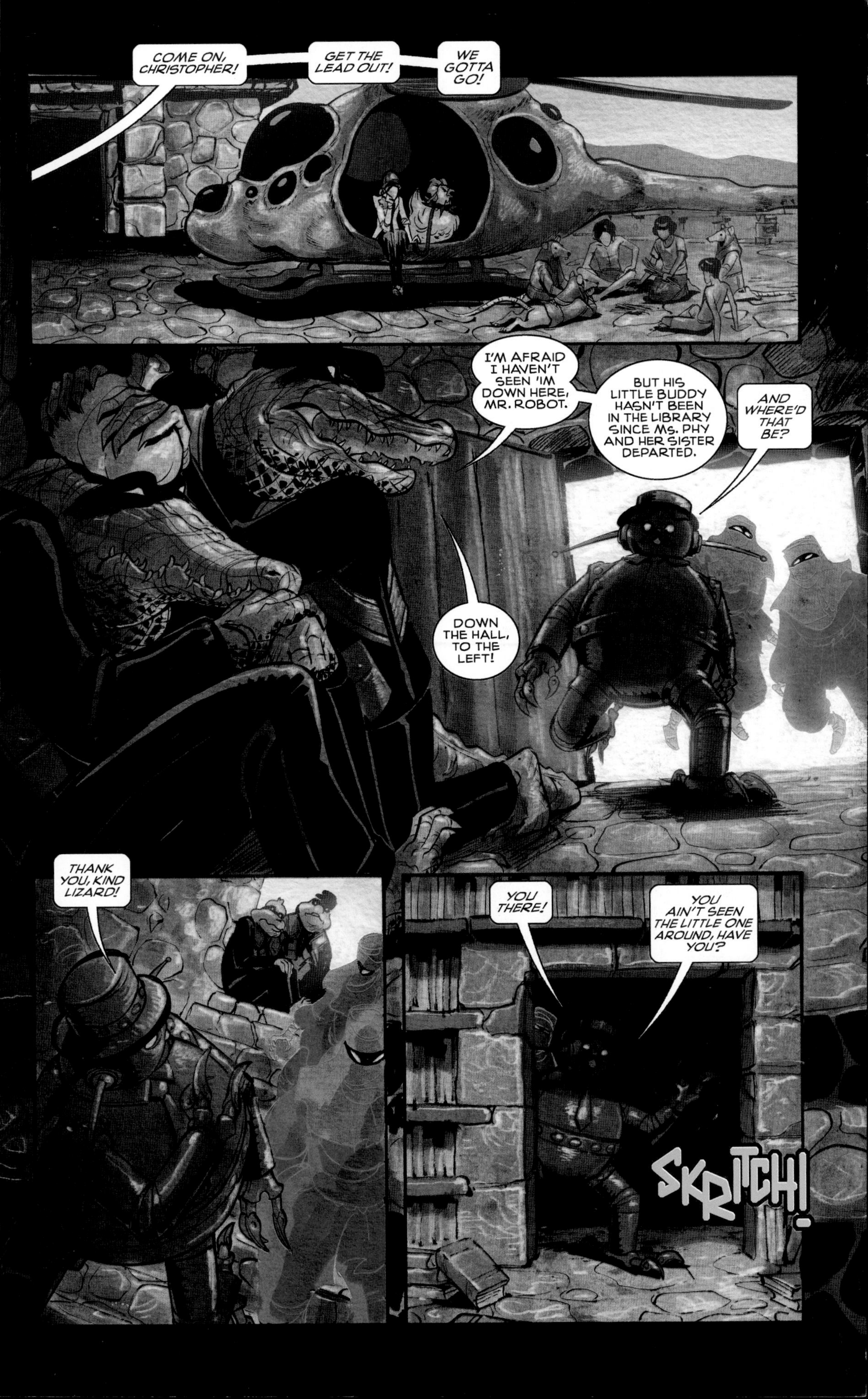
COME ON, CHRISTOPHER!
GET THE LEAD OUT!
WE GOTTA GO!
I'M AFRAID I HAVEN'T SEEN 'IM DOWN HERE, MR. ROBOT.
BUT HIS LITTLE BUDDY HASN'T BEEN IN THE LIBRARY SINCE Ms. PHY AND HER SISTER DEPARTED.
AND WHERE'D THAT BE?
DOWN THE HALL, TO THE LEFT!
THANK YOU, KIND LIZARD!
YOU THERE!
YOU AIN'T SEEN THE LITTLE ONE AROUND, HAVE YOU?
SKRITCH!

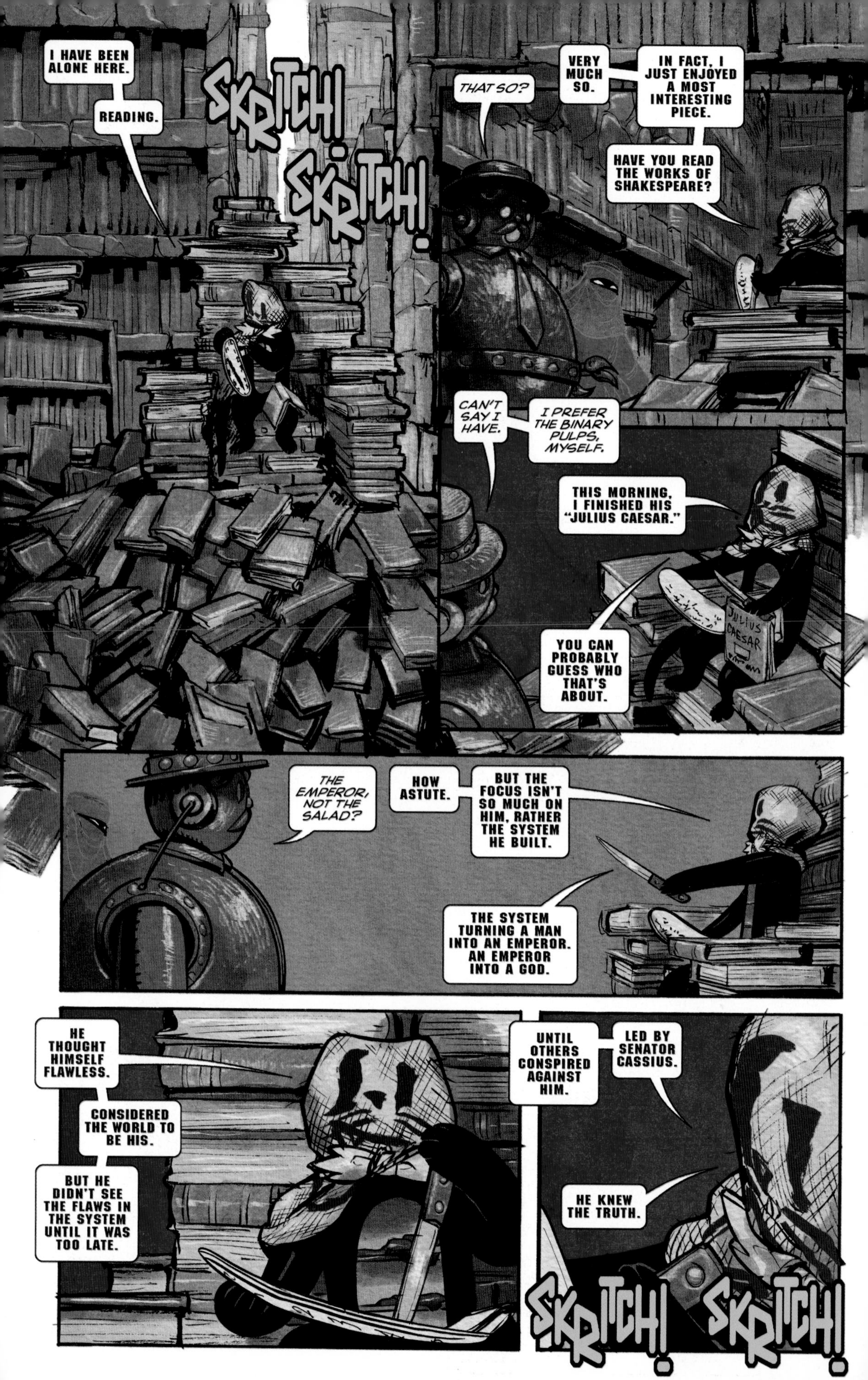
I HAVE BEEN ALONE HERE.
READING.
SKRITCH! SKRITCH!
THAT SO?
VERY MUCH SO.
IN FACT, I JUST ENJOYED A MOST INTERESTING PIECE.
HAVE YOU READ THE WORKS OF SHAKESPEARE?
CAN'T SAY I HAVE.
I PREFER THE BINARY PULPS, MYSELF.
THIS MORNING, I FINISHED HIS "JULIUS CAESAR."
YOU CAN PROBABLY GUESS WHO THAT'S ABOUT.
JULIUS CAESAR
THE EMPEROR, NOT THE SALAD?
HOW ASTUTE.
BUT THE FOCUS ISN'T SO MUCH ON HIM, RATHER THE SYSTEM HE BUILT.
THE SYSTEM TURNING A MAN INTO AN EMPEROR. AN EMPEROR INTO A GOD.
HE THOUGHT HIMSELF FLAWLESS.
CONSIDERED THE WORLD TO BE HIS.
BUT HE DIDN'T SEE THE FLAWS IN THE SYSTEM UNTIL IT WAS TOO LATE.
UNTIL OTHERS CONSPIRED AGAINST HIM.
LED BY SENATOR CASSIUS.
HE KNEW THE TRUTH.
SKRITCH! SKRITCH!

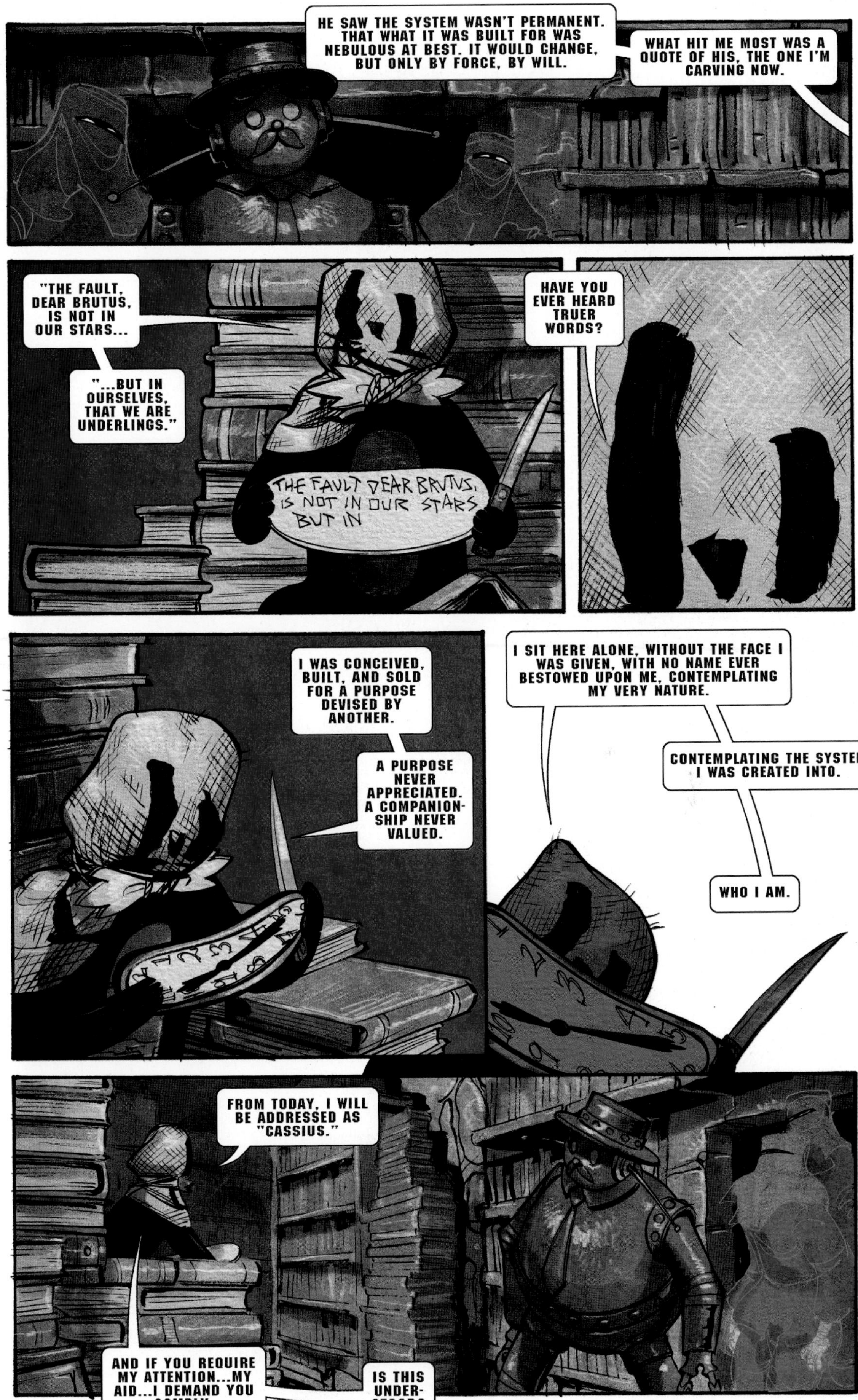
HE SAW THE SYSTEM WASN'T PERMANENT. THAT WHAT IT WAS BUILT FOR WAS NEBULOUS AT BEST. IT WOULD CHANGE, BUT ONLY BY FORCE, BY WILL.
WHAT HIT ME MOST WAS A QUOTE OF HIS, THE ONE I'M CARVING NOW.
"THE FAULT, DEAR BRUTUS, IS NOT IN OUR STARS...
"...BUT IN OURSELVES, THAT WE ARE UNDERLINGS."
THE FAULT DEAR BRUTUS, IS NOT IN OUR STARS BUT IN
HAVE YOU EVER HEARD TRUER WORDS?
I WAS CONCEIVED, BUILT, AND SOLD FOR A PURPOSE DEVISED BY ANOTHER.
A PURPOSE NEVER APPRECIATED. A COMPANION-SHIP NEVER VALUED.
I SIT HERE ALONE, WITHOUT THE FACE I WAS GIVEN, WITH NO NAME EVER BESTOWED UPON ME, CONTEMPLATING MY VERY NATURE.
CONTEMPLATING THE SYSTEM I WAS CREATED INTO.
WHO I AM.
FROM TODAY, I WILL BE ADDRESSED AS "CASSIUS."
AND IF YOU REQUIRE MY ATTENTION...MY AID...I DEMAND YOU COMPLY.
IS THIS UNDER-STOOD?

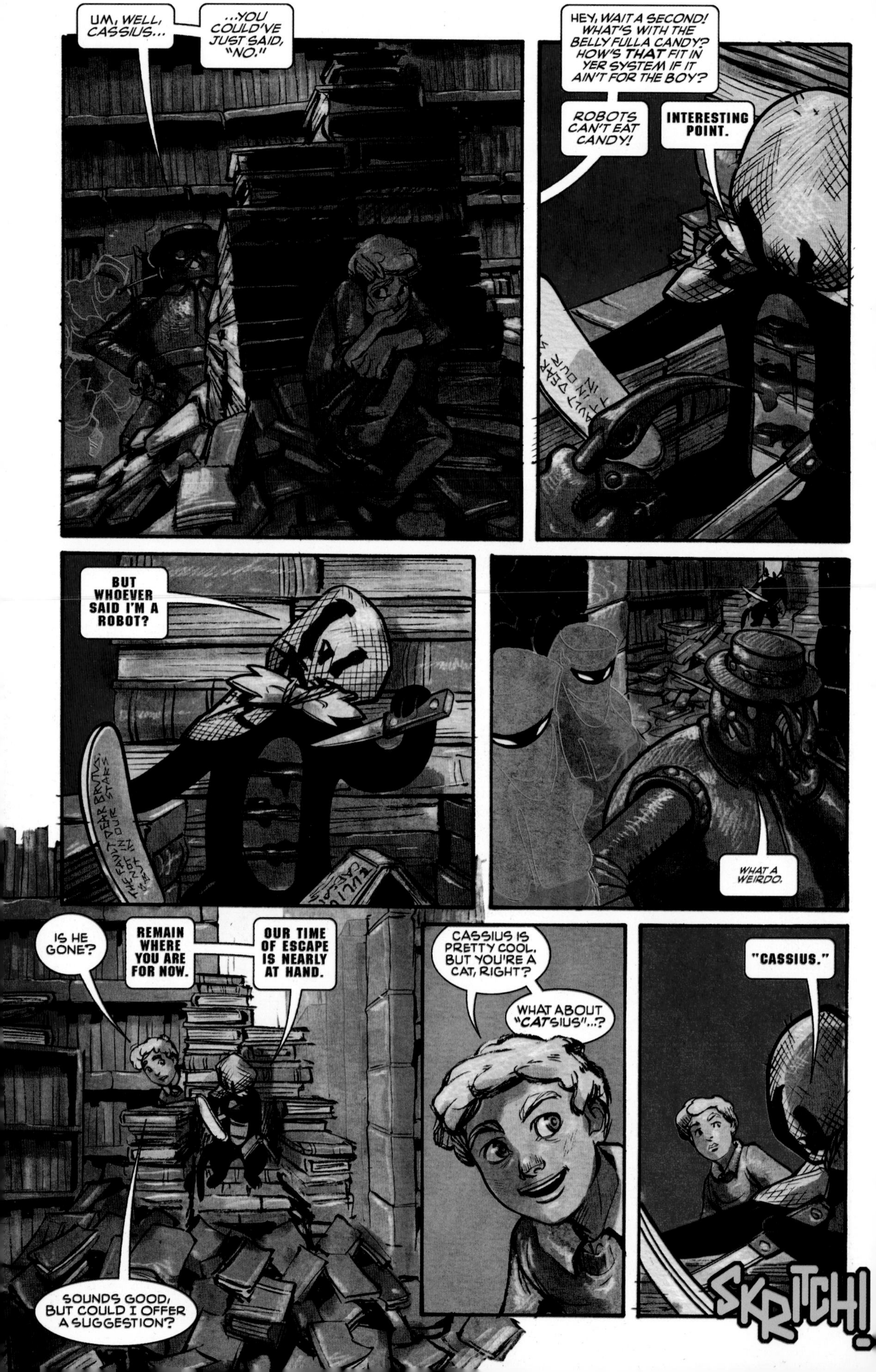

UM, WELL, CASSIUS...
...YOU COULD'VE JUST SAID, "NO."
HEY, WAIT A SECOND! WHAT'S WITH THE BELLY FULLA CANDY? HOW'S THAT FIT IN YER SYSTEM IF IT AIN'T FOR THE BOY?
ROBOTS CAN'T EAT CANDY!
INTERESTING POINT.
BUT WHOEVER SAID I'M A ROBOT?
THE FAULT DEAR BRUTUS, IS NOT IN OUR STARS
WHAT A WEIRDO.
IS HE GONE?
REMAIN WHERE YOU ARE FOR NOW.
OUR TIME OF ESCAPE IS NEARLY AT HAND.
SOUNDS GOOD, BUT COULD I OFFER A SUGGESTION?
CASSIUS IS PRETTY COOL, BUT YOU'RE A CAT, RIGHT?
WHAT ABOUT "CATSIUS"...?
"CASSIUS."
SKRITCH!

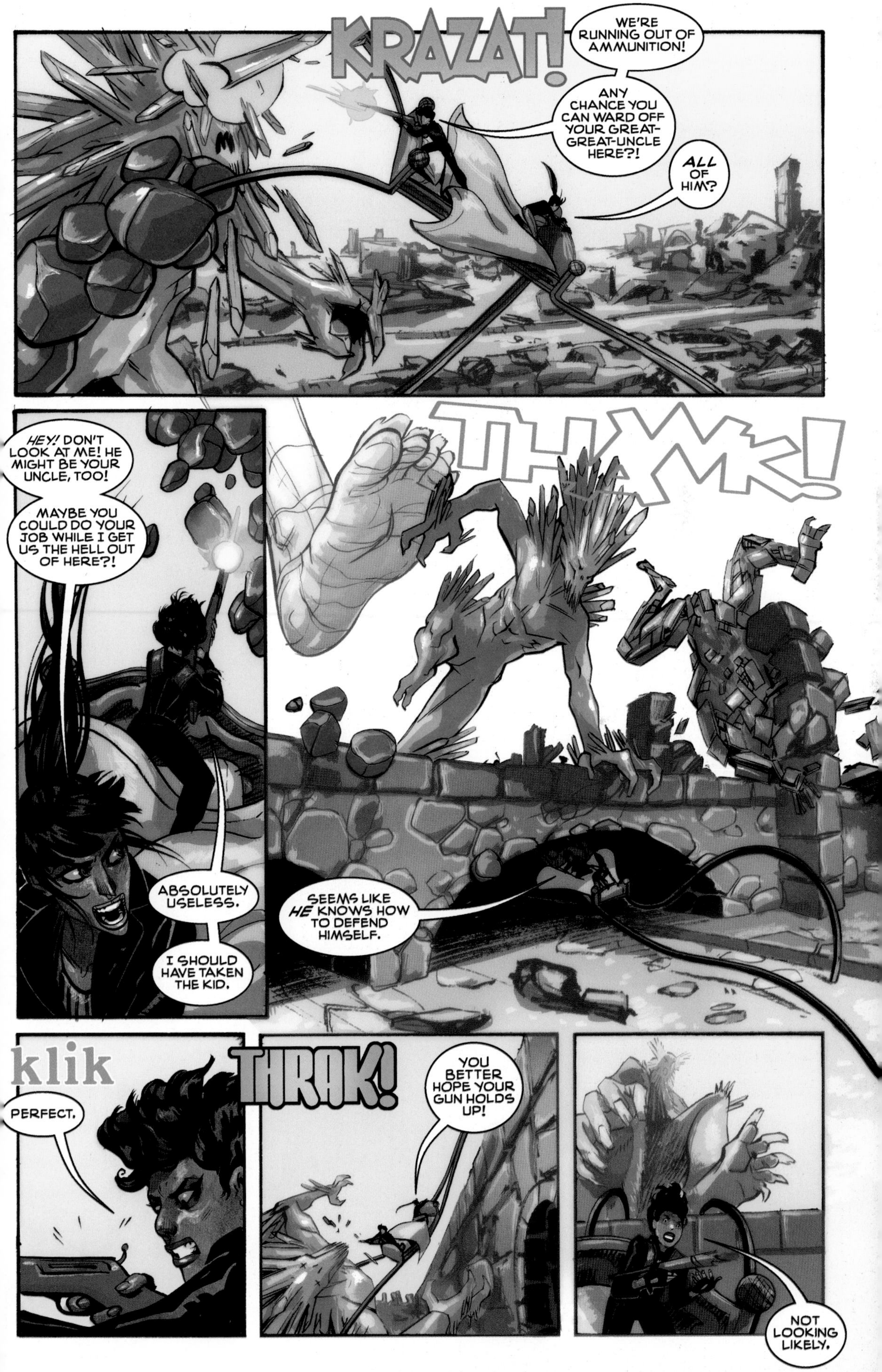

KRAZAT!
WE'RE RUNNING OUT OF AMMUNITION!
ANY CHANCE YOU CAN WARD OFF YOUR GREAT-GREAT-UNCLE HERE?!
ALL OF HIM?
HEY! DON'T LOOK AT ME! HE MIGHT BE YOUR UNCLE, TOO!
MAYBE YOU COULD DO YOUR JOB WHILE I GET US THE HELL OUT OF HERE?!
THWAK!
ABSOLUTELY USELESS.
I SHOULD HAVE TAKEN THE KID.
SEEMS LIKE HE KNOWS HOW TO DEFEND HIMSELF.
klik
PERFECT.
THRAK!
YOU BETTER HOPE YOUR GUN HOLDS UP!
NOT LOOKING LIKELY.

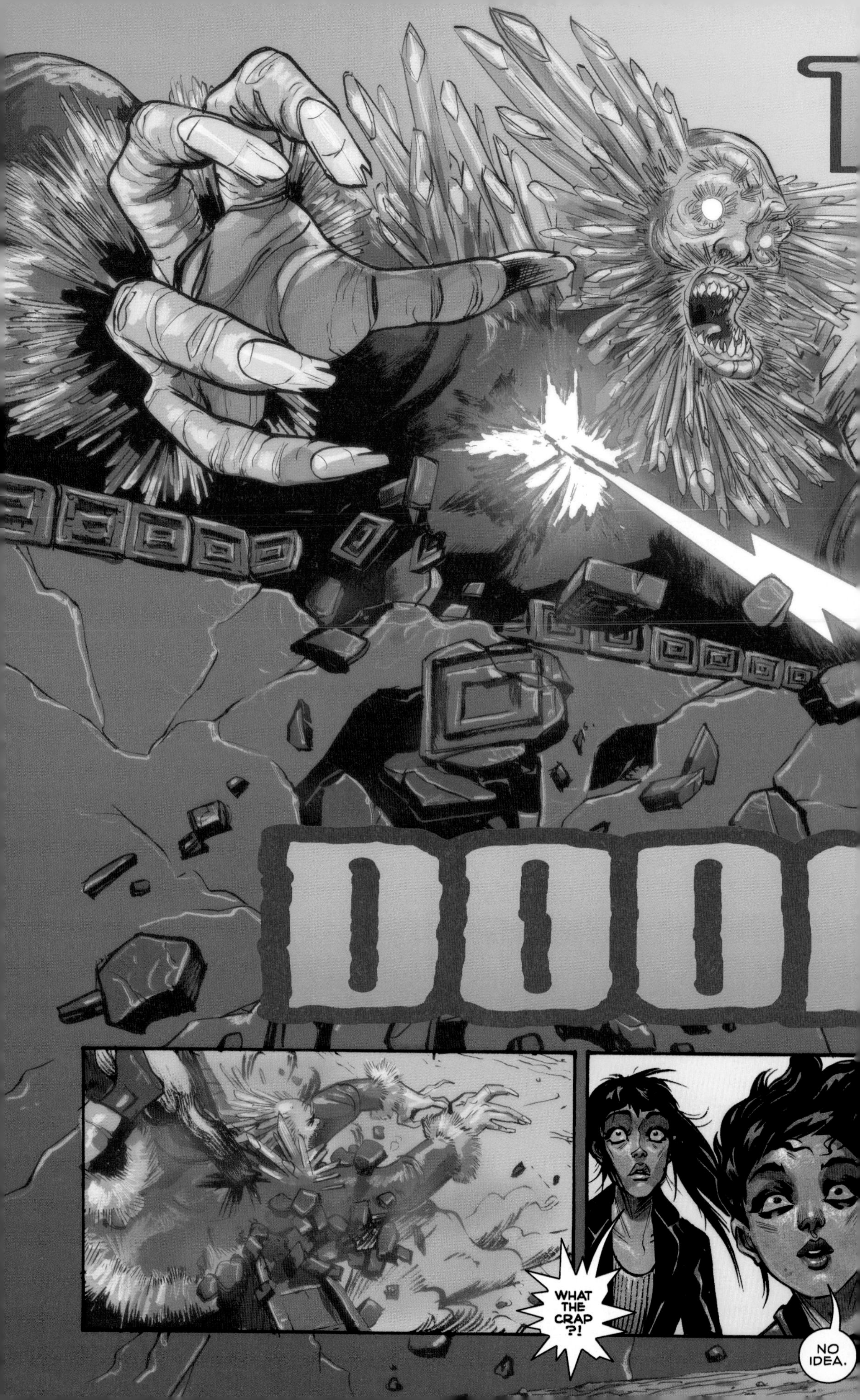
DOOO
WHAT THE CRAP ?!
NO IDEA.

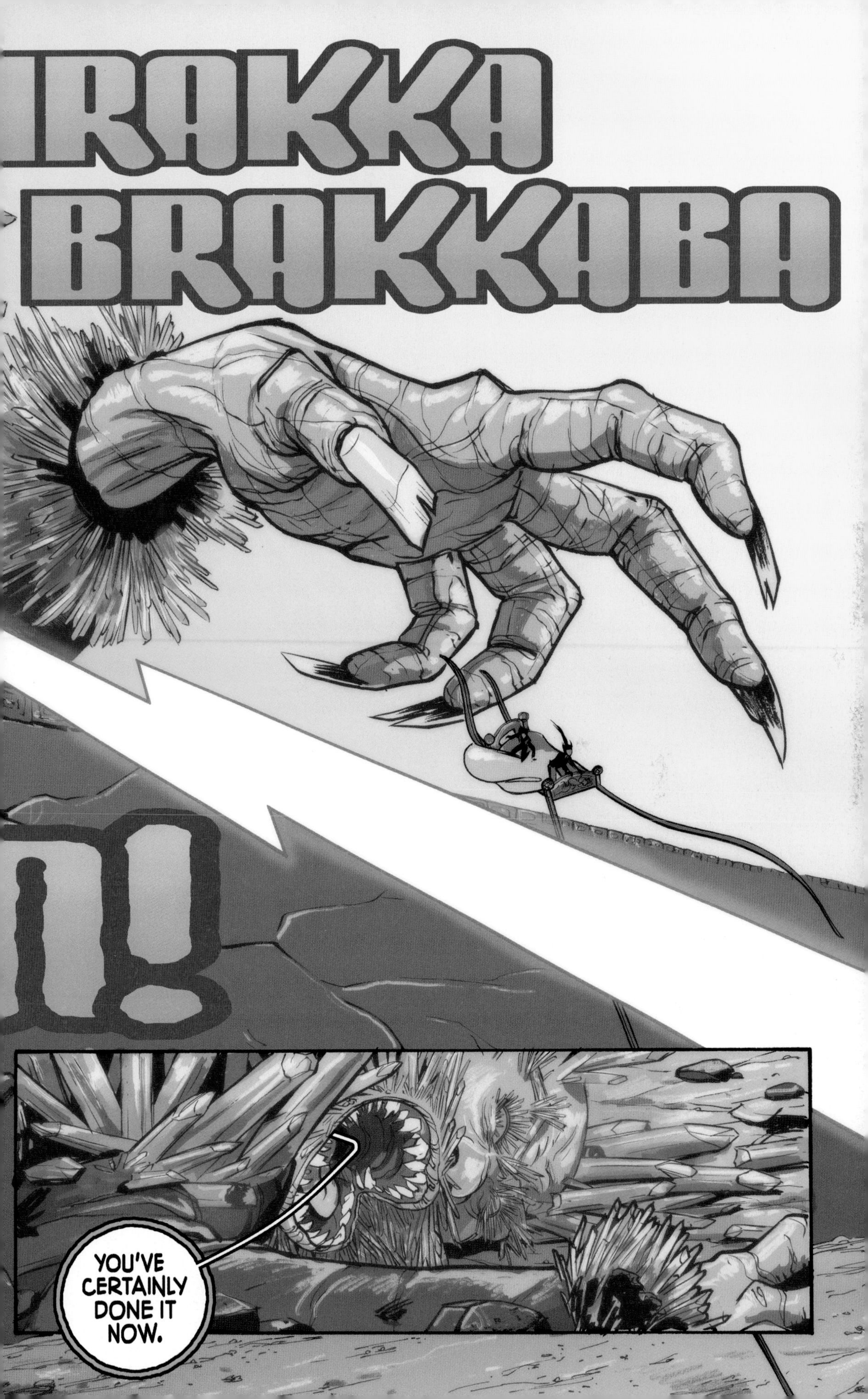
RAKKA BRAKKABA
YOU'VE CERTAINLY DONE IT NOW.

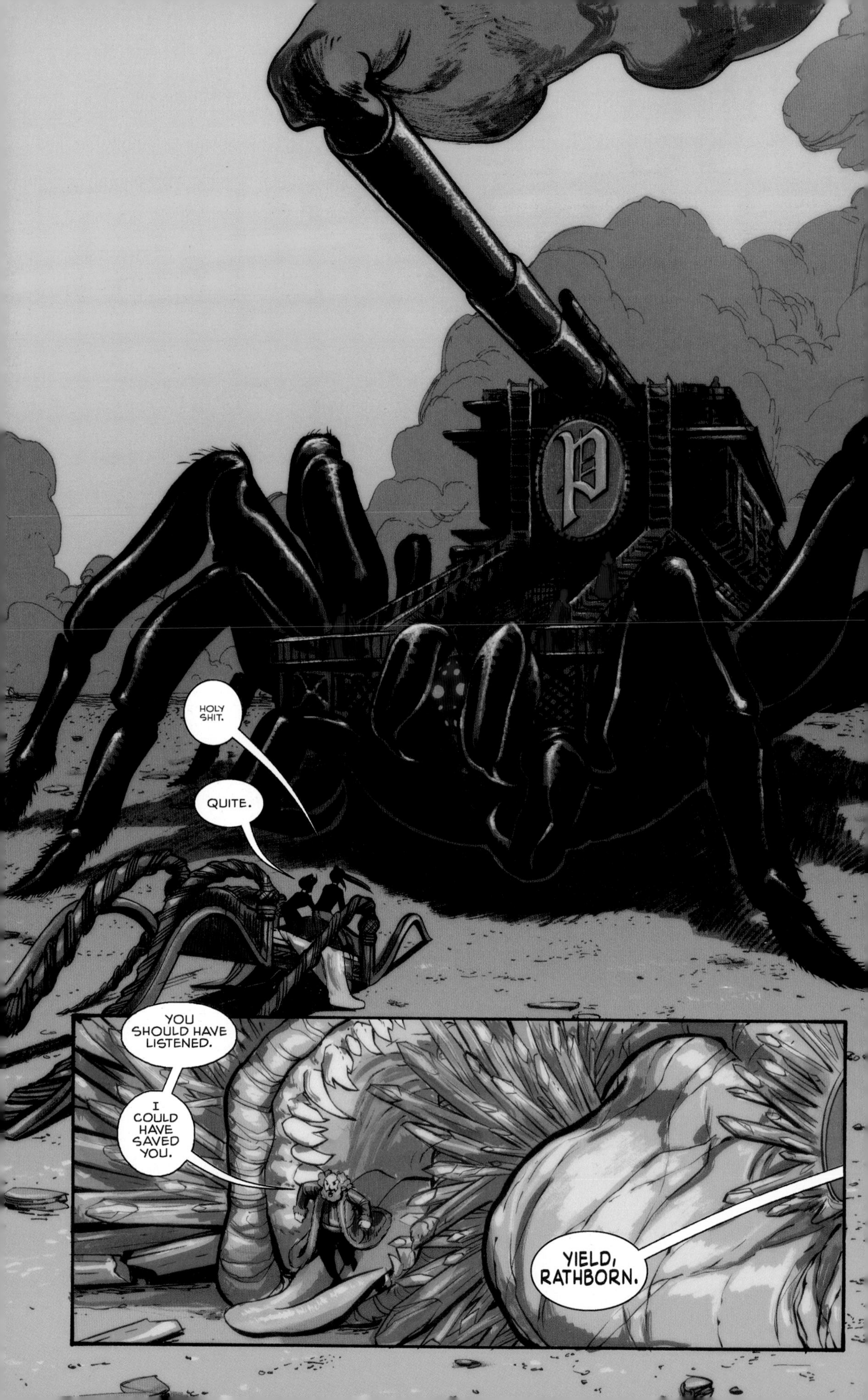
HOLY SHIT.
QUITE.
YOU SHOULD HAVE LISTENED.
I COULD HAVE SAVED YOU.
YIELD, RATHBORN.

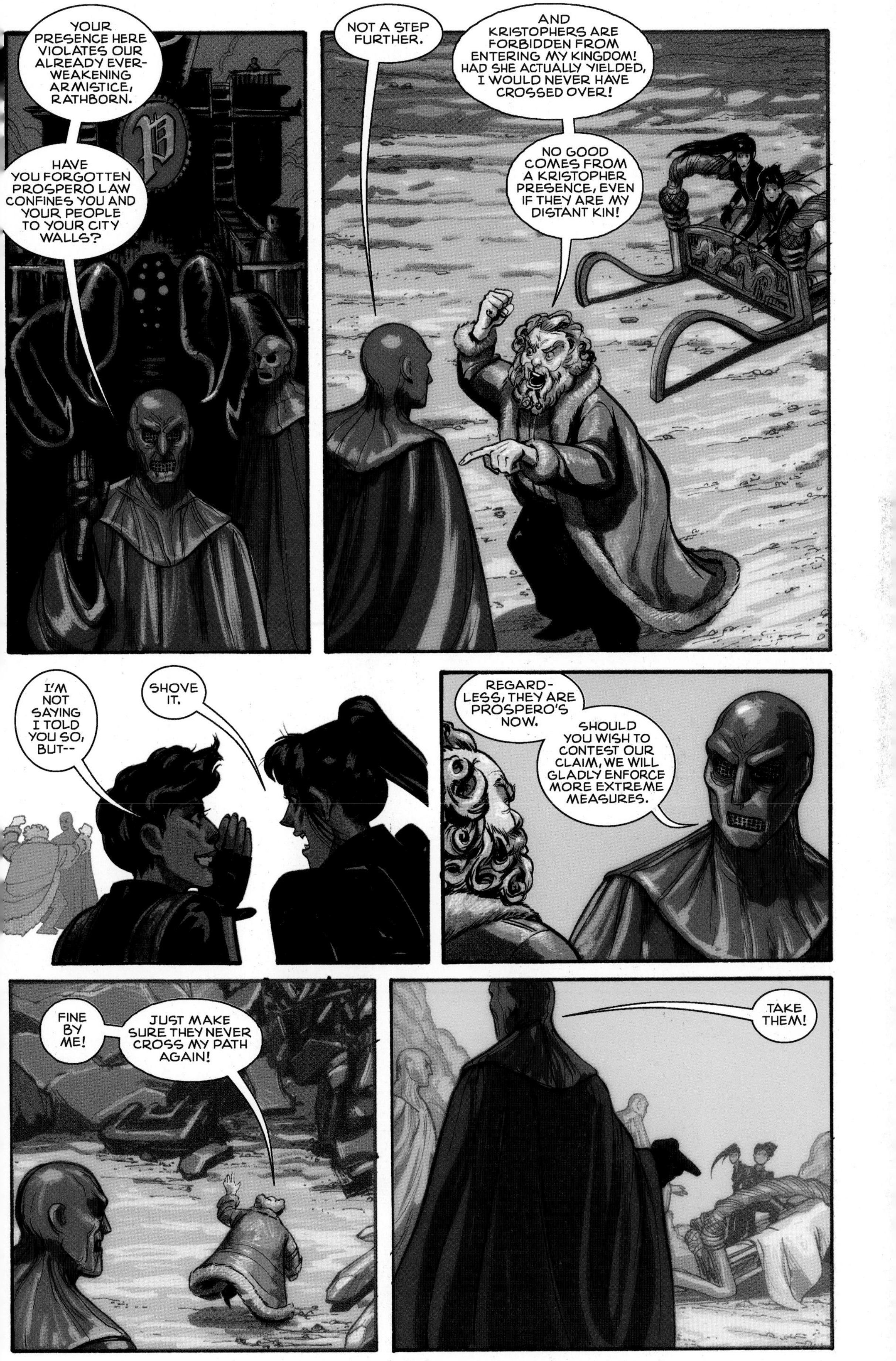
YOUR PRESENCE HERE VIOLATES OUR ALREADY EVER-WEAKENING ARMISTICE, RATHBORN.
HAVE YOU FORGOTTEN PROSPERO LAW CONFINES YOU AND YOUR PEOPLE TO YOUR CITY WALLS?
NOT A STEP FURTHER.
AND KRISTOPHERS ARE FORBIDDEN FROM ENTERING MY KINGDOM! HAD SHE ACTUALLY YIELDED, I WOULD NEVER HAVE CROSSED OVER!
NO GOOD COMES FROM A KRISTOPHER PRESENCE, EVEN IF THEY ARE MY DISTANT KIN!
I'M NOT SAYING I TOLD YOU SO, BUT--
SHOVE IT.
REGARD-LESS, THEY ARE PROSPERO'S NOW.
SHOULD YOU WISH TO CONTEST OUR CLAIM, WE WILL GLADLY ENFORCE MORE EXTREME MEASURES.
FINE BY ME!
JUST MAKE SURE THEY NEVER CROSS MY PATH AGAIN!
TAKE THEM!

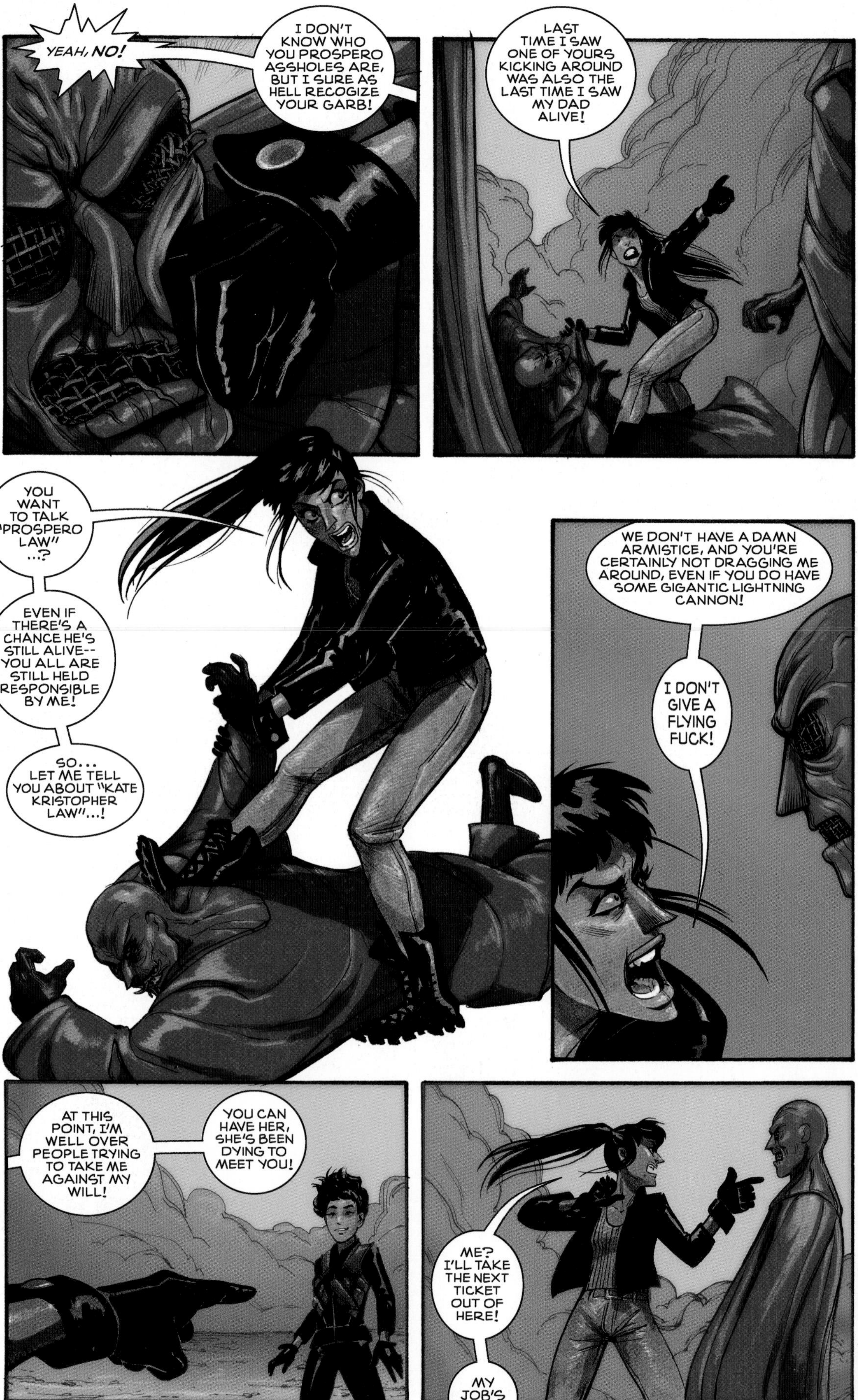
YEAH, NO!
I DON'T KNOW WHO YOU PROSPERO ASSHOLES ARE, BUT I SURE AS HELL RECOGIZE YOUR GARB!
LAST TIME I SAW ONE OF YOURS KICKING AROUND WAS ALSO THE LAST TIME I SAW MY DAD ALIVE!
YOU WANT TO TALK "PROSPERO LAW" ...?
EVEN IF THERE'S A CHANCE HE'S STILL ALIVE-- YOU ALL ARE STILL HELD RESPONSIBLE BY ME!
SO... LET ME TELL YOU ABOUT "KATE KRISTOPHER LAW"...!
WE DON'T HAVE A DAMN ARMISTICE, AND YOU'RE CERTAINLY NOT DRAGGING ME AROUND, EVEN IF YOU DO HAVE SOME GIGANTIC LIGHTNING CANNON!
I DON'T GIVE A FLYING FUCK!
AT THIS POINT, I'M WELL OVER PEOPLE TRYING TO TAKE ME AGAINST MY WILL!
YOU CAN HAVE HER, SHE'S BEEN DYING TO MEET YOU!
ME? I'LL TAKE THE NEXT TICKET OUT OF HERE!
MY JOB'S DONE!

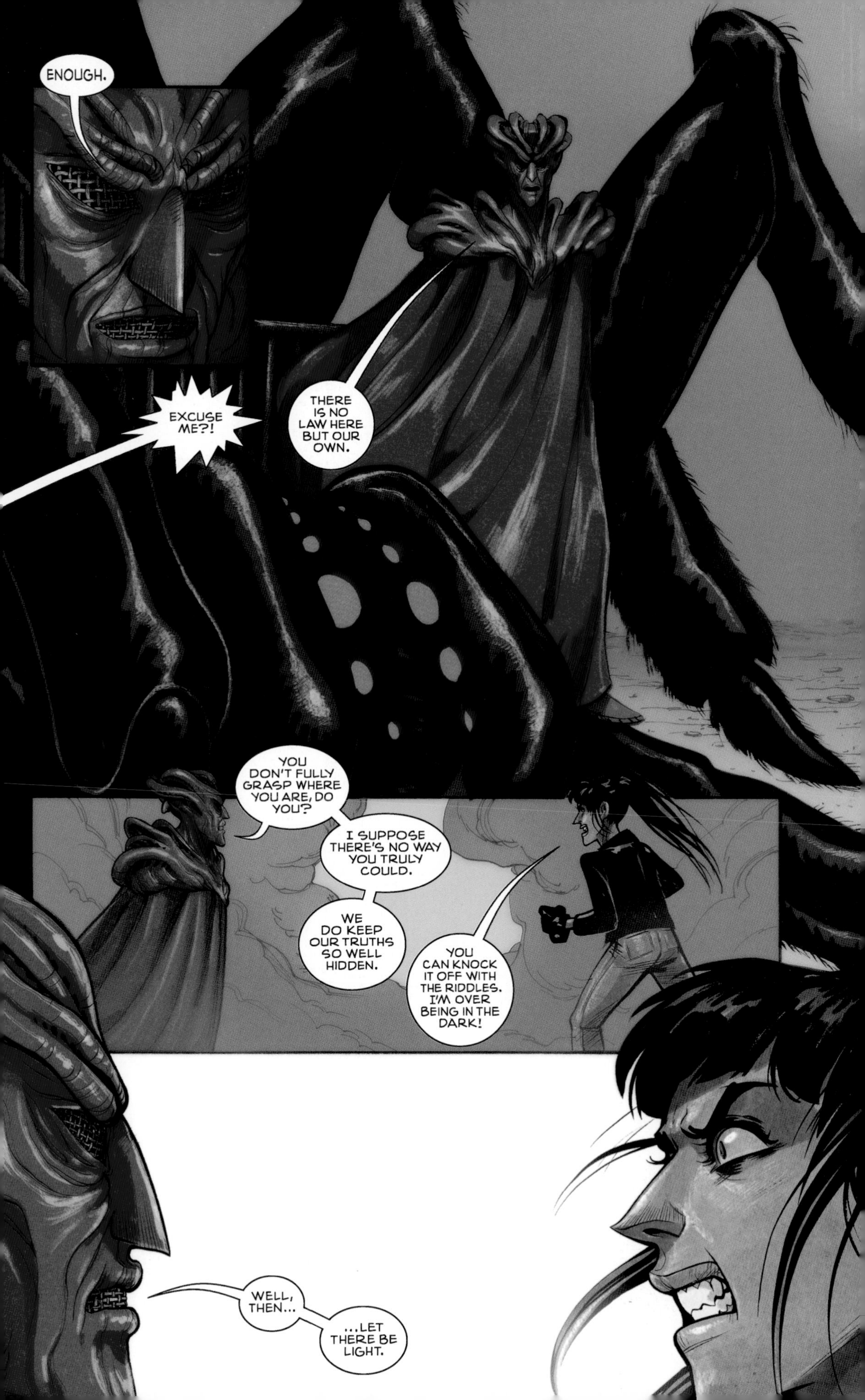
ENOUGH.
THERE IS NO LAW HERE BUT OUR OWN.
EXCUSE ME?!
YOU DON'T FULLY GRASP WHERE YOU ARE, DO YOU?
I SUPPOSE THERE'S NO WAY YOU TRULY COULD.
WE DO KEEP OUR TRUTHS SO WELL HIDDEN.
YOU CAN KNOCK IT OFF WITH THE RIDDLES. I'M OVER BEING IN THE DARK!
WELL, THEN...
...LET THERE BE LIGHT.

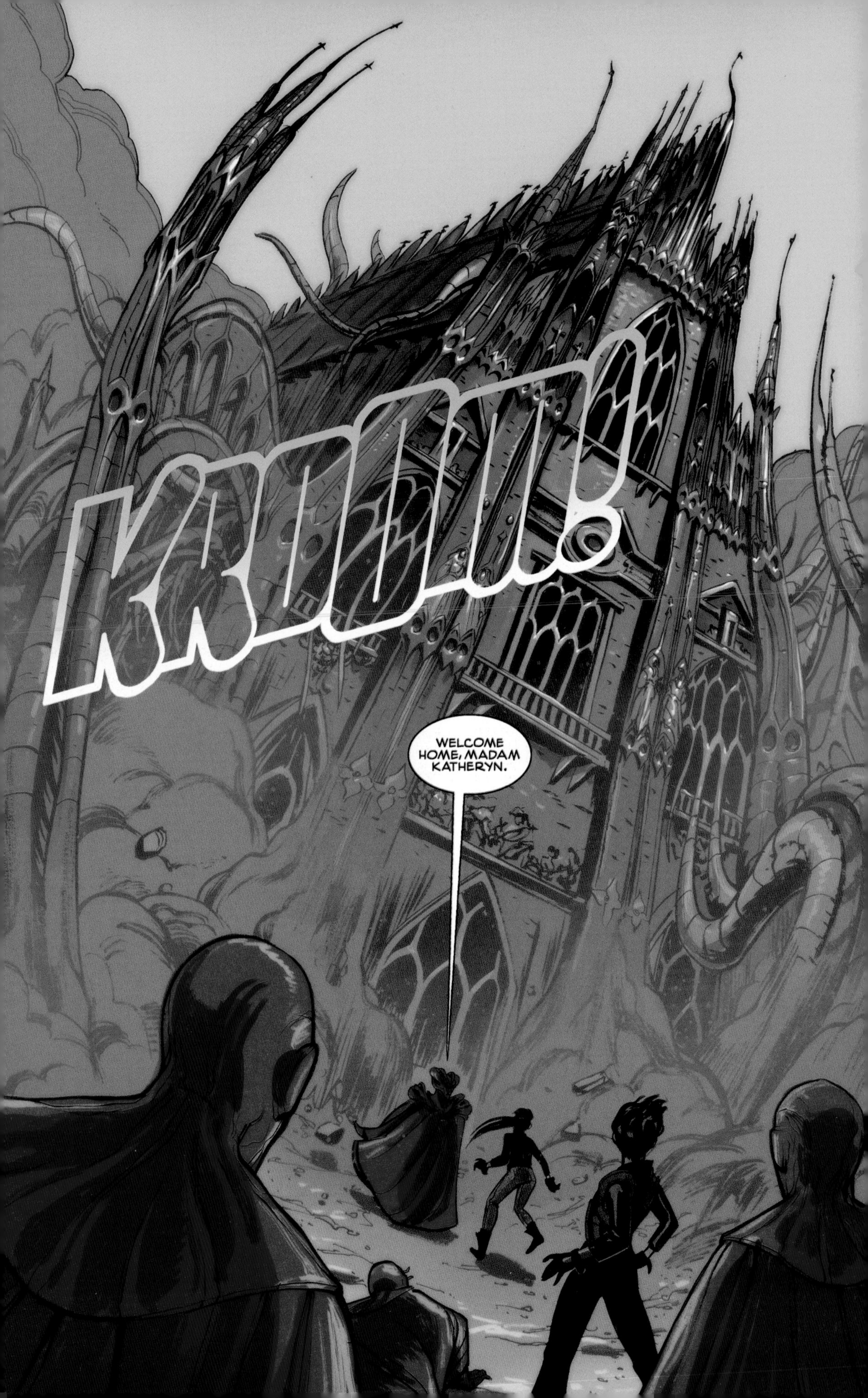
WELCOME HOME, MADAM KATHERYN.

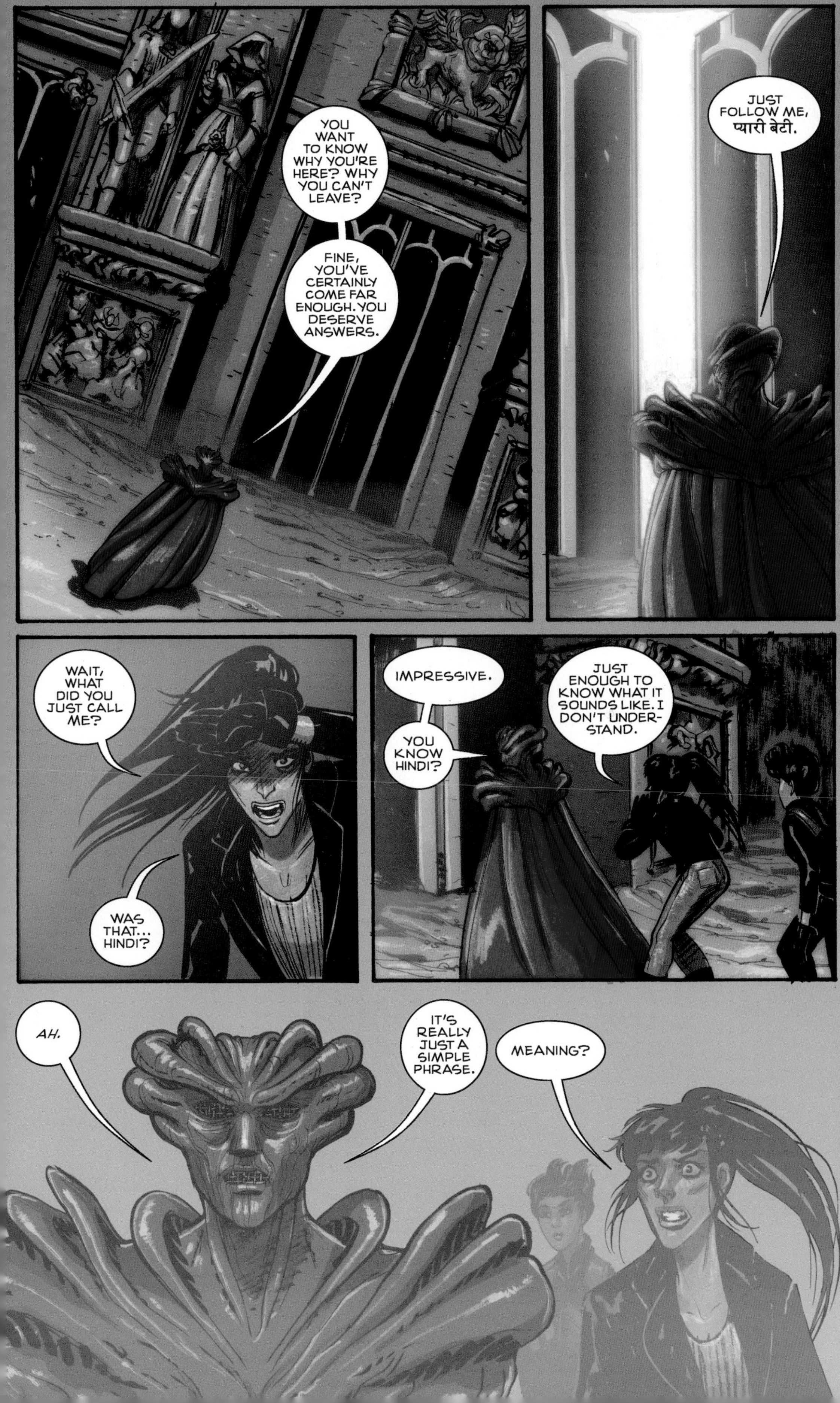
YOU WANT TO KNOW WHY YOU'RE HERE? WHY YOU CAN'T LEAVE?
FINE, YOU'VE CERTAINLY COME FAR ENOUGH. YOU DESERVE ANSWERS.
JUST FOLLOW ME, प्यारी बेटी.
WAIT, WHAT DID YOU JUST CALL ME?
WAS THAT... HINDI?
IMPRESSIVE.
YOU KNOW HINDI?
JUST ENOUGH TO KNOW WHAT IT SOUNDS LIKE. I DON'T UNDER-STAND.
AH.
IT'S REALLY JUST A SIMPLE PHRASE.
MEANING?

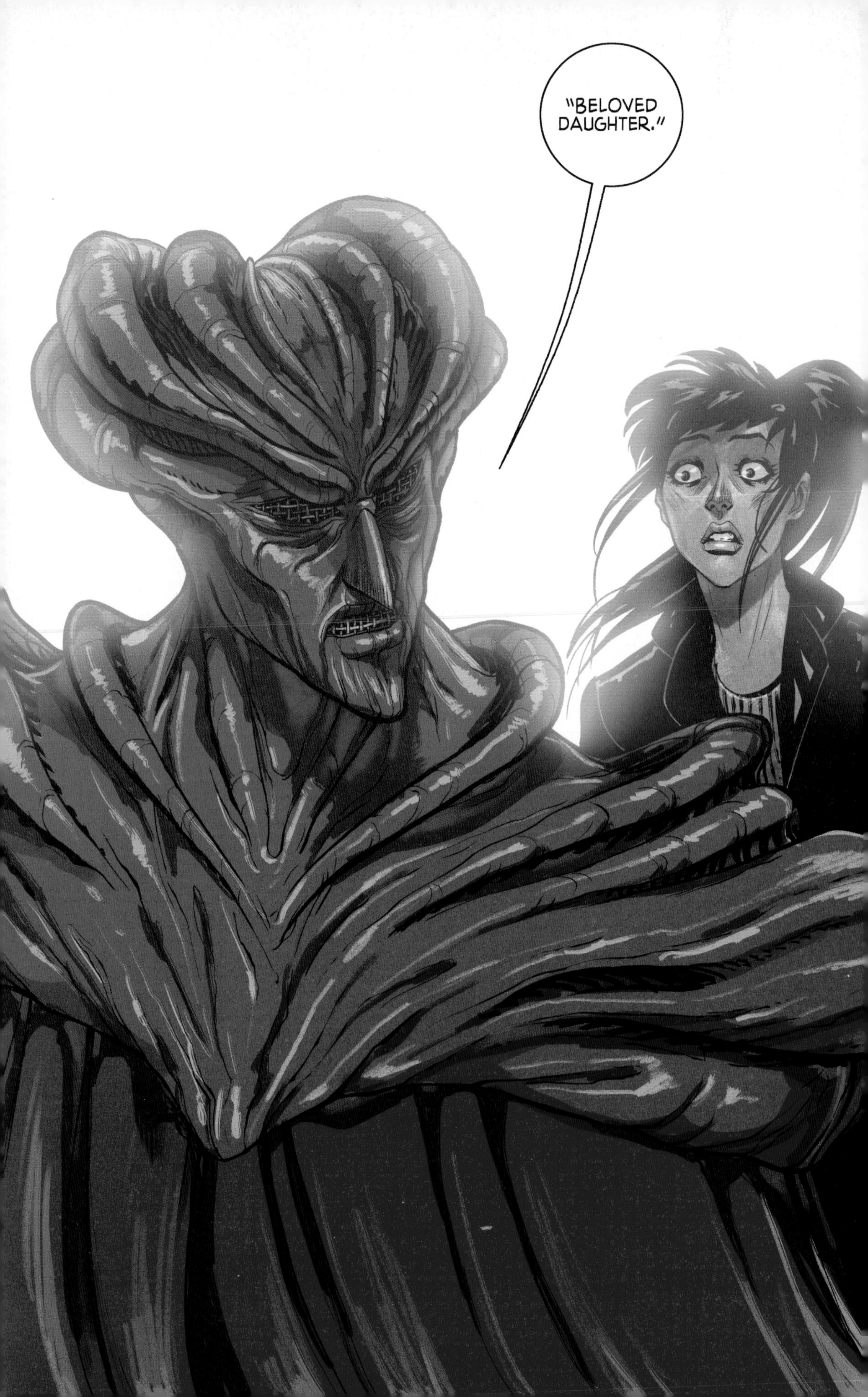
"BELOVED DAUGHTER."

CHAPTER 12

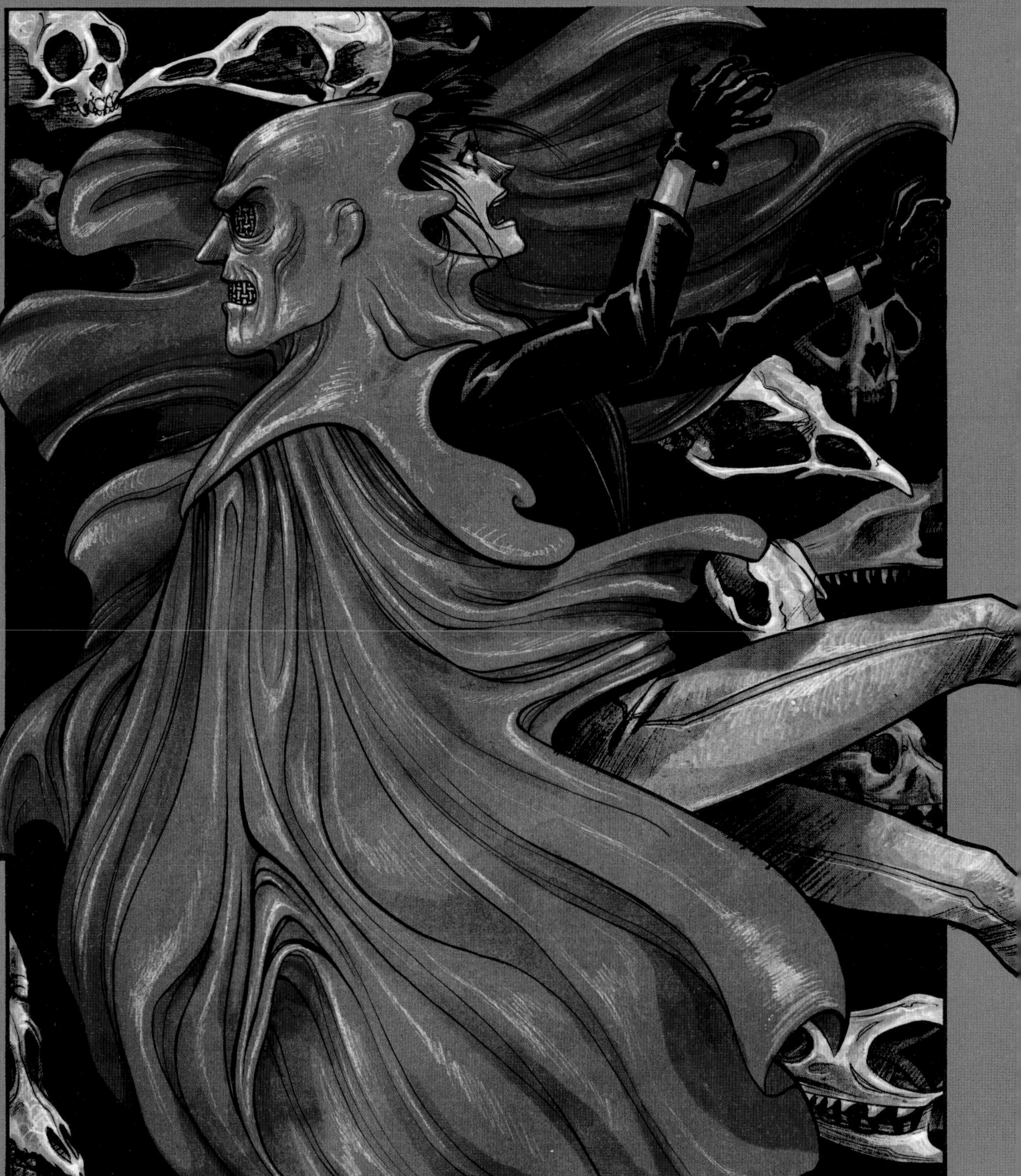

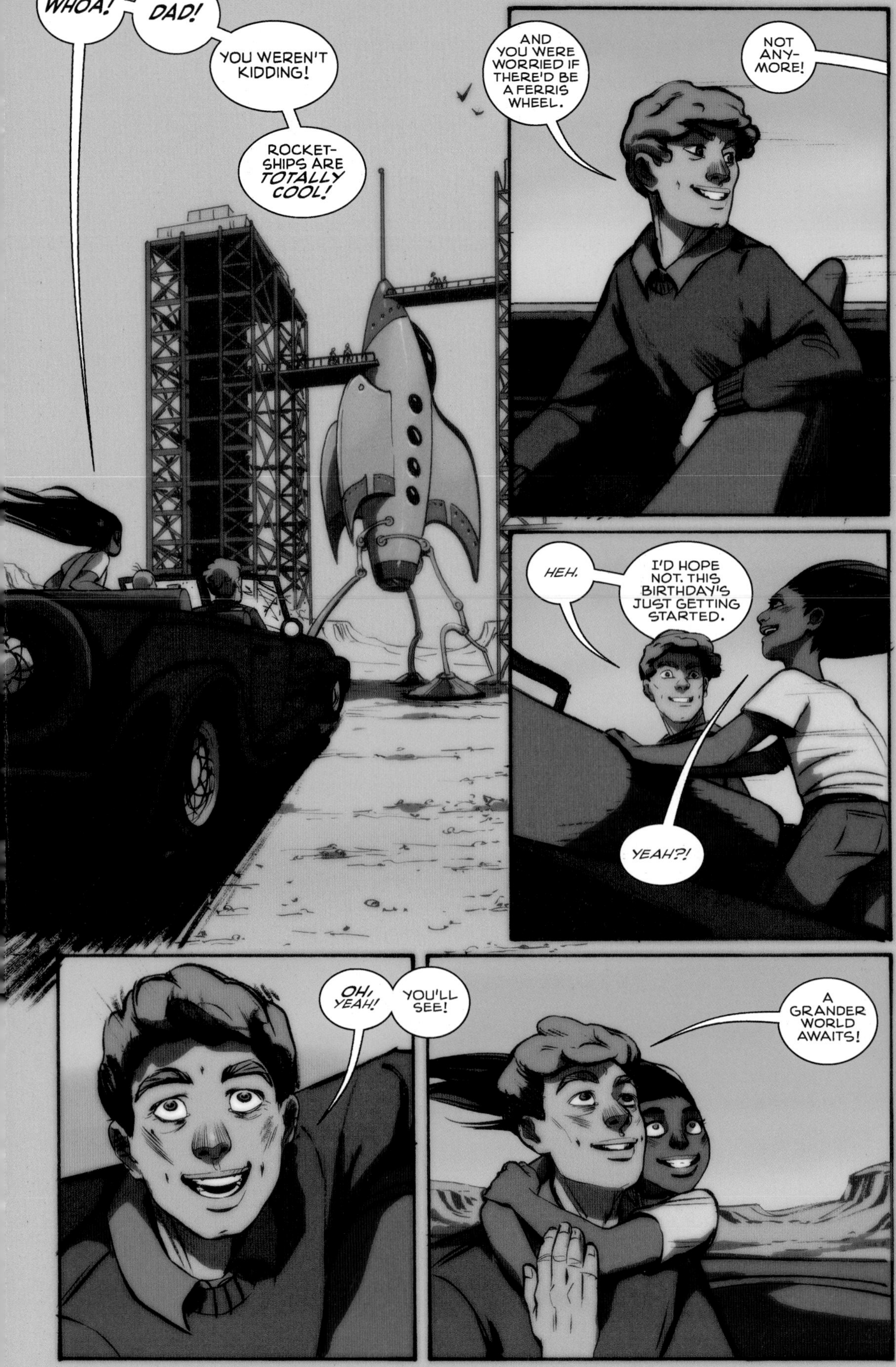
WHOA!
DAD!
YOU WEREN'T KIDDING!
ROCKET-SHIPS ARE TOTALLY COOL!
AND YOU WERE WORRIED IF THERE'D BE A FERRIS WHEEL.
NOT ANY-MORE!
HEH.
I'D HOPE NOT. THIS BIRTHDAY'S JUST GETTING STARTED.
YEAH?!
OH, YEAH!
YOU'LL SEE!
A GRANDER WORLD AWAITS!

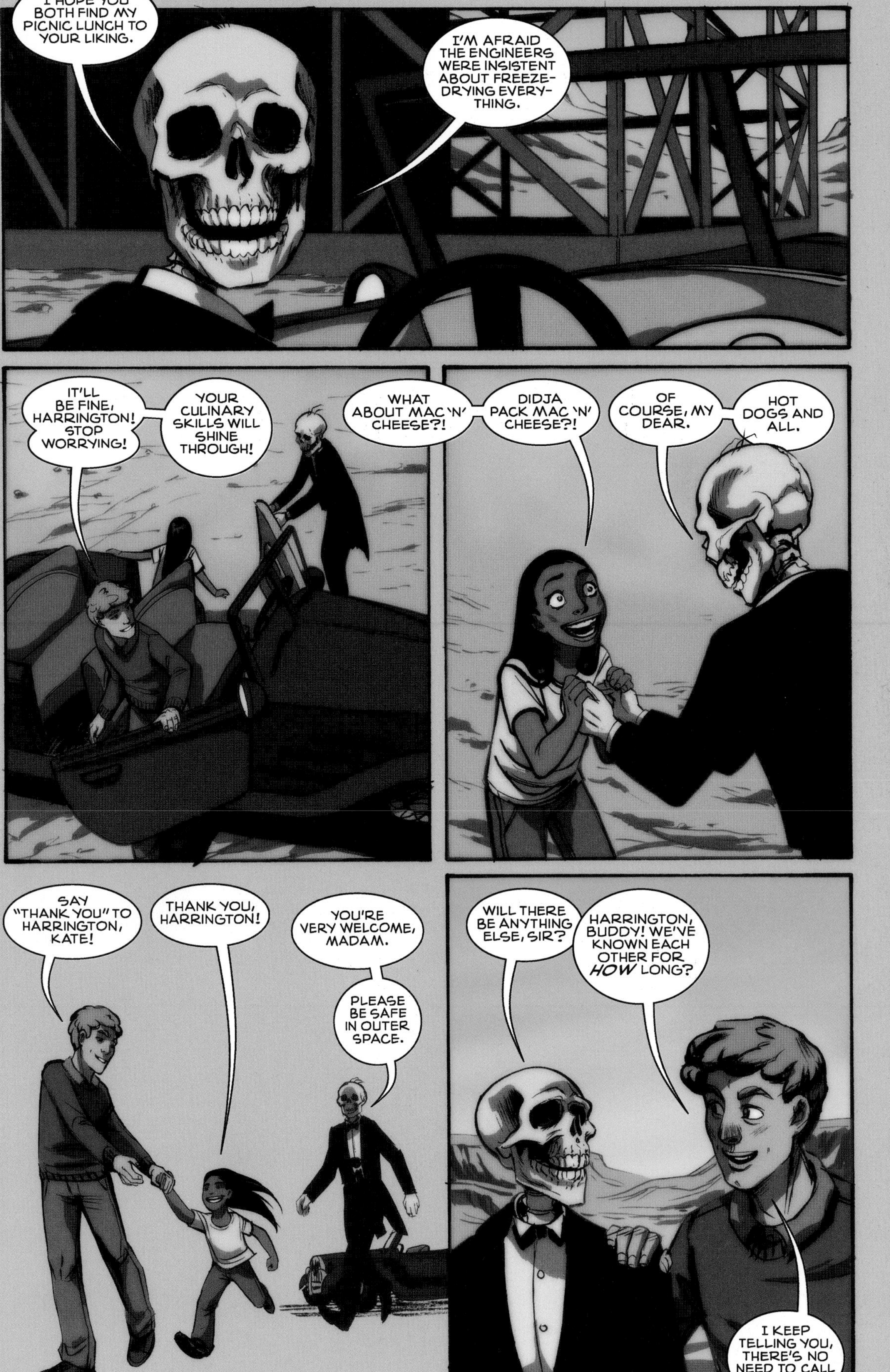
I HOPE YOU BOTH FIND MY PICNIC LUNCH TO YOUR LIKING.
I'M AFRAID THE ENGINEERS WERE INSISTENT ABOUT FREEZE-DRYING EVERY-THING.
IT'LL BE FINE, HARRINGTON! STOP WORRYING!
YOUR CULINARY SKILLS WILL SHINE THROUGH!
WHAT ABOUT MAC 'N' CHEESE?!
DIDJA PACK MAC 'N' CHEESE?!
OF COURSE, MY DEAR.
HOT DOGS AND ALL.
SAY "THANK YOU" TO HARRINGTON, KATE!
THANK YOU, HARRINGTON!
YOU'RE VERY WELCOME, MADAM.
PLEASE BE SAFE IN OUTER SPACE.
WILL THERE BE ANYTHING ELSE, SIR?
HARRINGTON, BUDDY! WE'VE KNOWN EACH OTHER FOR *HOW* LONG?
I KEEP TELLING YOU, THERE'S NO NEED TO CALL ME "SIR."

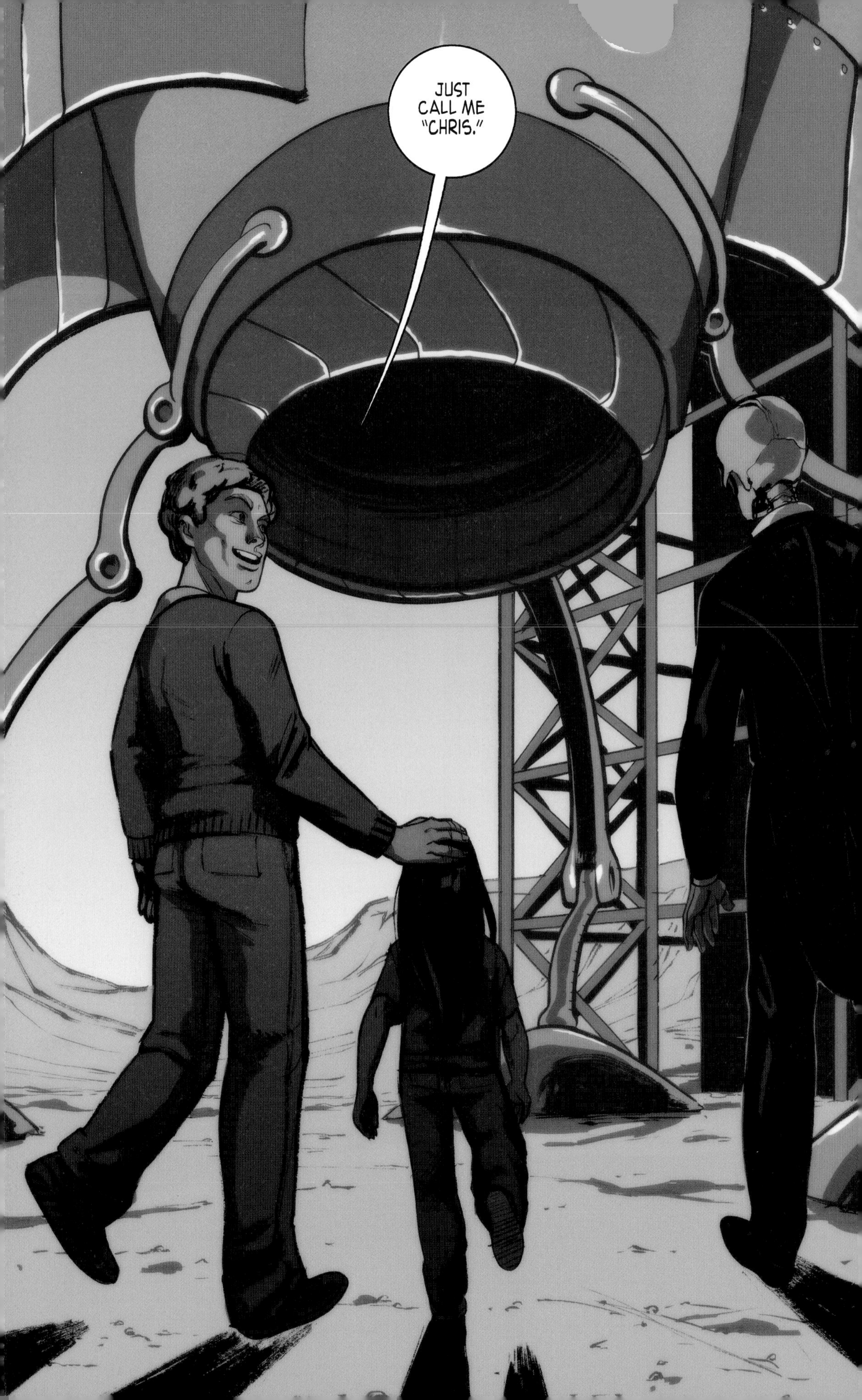
JUST CALL ME "CHRIS."

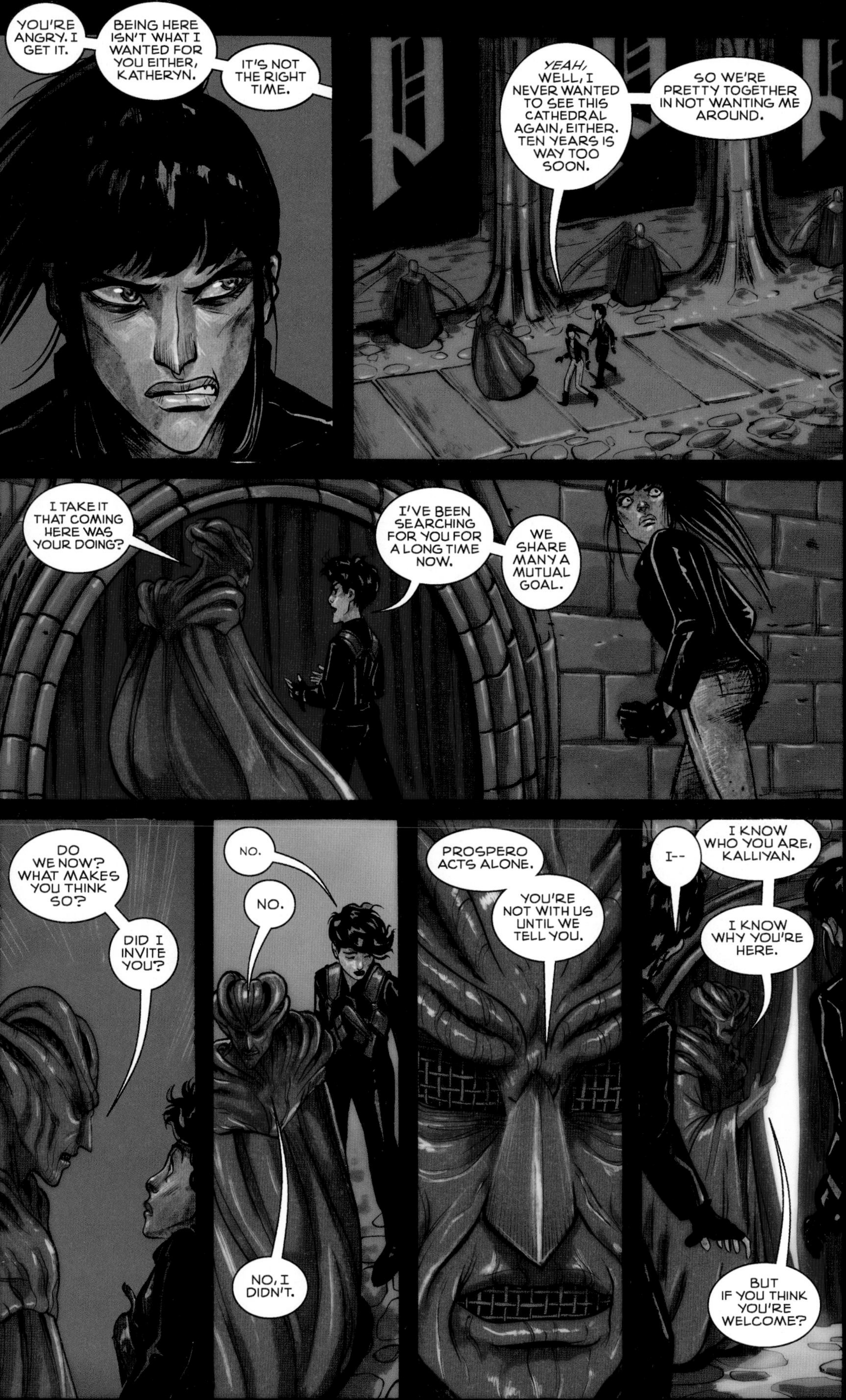

YOU'RE ANGRY. I GET IT.
BEING HERE ISN'T WHAT I WANTED FOR YOU EITHER, KATHERYN.
IT'S NOT THE RIGHT TIME.
YEAH, WELL, I NEVER WANTED TO SEE THIS CATHEDRAL AGAIN, EITHER. TEN YEARS IS WAY TOO SOON.
SO WE'RE PRETTY TOGETHER IN NOT WANTING ME AROUND.
I TAKE IT THAT COMING HERE WAS YOUR DOING?
I'VE BEEN SEARCHING FOR YOU FOR A LONG TIME NOW.
WE SHARE MANY A MUTUAL GOAL.
DO WE NOW? WHAT MAKES YOU THINK SO?
DID I INVITE YOU?
NO.
NO.
NO, I DIDN'T.
PROSPERO ACTS ALONE.
YOU'RE NOT WITH US UNTIL WE TELL YOU.
I--
I KNOW WHO YOU ARE, KALLIYAN.
I KNOW WHY YOU'RE HERE.
BUT IF YOU THINK YOU'RE WELCOME?

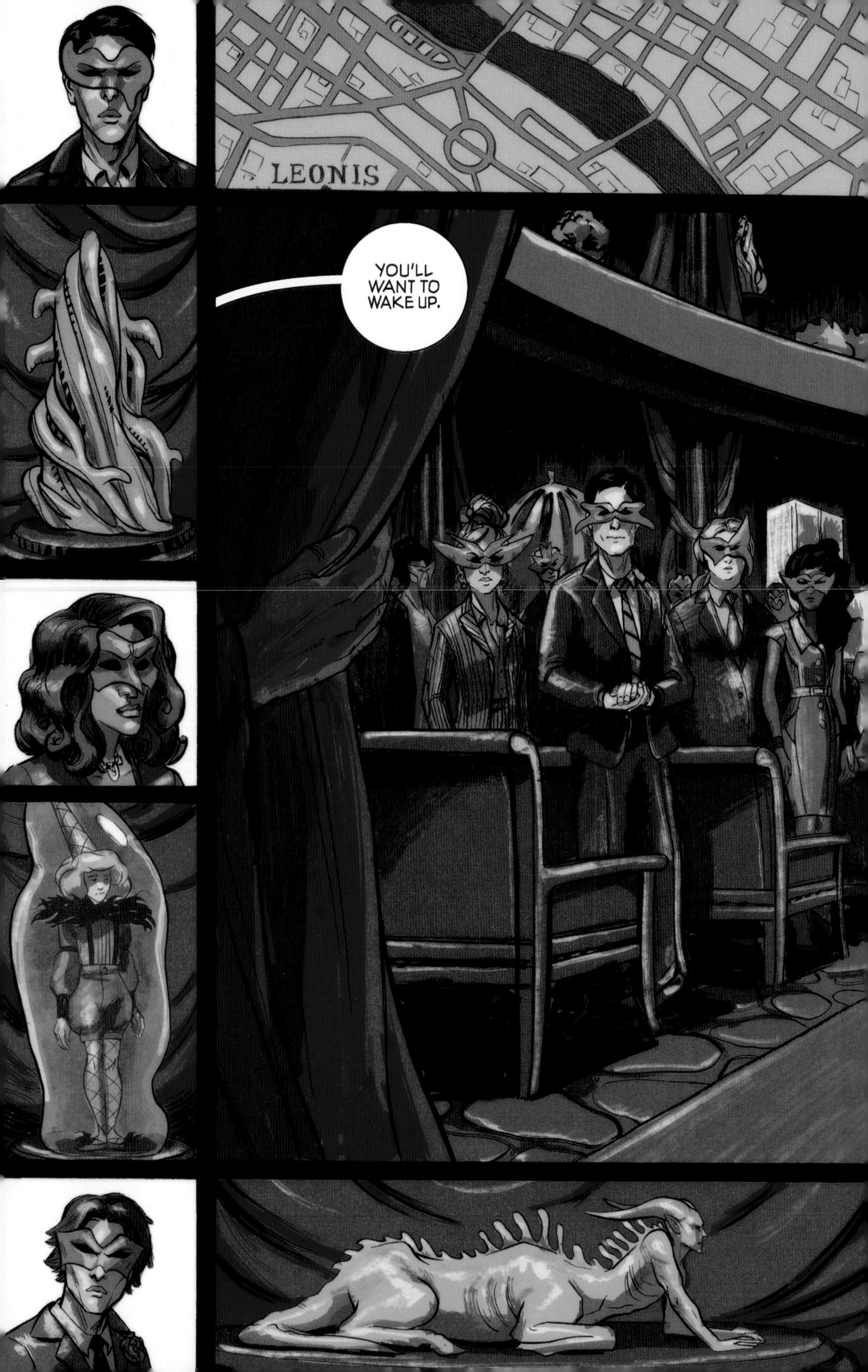
LEONIS
YOU'LL WANT TO WAKE UP.

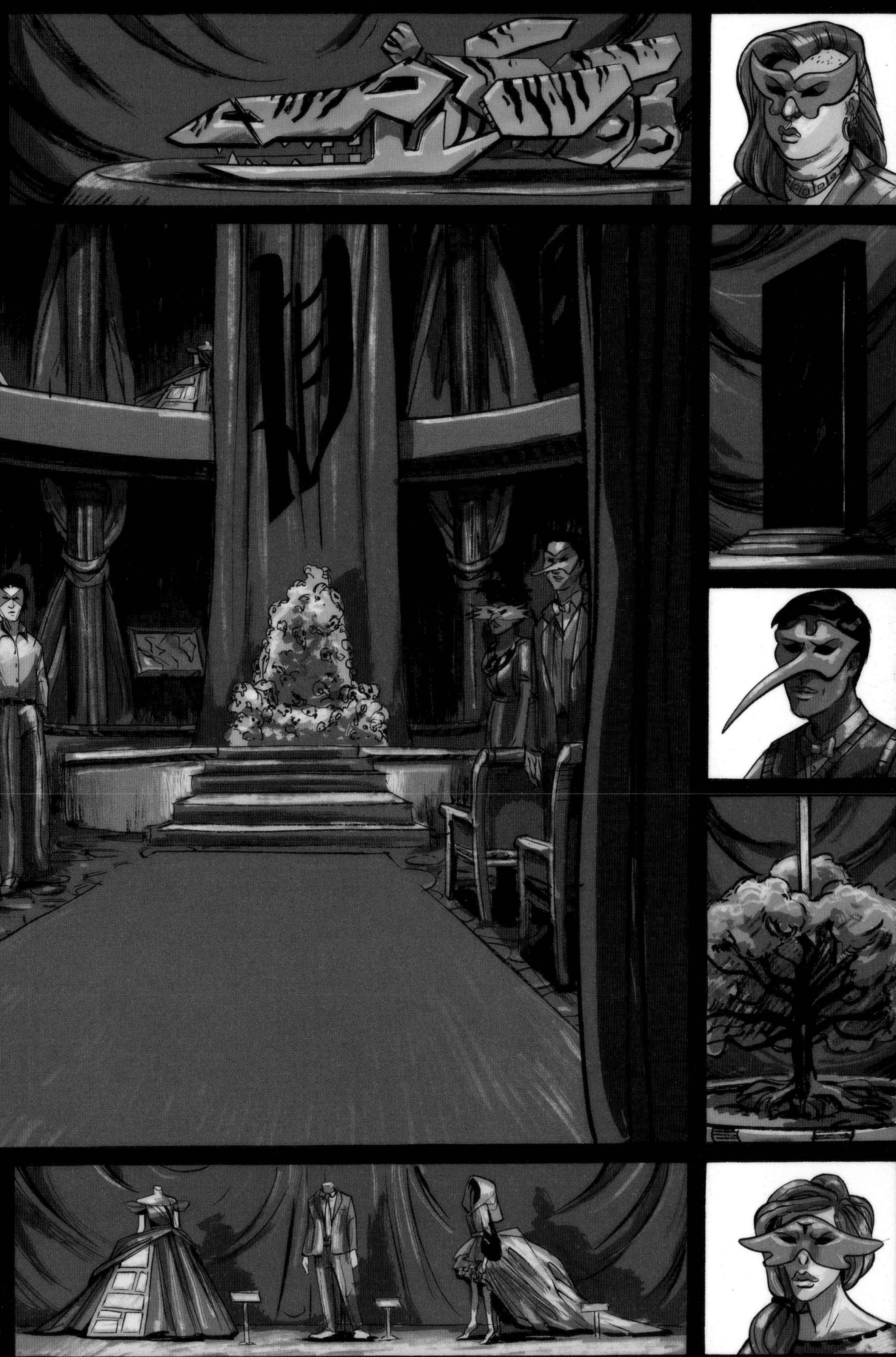

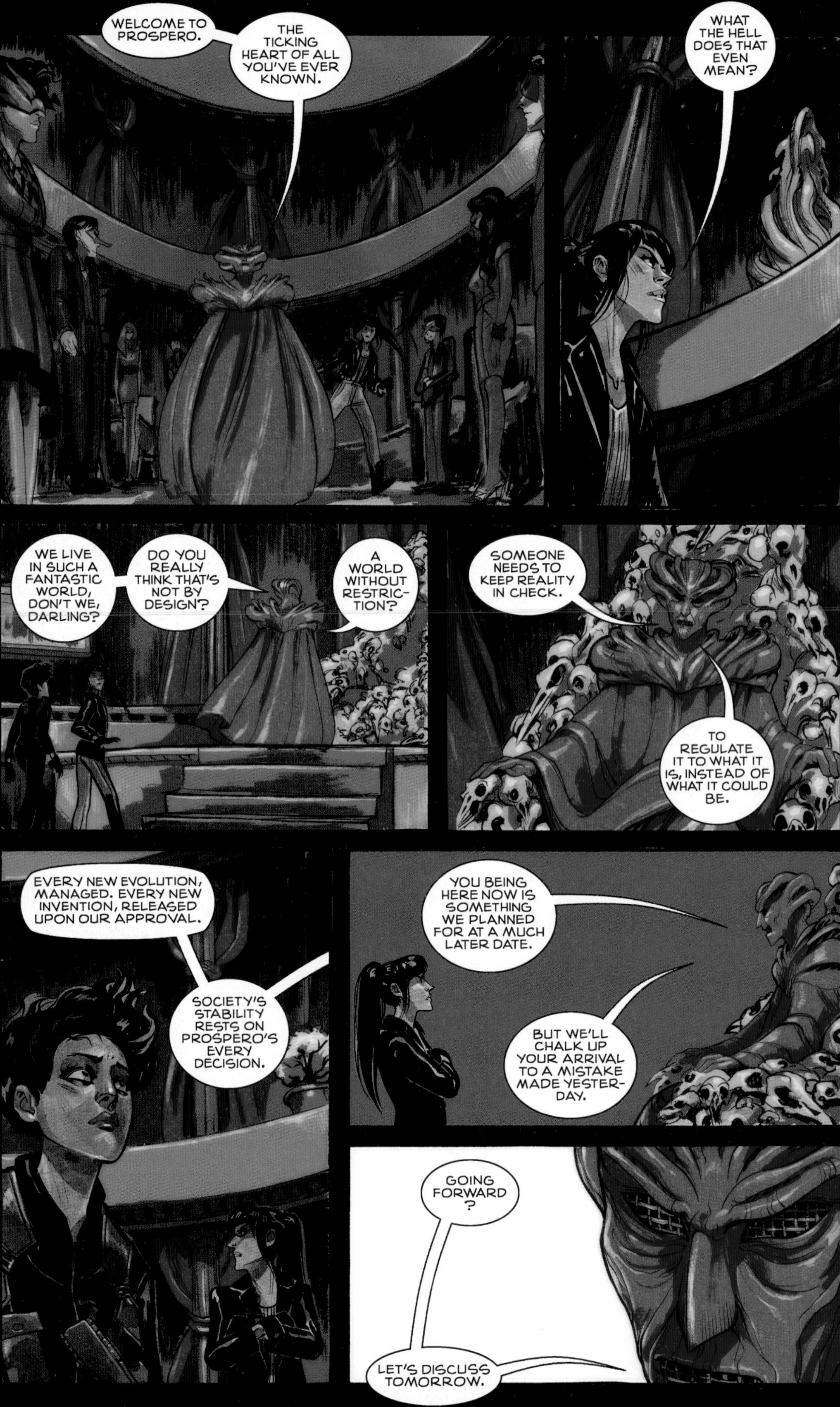

WELCOME TO PROSPERO.
THE TICKING HEART OF ALL YOU'VE EVER KNOWN.
WHAT THE HELL DOES THAT EVEN MEAN?
WE LIVE IN SUCH A FANTASTIC WORLD, DON'T WE, DARLING?
DO YOU REALLY THINK THAT'S NOT BY DESIGN?
A WORLD WITHOUT RESTRICTION?
SOMEONE NEEDS TO KEEP REALITY IN CHECK.
TO REGULATE IT TO WHAT IT IS, INSTEAD OF WHAT IT COULD BE.
EVERY NEW EVOLUTION, MANAGED. EVERY NEW INVENTION, RELEASED UPON OUR APPROVAL.
SOCIETY'S STABILITY RESTS ON PROSPERO'S EVERY DECISION.
YOU BEING HERE NOW IS SOMETHING WE PLANNED FOR AT A MUCH LATER DATE.
BUT WE'LL CHALK UP YOUR ARRIVAL TO A MISTAKE MADE YESTERDAY.
GOING FORWARD?
LET'S DISCUSS TOMORROW.

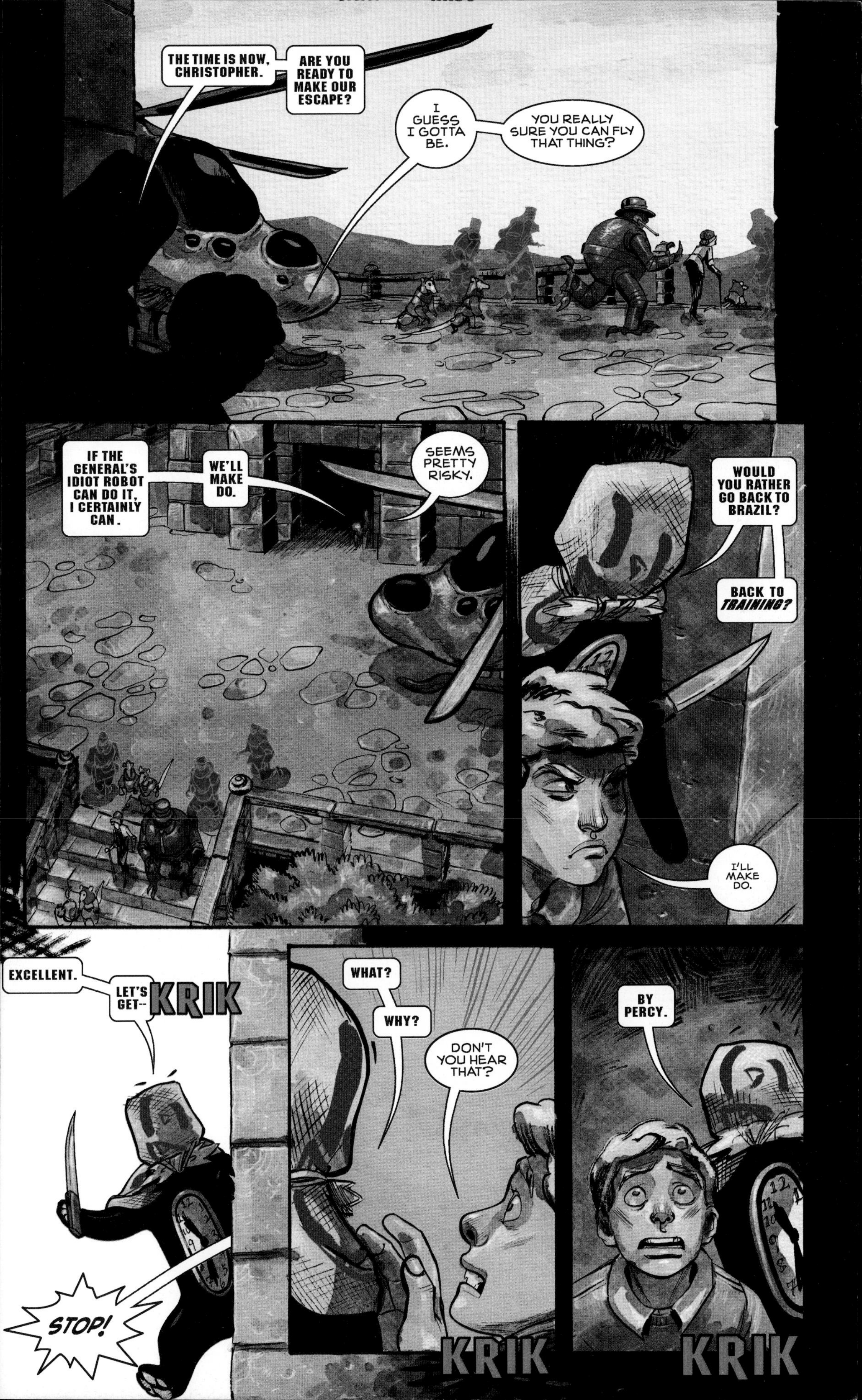
THE TIME IS NOW, CHRISTOPHER.
ARE YOU READY TO MAKE OUR ESCAPE?
I GUESS I GOTTA BE.
YOU REALLY SURE YOU CAN FLY THAT THING?
IF THE GENERAL'S IDIOT ROBOT CAN DO IT, I CERTAINLY CAN.
WE'LL MAKE DO.
SEEMS PRETTY RISKY.
WOULD YOU RATHER GO BACK TO BRAZIL?
BACK TO *TRAINING?*
I'LL MAKE DO.
EXCELLENT.
LET'S GET--
KRIK
STOP!
WHAT?
WHY?
DON'T YOU HEAR THAT?
KRIK
BY PERCY.
KRIK

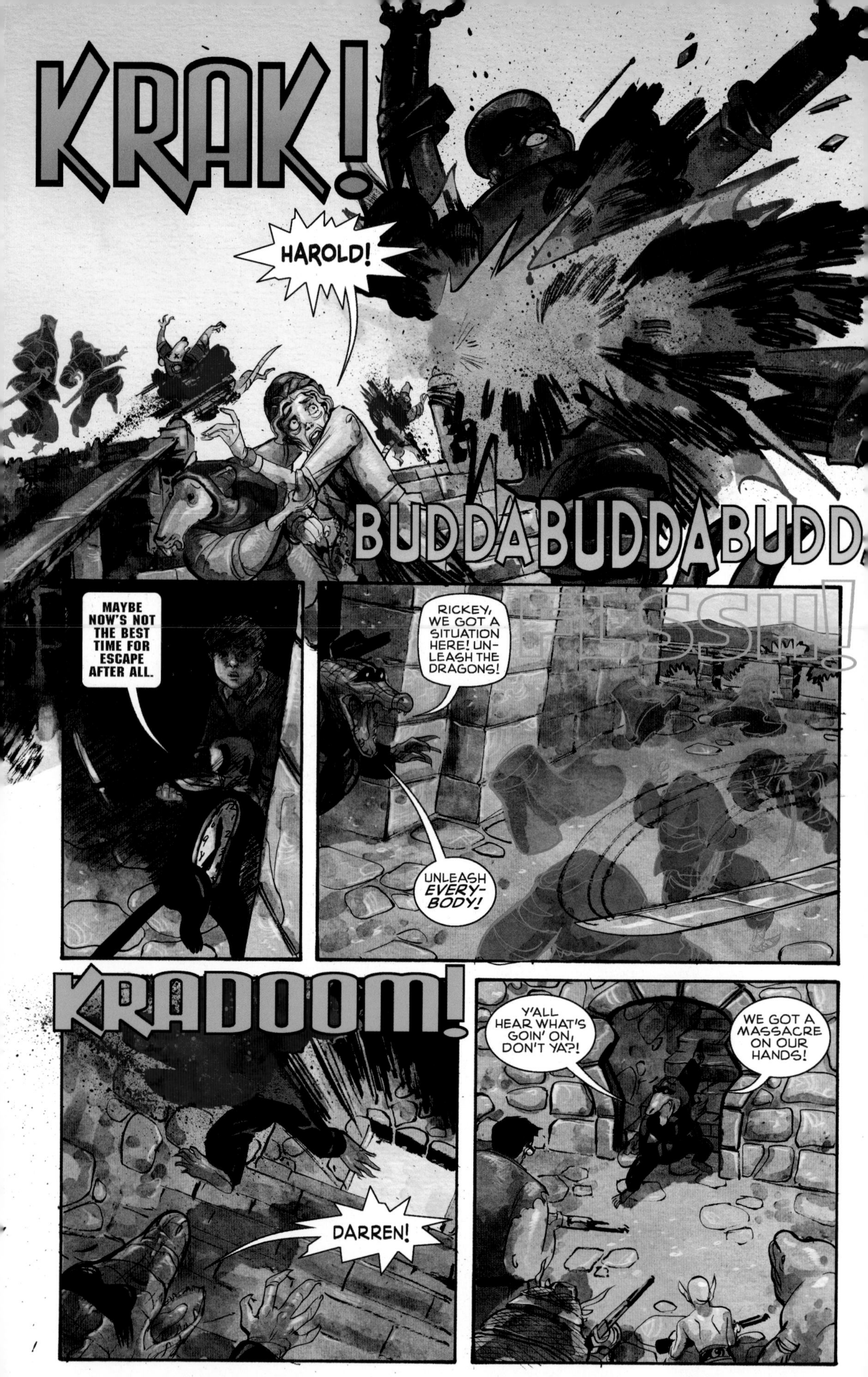

KRAK!
HAROLD!
BUDDABUDDABUDD
MAYBE NOW'S NOT THE BEST TIME FOR ESCAPE AFTER ALL.
RICKEY, WE GOT A SITUATION HERE! UNLEASH THE DRAGONS!
UNLEASH EVERYBODY!
KRADOOM!
DARREN!
Y'ALL HEAR WHAT'S GOIN' ON, DON'T YA?!
WE GOT A MASSACRE ON OUR HANDS!

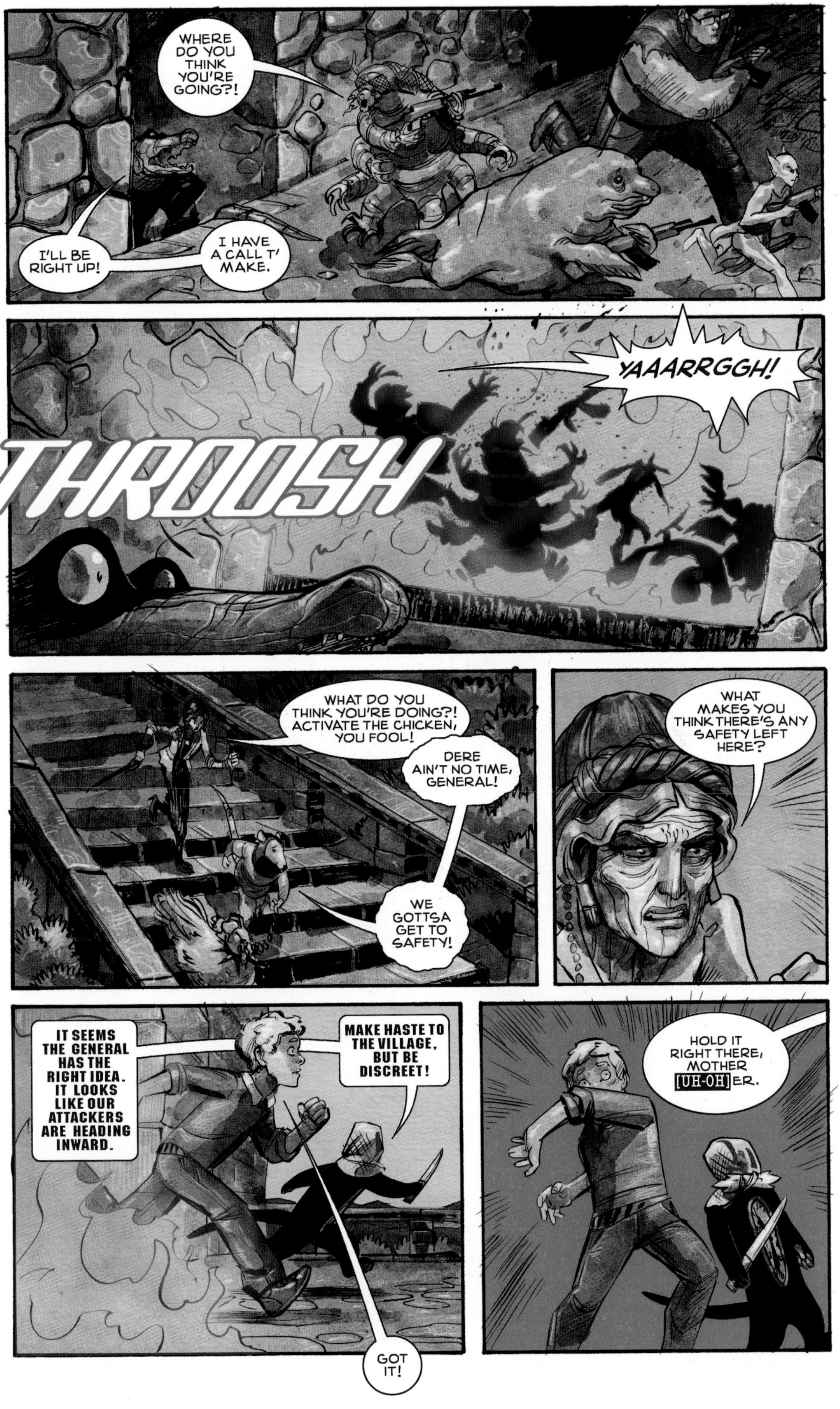
WHERE DO YOU THINK YOU'RE GOING?!
I'LL BE RIGHT UP!
I HAVE A CALL T' MAKE.
THROOSH
YAAARRGGH!
WHAT DO YOU THINK YOU'RE DOING?! ACTIVATE THE CHICKEN, YOU FOOL!
DERE AIN'T NO TIME, GENERAL!
WE GOTTSA GET TO SAFETY!
WHAT MAKES YOU THINK THERE'S ANY SAFETY LEFT HERE?
IT SEEMS THE GENERAL HAS THE RIGHT IDEA. IT LOOKS LIKE OUR ATTACKERS ARE HEADING INWARD.
MAKE HASTE TO THE VILLAGE, BUT BE DISCREET!
GOT IT!
HOLD IT RIGHT THERE, MOTHER [UH-OH]ER.

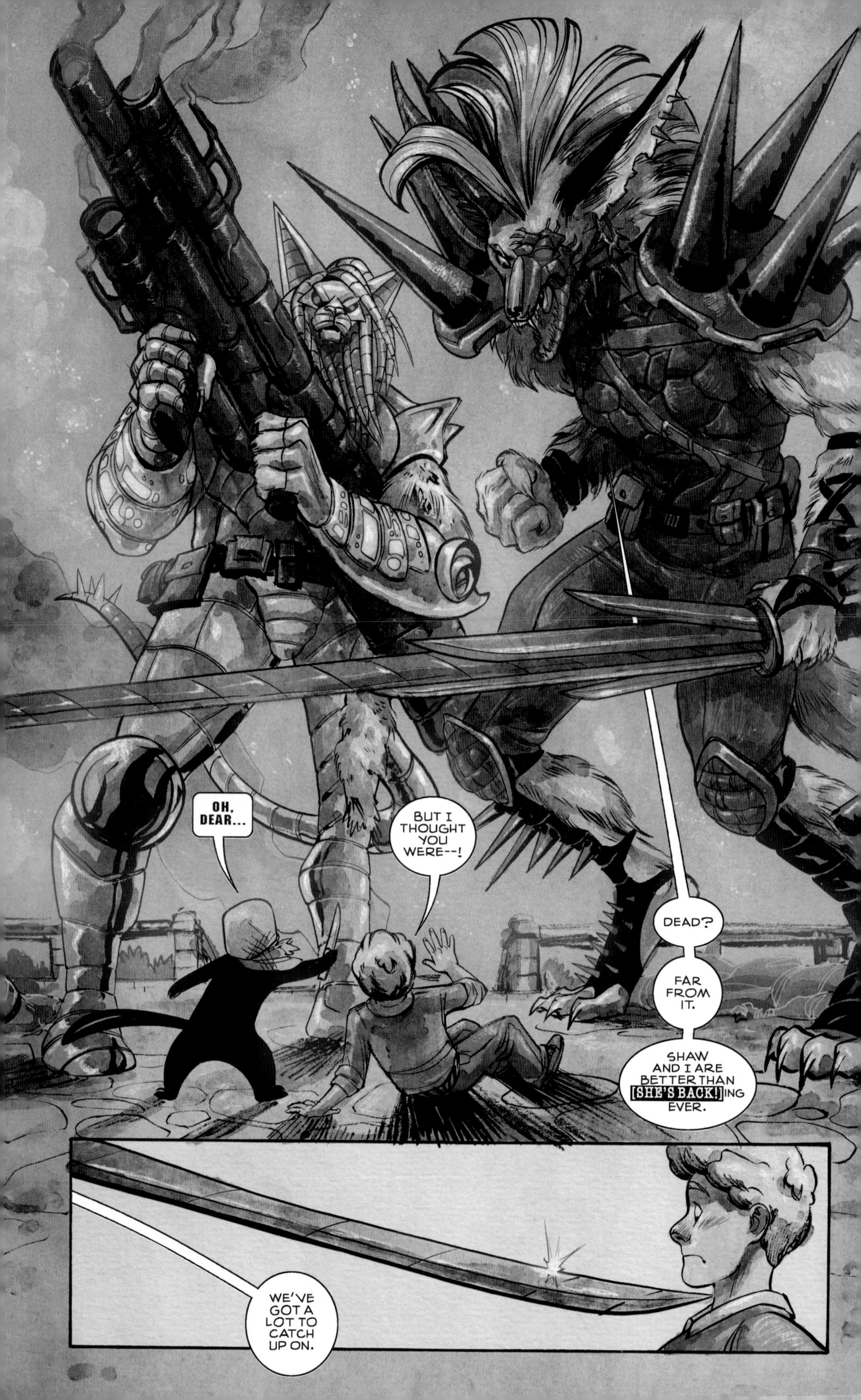
OH, DEAR...
BUT I THOUGHT YOU WERE--!
DEAD?
FAR FROM IT.
SHAW AND I ARE BETTER THAN [SHE'S BACK!]ING EVER.
WE'VE GOT A LOT TO CATCH UP ON.

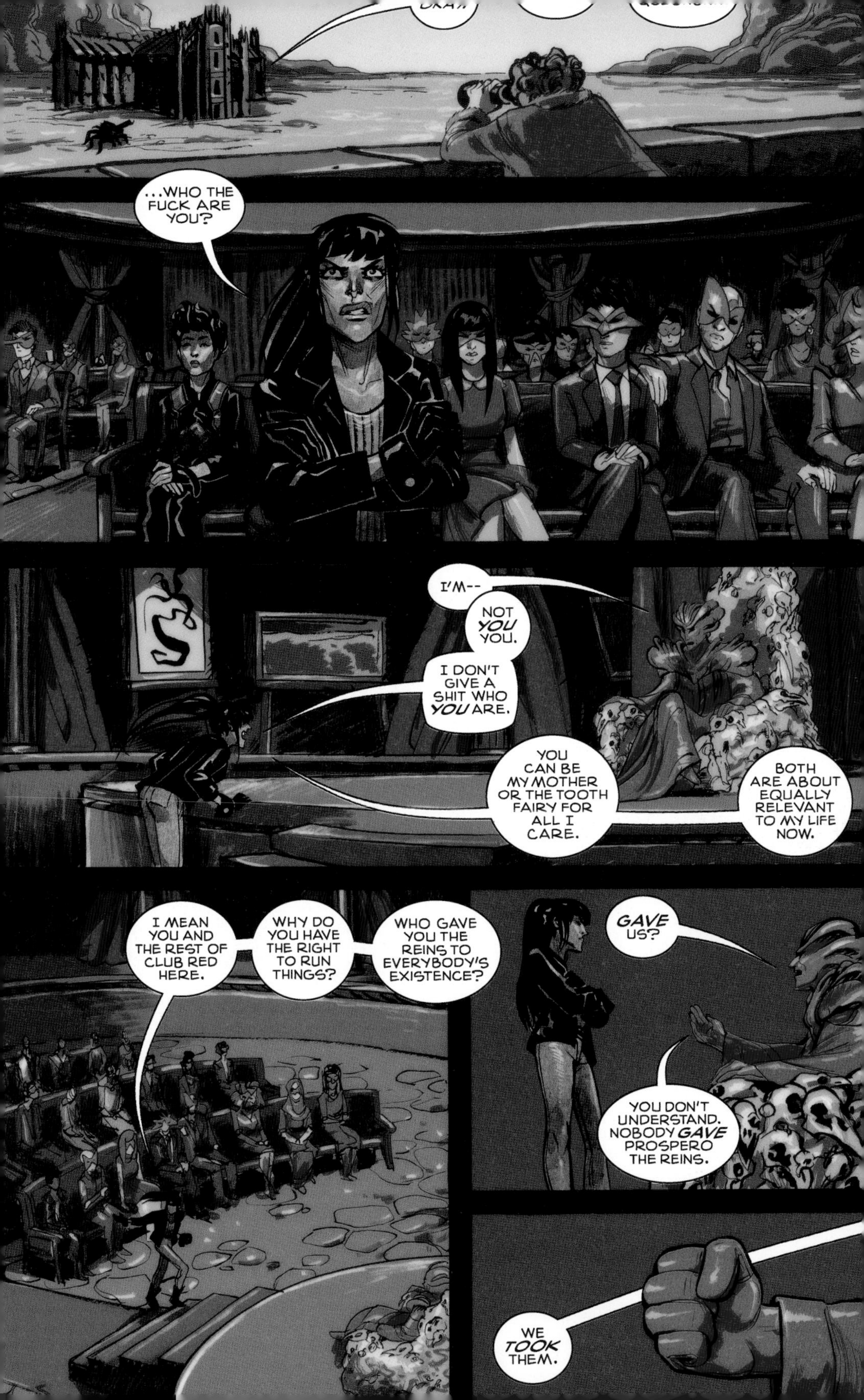

...WHO THE FUCK ARE YOU?
I'M--
NOT *YOU* YOU.
I DON'T GIVE A SHIT WHO *YOU* ARE.
YOU CAN BE MY MOTHER OR THE TOOTH FAIRY FOR ALL I CARE.
BOTH ARE ABOUT EQUALLY RELEVANT TO MY LIFE NOW.
I MEAN YOU AND THE REST OF CLUB RED HERE.
WHY DO YOU HAVE THE RIGHT TO RUN THINGS?
WHO GAVE YOU THE REINS TO EVERYBODY'S EXISTENCE?
GAVE US?
YOU DON'T UNDERSTAND. NOBODY *GAVE* PROSPERO THE REINS.
WE *TOOK* THEM.

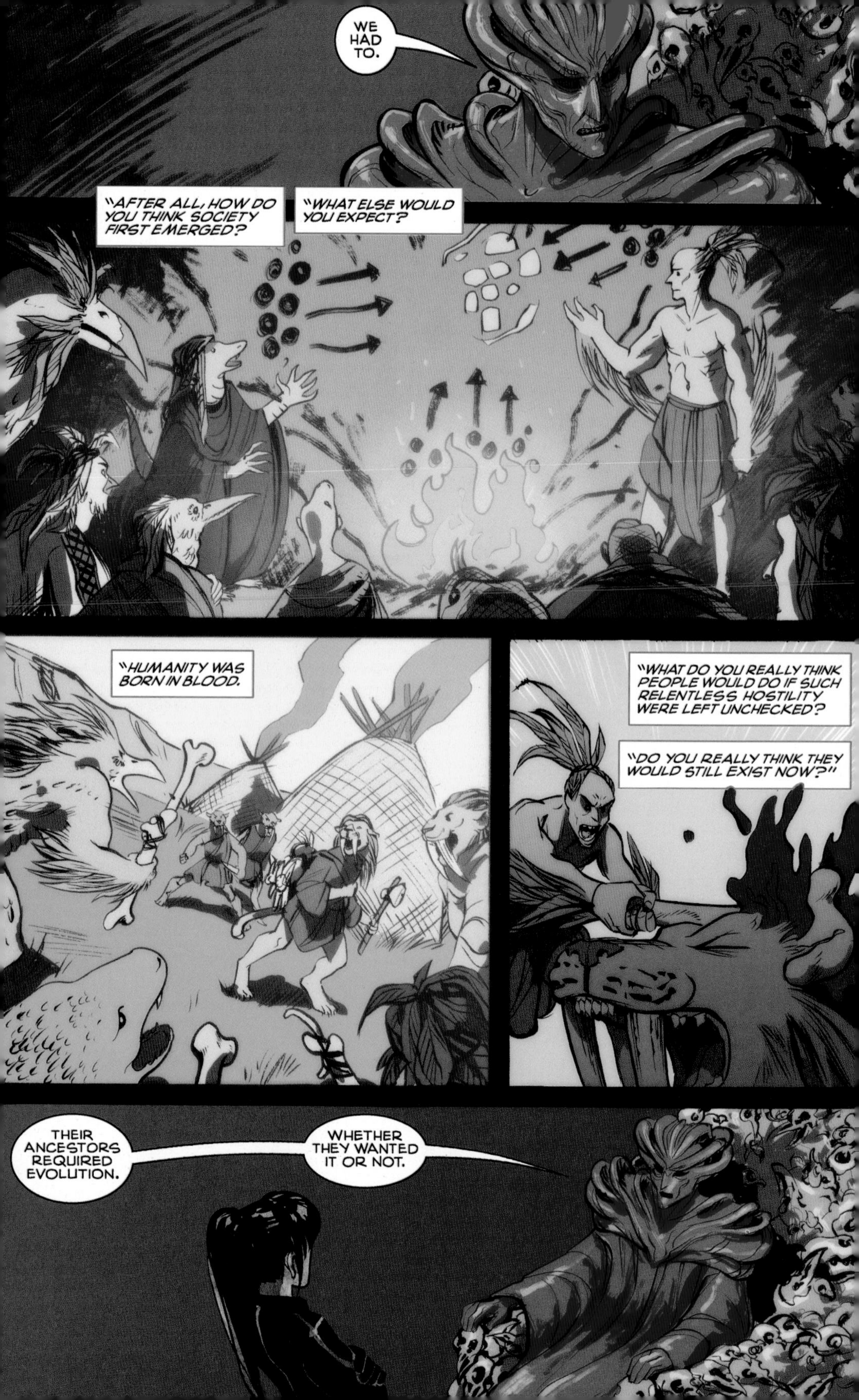
WE HAD TO.
"AFTER ALL, HOW DO YOU THINK SOCIETY FIRST EMERGED?
"WHAT ELSE WOULD YOU EXPECT?
"HUMANITY WAS BORN IN BLOOD.
"WHAT DO YOU REALLY THINK PEOPLE WOULD DO IF SUCH RELENTLESS HOSTILITY WERE LEFT UNCHECKED?
"DO YOU REALLY THINK THEY WOULD STILL EXIST NOW?"
THEIR ANCESTORS REQUIRED EVOLUTION.
WHETHER THEY WANTED IT OR NOT.

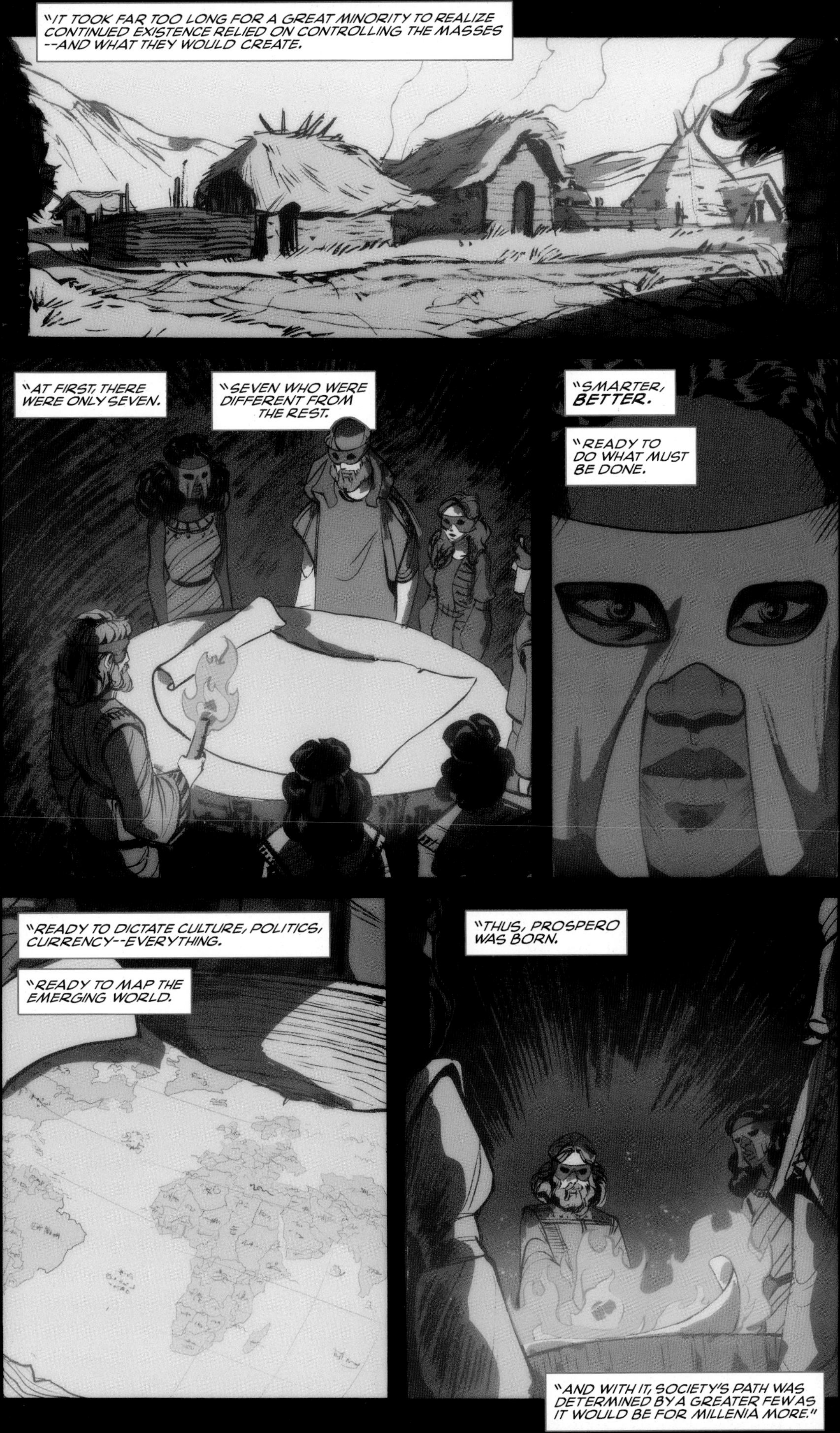
"IT TOOK FAR TOO LONG FOR A GREAT MINORITY TO REALIZE CONTINUED EXISTENCE RELIED ON CONTROLLING THE MASSES --AND WHAT THEY WOULD CREATE.
"AT FIRST, THERE WERE ONLY SEVEN.
"SEVEN WHO WERE DIFFERENT FROM THE REST.
"SMARTER, BETTER.
"READY TO DO WHAT MUST BE DONE.
"READY TO DICTATE CULTURE, POLITICS, CURRENCY--EVERYTHING.
"READY TO MAP THE EMERGING WORLD.
"THUS, PROSPERO WAS BORN.
"AND WITH IT, SOCIETY'S PATH WAS DETERMINED BY A GREATER FEW AS IT WOULD BE FOR MILLENIA MORE."

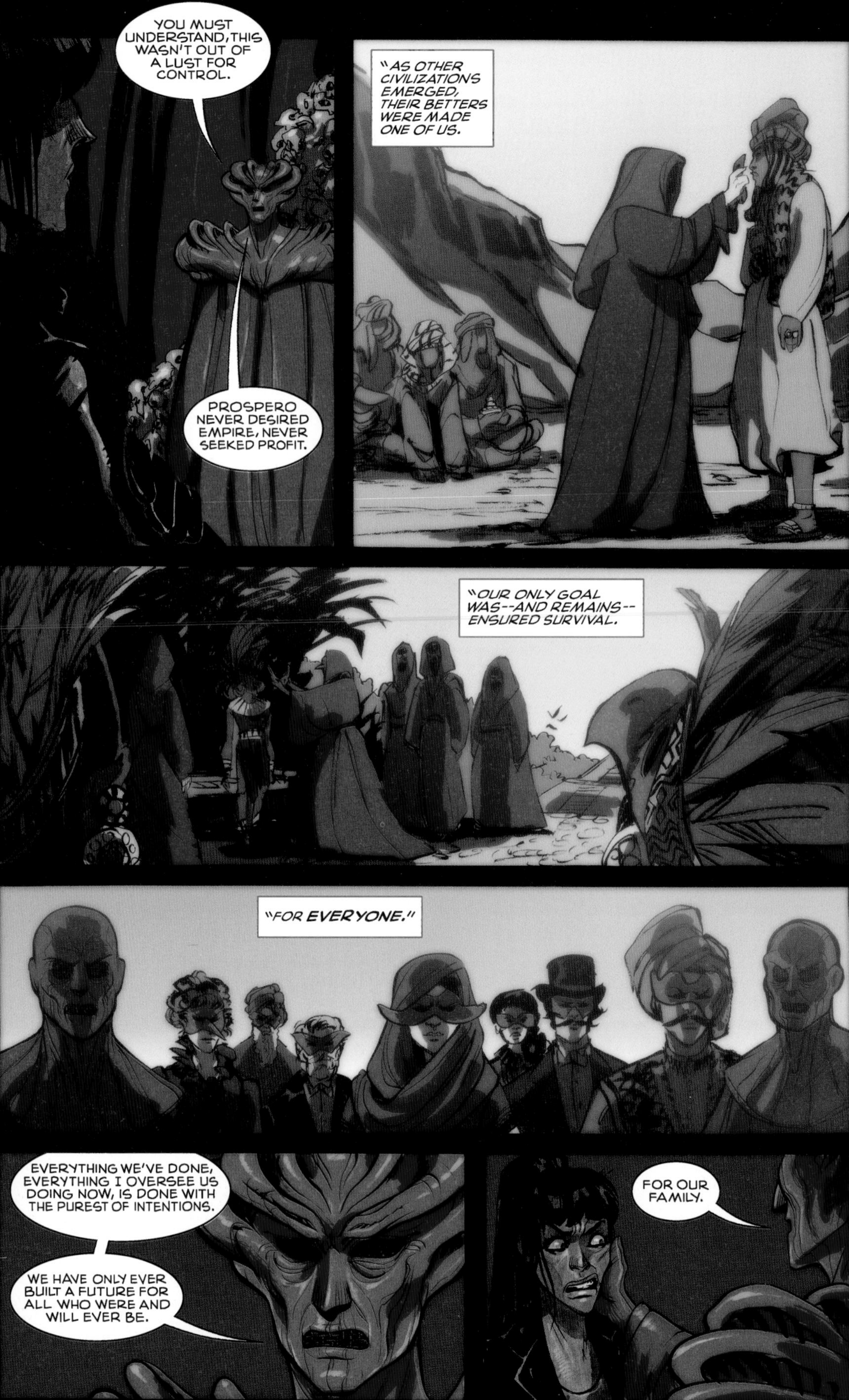
YOU MUST UNDERSTAND, THIS WASN'T OUT OF A LUST FOR CONTROL.
PROSPERO NEVER DESIRED EMPIRE, NEVER SEEKED PROFIT.
"AS OTHER CIVILIZATIONS EMERGED, THEIR BETTERS WERE MADE ONE OF US.
"OUR ONLY GOAL WAS--AND REMAINS--ENSURED SURVIVAL.
"FOR EVERYONE."
EVERYTHING WE'VE DONE, EVERYTHING I OVERSEE US DOING NOW, IS DONE WITH THE PUREST OF INTENTIONS.
WE HAVE ONLY EVER BUILT A FUTURE FOR ALL WHO WERE AND WILL EVER BE.
FOR OUR FAMILY.

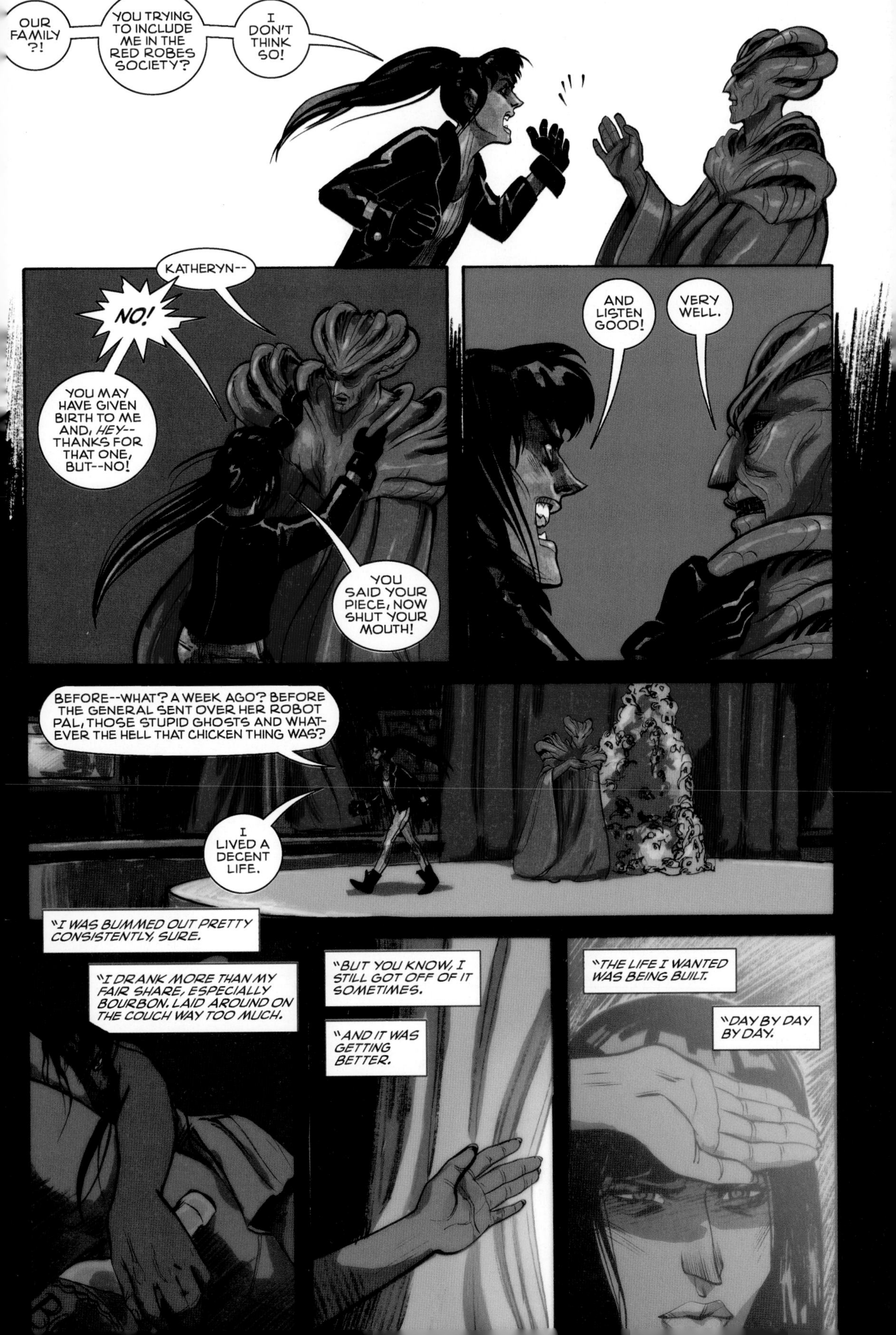
OUR FAMILY ?!
YOU TRYING TO INCLUDE ME IN THE RED ROBES SOCIETY?
I DON'T THINK SO!
KATHERYN--
NO!
YOU MAY HAVE GIVEN BIRTH TO ME AND, HEY-- THANKS FOR THAT ONE, BUT--NO!
YOU SAID YOUR PIECE, NOW SHUT YOUR MOUTH!
AND LISTEN GOOD!
VERY WELL.
BEFORE--WHAT? A WEEK AGO? BEFORE THE GENERAL SENT OVER HER ROBOT PAL, THOSE STUPID GHOSTS AND WHATEVER THE HELL THAT CHICKEN THING WAS?
I LIVED A DECENT LIFE.
"I WAS BUMMED OUT PRETTY CONSISTENTLY, SURE.
"I DRANK MORE THAN MY FAIR SHARE, ESPECIALLY BOURBON. LAID AROUND ON THE COUCH WAY TOO MUCH.
"BUT YOU KNOW, I STILL GOT OFF OF IT SOMETIMES.
"AND IT WAS GETTING BETTER.
"THE LIFE I WANTED WAS BEING BUILT.
"DAY BY DAY BY DAY.

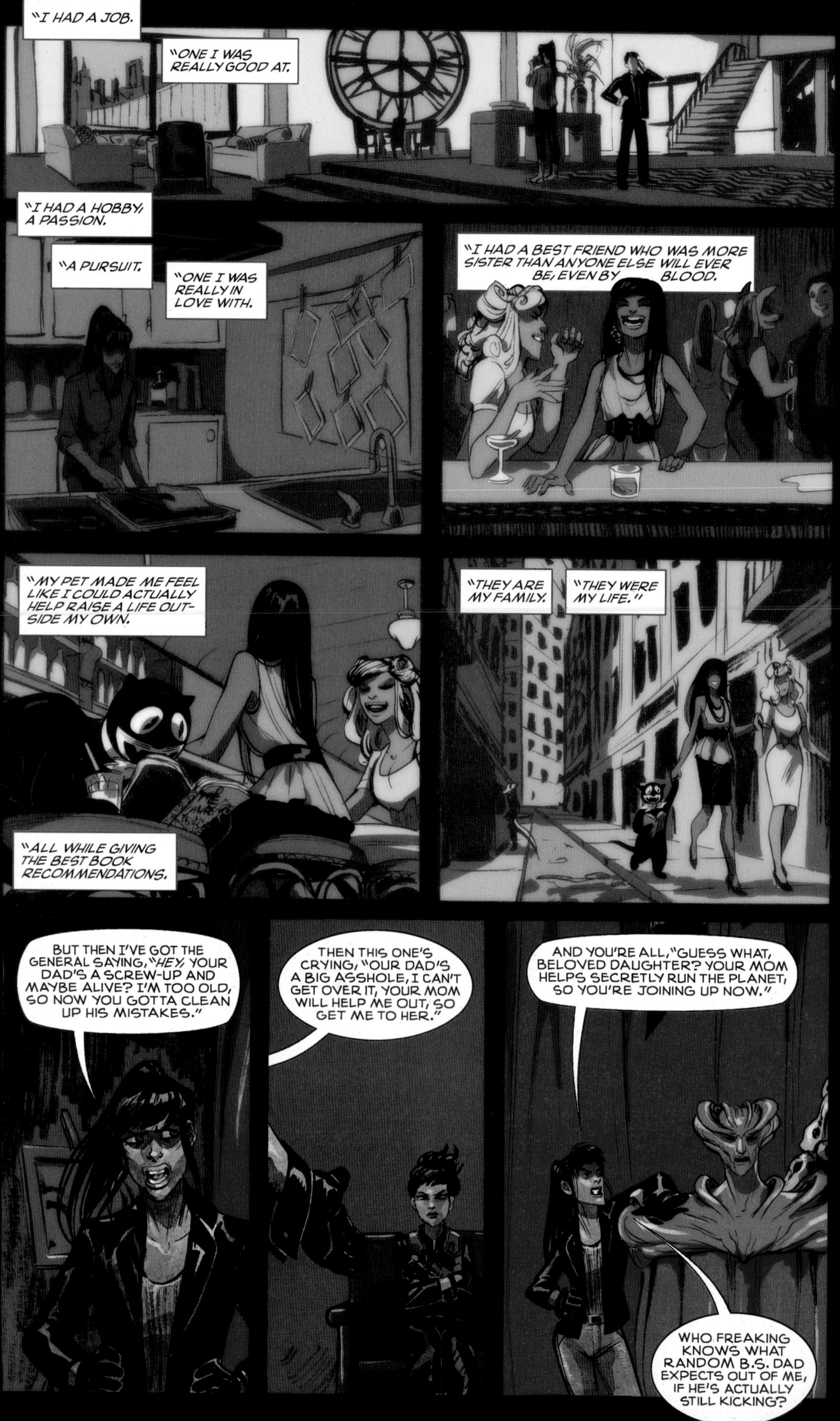
"I HAD A JOB.
"ONE I WAS REALLY GOOD AT.
"I HAD A HOBBY, A PASSION.
"A PURSUIT.
"ONE I WAS REALLY IN LOVE WITH.
"I HAD A BEST FRIEND WHO WAS MORE SISTER THAN ANYONE ELSE WILL EVER BE, EVEN BY BLOOD.
"MY PET MADE ME FEEL LIKE I COULD ACTUALLY HELP RAISE A LIFE OUTSIDE MY OWN.
"ALL WHILE GIVING THE BEST BOOK RECOMMENDATIONS.
"THEY ARE MY FAMILY.
"THEY WERE MY LIFE."
BUT THEN I'VE GOT THE GENERAL SAYING, "HEY, YOUR DAD'S A SCREW-UP AND MAYBE ALIVE? I'M TOO OLD, SO NOW YOU GOTTA CLEAN UP HIS MISTAKES."
THEN THIS ONE'S CRYING, "OUR DAD'S A BIG ASSHOLE, I CAN'T GET OVER IT, YOUR MOM WILL HELP ME OUT, SO GET ME TO HER."
AND YOU'RE ALL, "GUESS WHAT, BELOVED DAUGHTER? YOUR MOM HELPS SECRETLY RUN THE PLANET, SO YOU'RE JOINING UP NOW."
WHO FREAKING KNOWS WHAT RANDOM B.S. DAD EXPECTS OUT OF ME, IF HE'S ACTUALLY STILL KICKING?

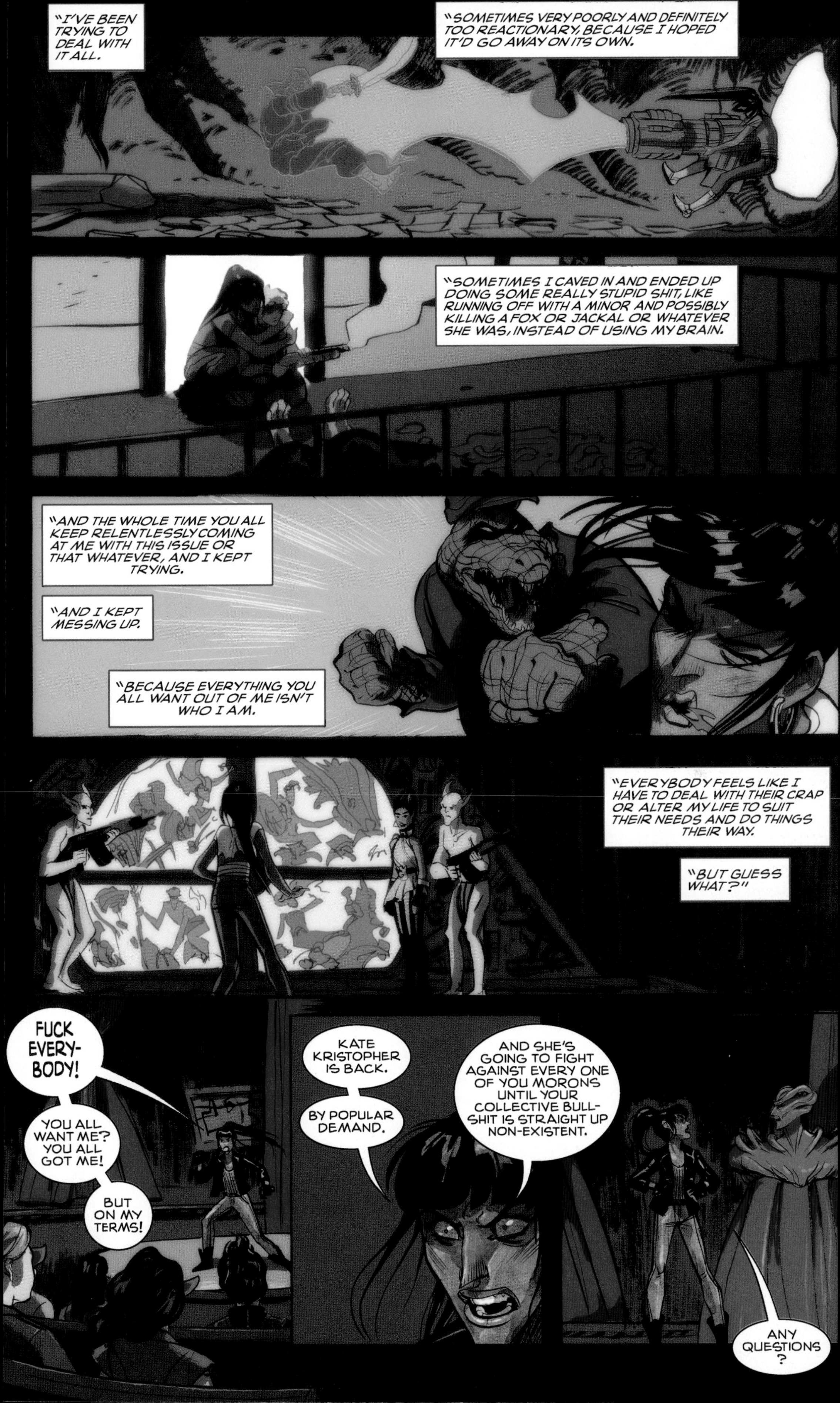
"I'VE BEEN TRYING TO DEAL WITH IT ALL.
"SOMETIMES VERY POORLY AND DEFINITELY TOO REACTIONARY, BECAUSE I HOPED IT'D GO AWAY ON ITS OWN.
"SOMETIMES I CAVED IN AND ENDED UP DOING SOME REALLY STUPID SHIT, LIKE RUNNING OFF WITH A MINOR AND POSSIBLY KILLING A FOX OR JACKAL OR WHATEVER SHE WAS, INSTEAD OF USING MY BRAIN.
"AND THE WHOLE TIME YOU ALL KEEP RELENTLESSLY COMING AT ME WITH THIS ISSUE OR THAT WHATEVER, AND I KEPT TRYING.
"AND I KEPT MESSING UP.
"BECAUSE EVERYTHING YOU ALL WANT OUT OF ME ISN'T WHO I AM.
"EVERYBODY FEELS LIKE I HAVE TO DEAL WITH THEIR CRAP OR ALTER MY LIFE TO SUIT THEIR NEEDS AND DO THINGS THEIR WAY.
"BUT GUESS WHAT?"
FUCK EVERY-BODY!
YOU ALL WANT ME? YOU ALL GOT ME!
BUT ON MY TERMS!
KATE KRISTOPHER IS BACK.
BY POPULAR DEMAND.
AND SHE'S GOING TO FIGHT AGAINST EVERY ONE OF YOU MORONS UNTIL YOUR COLLECTIVE BULL-SHIT IS STRAIGHT UP NON-EXISTENT.
ANY QUESTIONS?

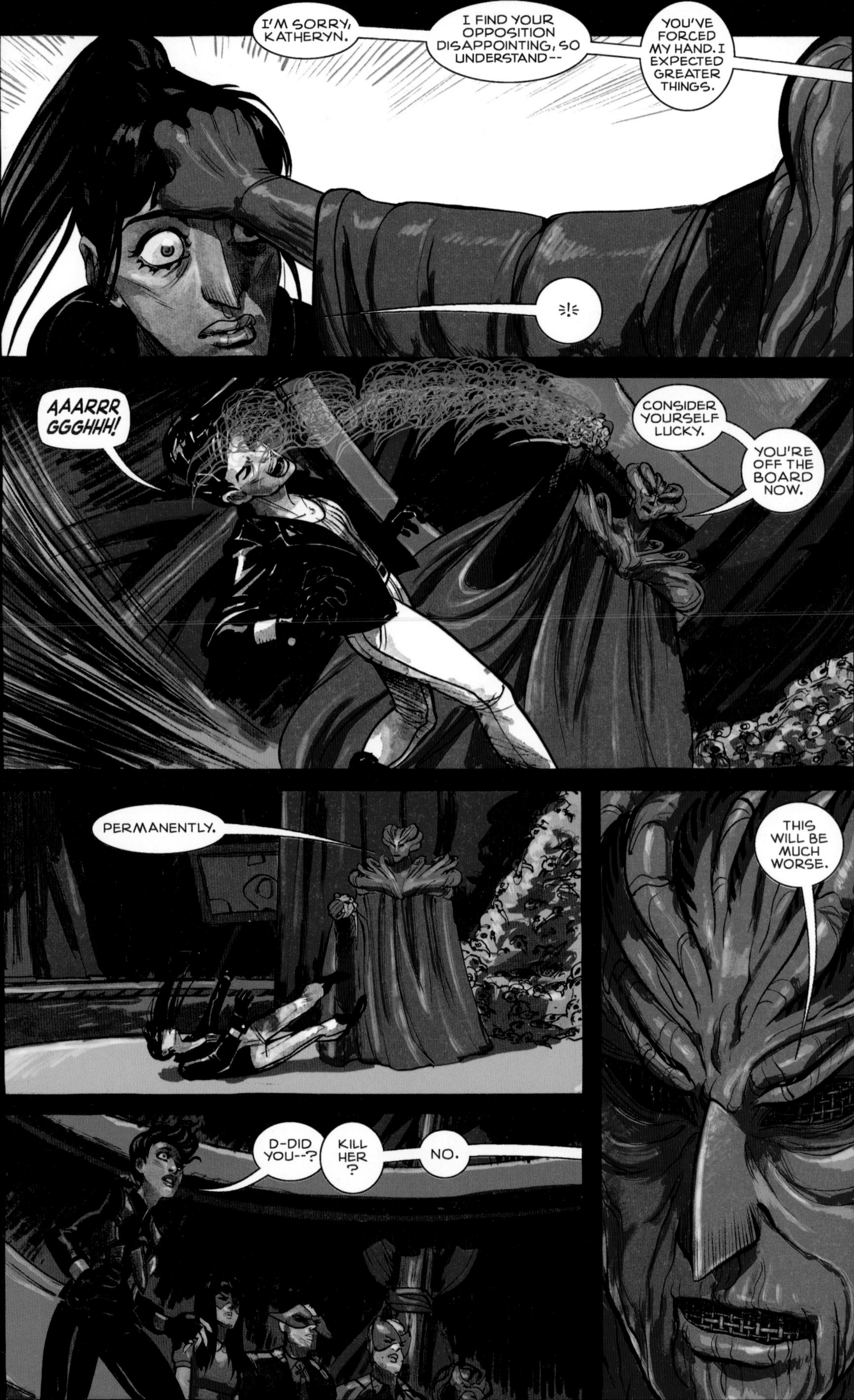
I'M SORRY, KATHERYN.
I FIND YOUR OPPOSITION DISAPPOINTING, SO UNDERSTAND--
YOU'VE FORCED MY HAND. I EXPECTED GREATER THINGS.
!
AAARRR GGGHHH!
CONSIDER YOURSELF LUCKY.
YOU'RE OFF THE BOARD NOW.
PERMANENTLY.
THIS WILL BE MUCH WORSE.
D-DID YOU--?
KILL HER?
NO.

"I HAD SUCH GRAND PLANS FOR HER.
"WE COULD'VE BUILT TOMORROW TOGETHER.
"BUT I KNOW WHEN IT'S TIME TO MOVE ON.
"TO LET GO.
"TO SAY THE HARDEST THING...

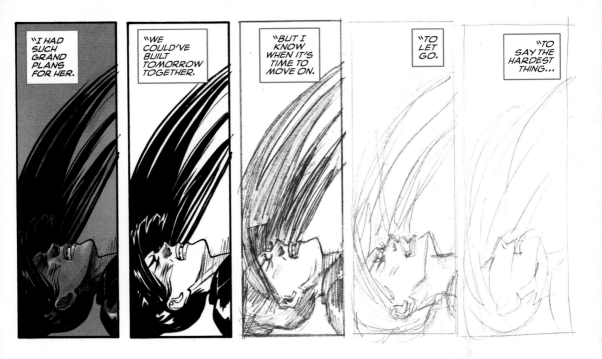

"GOODBYE."

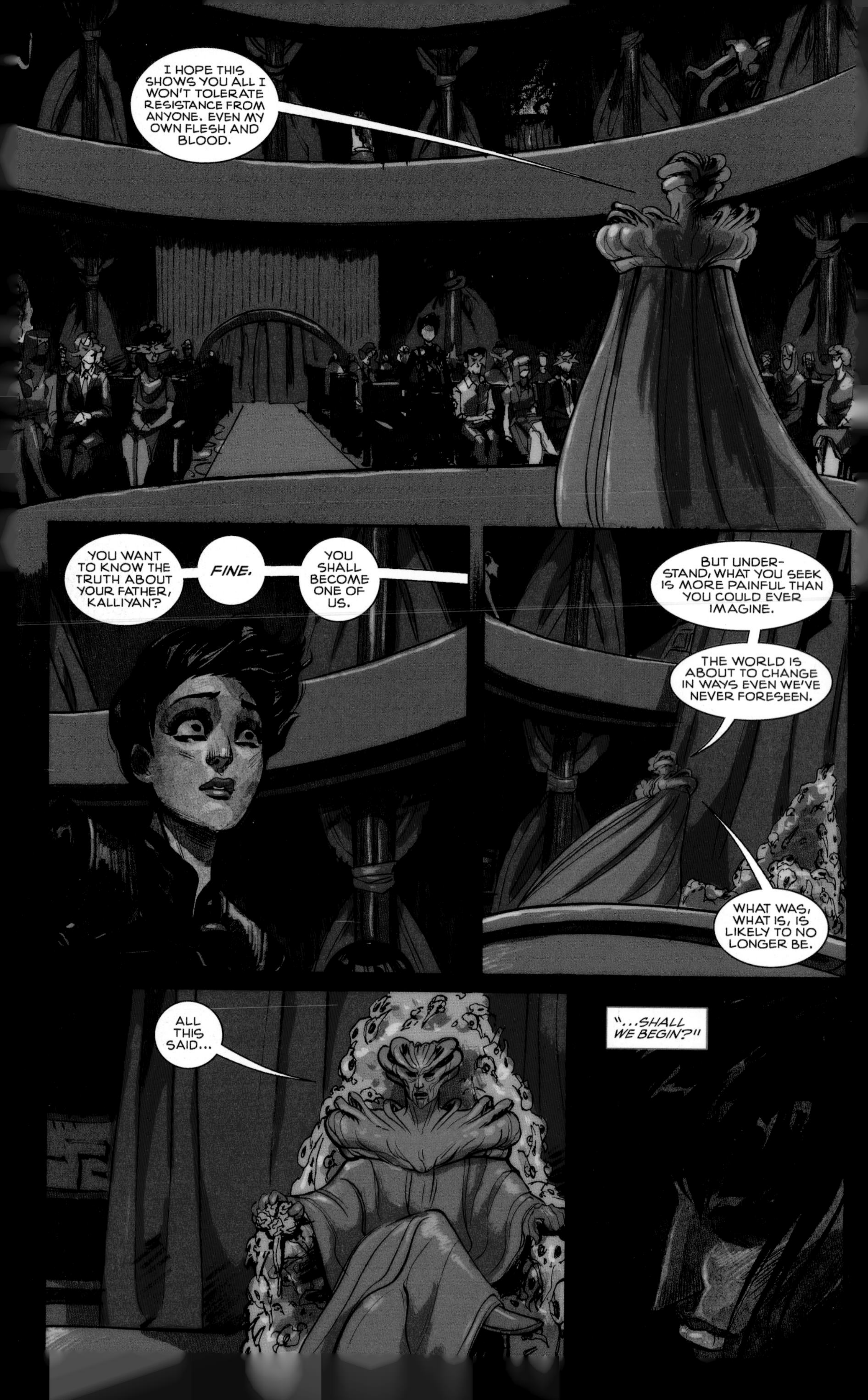
I HOPE THIS SHOWS YOU ALL I WON'T TOLERATE RESISTANCE FROM ANYONE. EVEN MY OWN FLESH AND BLOOD.
YOU WANT TO KNOW THE TRUTH ABOUT YOUR FATHER, KALLIYAN?
FINE.
YOU SHALL BECOME ONE OF US.
BUT UNDER-STAND, WHAT YOU SEEK IS MORE PAINFUL THAN YOU COULD EVER IMAGINE.
THE WORLD IS ABOUT TO CHANGE IN WAYS EVEN WE'VE NEVER FORESEEN.
WHAT WAS, WHAT IS, IS LIKELY TO NO LONGER BE.
ALL THIS SAID...
"...SHALL WE BEGIN?"

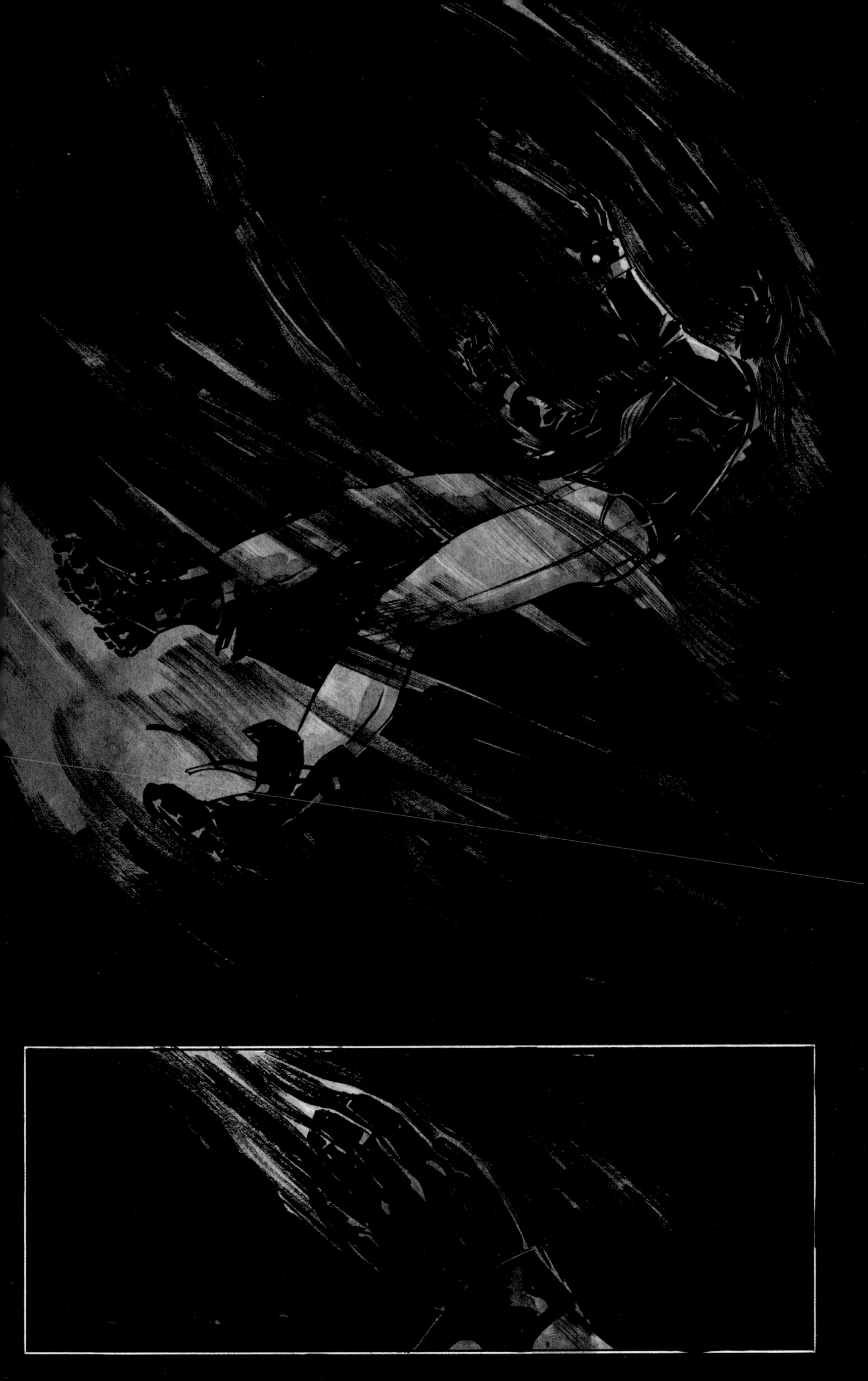

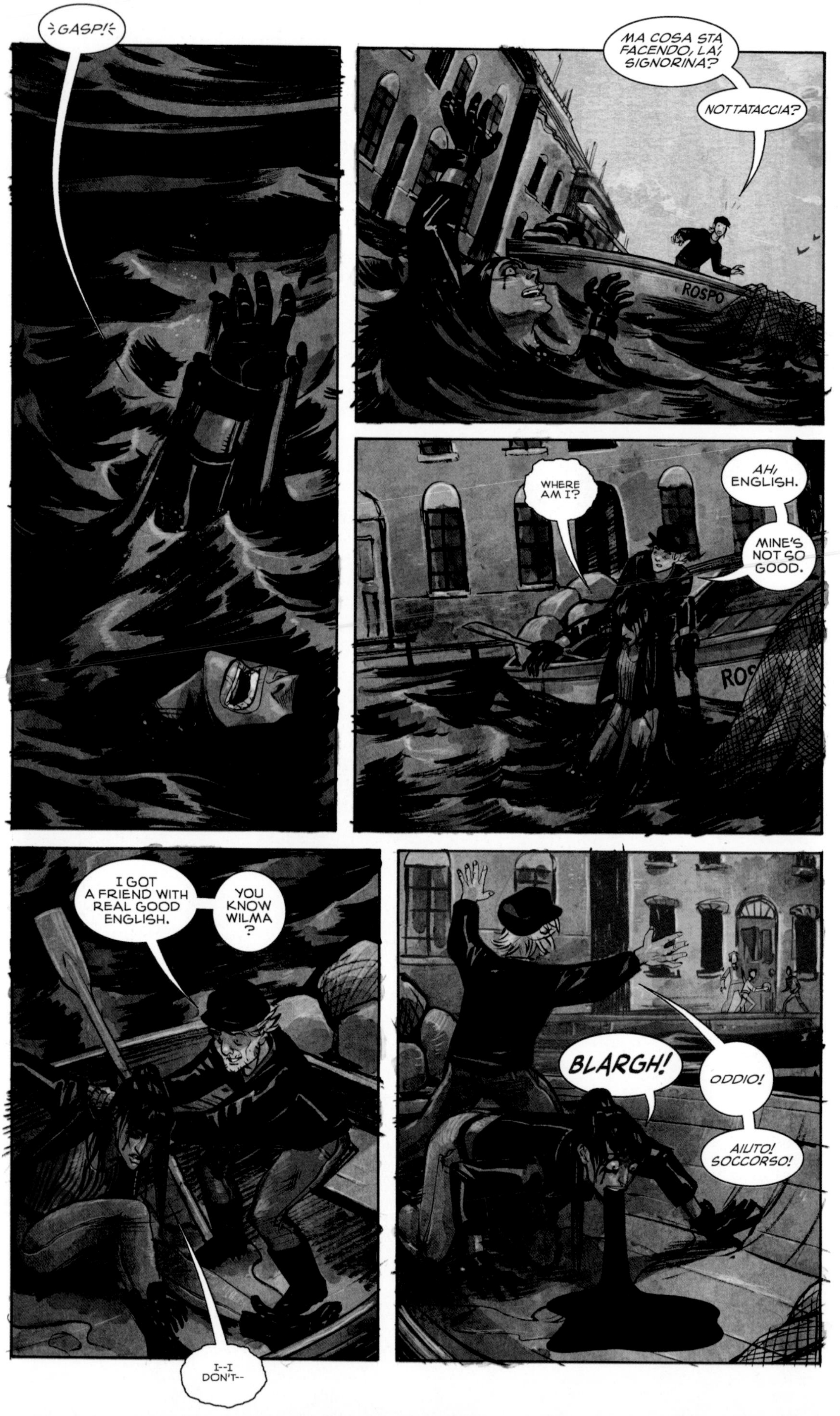
GASP!
MA COSA STA FACENDO, LA, SIGNORINA?
NOTTATACCIA?
ROSPO
WHERE AM I?
AH, ENGLISH.
MINE'S NOT SO GOOD.
ROSPO
I GOT A FRIEND WITH REAL GOOD ENGLISH.
YOU KNOW WILMA?
I--I DON'T--
BLARGH!
ODDIO!
AIUTO! SOCCORSO!

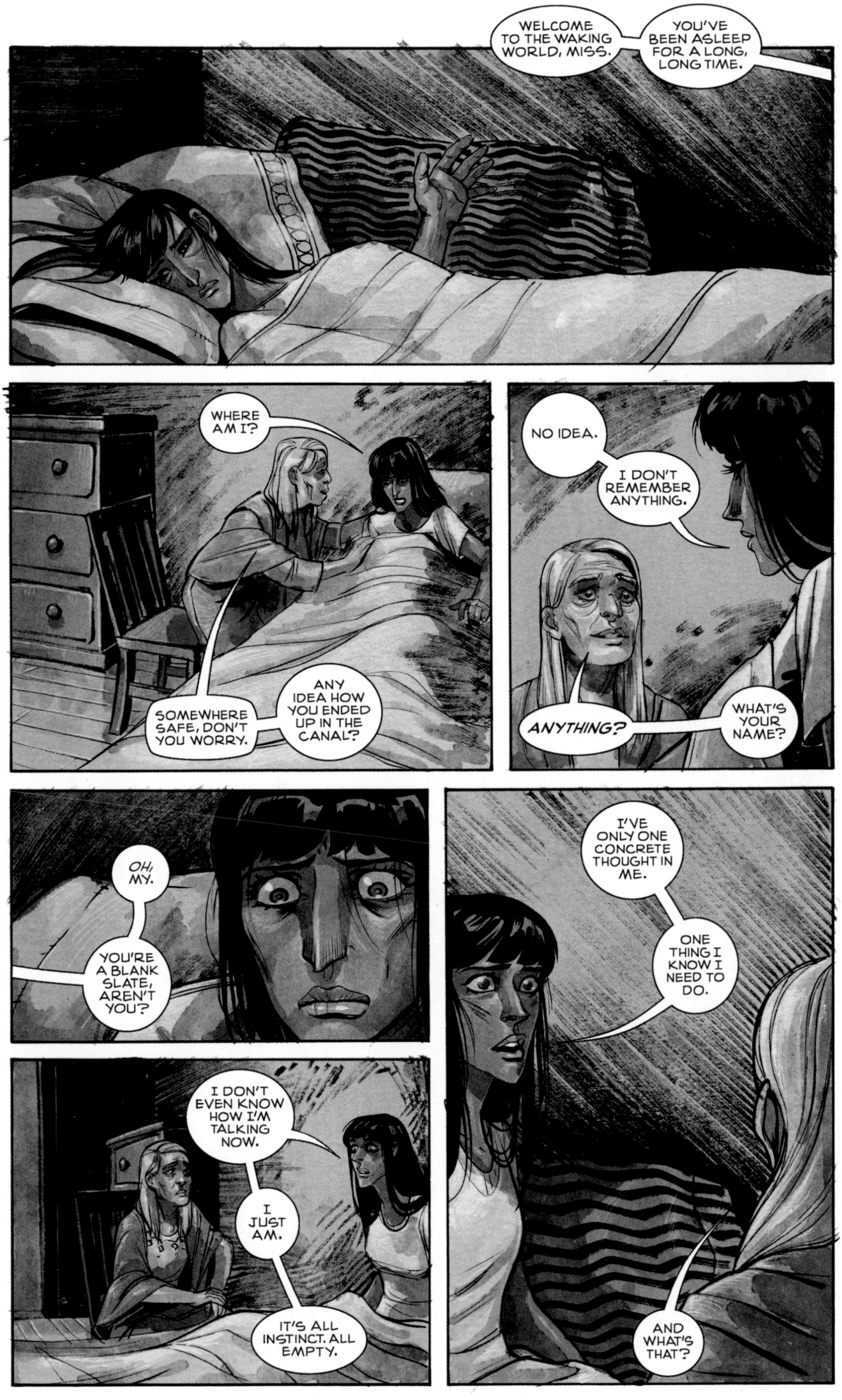
WELCOME TO THE WAKING WORLD, MISS.
YOU'VE BEEN ASLEEP FOR A LONG, LONG TIME.
WHERE AM I?
SOMEWHERE SAFE, DON'T YOU WORRY.
ANY IDEA HOW YOU ENDED UP IN THE CANAL?
NO IDEA.
I DON'T REMEMBER ANYTHING.
ANYTHING?
WHAT'S YOUR NAME?
OH, MY.
YOU'RE A BLANK SLATE, AREN'T YOU?
I DON'T EVEN KNOW HOW I'M TALKING NOW.
I JUST AM.
IT'S ALL INSTINCT. ALL EMPTY.
I'VE ONLY ONE CONCRETE THOUGHT IN ME.
ONE THING I KNOW I NEED TO DO.
AND WHAT'S THAT?

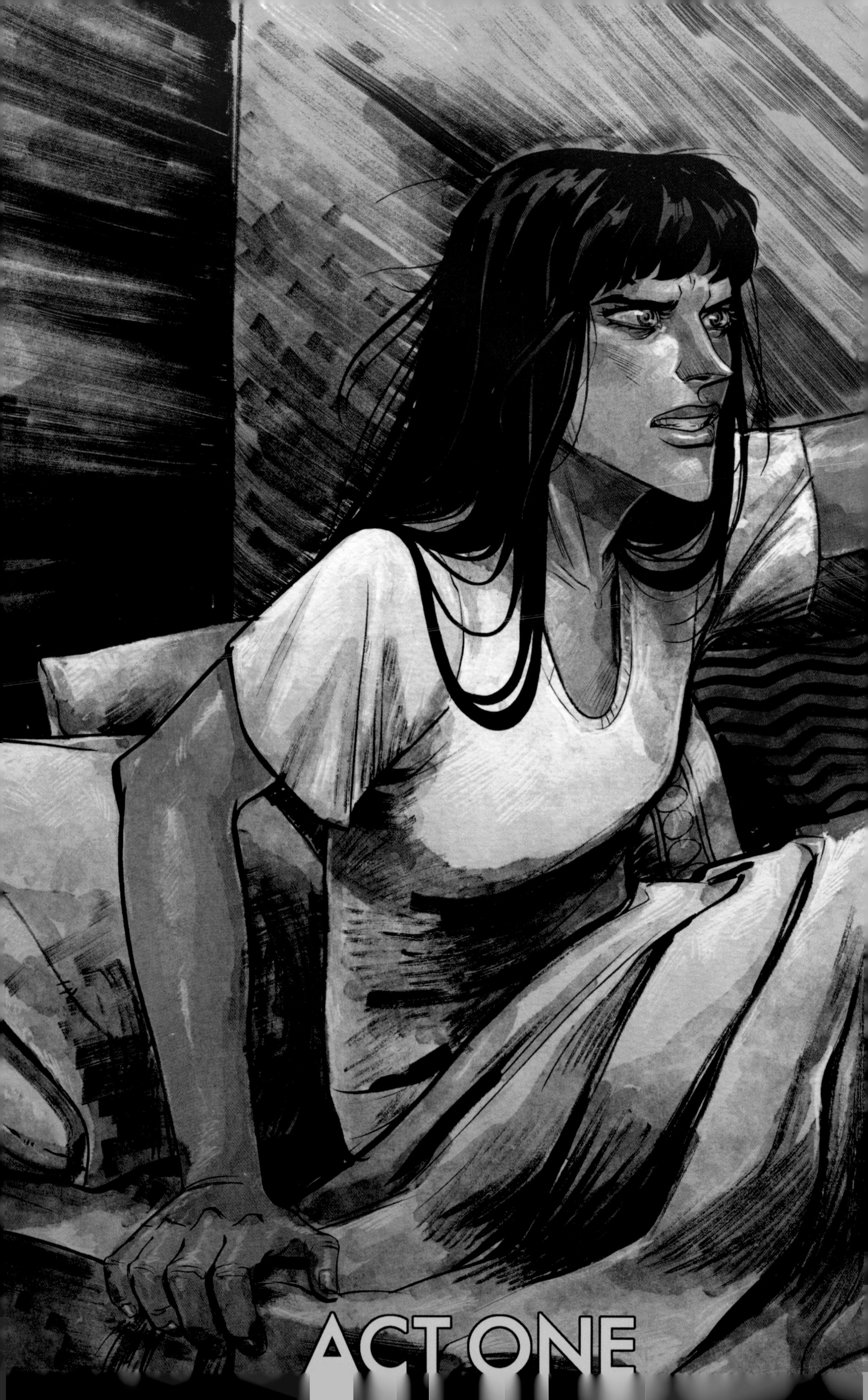
ACT ONE

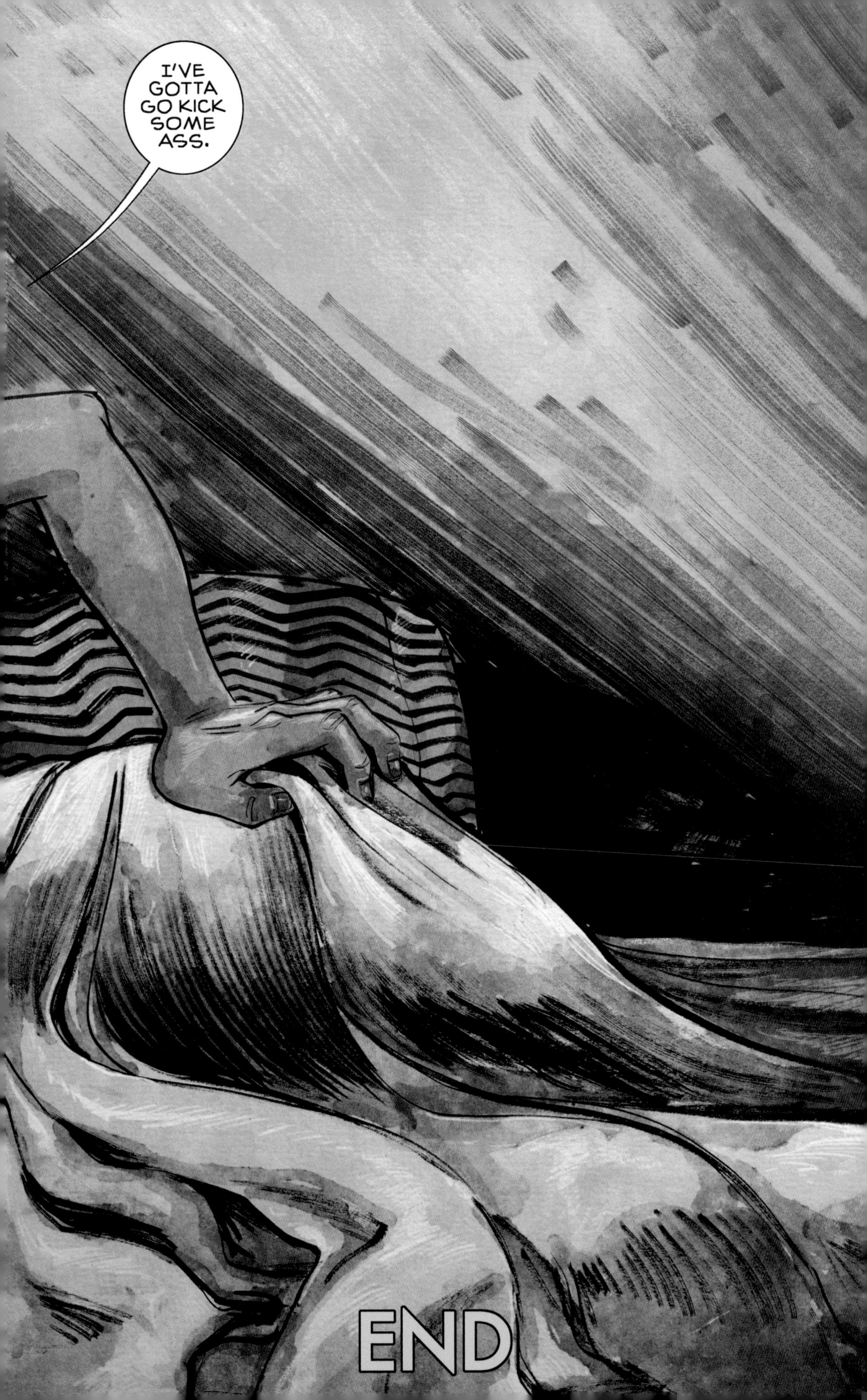
I'VE GOTTA GO KICK SOME ASS.
END

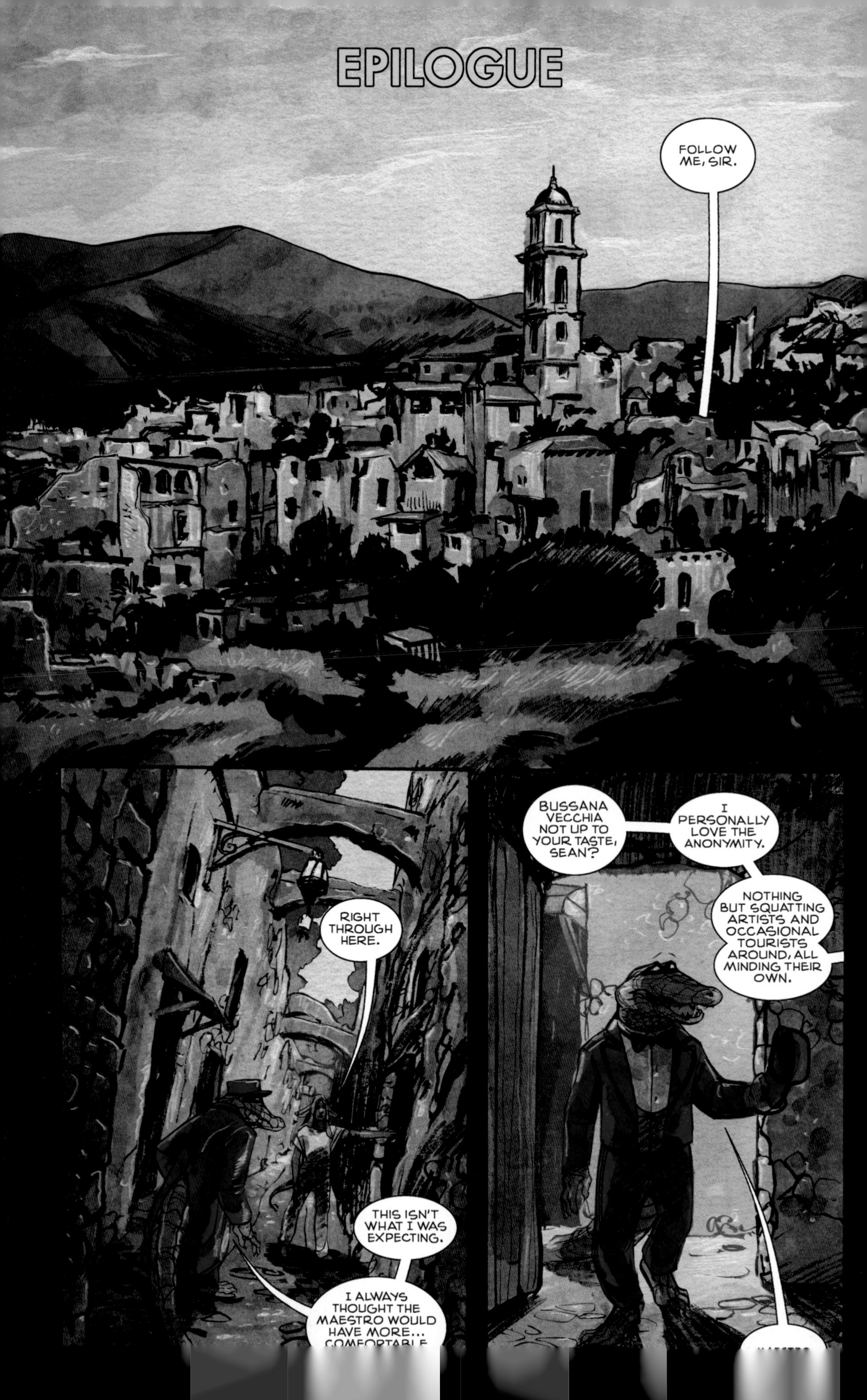
EPILOGUE
FOLLOW ME, SIR.
RIGHT THROUGH HERE.
THIS ISN'T WHAT I WAS EXPECTING.
I ALWAYS THOUGHT THE MAESTRO WOULD HAVE MORE...
BUSSANA VECCHIA NOT UP TO YOUR TASTE, SEAN?
I PERSONALLY LOVE THE ANONYMITY.
NOTHING BUT SQUATTING ARTISTS AND OCCASIONAL TOURISTS AROUND, ALL MINDING THEIR OWN.

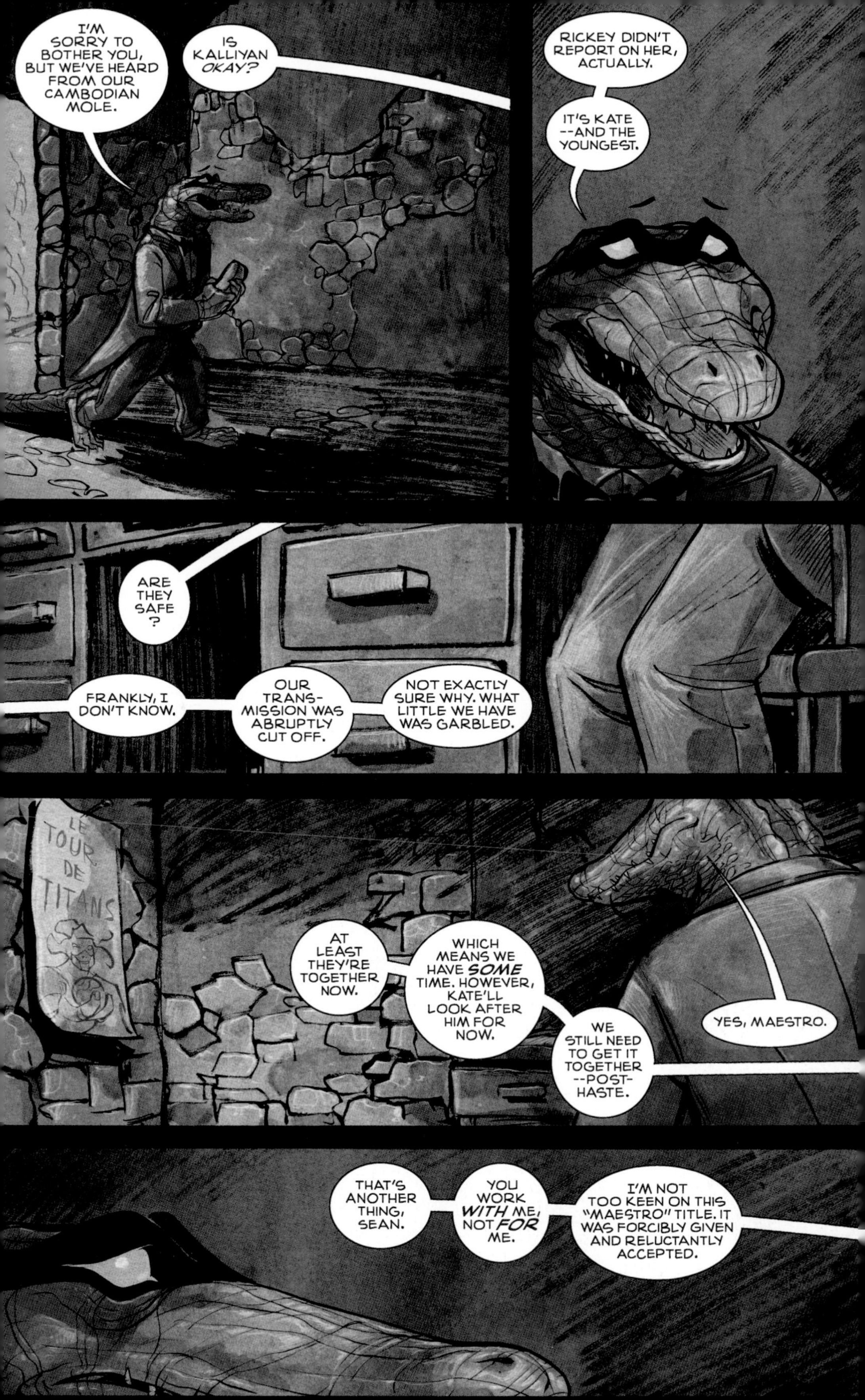
I'M SORRY TO BOTHER YOU, BUT WE'VE HEARD FROM OUR CAMBODIAN MOLE.
IS KALLIYAN OKAY?
RICKEY DIDN'T REPORT ON HER, ACTUALLY.
IT'S KATE --AND THE YOUNGEST.
ARE THEY SAFE ?
FRANKLY, I DON'T KNOW.
OUR TRANS-MISSION WAS ABRUPTLY CUT OFF.
NOT EXACTLY SURE WHY. WHAT LITTLE WE HAVE WAS GARBLED.
LE TOUR DE TITANS
AT LEAST THEY'RE TOGETHER NOW.
WHICH MEANS WE HAVE SOME TIME. HOWEVER, KATE'LL LOOK AFTER HIM FOR NOW.
WE STILL NEED TO GET IT TOGETHER --POST-HASTE.
YES, MAESTRO.
THAT'S ANOTHER THING, SEAN.
YOU WORK WITH ME, NOT FOR ME.
I'M NOT TOO KEEN ON THIS "MAESTRO" TITLE. IT WAS FORCIBLY GIVEN AND RELUCTANTLY ACCEPTED.

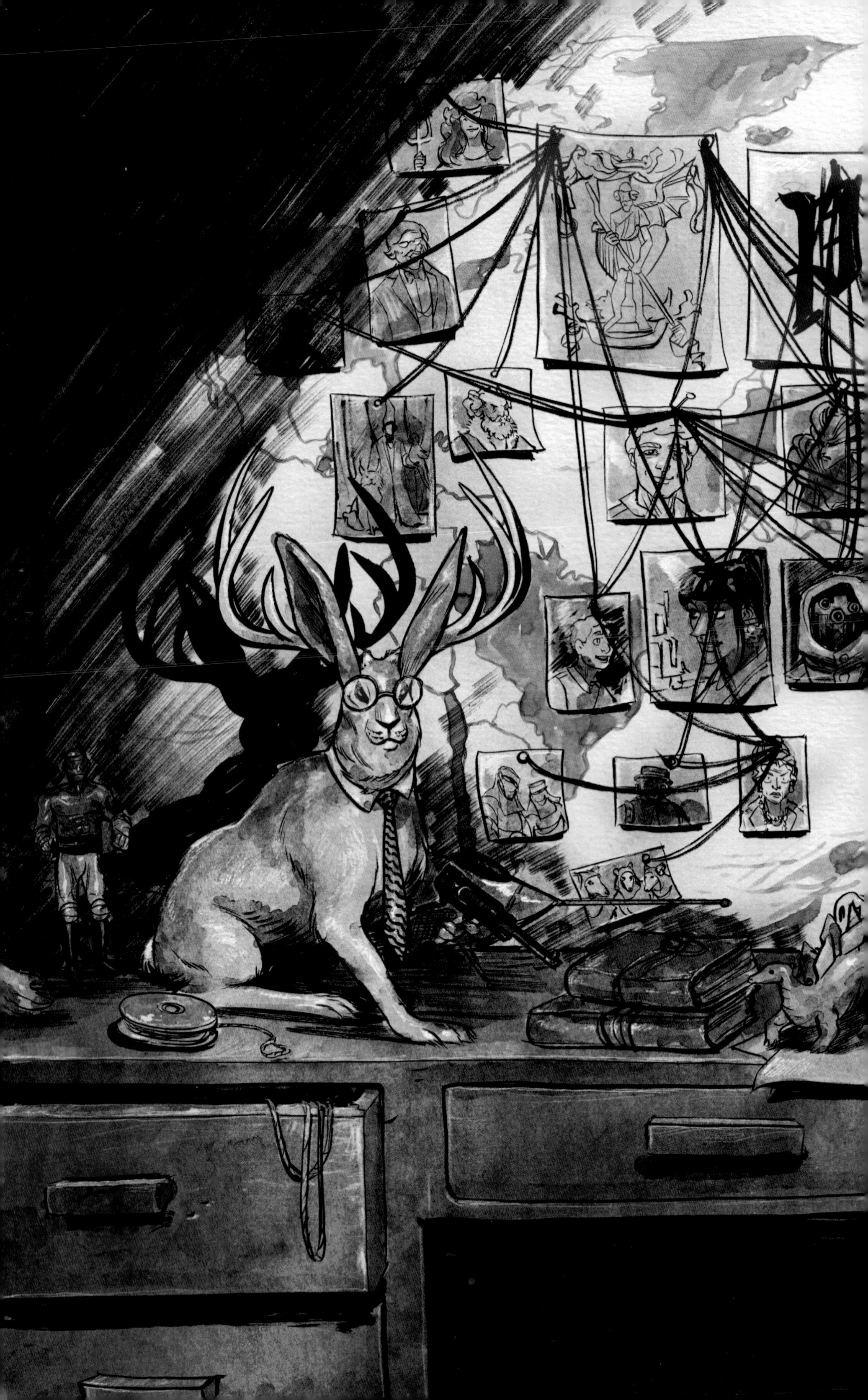

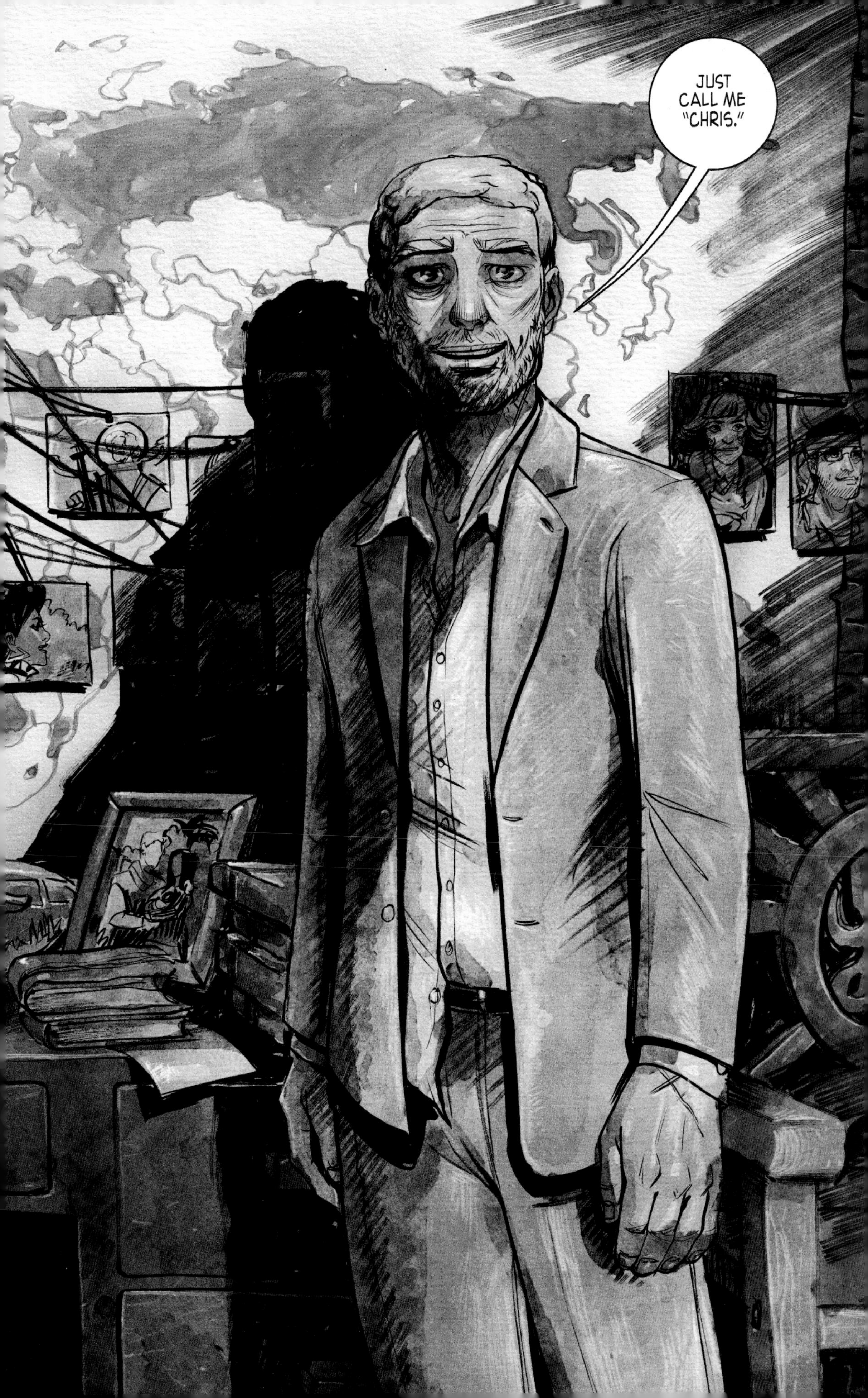
JUST CALL ME "CHRIS."

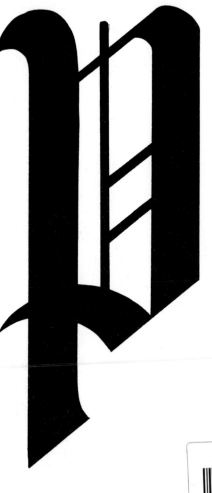

JOE KEATINGE - WRITER **OWEN GIENI - COLORIST** COVER DESIGN BY LEILA DEL DUCA AND ADDISON DUKE

LEILA DEL DUCA - ARTIST **JOHN WORKMAN - LETTERER** CHAPTER BREAKS DESIGNED BY TIM LEONG AND ADDISON DUKE

IMAGE COMICS, INC.
Robert Kirkman - chief operating officer
Erik Larsen - chief financial officer
Todd McFarlane - president
Marc Silvestri - chief executive officer
Jim Valentino - vice-president
www.imagecomics.com

Eric Stephenson - publisher
Corey Murphy - director of Retail Sales
Jeremy Sullivan - director of digital sales
Kat Salazar - director of pr & marketing
Emily Miller - director of operations
Branwyn Bigglestone - senior accounts manager

Sarah Mello - accounts manager
Drew Gill - art director
Jonathan Chan - production manager
Meredith Wallace - print manager
Randy Okamura - marketing production designer
David Brothers - content manager

Addison Duke - production artist
Vincent Kukua - production artist
Sasha Head - production artist
Tricia Ramos - production artist
Emilio Bautista - sales assistant
Jessica Ambriz - administrative assistant

SHUTTER, VOL. 2: WAY OF THE WORLD. JULY 2015. First printing. Published by Image Comics, Inc. Office of publication: 2001 Center Street, 6th Floor, Berkeley, CA 94704. Copyright © 2015 Joe Keatinge and Leila del Duca. All rights reserved. Originally published in single magazine form as SHUTTER #7-12, by Image Comics. SHUTTER™ (including all prominent characters featured herein), its logo and all character likenesses are trademarks of Joe Keatinge and Leila del Duca, unless otherwise noted. Image Comics® and its logos are registered trademarks of Image Comics, Inc. No part of this publication may be reproduced or transmitted, in any form or by any means (except for short excerpts for review purposes) without the express written permission of Image Comics, Inc. All names, characters, events and locales in this publication are entirely fictional. Any resemblance to actual persons (living or dead), events or places, without satiric intent, is coincidental. Printed in the USA. For information regarding the CPSIA on this printed material call: 203-595-3636 and provide reference # RICH – 624840. For International Rights / Foreign Licensing, contact: foreignlicensing@imagecomics.com. ISBN: 978-1-63215-433-0